Praise for the novels of *New York Times* bestselling author
Erica Spindler

THE LOOK-ALIKE

"In a word: riveting. An intense psychological thriller about love, betrayal, mental illness, and fear; a twisty, atmospheric suspense that will have you questioning the troubled heroine and flipping pages to find out what happened. Spindler is at the top of her game."

—Allison Brennan, *New York Times* bestselling author

"Twisty plots, chilling suspense, true-to-life characters—Erica Spindler's taut thrillers are a must-read."

—Brenda Novak, *New York Times* bestselling author

"Spindler keeps the pages turning with a taut plot and multiple suspects who appear suspicious right up to the end."

—*Library Journal,* starred review

THE FIRST WIFE

"[A] heated romantic thriller . . . strong personalities make for some wonderfully tense revelations."

—*Publishers Weekly*

"Spindler hooks readers into her latest . . . the mystery is engaging."

—*RT Book Reviews*

JUSTICE FOR SARA

"A spine-tingling romantic thriller . . . Spindler keeps the reader guessing until the last page." —*Publishers Weekly*

"Spindler's chilling novels explore our deepest fear—that danger is closer than we think. She is a master of addictive suspense."
—*New York Times* bestselling author Lisa Gardner

WATCH ME DIE

"Guaranteed to chill your blood and set your teeth on edge."
—#1 *New York Times* bestselling author Lisa Jackson

"A gripping thriller [with] numerous twists and turns until the startling conclusion."
—*Publishers Weekly*

BLOOD VINES

"*Blood Vines* is as mysterious and delicious as a fine cabernet . . . TOP-NOTCH SUSPENSE."
—*New York Times* bestselling author Linda Castillo

"A fast-paced, intense story that's hard to put down."
—*RT Book Reviews* (4 stars)

BREAKNECK

"A gripping story that unfolds with breakneck speed, heart-quickening suspense, and characters you can't help but root for."
—Bookreporter.com

"Filled with well-developed, multidimensional characters, Spindler's latest boasts fast-paced action and emotional tension . . . The intricately woven plot makes this novel a sure winner for readers who like to keep guessing all the way to the end."
—*RT Book Reviews* (Top Pick!)

Also by Erica Spindler

THE LOOK-ALIKE

ERICA SPINDLER

St. Martin's Paperbacks

Published in the United States by St. Martin's Paperbacks, an imprint of St. Martin's Publishing Group.

THE LOOK-ALIKE

For information, address St. Martin's Publishing Group, 120 Broadway, New York, NY 10271.

www.stmartins.com

ISBN: 978-1-250-78341-7

Our books may be purchased in bulk for promotional, educational, or business use. Please contact your local bookseller or the Macmillan Corporate and Premium Sales Department at 1-800-221-7945, ext. 5442, or by email at MacmillanSpecialMarkets@macmillan.com.

Printed in the United States of America

St. Martin's Press hardcover edition / January 2020
St. Martin's Paperbacks edition 2021

10 9 8 7 6 5 4 3 2 1

ACKNOWLEDGMENTS

Special thanks to Linda Collings, Ph.D., M.P., for her assistance in the creation of *The Look-Alike*. She deepened my understanding of the persecutory delusional disorder, and brought to life how the disorder affects the lives of both the afflicted and those who love them.

Thanks to my publishing team at St. Martin's Press, particularly Jennifer Weis, and to my agent, Scott Miller. I appreciated the guidance, encouragement, and understanding more than you know.

And as always, thanks to my family for the love and support. I couldn't do it without you.

PROLOGUE

Sienna Scott nearly tripped over the body. With her hood up and head down against the driving snow, she couldn't see more than a few inches in front of her feet.

It was the blood that stopped her, although she didn't realize that's what it was, not at first. No, stopping short had been an automatic reaction to coming upon something she immediately recognized as *wrong*. The move had been so sudden and unexpected, she lost her balance on the slippery walkway and fell to her knees, her gloved hands sinking into the dark snow.

She began to right herself and froze, staring at her gloved hands. The gloves were white. They matched her parka and the snow-covered landscape around her. Only they weren't. White. Not anymore.

Red. Dark, ugly red.

A sob broke from her throat, the sound guttural. A girl, sprawled on the path. Unmoving. Stained by the same red as her gloves. It felt to Sienna as if she might never breathe again. The seconds ticked past, her heart thundering against the wall of her chest, then the air barreled into her lungs, filling them to bursting.

She released it on a scream that shattered the night.

CHAPTER ONE

Whenever Sienna Scott thought back to that night—and that was more often than she cared to admit—a single, horrific image jumped out at her, of deep red creeping across brilliant white. As if the entire event had coalesced into a single, terrifying mental photograph.

Sensory memories always accompanied the image. Of every hair on her body standing up in awareness that she had stumbled upon something terribly, horribly *wrong*. And of cold. Bitter, cutting clear to her bones.

Sienna hunched deeper into her coat, gloved hands curled into tight fists in her pockets. Her heart beat wildly in her chest, same as it had that night. She stared at the spot—where the walkway passed an alcove at the back of the Humanities building. Nondescript. No marker. Nothing to indicate the most shocking crime in the college's history had occurred here.

How could such violence be erased in ten short years?

God, she wished she could erase it. What would it take to strip the event from her consciousness? Ten years on an entirely different continent hadn't done it.

But those years away had changed *her*. One didn't forget the unforgettable, but time and distance diminished its impact. Memories faded. Details grew fuzzy, then escaped altogether, disappearing into the ether.

"Sienna Scott?"

Sienna looked up. A petite woman in a light blue down jacket and matching hat stood not three feet away. Blond curls peeked out from under the knit cap and her blue eyes were wide with surprise.

"Oh, my God," she said. "It *is* you."

"Kim?" Sienna smiled. "Kim Meyers?"

"Peterson now. Going on two years. My goodness, you look even more like your mom than you used to."

Sienna had wondered how long before someone would comment on how she was the mirror image of her beautiful, auburn-haired mother. It used to bother her, the speculative looks, the feeling that they were just waiting for her to go off the rails. As if by inheriting her mother's features and coloring, she had inherited her mental illness as well.

But the truth was, back then she had been watching and waiting herself. Terrified that her mother's present was her own future.

Not anymore. She was her mother's daughter. Not her clone.

"Thanks, Kim. So what are you up to besides being married? Still helping your parents run the restaurant?"

"Gosh, no." She laughed and shook her head. "After working at The Wagon Wheel my whole life, that was the *last* thing I wanted to do. I work here on campus. Hey, didn't I hear you'd become a chef?"

"Sure did." Sienna smiled. "Fell in love with food. Who knew?"

Kim laughed again and Sienna remembered that she had been that kind of girl, exuberance and giggles, twenty-four seven.

"Wait!" she said, and clapped her gloved hands together. "I just thought of something. If you're going to stay around, you should talk to my folks. They're planning to put the restaurant up for sale."

"No kidding? The Wheel's an institution here."

"They're tired of running it and want to retire and move to Florida. I don't want to take it over and neither does Rob." Kim looked at her watch. "Crap, I've got to go, I'm late. Welcome home, Sienna. Call me."

Sienna watched her hurry off, then turned and started for the visitor parking lot. The Wagon Wheel for sale? She had thought of opening her own place, had even fantasized about it being located on Main Street in Old Town. And now, the perfect location could be dropping in her lap? Right off the bat?

Sienna reached her rental car, climbed in, and started it up. While the engine warmed, she flipped down the visor, peered into the mirror. Her mother's heart-shaped face and classic features stared back at her with large, wide-set green eyes.

She couldn't believe she'd spent all those years running away from who she might be instead of enjoying who she was. Years wasted on fear.

That was then. Sienna smiled at her reflection, then closed the visor. It wasn't now.

And she meant to prove it to everyone who thought otherwise.

Starting with her brother. Half brother really, though she'd never thought of him that way.

She grabbed her cell phone and punched in his number.

He answered, sounding worried. Of course he was. Almost ten years older than she, he'd made protecting her his job, from the day she came home from the hospital.

"Half-pint? You okay?"

She supposed she should have warned him she was coming. He'd never liked surprises. "I'm fine. Just excited. I have news."

"News?" She heard a rustle, probably him checking his watch, doing the math. "What time is it there?"

"Same time as it is in Tranquility Bluffs." At his silence, she went on. "I'm here, Bradley. In Tranquility. I've come home."

CHAPTER TWO

Sienna eased into the parking space in front of the re-purposed storefront that housed her brother's Old Town office. The sign above the door read: SCOTT PROPERTY DEVELOPMENT. RESIDENTIAL & COMMERCIAL.

She flung open her car door at the same moment her brother strode out. They met at the sidewalk; he pulled her close in a big bear hug. For a moment they stood that way, then he held her at arm's length.

"All grown up," he said with a grin. "Making all your own decisions."

She smiled back at him. "That's the way it's supposed to be, right?"

"Maybe so, but you'll always be my little Half-pint."

"Following you around, wanting to do everything big brother could do. I know I made you crazy."

"And that's the way *that's* supposed to be. C'mon, let's go inside." He laid his arm across her shoulder. "It's too damn cold out here."

It was her first time in his office. The interior was an attractive blend of modern meets north woods. The open concept was broken up by a conversation area arranged around a gas fireplace; the reception desk; and three large wooden worktables, big enough to spread out maps and blueprints. The gleaming wooden floors were dotted with area rugs in coordinating colors and patterns.

On the walls hung framed photos and plans from the projects his firm had spearheaded. Among them: upscale condos in Madison; a New Urbanism community near Belvidere, Illinois; and concept renderings of a resort proposed for Door County, right on Lake Michigan.

Over the years, he'd talked about his work, but she hadn't realized the scale of these projects.

She met his eyes over her shoulder. She noticed that the hair at his temples had gone gray since she'd last seen him. "These are amazing."

"Thanks." He smiled and crossed to stand beside her. "I'm especially excited about the Door County project. It's totally my baby, and is the most expansive—and expensive—development I've proposed. I'm in the process of securing investors now."

"You've done so well, Brad. I'm really proud of you."

"I couldn't have done it without Dad's help."

Their dad; it was hard to believe he'd been gone five years now. "That's not true. You had the brains and determination, and he believed in you."

"He was the first one who did." His voice thickened. "I miss him."

Tears stung her eyes. "I do, too."

He cleared his throat. "And how about you? A classically trained chef? Le Cordon Bleu? Damn, girl, I'm proud of *you*."

Sienna knew she was beaming. She couldn't help it. It had been the first time in her life she had truly let go of her doubts and let passion lead her. "Tell you the truth, I'm proud of myself."

"You should be. I know Dad would be, too."

"That means a lot, Brad. Thank you."

"How about a cup of coffee?"

"God, yes. I didn't sleep on the flight, and I'm pretty close to being toast right now."

He turned to go, then stopped and looked back at her, expression serious. "Why didn't you let me know you were coming?"

"I thought you'd try to talk me out of it."

He nodded, a smile tugging at the corners of his mouth. "I would have. I'll get the coffee. We'll talk."

She watched him go, then sat, choosing a spot on the cozy love seat in the conversation area. She turned her gaze to the fireplace and its flickering flames. The two of them were so different. Not surprising, she supposed. Not only was he ten years older and a male, he was the product of their father's first marriage.

He hadn't had it easy, shuffled between the two households, dealing with one mother who was angry at her ex-husband and resentful of his new wife, and one who suffered from persecutory delusions and was constantly in and out of treatment.

It was amazing he'd turned out as grounded as he had. She smiled to herself. Ditto for her.

He returned with two beautiful cappuccinos and a plate of small biscotti. "So fancy," she said, surprised.

"I let Liz talk me into one of those Nespresso machines that do everything but drink the beverage for you. I remembered you used to like these."

"I still do. Thanks."

He handed her a cup, then took the seat opposite hers. Suddenly tongue-tied, she dunked a biscotti in the frothy drink and took a bite. She sensed him watching her, waiting. She'd obviously come a long way for something; no doubt he was curious what it was.

She didn't want to go there, not just yet. For this

moment, it felt good just being here, reconnecting with him. Besides, she was pretty sure he wasn't going to be happy with her decision.

He broke the silence. "How's Mimi?"

Sienna thought about their paternal grandmother, a tiny dynamo who refused to accept "No" or "I can't" from anyone, including herself. Mimi's influence had been exactly what Sienna's then eighteen-year-old self needed.

"Really well. She said to tell you hello and that she loves you."

"I'll have to give her a call."

"She'd like that."

They fell silent again. Sienna took another sip of her coffee, then broke the silence. "What time's Liz coming in? I'm looking forward to seeing her."

"She's not."

Sienna frowned at the brusque reply. "Is she ill? Or—"

"She left me."

"Oh, Bradley. I'm so sorry."

"On our fifth anniversary. How's that for a kick in the gut?"

"When you visited, you seemed so happy."

"We were. Then." He stood and crossed to the fireplace. He stood, back to her, hands jammed in his pockets, spine ramrod straight. "She said she couldn't take Viv anymore."

Brad had never called his stepmother by anything but her given name, because he'd never thought of her as his mother. Yet, because Sienna had been hiding away in England, the role of her mother's chief caregiver had been forced on him.

Guilt pinched at her. Hard. She stood and crossed to him, laying a hand on his arm. "I'm sorry."

"It's not your fault."

"Isn't it? If I'd been here to help—"

"When he died, Dad entrusted her care to me." He stepped away; she dropped her hand. "Not to you."

"Maybe that wasn't fair?"

"Whatever, Sienna. It's done."

Which didn't absolve her of responsibility. "Well, I'm here now."

"And she'll enjoy seeing you."

"You misunderstand, Brad. This isn't a visit. I'm staying."

"Staying?" he repeated, brow furrowing again. "How long?"

"Permanently."

He looked her in the eyes. "Is this a joke?"

The question stung. "No. Why would you even think that?"

"C'mon, sis. We both know it's not healthy for you to be around your mother."

"I can handle it."

"That's what Liz said, and *she* wasn't the focus of Viv's delusions." He looked her in the eyes. "She hasn't let them go, Sienna. She still believes my mother and her family are out to punish her by hurting you. They 'drive by' the house. They've 'bugged' her phone in an attempt to trace your calls to her. She routinely searches for hidden cameras. I can go on if you'd like?"

"Don't bother. It's all standard Mom."

"You're sure you've thought this through?"

"Obviously."

"Really? Not obvious to me." He made a sound of frustration. "But why would it be? I didn't even know you were coming."

Another prickle of guilt. "I should have told you. I see that now, and I apologize."

"What about living arrangements? You're welcome to stay with me but, again, a little notice would have been nice."

"I'm staying at the house."

"The house?"

"With Mom."

For a moment, he simply gazed at her in that measured way of his. Then he shook his head. "You can't be serious."

"Dead serious. She's my mother, and that's my childhood home."

"That's right, she *is* your mother. The same one you ran away from."

"Dad sent me away."

"You didn't put up a fight, did you?"

"No," she agreed, "I didn't. But that was then. And I'm not that girl anymore. I've grown up, Brad."

She could see he was struggling with the idea. She went on, "Don't you want me here?"

"You're my sister, my only sib. Of course I want you nearby." He drew a resigned-sounding breath. "Mimi was okay with this?"

"She encouraged it. She knew how important it was for me to do this."

"A 'can't move forward before you go back' sort of thing?"

"Yes."

He dragged a hand through his hair. "I guess I get that. But you can't surprise Viv the way you did me. I have to give her a heads-up. This could trigger an episode."

With her mom, almost anything could trigger an episode. A thrumming started in her temple, like a silent drumbeat, pounding out a warning. It was a call she hadn't heard in a long time. "Seems to me an episode is unavoidable, whether you give her a heads-up or I simply show up on her doorstep. And the fact is, I'm here. What am I going to do? Hide?"

"It's your decision, sis." He paused, then went on. "But there's one more thing I think you should know."

"What's that?"

"They've reopened the investigation. A couple weeks ago."

CHAPTER THREE

The night of the murder

The man seemed to come out of nowhere. He emerged from the blinding snow like some sort of monster, and for one, terrifying moment, Sienna thought it must be the killer, come back for her. As she opened her mouth to scream again, the beam of a flashlight blinded her.

"Campus police," he called. "Stay where you are."

Sienna nodded and hugged herself. As if in a dream, she saw him kneel beside the body, check her pulse. Heard him swear softly.

That muttered curse proof the girl was dead.

She started to cry, great racking sobs from the depth of her being. She shook violently and the cop stood and wrapped his arms around her.

He had a gentle touch. And a kind voice. "Shh . . . shh . . . It's going to be all right. You're safe, I'm here."

She was safe.

Safe.

As the thought penetrated, her hysteria evaporated. Her legs went weak, and he tightened his grip on her.

"That's right," he murmured. "Now look at me. Not at her, at me."

She wanted to, more than anything, but couldn't seem to drag her gaze from the girl in the red snow.

"Wh . . . who . . . is she?"

"I don't know. Now, look at me." This time he said it forcefully, the way her father would. Startled, she met his eyes. Brown, she saw. A warm, deep brown.

"You recognize me, don't you? From around campus?"

He looked familiar, but she could hardly think, let alone put a name to a face.

"Officer Randall Clark. Campus police."

Then she remembered. He'd helped her one time, when she fell and twisted her ankle. He'd been kind that time as well.

"Good girl," he said. "What's your name?"

"Sienna Scott."

"Did you see what happened here?"

The image of the red snow, and the girl lying face-down in it, filled her head. She looked that way and a squeak of terror slipped past her lips.

"Sienna," he said again, gently but firmly, "keep your eyes on my face. I need to ask you a couple questions. Think you can handle that?"

She managed to nod, and he went on, "Did you see anyone? Perhaps fleeing the scene?"

"No," she whispered.

"How about voices? Did you hear an argument or—"

His radio crackled. "Randy, buddy, you there?"

He unclipped the device without completely loosening his grip on her. "Yeah, I'm here."

"We've gotten some calls, reports of hearing screams. It's probably nothing but—"

Officer Clark cut him off. "It is most definitely something. You better get over here. Behind the library, between the Humanities and Social Sciences buildings."

"In this weather? You've got to be out of your damn mind. Whatever it is, take care of it."

"And call the local PD. A female student has been murdered. It's bad. Real bad."

Murdered. The word reverberated in Sienna's head, blocking out the reply of the man on the radio. She shifted her gaze to the dead girl, taking in the hooded parka, once white, now stained red. She looked down, at her own white jacket and gloves, now also stained red, and a weird and horrible realization planted in the back of her head:

She and the dead girl were wearing the same coat.

CHAPTER FOUR

Sienna couldn't stop shaking. She couldn't keep her gaze from straying to the dead girl and the white, bloodstained jacket. Tears rolled down her cheeks, freezing before they could splash onto her high collar. "I'm . . . so . . . cold." She managed the words around her chattering teeth. "I . . . want-t . . . t-to g-go home."

"I have to wait for backup. I can't leave her." The officer sounded distressed. Confused.

The body. Sienna closed her eyes. Her head filled with the image of deep red creeping across stark white. Pooling in the snow. Seeming to have a life of its own as it drained another's.

"I think I'm going to be sick!"

The cop quickly ushered her to a corner shielded from the wind. She doubled over and retched with such force it felt as if her very soul were being expelled from her body.

"Come on," Officer Clark said, "we'll wait for my backup in the cruiser."

He led her around the Social Sciences Building, to the parking lot just beyond. His FREDRICKS COLLEGE POLICE cruiser was one of the only vehicles in the lot.

He unlocked the car, then opened the front passenger

door for her. "Climb in. I'll start her up, get the heat going."

She did and he slammed the door behind her, then went around to the other side. A few seconds later, he had the engine fired up and the heat on full blast. It didn't take long for the air blowing out the vents to go from cold to downright warm.

"That's one of the things these cruisers have going for them, great heaters."

She didn't respond and he held his hands up to one of the vents. He wasn't wearing gloves and they looked painfully chapped from the cold.

He rubbed them together. "Take off your gloves. Do this."

Sienna nodded and went to tug off her gloves. And froze, staring at the blood. For a moment, she'd forgotten. But now it came rushing back. Tripping, landing on her hands and knees, seeing the blood.

Deep red creeping across pristine white.

"I'll do it for you."

He carefully peeled off her gloves. She saw that her fingers were stained red. She started to shake.

He gently guided her hands to air rushing out of the vent. "See? Feels better, doesn't it?"

She nodded.

They sat silently, hands stretched out. As her hands and face warmed, they tingled, as if coming back to life.

Something the girl in the snow would never do.

She held back tears. Her nose began to run and she sniffled. "Do you have a tissue?"

"I'll do you better than that." He opened his console, drew out a folded square of plaid fabric, and handed it to her. "Keep it. I buy 'em by the dozen this time of year."

Headlights slashed across the night; a vehicle pulled up alongside them, on her side. A police car, she realized. Not campus police; Tranquility Bluffs cops.

Without a word, Officer Clark climbed out of the car and went around to meet the other cop.

"Randall Clark, Fredricks Campus Police."

"Detective Troy Furst, TBPD. Who's that?"

"Girl who found the victim. Student here on campus."

"Name?"

"Sienna Scott."

"Where's the victim?"

"Up ahead, just to the left of the building."

Officer Clark sounded different now, she thought. Tense. On edge.

"Who else is here?"

"You're the first."

"You left the victim unattended?"

"The kid was freezing, brought her around to let her warm up. I just got her situated."

He sounded defensive. The other cop, disapproving.

"If you're going to leave the car running, put her in the back. That's protocol one-oh-one."

"It's warmer in the front, I was just—"

"She'll be fine in the back."

Sienna decided she didn't like the city cop. Officer Clark was just being nice to her, and he was being such a jerk to him.

"Get this one squared away, meet me by the victim."

Officer Clark mumbled something under his breath that Sienna couldn't make out.

The other cop stopped, looked back. "Clark? You got a name?"

"What?" He sounded flustered.

"The victim's."

"Madison Robie."

Officer Clark opened the rear passenger door, reached in and pushed something out of the way, then helped her out of the front seat and into the rear one.

"I'll be back soon. Okay?"

She nodded. But as he walked away, he locked the car.

The sound of all four doors' levers simultaneously snapping into place reverberated through her like a gunshot. Sienna grasped for the door handle and yanked.

Nothing.

She slid across the seat and grasped the other door handle and got the same result.

She was locked in!

Heart thundering, she searched for a way to lower the window, but there was none. With a cry, she grabbed the metal divider between the front and back seat, poking her fingers through the spaces and tugging. It didn't budge.

Calm down, Sienna. He said he'd be right back.
But why'd he lock her in?

She struggled to catch her breath. She closed her eyes, concentrating on her breathing. On being calm.

Instead, the image of the girl in the snow filled her head. The girl in the white coat, so much like hers. Stained red.

Sienna looked down at herself. Her coat, stained red. Her hands, too.

Hysteria rose up in her. Her breath came in short, shallow gasps. She pounded the window with her fists, the last vestige of her rational self giving way to something stronger. Primal. Like a caged animal fighting for its life.

"Somebody help!" Her head swam; she saw stars. "Let . . . me . . . out!"

Headlights pinned her from behind. She swung around at the same time the door flew open. She scrambled to get out, her foot catching on a bag of gear protruding from under the seat.

Ice-cold hands cupped her cheeks. "Ms. Scott! It's me, Officer Clark."

"You locked me in!"

A door slammed. Another figure, she saw. Then another car, this one with flashing lights, the blue bouncing wildly off the snow.

"I'm sorry," he said. "I didn't mean to frighten—"

"Officer Clark? Chief Thompson, TBPD. Step aside."

The chief laid his hands gently on her shoulders. "Take a deep breath, Sienna. Good girl. Just breathe. That's right."

Confused and frightened, she struggled to do as he said.

"I don't know if you remember me," he went on, "but I'm a friend of your father's. Chief Fred Thompson."

A friend of her dad's? She thought of him and a knot of tears lodged in her throat. "I want my dad."

"I've called him." His voice was strong but soothing. "He's going to meet you at the police station. See that cruiser there, that's one of my guys. I'm going to have him drive you there."

She nodded, blinking against tears. "Yes, please."

He waved the other officer over. "Phelps, I need you to take Ms. Scott down to the station. Make her comfortable until her dad arrives. And look, let her ride up front with you. She's had a tough night."

CHAPTER FIVE

Thirty minutes later

The Tranquility Bluffs Police Department was located in old downtown, a block off Main and on the corner of State and Elm. Sienna had hardly even noticed the redbrick and austere building, before, let alone been inside.

She sat on a wooden chair in the small waiting room. They'd taken her coat and gloves into evidence, then offered her a small, scratchy blanket. She'd wrapped it around herself as tightly as possible, but she was still cold. So cold she trembled and her teeth chattered.

"Sienna!" Her dad burst into the police department, rushing to her side. "Sweetheart, are you all right?"

She nodded and he squatted in front of her. Gathering her ice-cold hands in his, he began rubbing them. "My God, you're shaking like a leaf. Where's your coat?"

"They t . . . t . . . took it."

He frowned. "What in God's name for?"

"Evi . . . d . . . ence."

"Evidence? This is ridiculous. I'm taking you home."

"But they said—"

"Never mind what they said. We're leaving."

He helped her to her feet. With his arm securely around her, they started for the door.

"Sir?" the desk officer called, jumping to her feet. "Excuse me? Where do you think you're going?"

"I'm taking my daughter home."

"Mr. Scott, Chief Thompson's orders were explicit: keep her here until he had a chance to interview her."

"It's *Dr.* Scott, and why the hell does he need to interview her?"

The woman looked flustered. "Dr. Scott, my apologies, but obviously, they need to question her about what transpired tonight."

"What happened tonight had nothing to do with my daughter. Obviously."

One of the uniformed officers working a desk stepped in. "I'm sorry, Dr. Scott, protocol—"

"I don't give a damn about your protocol. You tell Thompson—"

"Dad, it's okay—"

"The hell it is." He nudged her toward the door. "Tell Thompson if he wants to interview my daughter, he can come to the house to do it. He knows where I live."

Her dad hustled her out of the building and to his car. It was still warm inside, and the luxurious leather seat felt like a hug as Sienna sank into it.

"Buckle up," he said, starting the engine. "The roads are a mess."

They crept along, snow falling so heavily the wipers couldn't keep up. She saw that his knuckles were white from gripping the wheel so tightly.

"I'm sorry you had to come out in this weather, Dad."

"Thank God you're okay." He didn't take his eyes from the road. "But we do need to talk about your mother."

"About Mom?" she repeated, confused.

"About how we break this to her." He approached a stop sign and eased through it without stopping. "I'm not sure how she'll react to this. We need to prepare for the worst."

The worst. A full-blown paranoiac episode. Sienna shuddered. "We could keep it a secret?"

"That won't work. It'll be in the newspaper. On the TV. Even if I ask the police to keep your name out of it, it'll get out."

"I'm sorry," she said again.

"She's sleeping now. That's good. I'll tell her about the murder in the morning. Play down how you were involved. If you need anything or have any questions, nightmares, anything, come to me. Not a word to her. Okay?"

"Okay." She hugged herself, wondering how he would have "played it down" if she had been the one lying dead in the snow. How would he have protected her mother then? "When it comes to Mom, you always know best."

They drove the rest of the way in silence and without incident. They had no sooner gotten inside than Chief Thompson rolled into the drive. The headlights of his GMC Yukon sliced across the front window, followed a moment later by the sound of a car door slamming.

Sienna hovered just inside the front parlor, peering around the door casing, watching. As expected, her dad opened the door before the chief had the chance to ring the bell and wake up her mother.

Her father greeted the man at the door, though his voice was far from welcoming. "Fred."

"Dan." The chief sounded angry. "You know why I'm here."

"I do."

"That move you pulled at the station, you were out of line. A girl is dead."

"And Sienna is traumatized."

"She may have seen or heard something."

"She didn't."

"How do you know?" Her dad didn't have a response, and the chief pressed his advantage. "Can I come in?"

Her father didn't answer and Sienna wondered if he was going to refuse. Apparently, the same thought crossed the chief's mind because he added, "I have the right to question her. Here. Or back at the station. It's your choice."

"Damn right it's my choice. She's *my* daughter."

"She's eighteen, Dan. In the eyes of the law, an adult."

"Dammit, Fred!" He lowered his voice. When he spoke again, it shook with emotion. "It could have been . . . My God, she was right there."

"I understand. You're scared. What parent wouldn't be? But I have a responsibility to that other girl—and to *her* family—to do everything in my power to find whoever did this and bring them to justice."

Her father's voice lowered more. She had to strain to hear him.

"Sienna's fragile. You know that."

Fragile. Her cheeks heated. *The way her mother was fragile.*

"How would you feel in the other family's shoes, Dan? Wouldn't you want me to do my job?"

Sienna stepped into the doorway, hands curled into tight fists. "I want to help, Dad."

"Sienna—"

"He's right, what if it had been me?"

His face seemed to cave in on itself, as if just the thought was too painful to contemplate. "Okay. But I'm staying."

The chief stomped the snow from his boots and stepped inside. "I have to question her alone, Dan."

"That's ridiculous!"

"It's protocol."

"I don't give a damn if it's etched in stone on your mother's grave—"

"Dad!" Sienna took another step into the room. "It's okay."

"The hell it is." He glowered at the lawman, who seemed unperturbed.

"Thank you, Sienna." He shrugged out of his coat, removed his scarf and gloves, and handed them to her father. "Dan, close the door behind you."

Her father nodded curtly, then crossed to her, looked her in the eyes. "If you need me, I'll be right outside the door."

"I'll be fine," she said with forced bravado. "I'm stronger than you think I am, Dad."

She saw in his eyes that he didn't believe her. She couldn't blame him; truthfully, she didn't believe it either.

CHAPTER SIX

Chief Thompson ushered her across to the couch, then took a seat directly across from her. He met her eyes. "I have to ask you some questions. About tonight. Do you understand why?"

"I think so." Her voice sounded wooden to her own ears. The way her mother's sometimes did, after one of her flare-ups.

"You were first to the scene. You know what that means, right?"

Like everyone else, she watched crime shows. She swallowed hard and nodded, head filling with the image of red snow. "Am I a suspect?"

"In terms of investigative protocol, yes. But do I think you killed her? No, of course I don't." He shifted in his seat, but didn't take his gaze off her. She had a feeling that gaze missed nothing. Like he could see her wildly beating heart, read her fearful thoughts.

"But," he continued, "I can't summarily dismiss anything. That would make me a very poor cop."

"And you're not."

He smiled slightly. "That's right. That's also why I'm going to make notes of what you say. I don't want you to be nervous about that. It's part of the process."

"Okay." She folded her hands in her lap. She realized how cold they were. "I'll try not to be."

He reached into his jacket pocket and brought out a photo. He held it out. "Do you know this girl?"

Brown eyes and hair. A dusting of freckles across a pert nose. An earnest smile.

Red snow. A white parka. A sensation like ice cracking beneath her skates. Her hands began to shake.

"Yes. From the library. Her name's Madi."

"Madison Robie," he said. "Yes."

Her head went light. Sienna told herself to breathe. "I saw her tonight."

"At the library?"

"She works there. I see her every Wednesday night."

"Were you friends?"

Sienna shook her head. "I know her from there. She's older. A junior, I think."

"How did you happen to be out so late in such bad weather?"

"I have study group every Wednesday night."

"You didn't consider skipping tonight, because of the snow?"

"No."

"Why not?"

"There's a test scheduled tomorrow. We figured classes would be canceled, but none of us wanted to take a chance."

"How many in your group?"

"Four."

"All girls?"

She found it an odd question. "No. Two girls, two guys."

"Their names?"

"I don't understand, why would you need their names?"

He didn't seem at all offended by her question. "A couple reasons. The first, to corroborate your story. And second, they were out around the time of the murder. I want to talk to everyone who might have seen or heard something."

She swallowed hard. "Oh, okay." She rattled off her study partners' names. "And me, of course."

When he finished writing them down, he looked back up at her. "They didn't walk out with you?"

"We walked out together, but they all live in Parker Hall. I'm in Manchester."

"By the way, what subject were you studying?"

"Biology."

He nodded slightly. "You said you saw Madison tonight?"

"I did. She smiled at me."

"You didn't speak?"

She shook her head. "She wasn't at the circulation desk when I left."

He looked at her oddly, then made a note in his notebook. He'd told her not to be bothered by his note taking, but it made her feel weird. Like she was guilty of something.

"You left the library. What time was that?"

"Midnight. That's what time group ends."

"You didn't stop to talk to anyone?"

"I was anxious to get back to the dorm, because of the weather. Besides, there was nobody around. The way I go, there rarely is. It's a shortcut."

"You always go the same way?"

"The same way. Every Wednesday night."

Again, the odd look. "That cut-through is pretty isolated. You don't worry about that, especially at night?"

"Sometimes. But I force myself."

"You force yourself," he repeated. "Why's that?"

Sienna looked down at her clenched hands, then lifted her gaze back to his. "Because of my mom. Because she's always afraid."

She saw that he understood. Of course he did. Anyone who'd lived in Tranquility Bluffs any time at all would.

Poor, paranoid Vivienne Scott.

And such a shame her daughter's just like her.

"So, same as always, you take the path between the Humanities and Social Sciences buildings. Did you see anyone?"

"No."

"Hear any voices?"

"No voices."

"Something else?"

Sienna thought a moment, trying to pull out any detail she might have passed over at the time. After a moment, she shook her head. "The wind. I just wanted to get back to the dorm."

"How did you find the body?"

The body. That sounded so dispassionate. Like a thing, not the living, breathing person who had smiled at her only hours before.

Not breathing. Not anymore.

"I just . . . came upon . . . her." The icy shell around her crackled. She felt it giving way. "It was hard to see . . . because of the snow. And because I had my head down—"

Her voice changed. Seemed to vibrate. Like a finger on a too-tight wire. "My hood . . . I could only see the path right in front of my feet."

Her throat closed. She struggled to clear it. "I'm not sure what happened next. I don't know if I slipped or tripped. I went down. On my knees. And—"

She stopped.

"And what?" he prodded, tone gentle.

"My white gloves . . . they were red. And I real-ized . . . I knew—"

She started to cry, softly at first, turning to racking sobs.

Her father burst into the room. She saw her usually immaculately groomed brother was with him, tonight looking completely disheveled. In another situation, she would have teased him about the way his hair stuck out in every direction.

"That's enough!" Her father barked, both of them striding to her side. As they neared, she caught a whiff of alcohol. "You're done."

Chief Thompson didn't move. He held her gaze. "If you think of anything, recall anything, no matter how insignificant or outlandish you might think it is, bring it to me. Promise me you will."

She nodded and he handed her his card. "My num-ber's on this. If you think of anything at all, call me. Any time. Day or night."

CHAPTER SEVEN

Present day
1:15 P.M.

Sienna didn't have to ask her brother what investigation had been reopened. Her knees went weak, and she returned to the couch and sat down hard.

"It was in the news," Brad said. "Front page. Sorry, Half-pint. Your timing sucks."

Forget a conviction, the police had never even made an arrest. She looked up at him. "Why now?"

"I don't know. New evidence, I imagine."

The information had taken her by surprise, and she struggled to right herself. "They haven't talked to you?"

"No. But why would they?"

"Looking for me, I guess."

"So they haven't contacted you?"

"Not yet. I suspect they will." She expelled a pent-up breath. "Does Mom know?"

"She does."

"How'd she react?"

"Not good. Had an episode. A bad one, totally upended her."

"Crap. And now? How is she—"

"Not great."

"I hate hearing that."

"I should have let you know. It may have influenced your decision to come home."

"No." She shook her head. "It wouldn't have. This is where I need to be. And you know what? It's okay. In fact, I'm glad. I'd like nothing more than for them to find who killed Madison. For her family. And for me, too. It's still hanging out there, like a dark cloud, always threatening rain."

For a long moment he was silent, as if digesting her words. He crossed back to the couch and sat across from her. "Do you still think that maybe . . ."

He let the question trail off; she asked it for him. "That maybe the wrong girl was killed? That maybe the killer was waiting for me?"

He pursed his lips. "Do you?"

"No. I was young and excitable. Not delusional."

She heard the defensive edge in her voice and wished she didn't.

"I'm not judging."

"Maybe not now."

"Not then either."

"Then you were the only one."

He reached across and caught her hands. "This is what I was talking about. You being home, I'm just afraid—"

"I'm not, Brad. I'm done with being afraid."

He ignored her bravado. "And you haven't even seen your mother yet."

"Well then"—Sienna stood—"there's no time like the present."

Brad didn't argue. Instead, he offered to follow her to drop off her rental car, then drive her to her mom's. Sienna planned on using her mother's vehicle until she found her own place and bought one for herself. According to Brad, it wouldn't be a problem—her mom rarely left the house.

Now they rode in silence. Not an uncomfortable one, more that of two people lost in their own thoughts. Hers were on seeing her mother for the first time since the funeral. She wished she could convince herself otherwise, but she was anxious. And wrestling with doubt.

The things Brad said about her mother's state of mind, how news of the murder investigation being reopened had sent her on a downward spiral, made her wonder if she had made the right decision. She'd been away from her mother's chaos for ten years. Maybe the time away had blurred her memories? Made the idea of dealing with her mom's mental illness easier than it was going to be?

Sienna turned her face toward the side window, watching Tranquility Bluffs slip past her without really seeing it.

"You having second thoughts?"

"No," she lied, glancing back at her brother. "Just wondering how she's going to react."

"Your guess is as good as mine. But I'm leaning toward meltdown."

"Thanks."

"Just being real, sis."

He turned onto Winter Lane, and Sienna released a breath she hadn't realized she'd been holding. She'd grown up on this tree-lined street, with its wide sidewalk and deep front yards.

She caught sight of her childhood home, a large red-brick colonial with a sweeping front porch and a circular drive. He turned in, rolled to a stop, and cut the engine.

He met her eyes. She saw sympathy in his. "Ready?"

"As I'll ever be."

They climbed out of the car and started up the wide brick walkway. She noticed that all the front drapes were drawn and the Christmas wreath still hung on the door, battered and sad.

She rang the bell. After a few moments, she heard a shuffling from the other side of the door.

"Who's there?"

"Viv, it's Bradley."

"Who else is with you? Is it Liz?"

"No, Mom, it's me. Sienna."

A full ten seconds of silence followed, then the drape over the sidelight moved. Her mother peered out.

Sienna lifted a hand in greeting, and the drape fell back into place. A moment later the door opened and her mother waved them in. "Quickly."

As they crossed the threshold, her mother grabbed the door, peered outside, then shut it, twisting the dead-bolt lock.

She looked at Sienna, eyes wide. "It *is* you."

"Hi, Mom."

"I thought it was a trick."

"No trick." Sienna hugged her mother tightly. She felt so thin. "It's good to see you, Mom."

Her mother clung to her. "My beautiful girl's home. How I missed you."

"I missed you, too."

Her mother released her and held her at arm's length, studying her. It was like looking in a mirror, Sienna thought. One that bent time—herself thirty years from now.

"You shouldn't have come here. I warned you, it's—"

"Mom," she said evenly, "this is my home. I wanted to be near you." She looked at her brother. "And Brad."

"Sweetheart." She tightened her grip on Sienna's

shoulders, something dark and frightened creeping into her eyes. "It's not safe here."

"It's as safe here as it is in London." She covered her mom's hands with her own. "I'm staying."

Her mother's eyes widened. "They found you, didn't they? They discovered you were in London?"

She had wondered what the reality of living near her mom would be—this was it. Day in and out.

Sienna wanted to cry. The way she would when she was young and her mom talked like this. Because she had known, even when she was small, that something wasn't right with her mother.

She remembered when she'd been old enough to verbalize what she felt, and asked her father. She had to give him credit—he'd been honest with her. In his deep, warm voice, he'd explained that Mommy was sick, and because of that sometimes she said things that weren't right or didn't make sense. He made Sienna promise to come to him with everything, and in return, he promised her he would always tell her the truth.

"Nobody found me," Sienna said softly but firmly, "and nobody's after me. I just wanted to come home."

Sienna held her breath. Her mother blinked. Once. Twice. She did this, like a gambler's tell. A visual clue—not to what she was thinking, but that she was processing.

"For how long?" she asked.

"Maybe forever. And until I find my own place, I thought I'd stay here, with you. Would that be okay?"

She blinked again, then nodded and dropped her arms, wincing as she did. "We'll make this work. It'll be like old times."

Sienna smiled. "I think so, too."

"If I'd known you were coming, I would have

cleaned up." She looked pointedly at Brad. "You know I hate anyone seeing me look this way."

"She wanted to surprise you," Brad said, turning back to the door. "How about I get your bags?"

"I'll help."

He brushed Sienna off. "You visit with your mom. Viv, where should I put the suitcases?"

"In her old room, of course."

"Right," he agreed, winking at Sienna. "What was I thinking?"

"Thank you, Bradley," her mother said. "Come in, sweetheart. You've been away so long. And I want to hear all about your trip home. We'll have cookies and milk. Like we used to."

"I don't know about the cookies or milk, but I'd love a big glass of water."

Her mother nodded and Sienna followed her to the kitchen. The last time she'd been home was for her father's funeral, five years ago. She and Mimi had flown in, then out a couple days later. They'd stayed at the house, and she remembered it looking the same as always.

What a difference the last five years had made.

It was as dark as a tomb, with the drapes drawn at every window. And it smelled stale, as if it had been closed up for a very long time. What had once been impeccably decorated and immaculately kept was now dated, dusty, and frayed at the edges.

Her dad would be devastated to see the place this way. He'd been so proud of his home and family. He'd worked hard to fill it with love. And normalcy, she thought. He'd worked to give both her and Brad as normal a childhood as possible.

Her mother looked back at her. "What's wrong?"

"Just thinking about Dad. I miss him."

"I do, too."

"It's so dark in here, it's depressing. Do you mind if I open the drapes?"

"I'd rather you didn't. I don't like people looking in."

Her mother's reasoning should startle her, Sienna thought. Sadly, it didn't. She decided to start small, the way her dad used to. "How about just one window? It would make me feel so much better."

Her mother nodded. "In the kitchen."

They entered the room and Sienna crossed to the large window across from the table. She opened the blinds and light streamed in, falling across the oak tabletop.

"That is nice," her mother said. "Besides, if some-one sneaks into the backyard, it's better to know they're there."

Sienna let that pass, and her mother went to the pan-try. "Are you sure you don't want a cookie? I have Oreos. Your favorite."

The offer made Sienna smile. She hadn't had an Oreo in years. And truthfully, hadn't even thought of having one. "You go ahead, Mom. I'm not hungry. You want water? Or milk?"

She said milk, and while Sienna got out glasses and filled them, her mother arranged cookies on a plate. They carried them to the table and sat down, taking the seats that had always been theirs: her mother at one end, her dad at the other, and she and Brad across from each other.

Her mother reached for a cookie and her sleeve hiked up, revealing an ugly bruise that ran from her hand to her elbow, disappearing under the sleeve.

"Oh my God, Mom. You've hurt yourself."

"It's nothing."

"It's not nothing," Sienna said, recalling how she winced earlier. "What happened?"

"She fell," Brad said, entering the kitchen. He crossed to the table and plucked two cookies from the plate.

Sienna frowned. "What do you mean fell? Where?"

"Down the stairs. Caught her toe on carpeting that had come loose." He popped an entire cookie in his mouth. "Could've been a lot worse."

Sienna looked at her mother. "You fell down the stairs? When did this happen?"

Brad answered, reaching for another of the sandwich cookies. "A couple months ago. Right, Viv?" She nodded, and he went on, "In the middle of the night. I had the carpet at the top landing refastened the very next day. And added a safety light."

He sounded so casual about it. Like falling down the stairs was no big deal.

Sienna felt far from casual. "What were you doing up in the middle of the night, Mom?"

She shrugged. "I was hungry. I wanted a snack."

Brad checked his watch. "If you've got everything you need, sis, I'm going to head back to the office."

Sienna nodded and stood. "I'll walk you out."

"Thanks." He looked back. "Bye, Viv."

She didn't respond, and Sienna followed him to the front door and out to the porch, closing the door behind her. She caught his arm. "Why didn't you tell me about her fall?"

"There was nothing to tell. She's fine, thank God. Sprained wrist and some bruising. I had the problem corrected and added safety lights. What's the big deal?"

"I had a right to know."

"It wasn't that serious, I didn't want to worry you."

"Stop trying to protect me, Brad."

"With pleasure." He was angry. She saw it in the flush that stained his cheeks and the tight line of his jaw. He freed his arm and stepped away from her. "I hope you know what you're doing."

"You said that already."

"It needs saying again. Because I don't think I have the bandwidth to pick up the pieces if you don't."

CHAPTER EIGHT

2:25 P.M.

Sienna returned to the kitchen to find her mother gone. "Mom?" she called. Her mother didn't reply, so she called again, making her way through the downstairs. The living room. Her father's study. She even peeked in the bathroom and out at the patio—although why her mom would have headed out into the cold, she didn't know.

She went to the bottom of the stairs and looked up. "Mom? Are you up there?"

Although her mother didn't answer, Sienna acknowledged that of course she was. There was nowhere else she could be.

She started up. The upstairs hallway was dark as night, and when she reached the upstairs landing she saw why: every window on the second floor had been covered with blackout shades.

She started toward her old bedroom. The door stood partially open and a sliver of light spilled into the hall. Soft sounds of movement came from inside.

A heavy sensation settled in her chest. Her heart beat wildly around it, making it difficult to catch her breath. She found each step akin to another crank of a jack-in-the-box, and with each a growing anxiety for what was going to jump out at her.

Sienna stopped at the door, pushed it the rest of the way open. And found her mother bent over her open suitcases.

"Mom! What are you doing?"

She looked up. And smiled, her expression serene. "I'm unpacking you, sweetheart."

"I can do that myself. Please leave it." Sienna hadn't meant for the words to come out so sharply, so she softened the next. "But thank you, anyway. I appreciate the thought."

"You're welcome." She stood and crossed to sit on the edge of the bed. She smoothed a hand over the pink coverlet. "How do you like your room? I kept it just the way you left it."

Before her mother pointed it out, Sienna hadn't noticed, but it was exactly how she left it. *Exactly.*

She moved her gaze over the room. The bed was neatly made and, unlike downstairs, the furniture was dust free. She crossed to the corkboard above her desk. Ten-year-old notes to herself, a photo from her high school graduation, another with a group of friends. A crumbling corsage. Tickets stubs from a Nickelback concert. A calendar hung on it as well, open to April. She skimmed her notations—classes, work schedule, a psychiatric appointment.

She stopped on April tenth. The day she had been shipped off to London.

She hadn't even finished out the school semester. She frowned. Things had gotten that bad. *She* had gotten that bad.

Sienna shifted her gaze to the desktop. Homework in process. Her psychology text, open to a chapter on Axis I disorders. Other papers were scattered across its surface, as were several pens and a highlighter. She slid open the drawer on the right, wondering if it would still be there.

It was. Her journal. It had been a Christmas gift that year. After Madison's murder, she'd begun daily recording her thoughts and feelings.

Sienna slid the drawer shut. "It feels so strange," she murmured. "Being back."

She looked over her shoulder at her mother to find she wasn't even watching her, just staring at the open suitcase.

Her mother hadn't been unpacking her, Sienna realized. She had been looking for something. A bug, maybe?

"We have to be careful, Sienna. They're always watching. Always listening."

Sienna gave herself a mental shake. Her mother had the right to zone out, didn't she? It didn't mean she was on her way down the rabbit hole.

"What did you say, sweetheart?"

"Nothing important." Sienna began unpacking. She had taken the majority of her clothes with her when she left for London, so the closet and dresser drawers were mostly empty. She started filling the drawers first.

"Would you like me to hang these shirts?" her mother asked.

"That would be great. Thanks, Mom."

They worked together for a few minutes, the only sounds those of hangers being hung and drawers opening and closing.

Her mother broke the silence. "What did Bradley say about me?"

"Bradley? What do you mean?"

"Did he say I was doing well?"

"He said you were, up until a few weeks ago."

She nodded. "Since the fall."

"No, he thought you were upset about Madison Robie's murder investigation being reopened."

"Oh, that." She shook out a shirt, then slipped it onto a hanger. "Did he talk about Liz?"

Sienna nodded. "He told me she left him."

"That's what he told me, too. I miss her."

Sienna felt bad for her. Her mother's world was very small. Losing a piece of it would have a big impact. "I'm sorry. I liked her, too."

"She never talked about it."

"About what?"

"Being unhappy." Her mother trailed her fingers along the neckline of a pale pink sweater. "This is pretty."

"It's one of my favorites." Sienna went to the next bag. "She probably didn't want to upset you."

"Maybe." She neatly folded the sweater and handed it to Sienna. "She never said goodbye."

Sienna stopped what she was doing and frowned. That didn't sound like the woman she'd met. Of course, if her mother was the reason for the marriage ending, she could understand it. "Really? That's kind of surprising."

"He doesn't like me, you know. He never has."

"Who's that?"

"Bradley."

"That's not true, Mom. He's never thought of you as his mother, but he cares for you. It's just . . . complicated."

That was an understatement. He'd been saddled with a stepmother who had upended his childhood and, by his account, broken up his marriage. And even without those, her disorder made her difficult to love.

"I suppose. I do worry whether she's okay."

"I'm sure she is." Sienna shook out a pair of

trousers. "How about I check on her for you? I wanted to see her anyway. Would that give you some peace of mind?"

She brought a hand to her chest. "It really would. Thank you, sweetheart." She stood. "I'm feeling a little tired, do you mind if lie down while you finish unpacking?"

"Of course not. I'll check on you when I'm finished."

When Sienna checked on her, she found her sound asleep. She decided to use her time to compose a grocery list, then head to the store. She wanted to make something special for dinner, to celebrate her homecoming. Besides, maybe her mother would understand how much her daughter loved cooking after she tasted it.

The fridge, Sienna discovered, was nearly empty—a bag of sad-looking lettuce and past-its-prime cream. The pantry wasn't much better: breakfast cereal, sugary "protein" bars, and things like instant rice and boxed macaroni and cheese.

No wonder she's so thin, Sienna thought. She checked the freezer and was relieved to find a dozen frozen meals. At least she was getting some protein. For a moment there, she'd worried breakfast cereal might be her nutritional mainstay.

The car keys were hanging on a rack beside the door to the garage, same as they always had. After leaving a note so her mother wouldn't worry, she snatched them up and headed into the garage. The same Buick sedan from five years before sat waiting. Sienna climbed inside, wrinkling her nose at the stale smell. Obviously, it hadn't been driven in a while.

She inserted the key and twisted—the cold engine

whined and sputtered, then died. She tried again with the same result. The third time was the charm—it gasped its way to life.

She let it run a few minutes, then backed out of the garage, down the drive, and into the street.

Where the engine promptly died.

"Dammit," she muttered, trying to restart it. This time, she didn't even get a sputter out of it.

Her stomach sank. Great. The vehicle was angled in the street, blocking two-thirds of it. She'd have to call for a tow, so no groceries. No wonderful dinner, and only cereal for breakfast.

And no coffee.

The thought of going without her coffee in the morning severed her last nerve. She lowered her forehead to the steering wheel, fighting the urge to cry.

She jumped at the tap-tap on her window. A dark-haired guy with the most beautiful brown eyes stood beside her vehicle. His face was red from the cold, his expression concerned.

"You need some help?" he asked.

She nodded and cracked open the door. Cold air stung her cheeks. "It killed on me and won't start back up."

"Try starting it again."

She did. He listened, then nodded. "It sounds like either the battery or the alternator. Has it been sitting up awhile?"

"I think so. I'm visiting my mom and she doesn't get out much."

"I've noticed that." At her expression he smiled. "I'm not spying. I bought the house across the street." He pointed. "I'm in the process of renovating."

She nodded. "Gotcha."

"How about I try jumping it?"

"That would be *so* great. Thank you."

"Hold tight."

She watched him walk away. He looked to be somewhere in his early to mid thirties. He was tall, with the confident stride of a former athlete. Who knew, maybe he still was?

And maybe he was married and she should stop noticing things like his eyes and his backside.

A few minutes later, a big black pickup truck rolled down his driveway. She wondered at his profession. Perhaps he was one of those house flippers? Or he worked in construction and was laid off for the season? Or like a lot of folks in this part of the country, had been downsized.

Or maybe his wife was the breadwinner, and he was a stay-at-home dad? The kid, or kids, were at school, and he was left to save stranded women?

Which would make all of it none of her business.

He expertly maneuvered the truck, then hopped out. After lifting his own hood, he asked her to pop hers.

It took her a moment to find the lever; she did and he lifted the hood. She climbed out of the car and went to stand by him, stamping her feet and hugging herself to stay warm.

"Wait in the car, it's freezing out here." When she hesitated, he waved her toward the Buick. "I've got this. Besides, once I get the clamps connected, I'll need you to try starting it up."

She nodded and hurried back to the sedan. A few moments later, he signaled her to try cranking the engine.

It started. Sienna smiled and gave him a thumbs-up. After letting it run a minute, he disconnected the cables, slammed the hood, and came around to the driver's side window. She lowered it.

"I can't thank you enough," she said.

"Happy to help."

He smiled and his eyes crinkled at the corners in the most attractive way. She scolded herself for noticing.

"Go straight to Mack's Auto Stop. You know Mack's?"

She told him she did. Crazy how things in small towns didn't change.

"Good. He'll test the battery for you. If you need a new one, he'll install it right there, no extra charge."

"Sounds like the Mack's I used to know. Thank you—" She realized she hadn't asked his name, so she offered hers. "I'm Sienna."

His eyes did that too-charming crinkle thing again. "Jonathan," he said. "Good to meet you, Sienna."

"Tell your wife she's a lucky woman, being married to such a handsy guy."

She silently groaned at her word choice. Handsy? Did she really just say that? Slick, she was not.

"I'm not married. You?"

Her cheeks heated. "No. Free as a—"

She bit the last back.

"Bird," he finished for her, grinning. "Me, too." He took a step back from the window. "Remember, straight to Mack's."

Sienna nodded and raised the window. As she drove off, she checked in the rearview mirror and saw that he was watching her.

She acknowledged that pleased her way more than it should have.

CHAPTER NINE

5:45 P.M.

Sienna got the big sedan into her mother's narrow garage without incident. Per Jonathan's advice, Mack's had been her first stop. Mack had tested the car's battery, determined it was shot, sold her a new one, and installed it. He'd talked the entire time, catching her up on everything and everyone in Tranquility. Including the fact that Madison Robie's murder investigation had been reopened. As far as he knew, nothing new had turned up. But maybe now that she was home, something would.

Sienna hadn't known exactly how to respond to that, so she'd left it alone, paid him, and headed for her groceries. While perusing the aisles, she'd run into no less than a dozen different folks she knew; they all wanted to stop and chat a minute. Or five. Or ten. Some were interested in her, how she was and why she'd come back, but others were like Mack—happy to talk about themselves and Tranquility Bluffs.

Her final stop was the package store for a bottle of wine to thank her neighbor for helping her. Nearby Rockford was home to the original Sock Monkey, and the store had a locally crafted Sock Monkey wine bag, so she bought that too.

She planned to quickly drop off the wine before she unloaded the groceries and started cooking. She grabbed the ridiculous-looking wine bag and climbed out of the car. A minute later, she was at his front door. She rang the bell. When she got no answer, she tried again. When she still got no response, she rummaged in her purse for a pen and something to write on. When she found both, she penned *Thank you,* signed her name, and left the bottle propped up against the door.

She headed back to her trunkful of groceries, unsure whether she was relieved or disappointed he hadn't been home.

A couple minutes later, juggling the half-dozen bags, she stepped into the kitchen. Her mother sat at the kitchen table, clenching and unclenching her hands.

"Hi, Mom."

"Where have you been?"

"The grocery. Mostly." Sienna dumped the bags on the counter. "I left you a note. You didn't see it?"

"You've been gone hours."

"Has it been that long?" She glanced at her watch. Nearly three hours, she realized, shocked. Although with everything she'd accomplished, she supposed she shouldn't be.

"I'm sorry. I had no idea it'd been that long." She started unpacking the bags. "I had to stop at Mack's for a new battery for your car. It killed when—"

"I was so worried." Her voice shook. "I thought I'd lost you."

"Oh, Mom." Sienna went to the table and took the chair directly across from her. She reached for her mother's tightly clenched hands. They were ice cold. "I'm really sorry you were worried. I'm fine."

She didn't respond and Sienna went on. "I'm grown

up now, I can take care of myself. I've been living in a big city for ten years, and had no problem." She searched her mother's eyes. "Surely I'll be fine in little bitty Tranquility Bluffs. Trust me on this, Mom. You think you can do that?"

"I'll try."

"Good." Sienna squeezed and released her hands, then stood and went back to unpacking the bags.

As she worked, she talked. "I'd planned to make us Croque Monsieur for dinner and a strawberry Napoleon for dessert. But it's so late now, how about a couple omelets instead? I'll plan on the other for tomorrow night."

She crossed to the refrigerator with the eggs, cream, and butter. "I've never been able to cook for you, so I'm looking forward to—"

"It must be nice."

Sienna stopped and looked over her shoulder at her mother. "What's that, Mom?"

"To be so carefree."

Her words were like a punch to her gut. Is that how she sounded to her mother? To her own ears, she sounded desperate.

Desperate for their exchange to be pleasant. Normal. "Oh, Mom."

"I don't know if I can do it," she added, voice shaking.

"Do what?"

"Protect us both."

A lump formed in Sienna's throat. She wondered what it was like to be on guard all the time. To see the world, and everyone in it, as dangerous. She hurt for her mother.

"I can protect myself, Mom."

"You can't protect yourself from what you don't

see. I see them, you don't. Your dad couldn't either, no matter how hard he tried."

"You're right, Mom. I don't see what you see. And I don't want to. I love you, but I can't live my life in fear."

For a long moment, her mother was quiet. When she finally spoke, the words broke Sienna's heart. "You can't live in fear. And I can't seem to live without it."

CHAPTER TEN

2:50 A.M.

"Sienna, wake up."

The voice reached into her dreams and pulled hard at her. In the dream, the voice coiled around her like octopus tentacles, but instead of dragging her deeper, it pulled her closer to the surface.

She resisted. She was so tired. So very tired.

"Sienna! You have to wake up."

With a moan, Sienna opened her eyes.

Her mother, kneeling beside the bed. Eyes wild.

"Mom? What's—"

"It wasn't true. None of it."

Sienna blinked and shook her head, trying to clear the cobwebs. "What wasn't true, Mom?"

"That I fell down the stairs."

"What time is it?"

"It doesn't matter. I had to tell you." She shook her head. "It couldn't wait until morning. I didn't fall, Sienna."

"Then, what—"

"I was pushed."

The last remnants of sleep evaporated. Sienna struggled into a sitting position. "Mom, you caught your toe on the carpet—"

"No." She grabbed Sienna's arm, nails digging into her skin. "I made all that up. About wanting a snack and about the carpet, all of it."

"Why would you lie to Bradley about that, Mom? If someone was in the house, he needs to know. The police should have been called."

"He's not on my side. Neither are the police."

"That's just not true."

"It is true. He doesn't believe anything I tell him."

This was the deterioration of her mother's condition Bradley had been talking about. She understood now—everything from his fatalistic attitude to his concern over her well-being.

Sienna gently removed her mother's hand. "We'll talk about it some more in the morning. You need to get some sleep. Okay?"

"I was pushed." Tears filled her eyes and her chin trembled. "You don't believe me either, do you?"

"We'll figure this out tomorrow. You need some sleep. And so do I."

"I can't sleep." Her voice broke. "I'm so tired, but what if they come back? I have to be ready."

"I'm here now, Mom. You don't need to worry anymore."

Sienna scooted off the bed. She helped her mom to her feet and with an arm around her waist, led her into the hall. "I'll make sure we're safe."

"You promise?"

"I promise. Come on, I'll tuck you in the way you used to tuck me in."

The fight seemed to go out of her mother. Sienna guided her to her bedroom and helped her into bed.

Sienna kissed her forehead and stood. As she turned, she noticed one of the dining room chairs stood near the door. How had that made its way up here? It was hard to imagine her frail mother hauling it up by herself.

Sienna looked back at her. "I can take this downstairs for you, if you'd like?"

"No, I like it here."

Sienna frowned slightly. "Okay. Just let me know if you want it moved."

She nodded and pulled the blankets up to her chin.

"Goodnight, then. See you in the morning."

"Close the door behind you, okay?"

Sienna said she would and stepped into the hallway. The door shut with a soft click and she started for the stairs, then stopped and turned back, frowning. It didn't add up. She liked the heavy dining chair where it was? Nearly blocking the bedroom door? And she'd looked almost panicked when Sienna suggested moving it.

Sienna tiptoed back to the door, leaned close, and listened.

She didn't have long to wait. She heard the rustle of the bedclothes being moved aside, then the sound of something being dragged across the floor, her mother's elevated breathing. A moment later, a thump against the door.

As if something heavy had just knocked against it.

The chair. Her mother had barricaded herself in her room.

And it wasn't the first time.

The realization rolled over her in a debilitating wave. It felt as if the walls were closing in on her; as if she would suffocate if she didn't get out of this house and into the fresh air. It didn't matter what the windchill was.

Sienna ran down the stairs, threw on her coat and boots, and stepped out into the crystal night. The moon was full and the crisp new snow sparkled in its light. She sucked in a lungful of the frigid air, so cold it burned. She drew in another and another, each less panicked than the previous one.

Her mother's disorder had gotten so much worse. Barricading herself in her room? Believing she was pushed down the stairs?

During and after the funeral she had seemed fairly stable. Able to care for herself. Brad had been confident that he and Liz would be able to look in on her, make sure she was okay.

What had happened between then and now?

Stupid question, Sienna. It's been five years. A lot could happen in that time. Just living alone, with too much time spent with her own fearful thoughts, could have taken its toll. Liz was gone, and Brad had given up.

She would talk to him tomorrow, she decided. Call her mother's clinicians as well. Maybe her meds were wrong. And if she'd been lying to Bradley about taking them, he'd have no idea.

Across the street, her handsome neighbor's lights went on. The welcoming glow spilled out of the front window, and she wondered why he wasn't sleeping. Was he one of those nocturnal types, the folks that either required little sleep or preferred working at night? Or like her, was he being kept from sleep by worries about himself or those he loved?

He appeared at his front window, clearly silhouetted by the light behind him. Although she couldn't see his face, it felt as if he was looking directly at her.

But how could he be? She stood in the dark, only faint slivers of the light from inside to illuminate her. Maybe he sensed her here? Or was he watching her mother's house? Waiting for what? For every lamp to be extinguished? And then what?

Stop it, Sienna. You're losing it, big time.

She thought again of her mother's claim. That she'd been pushed down the stairs. If he was a night owl, maybe he had seen something?

He moved away from the window. His front door opened, and he stepped onto the porch, the light following him. He found the wine. She saw him bend to retrieve it, then straighten and look her way. Her cheeks went hot. Her heart skipped a beat. For the second time in a handful of minutes, she told herself she was being ridiculous.

What would he do if she strode across the street and knocked on his door? And if, when he answered, she asked if he wanted some company?

He would think she was a complete nutjob, that's what he would think. She was wearing her PJs, a coat, and snow boots. She hardly knew him. It was the middle of the night.

But some of that she could change.

Five minutes later, dressed in jeans and a bulky sweater, Sienna made her way across the snowy street. With every step, her heart thumped harder. And with each thrum, she doubted her decision a little more.

She ignored both and knocked on his front door.

He opened it, expression concerned. "Sienna? Is everything all right?"

"I saw you were up and took a chance." She sounded as out of breath as she felt.

He looked past her. "Is it your mom?"

"Nothing like that. I couldn't sleep and took a chance you wouldn't mind some company."

His eyebrows raised slightly, and she realized how

this looked and what he must be thinking. Showing up at the sexy neighbor's house—a guy she only just met—in the middle of the night?

Booty call.

"Not that," she said.

"Not what?"

"You know. I'm not coming on to you."

"You're not?"

"Yes. I mean, yes, I'm not. I'm not even flirting."

He folded his arms across his chest and tipped his head, studying her. Waiting.

"Okay, that's not one hundred percent true. I might be flirting a little. But that's not why I came over here."

"Then why did you?"

"Because it seems you're the only other human being on this block who's awake, and I really, really need another human being right now. And maybe a glass of wine."

He let out a bark of laughter, and stepped away from the door. "So you bought a bottle of wine for me, but not yourself? You realize that wasn't great planning?"

"Yeah, I see that now." She stepped inside and unzipped her jacket. The smell of fresh paint stung her nose. This house had been built around the same time as her parents', and she'd been in it many times over the years. The layout was similar to theirs—a series of individual rooms and a hallway that led to them.

Not anymore. He'd created an open concept by knocking out the walls between the living and dining rooms, and the kitchen. "You're doing all this yourself?"

"Pretty much."

"And you're living here full-time?" She gestured around her. "In all this?"

"I'm living in the efficiency in the basement."

She'd forgotten about the apartment the Collinses had built for one of their parents. After the parent passed away, they'd rented it out to college students.

She remembered it as being kind of scary down there, although it had a dedicated entrance and a couple small windows.

"Don't worry, I won't subject you to the dungeon." He'd set the sock monkey by the door, and bent to pick it up. "Help yourself to a lawn chair. I'll get us some wine."

A folding chair stood propped against the wall near the front window. One sat open, facing out, a small outdoor table beside it. She carried hers to the same spot, hung her jacket on the back of it, and sat.

And looked out at the street—and directly at her house. It wasn't . . . weird. But it was.

He returned with two plastic cups. He handed her one, his expression sheepish. "Sorry, I don't have any wineglasses."

She took it. "This is fine. Makes me feel like I'm in college again."

He laughed. "Good times."

She motioned to the window. "Our driveway. Not much of a view."

"I'd rather look out than in," he said. "Reminds me I'm not alone."

She angled a glance at him. "That's a little odd, don't you think?"

"Maybe. But I spend a lot of time alone in here. It's good to know life is happening outside these walls."

"It came in handy for me today. Thank you, again."

"Mack took care of it?"

"Yup. I've got a brand-new battery and am ready to roll."

"Good." He took a sip of the wine. "Tasty," he said. "Not that I'm an expert."

"But you know what you like."

"Exactly." He took another sip. "So, what's your story? Why're you awake at three in the morning?"

"What's yours?"

"I asked first. Besides, not to be a dick or anything, but I wasn't the one who walked across the street."

He had her there. She took the easy way. "Jet lag. I've been living in London for the past ten years. It's daytime there. Simple."

One corner of his beautifully shaped mouth—she had no idea when she'd noticed *that*—lifted. "If it had been that simple, Ms. Scott, you wouldn't have called on a complete stranger in the middle of the night. Am I right?"

He was. Again. "Not a *complete* stranger."

"This is your party. If you don't want to talk, that's cool."

Sienna looked down at her wine, which she'd hardly touched. It was almost surreal, sitting here with him, getting ready to spill her guts.

But it's why she'd crossed the street. Someone to talk to. Someone who *didn't* know her. Or her history. Oddly, she felt safer this way. Like he wouldn't judge her. Or if he did, the judgment would be based on the woman she was now rather than the girl she had been.

"How long have you been in Tranquility?" she began.

"Not long. Six months."

"Long enough, I bet. You know about my mother? That she suffers from mental illness?"

"I don't know the details. Heard it from the real estate agent first. She called her 'that crazy Mrs. Scott.' Said she was scary, but harmless."

Sienna winced at the description. "She has persecutory delusional disorder. Everyone's against her, plotting to hurt her or the people she loves."

Sienna set her wine on the small table between their chairs. She folded her hands in her lap. "It's mostly controlled with medication, although it was always a fight to get her to take it."

"Because she doesn't trust it."

"Give the man a gold star."

"It follows, that's all. You think everyone's out to get you, what better way than by drugging you?"

Funny how he understood that and she never had. Emotionally, anyway. "Tonight she woke me up to tell me the fall she took a few weeks ago wasn't an accident. Now she says she was pushed down the stairs."

"She didn't go to the police?"

Sienna shook her head. "Said they wouldn't believe her. After all, she is 'that crazy Mrs. Scott.'"

"Hell, I shouldn't have told you what the Realtor said. I'm—"

She held up a hand, stopping him from apologizing. "Don't. That's what people have been calling her for years." She clasped, then unclasped her hands. "She didn't even tell my brother. Because, she said, he wouldn't believe her either."

"Do you? Believe her?"

"No," she said. Then, when she heard how hesitant she sounded, she repeated it, this time firmly. "No, I don't."

"Then what? What aren't you saying?"

"That even though I know it's her illness making her think these things, I feel bad. Or guilty. That I don't believe her."

"What if someone did push her?"

"That's nuts. Why would someone push my addled old mother down the stairs?"

"I don't know. But if they did, it'd be a classic boy who cried wolf story."

"I suppose it would." She glanced away, then back. "I've been listening to her ravings all my life and I'm so . . . over it."

"Sounds like a difficult way to grow up."

"Lots of folks have it a lot worse."

"It's tough when someone you love is suffering."

Something in his tone suggested intimate knowledge of such suffering.

He offered before she asked. "My mom tried to drink her depression away. Refused to get counseling or get into rehab."

"What about your dad?"

"Not in the picture at that point. It was just me, trying to pick up the pieces."

"I'm sorry."

He shrugged. "We've all got our shit to deal with."

His was a deep wound, she realized. Just as hers was. Different but the same. She tipped her face toward his. "Thank you."

"For what?"

"For listening."

"Hate to break it to you, but you didn't say all that much."

She hadn't, Sienna realized. But she'd said enough. "I should go."

She stood and grabbed her coat. He followed suit. "So," he said lightly, "I guess you *really* weren't coming on to me."

"I really wasn't."

"Maybe next time?"

She liked him, she realized, and smiled. "Maybe."

He walked her to the door. She fastened her coat and tugged on her gloves, then stepped out into the cold night. Halfway down the walk, she looked back at him. He stood in the doorway, watching her go. And as earlier, he was silhouetted by the light behind him, tall and broad, his expression unreadable. "I appreciate the company, Jonathan. And the ear. Thanks."

A minute later, as she let herself into her house, she realized he'd never told her why he couldn't sleep.

CHAPTER ELEVEN

9:55 A.M.

The kitchen phone awakened Sienna from a deep sleep. She rolled off the couch and onto her feet, hurrying to catch it before the last ring. "H'llo."

"Sienna?"

"M'hmm."

"It's Kim Peterson. Formerly Meyers."

"Of course." She stifled a yawn. "How're you this morning?"

"Great. But it sounds like I woke you up. You want me to call back later?"

Sienna glanced at the mantel clock. Nearly ten. "No, this is good. What's up?"

"I told my mom and dad about running into you, and about you being a chef and all. They asked me to see if you wanted to come take a look at the restaurant. They really want to sell it and they love the idea of a local buying it. I'm mean, if you're at all interested."

Although opening her own place was a dream of hers, she hadn't planned on acting on it so soon. But The Wagon Wheel *was* the perfect location.

"Thanks, Kim, I think I would like to talk to them. Tell them I'll stop by this afternoon, after their lunch rush."

They said their goodbyes and Sienna hung up. She turned around to find her mother standing in the doorway, staring at her.

"Who was that?" she asked.

"Kim Meyers. Now Peterson. Her parents own The Wagon Wheel." She went to the coffeemaker, filled the water tank, then dropped in a filter and added coffee. "Her parents are wanting to retire to Florida, so they're going to sell the place. Kim wanted to know if I wanted to take a look at it."

"And you said yes?"

"I did." She got out a cup and the carton of half-and-half she'd bought the day before. "You want some toast?"

"I'd love a slice. I have some jam?" She went to the refrigerator, took it out, and held it up. "Strawberry."

"I like almond butter these days. But thanks." She gestured toward the table. "Sit down, Mom, I'll get everything."

Her mother did and Sienna noticed her iPhone on the kitchen table, not far from her mother's. She didn't remember leaving it there, but it was no wonder—she'd been so tired when she'd finally finished in the kitchen and headed up to bed.

After making them both toast, Sienna carried everything to the table, then went back for the coffee. She poured them both a cup, then sat. Her mother had gotten out pretty sunflower-print cloth napkins, and Sienna laid hers in her lap. They ate in silence.

"Did you leave the house last night?"

"Excuse me?"

"I thought I heard you go out."

"Just to get some air."

"I don't want you talking to that man across the street."

"Excuse me?"

"He's not a nice person."

"Why do you say that?"

"He's always watching me."

"Like a spy?"

"Yes."

She wasn't sure if she wanted to laugh or cry. "I don't think he's a spy, Mom."

"He moved in and two days later the police reopened your case."

"It's not *my* case, Mom. And his moving in then was just a coincidence."

She looked frustrated. "You really think *that's* a co-incidence?"

"Yes, I do." Sienna decided to change the subject. "You want to come with me this afternoon? To look at The Wagon Wheel? It'd be fun."

Her mother shook her head. "I need to stay here."

"I think it would be good for you to get out." She curled her hands around the coffee cup and breathed in the aroma, then took a sip. "When's the last time you left the house?"

"To go to the doctor's."

"And when was that?"

"I don't remember. A month or two ago."

"Then come with me. You need to get out."

"I would, sweetheart, but I can't give them the op-portunity."

"Them?"

"You know. Margaret."

"Brad's mother?"

"And her clan."

"Clan Margaret?" Sienna sighed. "Because they're all out to get you?"

"Yes. Through you." She looked frustrated. "Nothing's changed, just because you've been gone."

"That's obvious, Mom." Sienna wasn't hungry anymore and pushed her plate away. "Painfully obvious."

"That's why I don't trust him."

"Who? Your new neighbor?"

"No." She shook her head. "Bradley. He's on her side. He always has been. Your dad didn't want to believe it."

"And I don't either." Sienna stood, gathered their plates, and carried them to the sink. "He's my brother. Your stepson, who has taken very good care of you these last few years. He wouldn't hurt either of us."

"It's about the money. It always has been."

"Mom—"

"And about you. Listen to me!" Her voice rose. "Your dad left Margaret for me, and took his money with him. Then we had a baby together—you, a girl—and she couldn't take it anymore."

She crossed to Sienna, caught her hands. "Don't you see? She always wanted another baby. A girl. Then, not only did I have him and his money . . . I had you, too."

She searched Sienna's gaze, as if desperately looking for agreement. "So she set out to hurt me. Punish me for having what she couldn't. What better way to do it than through you? The baby, the daughter, she couldn't have?"

Sienna knew her mother. After a certain point of agitation, she couldn't calm herself down. Only her dad had been able to do it. And even then, he'd had to sometimes call for help.

Sienna calmly eased her hands free. She turned to the sink, rinsed her plate and placed it in the dishwasher, then reached for her glass. "Mom," she said carefully, setting the glass in the machine's top rack, "have you been taking your meds?"

"You know how I feel about taking pills."

"I do." She scraped the remains of her mother's toast into the garbage. "And you know how you feel when you take them." She looked over her shoulder at her. "Better, right?"

"How do I know what's really in them?"

Sienna worked to keep her unease from showing. When she spoke, her voice was steady, her tone soothing. Although it had been many years, Sienna had been through this process hundreds of times, via watching her father. Listening to what he said.

She mimicked him now. "You take all the precautions, don't you? You pick up the prescription from your doctor and take it over to Walton's Pharmacy yourself. Right?"

"Yes. Of course."

"You wait while Steve Johnson fills it. He hands it directly to you. You check the label to make certain you have the correct medication."

Her mother's forehead wrinkled at the logic. She made a sound of frustration. "But how do I *know*?"

"How do you know what, Mom?"

"What's *really* in it. How do I know they haven't gotten to him? Or my doctor?"

A lump formed in Sienna's throat. It was the conundrum of delusional disorder. The person believed what they believed, despite logic or evidence.

She cleared her throat, turned, and met her mother's eyes. "I guess you have to trust, Mom. I know it's hard for you, but when you don't it makes it really hard for anyone to be close to you. Even the people who love you. Like me."

Her mother's eyes filled with tears. "I want to. I just . . . can't."

"The meds help, Mom. You know they do. *That's* why you take them." She paused. "I want to be close to you. It's all I really want."

Tears rolled slowly down her mother's cheeks. "I want that, too."

"Then you need to take your meds. Can you do that for me?"

Her mother nodded. "Okay. I'll do it for you."

CHAPTER TWELVE

Sunshine poured through the driver's side window, warming Sienna. The brilliant day was almost too bright, but it matched her celebratory mood. She and her mother had gotten the medicine, checked the vial carefully—it was indeed the antipsychotic drug Zyprexa—and her mother had taken it.

It felt like a major victory. Not just because her mom had taken the medicine, but because Sienna had stopped her mother from cycling into a full-blown paranoiac episode.

She could do this, she thought, smiling. Her decision to come home wasn't as boneheaded as she had started to fear it was.

Sienna turned onto Main Street, the heart of Old Town. She'd driven this path on the way to her brother's office just yesterday, but she had been too anxious to see him to take her time, and too distracted to soak it in even if she had.

She did now, swinging her gaze from side to side, taking in the old and the new, flooded with memories. Of Sunday-morning pancakes at the Morning Bell; of July Fourth celebrations, with games and a fireworks display; of shopping with her girlfriends, searching for that special dress and flirting with boys who were too old for them.

Main Street was still like a small slice of Americana, frozen in time. Ten years ago it had looked its age. Like a lot of American Rust Belt cities, left behind and fading, dotted with empty storefronts and failing businesses.

No longer. Many of the pre–twentieth century buildings had been repainted and rehabbed. The empty businesses had been replaced with new ones, a skate shop and a coffeehouse. She saw an upscale women's boutique and a children's store.

Brad had been talking about the changes. A billionaire had come to town with a vision of making the small Wisconsin community a tech mecca. Old industrial sites, like the foundry down by the river, had been not just rehabilitated, but modernized as well.

Many called the woman foolish—she'd proved them wrong. Young start-ups and creative thinkers from places like Seattle, Portland, Chicago, and Austin had come to Tranquility Bluffs.

And those sophisticated young people needed places to live. Brad had stepped in, developing trendy condo communities with all the features they desired— and his business had exploded.

Now, she thought, easing into a parking space across the street from The Wagon Wheel, it was her turn. Those very same people needed places to eat that provided the food, atmosphere, and service they were accustomed to.

Sienna climbed out of her car, working to tamp down her excitement. She couldn't get ahead of herself. This was happening way sooner than she had planned for, and frankly, sooner than she might be ready for.

But she couldn't *not* explore this opportunity. A

working restaurant with a full kitchen, located at the very heart of Main Street? It might never come her way again.

She locked the car and turned to look at the restaurant. The Wagon Wheel had not yet gotten a face-lift. It looked tired and shabby next to its shiny counterparts.

But it had good bones, she thought. And character. All the new paint in the world couldn't manufacture those.

Sienna crossed the street and stepped into the restaurant. The interior was exactly as she remembered it. Wagon-wheel light fixtures, sturdy wooden tables with red-and-white-checkered tablecloths. A lantern with a candle sat in the center of each.

She would bet the menu hadn't changed either. Simple, hearty dishes—like stew and chili—with beef the featured protein in most of them. Back in the day, the Friday-night sirloin steak special had been so popular, they'd begun offering it Wednesday nights, as well.

As she moved her gaze over the interior, she acknowledged that both the Old West concept and heavy-on-beef menu were not what current diners enjoyed. And she bet the hipsters pouring into town would like it even less than most.

But an updated French bistro? With lighter fare, complex flavor profiles, and a bright, contemporary atmosphere?

Yeah, she thought, smiling broadly. They would love it.

A waitress appeared from the swinging doors that led to the kitchen. She caught sight of Sienna and came over.

"I hope you weren't waiting long," she said.

Sienna smiled. "I'm here to see Donna and Ted. Could you let them know Sienna Scott's here?"

"You bet." She smiled and tucked her long bangs behind an ear. "They told me to be on the lookout for you. I'll be right back."

"Thanks." Sienna watched her go. The woman looked to be forty-something, with a pleasant face and a nice manner. She would have to remember her when she started staffing.

Donna Meyers came through the swinging doors, followed by her husband.

"Sienna," she said, giving her a hug. "It's so good to see you. All grown up, too." She looked over her shoulder at her husband. "Ted, can you believe it?"

"It's very nice to see you, Sienna," he said, holding out a hand.

She took it, remembering he was always the more reserved of the two of them. "It's good to see you, too."

"I hear you're a chef," he said.

"A fancy French one," Donna added.

"Honey, you're embarrassing her."

"I'm proud of her, that's all."

"Thank you, Donna. I appreciate that." Sienna moved her gaze between the two of them. "Kim tells me you're interested in selling the restaurant."

"We are," he said, "but we're not in a hurry."

"*He's* not in a hurry. I can't wait."

Ted rolled his eyes. "How about a tour of the old place?"

Sienna said she would love it. As they showed her every nook and cranny of the business they had run for forty years, their pride came through—not just in the things they said, but in the immaculate way they had maintained the facility. The floors, walls, and fixtures—all had been meticulously cared for.

The kitchen was a marvel. Old, sure. But it appeared to be in tip-top condition. She would have to make a few upgrades and additions, but otherwise, what was here was better than what she'd expected.

They finished the tour in the second-floor apartment. It was open concept, large and light. "I didn't realize this was an apartment up here," Sienna said. "I just assumed it was storage."

"It was, once upon a time. We've been renting to one of the college professors—"

"Dr. Isaac Warner," Donna offered.

"He retired the end of last semester—"

"He kept to himself. Rather eccentric."

"We didn't want to lease it again until we knew what we were doing."

Sienna only heard half of what they were saying. She turned in a slow circle, taking it in. Twelve-foot ceilings and large, old-fashioned roll-up windows that cast big rectangles of light on the wooden floors. This was perfect for her, absolutely perfect. She could live above the restaurant. It would make watching over the renovation and later, the operation, so much easier.

Excited, she moved on to the kitchen. Minimal, she saw. But that was okay. It had a good layout and she loved the bar with seating for three. One bathroom. Certainly not luxurious, but large with the appropriate fixtures—double sink, large mirror, tub and shower—with a private closet for the commode.

"I love it," she said.

Mr. Meyers's brow wrinkled. "Which part?"

"All of it. What are you asking?"

"We haven't gotten a valuation on the business yet. We weren't in a hurry—"

Donna cut him off. "Are you in a hurry?"

She hadn't been, Sienna acknowledged. But she

was now, fueled by excitement at the possibilities. "It's something I planned for the future, but this seems like a perfect fit for me. But price is going to be important."

"It always is," Donna said, and looked at her husband.

He nodded. "Okay, I'll get the ball rolling."

"And you won't offer it to anyone else?" Sienna knew she shouldn't be showing her hand this way, but she wasn't about to let this slip through her fingers. "You'll give me first refusal?"

Sienna held out her hand; he grasped it. "That we will. In fact, we'd be delighted to do that."

A few minutes later, Sienna was standing on the sidewalk outside the restaurant. Too excited not to share this news with someone, she dialed her brother. It went straight to voice mail. "I'm in town, thought I'd stop by. Call me back."

She crossed the street. From that vantage point she could see his Lexus sedan parked in front of his building. He was her brother; she was allowed to pop in. If he was in the middle of something, she'd wait or have him call her.

A couple minutes later, she stepped through his door. She found the waiting area empty and called out, "Brad? It's me."

She didn't get a response, and started for his office. The door was partially open; he was on the phone.

"—a little more time," he was saying. "In this climate—"

He stopped as if cut off by the person on the other end of the call. "I told you I'd take care of that. . . . You have to understand, financing a project as large as this—"

Realizing this was a conversation he wouldn't have

wanted her to hear, Sienna backed away from the door, then turned and hurried to the waiting area.

She started to write him a note when he appeared from the rear, expression thunderous. He saw her and stopped, expression clearing. "Hey sis, what're you doing here?"

"I came to share some good news. But I've got a confession to make first. When I came in I called out, but when I didn't get a response, I wandered back to find you."

"And heard my conversation."

"Part of it. I'm sorry about that."

"Nothing to be sorry for." He grinned. "I've got nothing to hide from my kid sister. Investors are such a pain. I'm always soothing someone's ruffled feathers." He smiled, though it didn't reach his eyes. "What's your good news?"

"I guess it's not really news, more like sharing my excitement. Did you know The Wagon Wheel's for sale?"

"I heard a rumor they were thinking of selling, but didn't know they had made a final decision."

"They have now, and I went to look at it."

"Look at it?" He drew his eyebrows together. "Why?"

"To buy it, of course."

He didn't respond and she went on. "You've got to admit, it's a great location. And a great live-and-work opportunity."

"You're considering taking over The Wheel? If they didn't own the property and had to pay rent all these years, that place would've gone under a long time ago."

"Not take it over, open my own place. It's something I've been thinking about for a while, although I hadn't planned to do it so soon."

He looked so incredulous, she laughed. "Sorry to

drop another bombshell on you. Like I said, I didn't have immediate plans, but with The Wagon Wheel up for sale . . . It's perfect, Brad."

He cleared his throat. "Wow . . . your own restaurant."

"A French bistro."

"Here? In Tranquility Bluffs, Wisconsin?"

"Yes. Just like you told me on the phone, Tranquility Bluffs has changed." When he only frowned, she went on, "I thought you'd be excited for me."

"It's not that." He paused, as if to carefully choose his words. "I know you're a chef, but what do you know about running a restaurant?"

"More than you might think. I've spent the last ten years around and in restaurants. I even helped a friend open his own place."

"Let me rephrase that. What do you know about running a business? It's no picnic, let me tell you. There's inventory and salaries, taxes, advertising. And above all, the bottom line."

"Like I said, I've been working in the industry for ten years. And I can learn. And hire the right people."

"Which takes money," he shot back.

"Which I have. Dad left me more than enough to do this. What's your problem?"

He let out a weary-sounding breath. "I just don't want you to blow your inheritance on a pipe dream."

"Opening my own bistro is not a 'pipe' dream," she said stiffly. "It's an attainable one."

He shoved his hands into his pockets. "Poor choice of words, I apologize. But Dad left me in charge, and I take his confidence in me very seriously."

Sienna met his eyes. "I appreciate that, Brad, I do. But I'm almost thirty years old. Don't you think it's about time I acted on my dreams?"

He gazed at her for a moment, then let out a sigh that sounded way too heavy for a man of his age. "You're right. You're not a kid anymore, and I need to get with the program. But damn, it's not going to be easy."

She gave him a quick hug. "I really do appreciate your concern, and I love you for it. I tell you what, how about you work on remembering I'm grown up, and I'll work on remembering how awesome it is to have a big brother who wants to protect me."

He grinned. "It's a deal. As long as you'll allow me to offer advice from time to time?"

"Are you kidding? I'm counting on your sage advice. Buying and rehabbing property is in your wheelhouse, not mine."

"Sage? Wow, that makes me feel old."

"How about amazing? Or brilliant?"

"Better. Much." He checked his watch. "Did you have lunch? I haven't, and I'm hungry enough to chew off my own arm."

At the thought of food, her stomach rumbled. Her meager breakfast was long gone. "I haven't and am starving, too. What do you have in mind?"

"There's a great little café on the riverfront. I think you'll like it."

"Sounds great. And I'll treat."

"Oh, hell no," he said. "I will."

CHAPTER THIRTEEN

"Welcome to Max's Table," a woman called out from the top of a stepladder. "Have a seat anywhere, I'll be right with you."

They chose a table by a window with a view of the river. "Cute place," Sienna said as they sat down. It was an eclectic mix of turn-of-the-century industrial—obviously a nod to Tranquility's past—and high-tech urban, reflecting its present.

The combination of elements—exposed ducting, scored concrete floors, and enlarged photographs from the town's manufacturing heyday, juxtaposed by neon light elements and shiny tables and chairs—shouldn't have gone together, but did.

Sienna turned back to her brother and found his eyes not on her, but on the woman who had greeted them, now on her way toward them with menus.

Something in his intent expression suggested interest that had nothing to do with lunch. She wondered if he was romantically involved with her. Or just wanting to be?

"Hi, Brad," she said. "I haven't seen you in a while."

Her gaze shifted to Sienna, and he quickly jumped

in. "This is my sister, Sienna. She just moved back to town. Sienna, Laura Maxwell."

The woman smiled and held out her hand. "Call me Max."

"Hi, Max," she said. "This is your place?"

She laid the menus on the table. "It is."

"Sienna's hoping to open her own restaurant soon."

"No kidding? You coming at it from the cooking side or business side?"

"Cooking, most definitely. Luckily, I have Brad to turn to for business advice."

Another group came in. Max called hello, then turned back to her. "I'd love to talk to you about it sometime."

Sienna smiled. "I'd love that, too."

"Take a look at the menu. I'll be out with water for both of you and will be happy to answer any questions you might have."

Sienna watched her walk away, then turned to her brother. "She's really nice," she said. "I like her. She's not from here, is she?"

"No, Chicago." He picked up his menu. "Everything's good, by the way. I particularly enjoy her turkey chili."

That sounded good to her, and she set the menu aside. "It's been an interesting twenty-four hours."

"Do I hear a hint of 'it seems way longer than that' in your voice?"

"You do. But it hasn't been all bad."

Max brought the water, took their order, then left them alone again. And again Sienna noticed how her brother's gaze followed the woman.

"You were saying? Not all bad?"

Sienna thought of her sexy neighbor, but talked about

her mother. "We had a much-needed breakthrough this morning. I got her to take her Zyprexa without a scene."

"No screaming? No accusations or threats?"

"Nope. None."

"Wow, that is a major victory."

"There is something I wanted to tell you. About her fall."

His expression turned guarded. "Yeah?"

"She says it wasn't an accident. She says she was pushed, Brad."

"Of course she did."

"She says she didn't tell you because—"

"I wouldn't believe her."

"No." Sienna lowered her voice. "Because you're one of 'them.'"

"I'm not surprised." He fiddled with his flatware. "But I am pissed. And hurt."

She didn't blame him for either emotion. "I'm sorry. I thought you should know."

"I've tried to be a good stepson, because that's what Dad wanted. Not a day goes by that I don't have some issue related to her to deal with. For God's sake, my marriage ended because of her. And I'm one of the imaginary *them*?"

The question was rhetorical; Sienna didn't respond. "Did she say I pushed her down the stairs?"

"No."

"I suppose I should be grateful for that."

"I'm sorry," Sienna said again.

He looked at her then, something akin to grief in his eyes. "You need to understand something, Sienna. This isn't going away. She's never getting better. And building a life here means shackling yourself to the crazy train."

He was being deliberately blunt and disrespectful. "I know that."

"I'm not so sure you do."

"Speaking about Mom, she's worried about Liz and asked if I'd give her a call, and since I wanted to touch base with her anyway—"

"Seriously?"

She took a sip of her water. "What?"

"She left me, Sienna. She's not family anymore."

"I get it. But you know Viv, the way she obsesses about things . . . so, if you don't mind, I could give her a call and—"

"I do mind." As if in reaction to her surprised expression, he softened his tone. "She and I are still negotiating a few things, and I don't want to muddy the water."

Max showed up with their chili and a basket of crackers. It smelled delicious, and something about the spicy aroma and the bright-colored crockery bowl calmed her.

It seemed to have the same effect on Brad, because as they ate they talked to each other in a way they hadn't since she'd been home. She shared her dreams for her restaurant and he, his longing for a family someday. They laughed, too. And teared up, as they recalled memories of times with their father.

It wasn't until later, in her mother's car and nearly back to the house, that his earlier warning came crashing back down on her.

"This isn't going away. She's never getting better."

Did she understand that? Intellectually, sure. But what it *truly* meant?

Never. Getting. Better. A lifetime riding the front car of the roller coaster of mental illness.

The words sank in. The emotional exhaustion. The helplessness. The frustration and grief.

The anger.

If she stayed, her mother's mental illness would be a day-to-day part of her life. It would never go away. Her mother would never be miraculously healed. The best she could hope for was managing her illness with medication.

For the rest of her life.

Sienna suddenly felt strange, light-headed and sweaty, and she gripped the steering wheel tighter. She thought of Mimi, of London, her friends and coworkers.

She longed for them. For her easy, confident life.

Her home was London. Not Tranquility Bluffs.

What had she done?

Her vision blurred and a panicked squeak slipped past her lips. Her heart beat wildly; she couldn't catch her breath. What was happening to her?

Pull over, Sienna.

She responded to her voice in her head, pulling over, shifting into park. She fought to breathe. Her mind raced.

The airport. She could drive straight there, catch the next available flight.

Brad would understand. It was almost as if he'd prefer her to go. So he wouldn't have to worry about her. And her mother? She would be better off without her nearby, stirring up her imaginary monsters.

Yes, she should go. Coming home had been a mistake. Look what was happening to her. Only home one day, and already falling apart. That's why her father had sent her away.

Because she had been falling apart.

The memories of that time came flooding back.

Not just of the murder or her interviews with the police; no, of *her*. How she had been. What she had been becoming.

Not what. Who. Her mother, she acknowledged. She'd been becoming like her mother.

And it was happening again.

CHAPTER FOURTEEN

Two weeks since the murder

Sienna tapped on her father's partially closed office door. "Dad, do you have a minute to talk?"

He looked up and smiled. "Of course, sweetheart. I always have time for you."

She crossed to the desk and sat in the wing chair across the expanse of mahogany from him. She realized her palms were damp, and rubbed them on her jeans. "It's been two weeks since, you know. And I think I'm ready to go back to school."

"But you're not sure?"

She wasn't. But she felt like she had to. Her professors had been great. They'd made sure all the lecture materials were available to her and had allowed her to test from home.

But the time had come.

And she wouldn't give in to fear. She couldn't.

"Yes." She nodded. "I'm sure. I thought I'd start tomorrow."

He looked at her over his steepled fingers. "Have you told your mother?"

"No." She drew in a quick, deep breath, then let it out. "I'd hoped . . . would you do it for me? You're the only one . . . you keep her calm."

For a long moment, he held her gaze. She wanted to look away—like a guilty child—but she didn't.

Finally, he nodded. "I'll do it. But on one condition." She nodded and he went on. "For now, for my peace of mind, you live at home instead of the dorm."

She had fought so hard for the right to stay in the dorm. Her mother had wanted her here, where she was "safe." Truthfully, Sienna had wanted to go away to school. She'd applied to, and been accepted by, the University of Chicago, Ohio State, even UW Madison, thinking that if the school was within driving distance, her mother would acquiesce.

She hadn't. The thought of Sienna out of her sight had triggered an episode so severe it landed her a seventy-two-hour stay at Evergreen Behavioral Health Hospital. So, to keep the peace, Sienna had agreed to Fredricks, the private liberal arts college ten minutes from home. But she'd insisted on the dorm.

Her heart sank. "Okay. Until they make an arrest."

"Thank you. I know—" His voice turned thick and he cleared his throat. "—it hasn't been easy for you, because of your mother's illness. And I appreciate the sacrifices you've had to make."

He looked tired, she thought. More tired than usual. And who could blame him? Keeping her mother functioning was a full-time job—on top of his busy medical practice.

She reached across the table and covered his hand with hers. "It's okay, Dad."

"Love you, pumpkin."

"Love you, too."

She released his hand and started to stand, then sat back down. "I wanted to ask you something else."

"Shoot."

She realized her hands were shaking and dropped

them to her lap. "You talk to Chief Thompson some-times, don't you?"

"I do."

"I was wondering, how come they haven't caught the guy who killed Madison?"

"I don't know, sweetheart. They're trying, I do know that."

"What about her boyfriend? I heard they had a big fight the same day she was killed."

"I'm sure they know that. I've checked in with Fred—they're interviewing everyone who knew her and knew her schedule. Family, friends, classmates. They'll find the guy who did it."

She jumped on the description. "Do they know it was a guy who did it?"

He looked surprised. "I don't know that. I guess I just assumed the killer was a male."

Sienna nodded, understanding. She had assumed the same thing. She couldn't picture a woman perpe-trating such violence, although intellectually she knew otherwise.

His brow furrowed with concern. "What's going on? Why're you asking me all this?"

She looked down at her hands, then back up at him. "It just seems like, if the boyfriend was the guy, they'd know it by now."

"Maybe they don't have enough to prove it yet. I'm no legal expert, but I know there are rules about how long you can hold someone before you formally charge them. Could be they're getting their ducks in a row."

"Maybe," she said, biting her lip.

"Are you afraid to go back to school because they haven't made an arrest?"

She shook her head. "No."

The truth was, she was terrified. But not of going

back to school; of something else, something darker. A thought that had wormed its way into her head.

Something she didn't want to share with him.

Because she didn't want him to think *it* was happening. That she was becoming like her mother.

"Pumpkin? What's wrong?"

"It's just weird, I think. That they haven't made an arrest."

"It's not. Give the police time."

"Thanks, Dad." She nodded and stood, the dark thought pressing, wanting out. As if it had a will of its own. "Sorry I bothered you."

She reached the door and stopped. Turned back. "Did you think it was . . . odd, that Madison and I were wearing the same coat?"

His expression took on a frozen quality. "What?"

"Our jackets. They were almost identical."

"I didn't realize that."

"Well, they were."

"It doesn't mean anything," he said sharply.

She understood the root of his sharp tone. She knew what he was thinking.

Because she was thinking the same thing. That the similarity of the coats wasn't the odd part—her question about them was.

Her mother would do the same thing. Then she would focus on the coincidence, and it would nag at her, and nag at her. And build until it was large, menacing . . . and in control of her life.

His expression softened. "You were wearing your ski jacket, right? The white one?"

She nodded. "With the hood."

"There you go. It's just a plain jacket in a generic color. I bet a lot of girls have a similar coat."

She wasn't so sure about that, but to ease his mind, she agreed with him anyway.

"You're right." She forced a smile. "It was a silly coincidence. Thinking about it freaked me out, that's all."

"You've experienced an awful shock. One I can only imagine. Don't give the jacket thing another thought. Okay?"

She agreed and left him to his work, although she knew he'd asked the impossible.

She would be unable to think of anything but.

CHAPTER FIFTEEN

One month since the murder

Sienna had begun counting off the days since that terrible, snowy night. Today was thirty. Exactly one month.

And still no arrest.

She'd kept Chief Thompson's card, making sure she had it with her at all times. Every so often she would take it out of her wallet and just look at it. She found seeing his name reassured her. Sometimes she read the phone number aloud, whispering it over and over, like a mantra.

If she needed him, he was there. He would save her.

But save her from what?

Sienna thought about the coat all the time. She dreamed about it. And about ugly red creeping across pristine white. She had taken to looking for other jackets like hers. On campus. Downtown. On the Internet.

Truth was, solid white hooded ski jackets weren't all that popular. Color was big. Bright, even neon. Orange. Lime. Electric blue.

She told herself it didn't mean anything. Coincidences happened. Didn't they?

Sienna sat on a bench at the edge of the college quad, watching the organizers of tonight's vigil set up. A news van arrived. A cameraman and reporter hopped out.

Sienna hunched deeper into her new jacket, this one pink, no hood.

Like the coincidence of the time. She thought about that a lot, too. Madi had been killed right around midnight, just minutes before Sienna found her. The killer could have still been close by. He could have been watching her.

The thought was chilling, but not nearly so chilling as another: if she hadn't left her study group late, it could have been she who was killed.

The thought nagged at her. It pounded in her head like a warning drumbeat.

You're missing something, Sienna. Something important.

That drumbeat mixed with another.

The coat, Sienna. Why did you both have the same coat?

Then another thrumming, far away but drawing closer.

Maybe it was supposed to be you, Sienna. Maybe you were the one who was supposed to die.

No. Sienna shook her head. She couldn't think that way. She wouldn't. That was her mother—seeing everything as a personal threat.

A long-ago memory popped into her head. Her father sitting her down and telling her that Mommy was sick. That her sickness was in her mind instead of her body. It caused her to sometimes say and do things that were scary. The important thing, he said, was to remember that it was the illness talking and to always come to him for the truth.

It wasn't until years later that he named the illness. Delusional disorder. He described it for her: a form of psychosis in which a person cannot tell what's real and what's imaginary. In her mom's case, the delusions were persecutory. She hadn't understood the word and he explained: her mother believed people were plotting against her, that they wanted to hurt her. And that they wanted to hurt the people she loved. Including Sienna.

"Am I like her, Daddy?"

"No, pumpkin, you're not. Never worry about that, not for a minute. Promise me you won't."

She promised, but even then she knew it was a promise she couldn't keep. He'd sounded so strange when he said it, his voice sort of tight and choked. Like he couldn't quite catch his breath. And he'd looked funny, too. Sad and worried and . . . scared?

She didn't really understand at the time. Now, she did.

He was afraid Sienna was her mother's daughter in every way.

And she feared it, too.

"Sienna?"

It took her a moment to recognize the man without his uniform. "Officer Clark?"

"That's me." He smiled and she realized he was much younger than she'd previously thought. More like her brother's age. Thirty, maybe.

"Mind if I sit by you?"

"Sure." She moved her backpack to the ground by her feet.

"I've been meaning to stop by and check on you. See if you were doing all right."

"I'm doing okay, I guess. How about you?"

He looked surprised by the question. "The same." He gazed down at his feet, shuffling them slightly.

She found the small sign of unease comforting. She reached over and laid her gloved hand over his. "I still see her, in my head," she said softly. "When I close my eyes."

"Me, too. I never thought I'd see anything like that." He curled his hand around hers.

"I sure wish they'd catch whoever did it." Her voice quivered. "It's hard being back on campus, knowing he could be anywhere. Maybe even following me."

He looked at her, eyebrows drawn together in a frown. "Why do you think he'd be following you?"

"I don't. Not really." She pulled her hand back, feeling exposed and weird. "I've got to go."

"Wait, Sienna. He's not following you. I know he's not."

The strangest sensation rolled over her, prickly and uncomfortable. "How do you know?" she asked, voice squeaky.

"'Cause that's not the way a killer operates."

She frowned slightly and he went on. "We've got two reasons for this murder. The first would be opportunity. Madison Robie was in the wrong place at the wrong time. Our killer saw his opportunity and took it."

Sienna shivered. It was a terrifying thought. She knew such things happened, but in places like Chicago and Detroit. Not here.

He pursed his lips and narrowed his eyes. "That theory doesn't hold water for me. Not on this campus. Not during a snowstorm. It doesn't make sense."

"What's the other reason?" she asked, mouth dry.

"It was personal."

"Personal?"

"Somebody was damn mad at her. Or jealous. We're talking strong emotions, love or hate. Passion."

"Love?" she asked, voice shaking. "I don't understand."

"Warped love. Love that wasn't returned. Or was betrayed."

"Which hurts."

"Sometimes enough to twist itself into something much darker."

"Hate." She nodded. "I see what you're saying."

"That's the way she was killed. Eighteen stab wounds? Nothing impersonal about that."

Eighteen stab wounds? Sienna's stomach turned over, and her head felt light.

He went on. "He was waiting for her. He knew she would walk by him, even on such a terrible night. He maybe figured the weather was a good thing. Nobody else would be around. Evidence would be hard to collect. That's my theory, anyway."

Sienna wrapped her arms around her middle. "But if it was personal," she said, voice quivering, "that means the killer had to be someone she knew."

"That's right. And knew well."

"So—" She cleared her throat, swallowing past the sour taste in her mouth. "—why haven't the police figured out who did it? It seems like it'd be lots easier to find the guy if she knew him well."

"Usually it is. Think about it, it's always easier to find something if you know where you lost it."

"But if they're wrong, they're looking in the wrong place."

He frowned. "What do you mean? Wrong about what?"

She couldn't say it. Couldn't voice her crazy thoughts aloud. "I don't feel so well, Officer Clark. I've got to go."

She jumped to her feet and started off, then stopped and glanced back. "Thanks. For talking to me. Nobody else has."

CHAPTER SIXTEEN

Seven hours later

Sienna didn't realize she'd forgotten her backpack until later that night when Officer Clark showed up at her door with it.

She took it from him. "Thank you! I have a test tomorrow, I would have panicked when I saw it wasn't here."

"Do you have a minute to talk?"

Sienna frowned slightly and glanced over her shoulder. Although it wasn't that late, her mother was sleeping and her dad had been called to the hospital for an emergency.

She opened the door wider and stepped aside anyway. "We just need to keep it low. My mom's not . . . feeling well."

He nodded and she closed the door behind them. She motioned toward the living room. He followed her and sat down in the same chair Chief Thompson had sat in when he interviewed her. And like that night, she took the same spot across from him on the couch.

"What's up, Officer Clark?"

"First, I wanted to thank you."

"Thank me? For what?"

"This afternoon, when you asked how I was doing. You're the first one who has."

"Oh." She wasn't certain what else to say, so she looked down at her hands.

He went on. "I'm a cop, so I guess I'm supposed to be hardened to all this. But I'd never seen, you know, anything like that before."

She did know, and nodded.

"And I wanted to apologize."

She looked up, surprised. "For what?"

"This afternoon. I think I scared you with all that stuff I said, and I'm sorry about that."

"You didn't scare me."

He laced his fingers together, looked down at them a moment before meeting her eyes once more. "I could see you were upset. And in such a hurry to go, you forgot your backpack."

She flushed. "I was upset. But not scared."

"Then I apologize for upsetting you. That certainly wasn't my intent."

She glanced away. Then back. "No, that's not . . . like I said, I'm glad you told me all that."

They fell silent. The seconds ticked past, becoming long and awkward. She once again dropped her gaze to her hands clenched in her lap.

"Sienna?"

She looked up.

"You can talk to me." He said it softly. When she didn't respond, he tried again. "Tell me what's bothering you."

"Nothing. It's just hard . . . to get it out of my head."

"I know. I'm right there with you." He paused a moment before going on. "What did you mean when you said that thing about the police looking in the wrong place?"

"I don't want to talk about it."

"You can trust me, Sienna."

"It makes me look . . . I'll sound crazy."

"How about I be the judge of that?" She didn't respond and he leaned forward. "Look, I know police work. You don't. What if the very thing you're thinking is what we need to know to make an arrest?"

She had been thinking the same thing. Wasn't it her responsibility to do everything she could to help the police? What if, by holding back she let Madison's killer get away?

She met his eyes. "I just wondered . . . I mean . . . what if—" Her throat closed over the words, and she cleared it. "What if it was supposed to be me?"

He stared blankly at her a moment before realization crossed his features. "You mean, like the killer was after you?"

Her cheeks burned. "Never mind, I'm being ridiculous." She jumped to her feet. "I really need to start studying."

"Wait." He followed her to her feet. "I want to know why you would even think that."

Because I'm crazy. Just like my mother.

Instead, she said, "Mostly because of the coat."

"The coat?"

"We were wearing the same jacket. With the hood up, her head down, and the snow, she could have been mistaken for me."

"And that's it?"

"Yes." She drew in a deep breath, then let it out. "No. There's the time, too. I take that cut-through every Wednesday night at midnight. That Wednesday I was late, because of the weather and because my study group ran long."

"Did Madison always take that route?"

"I don't know. I never saw her—or almost anybody using that path at that time of night."

He was quiet for several moments, eyebrows drawn together as if in thought. "She worked at the library, correct?"

"Yes. I saw her there every Wednesday night."

"The library closes at midnight."

"Yes."

"But you never crossed paths with her then. For what you're suggesting to work, Madison Robie either stayed at the library late or—"

"Left early," she finished for him. "Because of the weather."

"Or a third option, she never took that shortcut, but did that night hoping to get wherever she was going sooner. Because of the snowstorm."

They fell silent, the only sound in the room the ticking of the mantel clock. "Do you think I'm . . . crazy?"

"No. What you're suggesting is possible."

"But?"

"Not probable. In my opinion." He leaned forward, gaze trained on hers. "Tell me this, why would someone want to kill you?"

"I don't know."

"You break up with a boyfriend recently?"

"No. No boyfriend."

"You cross somebody recently? Dump a best friend or—"

"No!"

"So, no enemies that you know of."

"I have enemies."

Her mother. Standing in the doorway in her robe and slippers, hair disheveled.

"Mom! What are you doing up?"

But her mother didn't even glance her way. Instead, her gaze never strayed from Officer Clark.

"I have enemies," she said again. "And they'd love nothing better than to hurt me through Sienna."

Sienna stood. Cheeks hot, she crossed to her mother, slipped an arm through hers. "C'mon, Mom. You need to go back to bed. This has nothing to do with you."

She shook her arm free. "You're my daughter, of course it does."

Sienna looked at Officer Clark. "Could you please leave? It's not a good time."

She saw his confusion, and was grateful he stood up without question and prepared to go.

Her mother stopped him. "Who are you? What do you want with my daughter?"

"He doesn't want anything with me, Mom. I forgot my backpack at school, and Officer Clark was nice enough to bring it for me."

"You don't look like a cop. Where's your badge?"

"Mom! He's from the college. He's part of the campus force."

"I don't believe you. I heard you talking about enemies. You're hiding something from me."

Sienna's breathing quickened. Her cheeks burned with embarrassment. "Mom, for heaven's sake, stop it! We were talking about the girl who was killed on campus. I was wondering why they hadn't caught the killer. If *she* had enemies. That's all."

Officer Clark looked at her, and she saw the sympathy in his gaze. She understood that he might not know her mother's diagnosis, but he knew there was one.

"I'm going to go, Mrs. Scott. I'm sorry I disturbed you."

He headed to the front door; her mom grabbed his arm, stopping him. "Maybe that's why they haven't caught the killer . . . Maybe it was them . . . they meant to kill Sienna. They lay in wait—"

Headlights cut across the front window. Her father, Sienna saw, home from the hospital.

She ran to the door, yanked it open. He'd stopped alongside Officer Clark's SUV. "Dad!" she shouted. "Come quick!"

His door flew open, and he came at a run. Her mother had backed herself into a corner. "Lord help me . . . my little girl . . . they could have killed my little girl!"

"Viv!"

Sienna made way for her father. He passed her and Officer Clark without even a glance. He caught her shoulders and shook her. "Viv! Everything's fine! Sienna's fine."

"No!" she screeched. "Don't you see? It was them! They almost got her this time!"

Her dad pulled her into a bear hug. She fought him. Wailing and screeching.

He looked over his shoulder at her. "Get him out of here, Sienna! Now, please."

She didn't have to ask. Officer Clark reacted, heading for the door like a streak. Sienna followed him, wishing she could climb in his Suburban and go, too. Wherever. Anywhere but here.

And never come back.

He hopped in the vehicle and fired up the engine. Before he closed the door, he looked back at her. "I'm sorry, Sienna," he said, then slammed the door.

She watched him drive off, uncertain what he meant.

Was he sorry he'd come tonight? Or because he thought he had caused her mother's meltdown?

Or maybe neither of those. Maybe he was just plain sorry for her.

CHAPTER SEVENTEEN

Present day
4:55 P.M.

Tap. Tap, tap.

She turned toward the sound, struggling to breathe.

"Sienna? Are you okay?"

Jonathan. Bent over to look in her car window. She tried to speak, to tell him she wasn't okay, but couldn't find her voice.

He tried the door. Found it locked.

"Open the door, Sienna! Let me help you."

She nodded and yanked on the door handle, but nothing happened. She yanked again, panic overwhelming her. "I . . . can't . . . breathe!"

"It's locked," he called. "Find the switch."

Sienna frantically searched for the lock button. Where was . . . it? There had to be . . .

She found it and a moment later, the door flew open. Frigid air rushed over her and she half leaped, half tumbled out of the sedan.

He caught her. "Look at me, Sienna."

She did. Warm brown eyes so deep she could get lost in them.

"I think you're having a panic attack," he said calmly.

"Try to slow your breathing. Deep, even breaths. In and out. You can do this."

She followed his instructions, breathing slowly in, then slowly out. Minutes passed; her heart slowed, her vision cleared. Her panic retreated, leaving the sting of the cold—and the heat of embarrassment.

She forced herself to meet his eyes. "That's twice you've come to my rescue."

"That's me, just your everyday knight in shining armor."

"I feel like an idiot."

"Don't. Panic attacks are a natural reaction to extreme stress."

She took a step back, and he dropped his arms. "I haven't had one in years. Thank God I pulled over when I did."

"And that you were so close to home."

She looked past him, surprised. There it was, the redbrick colonial: 212 Winter Lane. Where she used to live. But not anymore. Brad was right, being here was not good for her.

"You know what brought the attack on?"

"Yeah, I do." She slid back into the car, looked up at him. "Thanks for coming to my rescue again."

A small frown formed between his eyebrows. "No problem. If you need to talk about it, you know where I am."

She did, indeed. Unfortunately, soon she would be thousands of miles away from there.

He straightened and stepped back. She pulled away from the curb. As she drove off, she glanced in her rearview and found him watching her. She couldn't make out his expression but had a pretty good idea what he was thinking.

That she was a complete whackjob. Just like that "crazy Mrs. Scott."

Sienna expected her mother to be anxiously waiting, half out of her mind with worry. She braced herself for the scene; instead, she found her mother in her favorite chair by the fire, quietly reading.

When she saw Sienna, she smiled and set her book aside. "Hi, sweetheart. How'd it go?"

"Really well. I'm sorry I'm so late."

"It's not a problem." She stood and smoothed a hand over her slacks. "How was lunch with Bradley?"

"Good. Really nice catching up."

Sienna frowned slightly. Besides her mother's behavior, something else about this scene was different. She moved her gaze over the room and realized what. The front drapes were open. Revealing a clear view of the street.

And the street a clear view of her mother.

"Are you all right, Sienna?"

She looked back at her. "A little tired, that's all. I didn't sleep much last night."

"Why don't you lie down for a bit? I thought I'd order us a pizza from that place you always liked so much."

"Mama Riggio's?"

"Yes. I'll wake you up when it arrives."

"That would be really nice, Mom."

Sienna started toward the stairs. As she passed the formal dining room, she glanced that way. All six dining chairs sat around the table.

She froze, breath catching in her chest. One pill. That's all it had taken to relieve her mother from the demons who tormented her.

Not all it had taken, not really. It had taken someone

here to coax her mother into taking it. Being here made a difference in her mother's life. *Her* being here made a difference.

"Sienna?"

She looked back at her mother, suddenly seeing her in a different light. She wanted to weep.

"Thank you, sweetheart."

"For what, Mom?"

"Coming home."

She was the only one who could do this, Sienna acknowledged. She was her mother's daughter.

She had to stay.

CHAPTER EIGHTEEN

Sienna awakened abruptly. Disoriented, she sat up, looked around the dark room. Her childhood bedroom. She was in Tranquility Bluffs. In her mother's house.

She pushed the hair away from her face and reached for her cell phone. Seven thirty? She couldn't believe she'd been asleep over two hours. The last thing she remembered was laying her head on the pillow.

Her poor mother had to be starving by now. Sienna stood, stretched, and crossed to her bedroom door. As she stepped into the hall, the doorbell sounded. A split second later, a telephone rang.

She jumped, startled. The hall phone, she realized. Her mother had never gotten rid of it, or the antiquated stand it sat on.

It rang again. She heard her mother at the door, quizzing the person there. Most probably the pizza delivery man. Poor guy, grilled with twenty questions when all he wanted was to leave the pie and get a tip.

She answered the phone. "Scott residence."

"Is this Sienna Scott?"

"Yes, it is. Who's this?"

"I've been waiting for you."

The voice was strange, slightly distorted. "Excuse me?"

"I'll see you soon."

"Who is—"

The caller hung up, leaving her with the receiver pressed to her ear but the only sound the blood rushing in her head.

"Sienna," her mother called, "who was that?"

"No one," she managed. "Just somebody trying to sell us something."

"Pizza's here."

"I'll be right down."

Sienna carefully set the receiver back in the cradle. Her hands shook. Her legs felt wobbly. She returned to her bedroom and sat on the edge of the bed.

What the hell was that all about? She drew in a deep breath, then let it out. Nothing. That's what it was about. Somebody's idea of a joke.

She started to stand, then stopped, eyes on her bulletin board. She frowned. Something about it looked different. What? She cocked her head, studying it. The arrangement of items tacked to it looked different.

She dropped her gaze to the desk. Two notebooks and a textbook. Her journal. Were those there before? Arranged that way?

Sienna shook her head to clear it. Now she was just being ridiculous.

Get a grip, Sienna.

"Sienna? Are you okay?"

"On my way down."

She stood, snatched up and pocketed her cell phone, then, noticing the lamp shade was askew, she righted it. At the door, she took a glance back, the oddest feeling of déjà vu coming over her. As if she had been not just in this place, but this very moment, before.

CHAPTER NINETEEN

11:20 A.M.

A week had passed since Sienna's panic attack and her mother's miraculous turnaround. The phone had been ringing nonstop, calls from old friends who'd heard she was back in town and wanted to say hello or schedule a time to get together.

For the first few days, every time the phone rang, Sienna paused before answering, wondering if it might be her mysterious caller again. But by mid-week, she'd convinced herself the call had been somebody's idea of a joke and all but forgotten about it.

She'd thrown herself into a top-to-bottom cleaning of the house. Her mother joined in, and as each day passed, she seemed healthier and stronger than the one before. By the end of the week, Sienna had even convinced her mother to go to the grocery with her—all the way to Rockford to collect some items the local stores didn't stock.

"Next time we should get mani-pedis," Sienna said as they unloaded the shopping bags.

"That would be fun." Her mother looked at her hands, and frowned. "I haven't had a manicure since before your dad died." She looked at Sienna. "Remember how nice my hands used to be?"

Sienna smiled. "I do remember. And there's no reason they can't be that way again." The phone rang. "I'll get it."

Her mother waved her to the phone. "I'm going to change my shoes. These pinch."

Sienna nodded and picked up. "Hello," she said. "Scott residence."

"Hi, Sienna."

Receiver propped between her shoulder and ear, she returned to unpacking the groceries. "Hi, who's this—"

No sooner were the words out of her mouth than she recognized the slightly distorted voice—it was the voice of her mystery caller from the other night.

"I have something important to tell you."

Sienna glanced in the direction her mother had gone, worried. She'd been doing so well; the last thing she needed was some sick jackass upending her progress. "This isn't funny. Goodbye—"

"Don't you want the truth?"

She hesitated, heart hammering against her ribs. "What truth?"

"About that night, of course."

Madison Robie, there, in the blood-soaked snow.

The night that changed the course of her life.

"Stop it," she said, voice low. "Don't call me again—"

"You were right. It was you. It was always supposed to be you."

The soft click of the call ending resounded in her ear. Sienna carefully returned the receiver to its cradle, then stopped, leaning against the counter for support. She drew in three deep, even breaths.

Somebody's sick joke. Cruel and ugly.

The case had been reopened. The details splashed across the media. Including her small part in the incident.

But what if it wasn't? What if all the media attention had drawn the killer out? What if she really had been the intended victim?

Her mother emerged from her bedroom and was staring at Sienna, eyes wide. "What's wrong?" she asked.

Sienna worked to smooth her expression. "Nothing."

"You look like you've seen a ghost."

"Just hungry. Blood sugar plummeted."

She pulled out one of the counter stools and sat, managing as best as she could to act normal.

"Let me get you something."

"Juice, please."

Her mother brought her a glass. Sienna took it and sipped, thoughts racing. Who would do this and why? She sorted through the options. Someone with a sick sense of humor, or someone with an ax to grind, with her or her family. Someone with a lot of anger or resentment toward her.

Only one option truly seemed likely to her. The killer, because ultimately, he was the only one who knew what had really happened that night. But why call her?

To finish the job. Do what he had intended to do ten years ago. If she'd been his intended victim. If Madison Robie was dead instead of her.

The thought made her feel sick. She swallowed past the sour taste in her mouth. Ten years ago, when she voiced that thought, her father sent her away. Then, she'd been the only one who didn't think she was crazy.

And now, someone else was voicing it.

"Sienna?"

She blinked. Looked at her mother. "Yes?"

"Who was that on the phone?"

She hated lying but feared telling her would undo all her progress. "Wrong number."

She looked at her oddly. "I thought I heard you talking to them?"

"They wanted to argue with me about it. I told them it wasn't funny." She finished the juice and stood. "There's something I just remembered I have to do. I'll be back in a bit."

"Go do? But we just got home."

"I know, I'm sorry." She grabbed her purse, then bent and kissed her mother's cheek as she passed her on the way to the garage. "I'll be home as soon as I can. Call my cell if you need me."

"Wait! Where're you going?"

Sienna looked over her shoulder, meeting her mother's eyes. "To see an old friend, one I should have contacted the moment I got home."

CHAPTER TWENTY

12:20 P.M.

The Tranquility Bluffs Police Department hadn't changed one bit in the ten years since Sienna's last visit. But Chief Thompson had. His long face was now heavily lined, and his hair, what was left of it, had gone completely gray.

His voice, however, was as deep and authoritative as ever. "Sienna," he said warmly, "come in. Have a seat."

She did, smiling at him. "I was worried you may have retired."

He laughed. "I should have, I suppose. But I've put it off as long as I can. I'm finishing out the year, then taking my Carol on a three-week cruise."

"That sounds nice."

"I heard you'd come home, wondered if you'd be in to see me."

Since he'd offered her the introduction, she took it. "My brother tells me you reopened the case."

"The Madison Robie murder, yes we have."

"May I ask why?"

He cocked an eyebrow. "Because we didn't solve it. And quite frankly, that bugs the hell out of me."

"But why now?" She searched his gaze. "Surely I'm not the first to ask."

He steepled his fingers, looked at her over the top of them. "No, you're not. And as I told the others, I wish I could tell you that new evidence has come to light or a new witness has come forth. But I can't. The truth is, my age and impending retirement is the reason."

"Your age and retirement?"

"I don't want to leave this post, let alone this world, without getting justice for that sweet girl and her family."

A lump settled in Sienna's throat, and she nodded. "I understand that more than you know."

"I'm sure you do." He made a soft sound of regret. "What you went through, it was tough on you. And your dad. Up until he died, he periodically checked in about the case. He wanted closure for you. So you could . . . let it go. Completely."

Tears stung her eyes, but she fought them. Being here wasn't about her, not really. And she wasn't going to make it about her.

He went on. "I've been on this force forty years, thirty of them as chief. Seen a lot of bad stuff, too much cruelty, too many lives ruined. But Madison Robie was the worst. It just never . . . added up. We never got past the boyfriend."

He stopped, as if realizing he was saying more than he meant to. He cleared his throat. "Was that all that brought you in today?"

"No." She laced her fingers together. "I've gotten a couple . . . disturbing phone calls. Thought I should bring them to you."

"Go on."

"The first was a week ago. The caller asked if it was me, then said they had been waiting for me to return and that they would see me soon. Then they hung up."

"And that was it?"

"For that call, yes."

"Did you recognize the caller's voice?"

"No. They were doing something to muffle or distort it."

"Was it a man or a woman, could you tell?"

"I'm not one hundred percent certain, but I'm thinking it was a man."

He made a note. "And the next call?"

"Was today, and prompted me to come see you. Same altered voice. Said I was right. I was the one who was supposed to die." As she recalled the words, goose bumps raced up her arms.

For a good ten seconds, Chief Thompson silently studied her. When he spoke, his tone was measured. "Somebody's idea of a joke."

"I'm not laughing."

"Nor should you be. But people do stupid things."

"But why even bother? Who would care enough to go to the trouble?"

"Look, the story has been in the news again. That stirs up memories, emotions. Could be kids heard their folks talking, and decided to have some fun."

"This wasn't kids. It was too sophisticated."

He arched his eyebrows. "A phone call?"

"The voice alteration. Teenagers wouldn't think of that."

"You're saying you think it was for real?"

"I'm saying I think it could be." She leaned forward. "Back then, you didn't put any credence in the idea that I was the actual target that night. Nobody did."

"Who would have wanted you dead?"

"Who wanted Madison dead?"

He didn't reply and she went on. "If there had been someone, you would have caught them by now."

"I thought you would have let this go," he said softly, "after all these years."

"I thought I had. Until today."

"Okay."

She made a sound of surprise. "Okay?"

He stood. "Come on, I'll get you fixed up with the detective in charge of the case. He's actually an old acquaintance of yours. Randall Clark."

CHAPTER TWENTY-ONE

One month and three days since the murder

The campus police were located in a small brick build-ing, smack dab in the middle of campus. She'd only been here twice before, both times to pay parking tickets.

Today, she'd come to apologize to Officer Clark for her mother's scene, and to ask him not to share the in-cident with anyone.

She stepped inside. The secretary looked up. "Hi, hon. How can I help you?"

"Is Officer Clark here?"

"Randy? He's on rounds right now." She checked the wall clock. "But he'll be by to punch out for lunch in about fifteen minutes. If you have the time, you can wait?"

"I will, thanks."

Sienna took one of the hard plastic chairs lined up against the wall directly across from the secretary. Sort of like a police lineup or a firing squad, she thought, shifting uncomfortably. It felt awkward to sit here like this, but it had taken three days to work up the courage to come to see him; if she left now she didn't think she could do it again.

"I know you."

Sienna looked up at the secretary.

"You're the one who found that poor Madison Robie." She clucked her tongue. "Such a tragic, terrible thing."

A lump formed in her throat. She nodded.

"You doin' okay since?"

She wanted to shout *"No! I'm not. How would you be if it happened to you?"* Instead, she nodded and looked down at her hands.

"I imagine you can't even close your eyes without picturing that poor girl. Like I always say, there are just some things you can't unsee."

Deep red, creeping across brilliant white.

Her stomach turned; a metallic taste filled her mouth. She mumbled something about having a class, jumped to her feet, and darted out the door.

And ran smack into Officer Clark.

"Whoa," he said, steadying her. "What the— Sienna?"

She looked at him, vision blurring with tears. She'd come to apologize for her mother, but now she looked every bit as out of control.

"What's wrong?"

"Nothing." She blinked furiously. "I've just . . . I'm only . . ."

The words trailed off helplessly, and he put an arm around her shoulder and steered her to a close-by bench. "Sit," he said.

She did and he sat beside her. "What's going on?"

She shook her head. "Nothing."

"I know that's a lie." He paused. "What were you doing at the CP?"

"Came to see you." Her nose was running and she sniffled. "Now I feel like an idiot."

"I'm not quite sure how those two things go together,

but okay." He gave her a moment, then said, "You know what the frat boys call the CP?"

She shook her head.

"The Pig Pen."

She laughed; she couldn't help herself.

"If you've ever been inside one of the frat houses, seems to me that's the pot calling the kettle black."

"I wanted to apologize," she blurted out. "For the other night, my mother's meltdown."

He was quiet a moment, then looked her dead in the eyes. "Seems to me there's nothing to apologize for. Your mom's obviously got issues. Not your fault."

Sienna wanted to cry again, but this time because he was being so sweet. "Thanks, Officer Clark."

"Considering what we've been through, I think you can call me Randy."

"I suppose so. Heck, after seeing my mom that way the other night, you're almost family."

He laughed. "You're funny, Sienna. I like you."

"I like you, too."

"So, what's your mom's deal?"

"She suffers from paranoid delusions. Unfortunately, they revolve around me being hurt or killed as a way to punish her."

"Figured it was something like that."

"Yeah."

"Must have made your life difficult."

"It's why I'm here at Fredricks instead of away at school." She hesitated, then added, "Could you do me a favor?"

"Sure thing."

"Please don't share what happened the other night or the stuff I told you about my mom. It's hard enough living in a town where everybody knows your mother's got, as you put it, issues. The last thing I want is for the entire campus to know."

"I won't talk about it, Sienna. I promise you that." He looked at his watch. "I'd like to revisit our conversation from the other night, if you're up for it. We could go over to the Commons, get a sandwich or something?"

"Can we go somewhere else? It's always so busy, and I don't want anyone to overhear us."

"You've got it. I know just the place."

At Fredricks College the campus police had several modes of transportation: cruisers, golf carts, and bicycles. The Barn was the storage facility for the carts and bikes, and was empty during the day.

Randy bought them both a sandwich and a drink, then drove them there in his cart. They sat next to each other on the bench just inside, eating their sandwiches in silence.

She broke the silence first. "I've been thinking about what you asked me the other night, before my mom . . . about me having any enemies. I didn't come up with any."

His brow furrowed, as if with deep thought. "That's good, right?"

"Yeah, I suppose it is."

"I talked to Madison's supervisor at the library. She let Madison go early that night. Because of the weather. It's usually after midnight by the time they clear the building and lock up."

"So he could have been waiting for either of us?"

"He could have, but the librarian also told me Madi was distraught that night, over her and her boyfriend breaking up. I also learned that the city police have been all over him, and he's withdrawn from school."

"Who did the breaking up?"

He looked surprised by the question. "I don't know. Why?"

"Well, if she broke up with him, I see him as being angry. But if he broke up, why would he go all psycho and kill her?"

"True, but my point is, I think they're going to make an arrest soon, Sienna. They're just getting their ducks in a row."

"Really?" She searched his expression, almost afraid to believe it.

"Yes, Sienna, really."

"Thank God!" She turned and hugged him. "Thank you! I can't explain how relieved that makes me feel!"

He carefully extricated himself from the hug, and held her at arm's length. He smiled. "I get it. This thing's been eating me alive. Once they get him behind bars, we'll both be able to breathe easy."

She looked away for a moment, then back at him. "Do you ever think about destiny?"

He looked surprised. "Like things happen for a reason, like people's paths being destined to cross, things like that?"

"Yeah. Things like that."

He nodded, searched her gaze. "I do, Sienna. How about you?"

"Yeah, I guess. It's weird, but I've been thinking that lately because of me and Madi, being almost in the same place at the same time."

"Not weird," he said softly. "Makes sense."

She stood. "Thanks for lunch."

"You bet. You need a ride back?"

"My car's parked on this side of campus, I'll walk."

"Sienna?" She looked back. "Let me give you my personal number, in case you need to talk to me about this."

She nodded and he jotted it down on the back of a card and handed it to her. She tucked it in her pocket. "Maybe I should give you my cell number? If you call the house, my mom might freak out."

"That'd be good."

She dug a piece of paper and a pen from her backpack, wrote the number down, and handed it to him. "You'll let me know if you hear anything?"

"I will. But my expectation is, it'll be all over the news before I have a chance to."

She thanked him again, and walked away, aware of him watching her go. Unable to help herself, she took a quick peek back over her shoulder. But he wasn't watching her, she saw. He sat with his chin resting on his fists, seeming to stare at nothing at all.

CHAPTER TWENTY-TWO

Forty-five days since the murder

Sienna sat cross-legged on her bed, her wall calendar in front of her. Still no arrest.

She counted off the days again, just to be certain. But the number didn't change. Forty-five. One month, fifteen days.

She couldn't stop thinking about it. She dreamed of red seeping across white and of running from a shadowy figure, one she couldn't escape, no matter how many shortcuts she took. She awoke every morning exhausted and panicked.

She hid it from her family as best she could. Threw herself into her studies. Pretended she was fine.

But she wasn't fine. She was falling apart.

Sienna shifted her gaze to her bedside table and the card with Randy's number on it. They talked every day. And every day he filled her in on the latest developments, if there were any to report. He'd shared that the boyfriend, Reed Shepard, had been cleared. Apparently, he had an ironclad alibi. The police had then turned their attention to a family member, an uncle with a history of violence and a rap sheet to prove it.

Randy hadn't said what "a history of violence"

meant, but a week later it hadn't mattered because he had been cleared as well.

Sienna dropped her head into her hands. She didn't know what to do. Randy kept saying "give it time," but she had this feeling time was running out.

"Half-pint?"

She looked up. Brad, standing in the doorway. Forehead wrinkled with concern.

"Hey," she said. "What're you doing here?"

"Came to see Dad."

"He took Mom for a drive. Thought that might calm her down."

"She having a bad day?"

"You could say that."

"What about you? Looks like you're having a bad one, too."

She started to cry and he came over and sat on the bed beside her. She leaned into him and he put his arm around her shoulders.

"What's going on?"

"I'm scared."

"About what?"

"There's something . . . a secret I've been keeping. And it's . . . I don't know what to do, Brad."

"Secrets are never good, sis. Get it off your chest, you'll feel better."

"But I'm afraid if I tell Dad—" She bit the last back.

"Afraid what?"

"He'll be really upset. He's got enough to deal with, he doesn't need me adding to his worries."

"Are you pregnant?"

"Pregnant?" She looked at him aghast. "Why would you think—" She bit the question back. She knew why. Wondering if she was pregnant made a bunch more sense than the secret she was keeping. "No," she answered, "I'm not pregnant."

"So, tell me. I'm always on your side, you know that."

He was. But this . . . She twisted her fingers together, afraid that voicing it to him would make it true.

She pulled in a deep breath, then let it out—her terrible fear with it. "I'm afraid I'm . . . that I'm like my mom."

"Half-pint, no." He hugged her to his side. "You're not. What's making you think that?"

A knot formed in her throat. She had to force the words past it. "I keep thinking the person who killed Madison might have been after me, not her."

She peeked up to see his face. And wished she hadn't. He looked horrified. As if his worst fear had just sprouted wings—not just one unbalanced woman to help look after, but two.

She hurried to explain, to prove to him that he'd been right a moment ago, that he could still believe in her. "She was wearing a coat just like mine, and that cut-through is the path I take every Wednesday night at midnight. She had her hood up, so he could have mistaken her for me."

"Half-pint—"

"And they still haven't made an arrest. Why, Brad?"

For a long moment, he was silent. When he finally spoke, his tone was cautious. "I don't know why. They probably need more evidence. Look, that poor girl was in the wrong place at the wrong time. It has nothing to do with you."

"No." She shook her head. "Officer Clark says that this wasn't a random crime. Because of the way she was killed, it was somebody she knew. And somebody who knew she would be there at that time. She was stabbed eighteen times." Her voice rose. "Eighteen, Brad! Officer Clark said that proves the killer knew her."

Brad turned her to face him. He looked pissed. "Who the hell is this Officer Clark?"

"The campus cop."

"The cop who got to you first?" She nodded. "Why've you been talking to him?"

"He's nice. He understands because he was there. He saw her, too."

Her brother made a choked sound. "He's been encouraging you in this?"

"No." She shook her head. "He thinks my theory is possible, but not probable."

Brad took her hands, squeezing them hard. "Well, he's wrong. Do you hear me? It's not possible. Not at all. Put it out of your mind."

"But what if—"

"There is no 'what if.'" He tightened his grip. "Do you understand me? This is your mom's influence on you. She's been feeding you her bullshit delusions all your life. Don't start believing them!"

Her eyes filled with tears. "I'm sorry."

"Don't be sorry, just believe me. You're not like your mother." He hugged her again, hard. "I love you, sis, and I don't want to lose you."

From downstairs came the sound of her mother and father arriving home. "Pull yourself together. Dad can't see you like this. And if Viv does, she'll fall apart."

"Sienna," her dad called from the bottom of the stairs, "we're home. Is Brad up there with you?"

Brad answered for her. "Sure am, Dad. Coming right down."

"Pull it together," he said again, and kissed her forehead. "I'll see you downstairs."

CHAPTER TWENTY-THREE

Present day
12:35 P.M.

When Randy saw her, he jumped to his feet, smiling broadly. "Sienna Scott. Boy, has it been a long time."

She returned his smile. "Yes, it has. Ten years."

He came around the desk and gave her a quick hug. "How have you been?"

"Really good."

She shifted from one foot to the other, feeling off-balance. When her dad sent her to London, something had been growing between them. Nothing that either of them acted upon—not only was there more than a decade between their ages, but he'd been an employee of the college as well—but it had been there nonetheless.

"How about you?" she asked.

"Got a big promotion. You can call me Detective Clark now." He ushered her into his office. "I sure can't complain."

The chief stepped in. "Yup, I hired him away from the college eight years ago. What I saw impressed me, and he hasn't let me down."

"Thank you, Chief."

"Sienna here has gotten a couple calls I think you

might be interested in. I'll let you decide how to move forward." He looked back at her. "It was good seeing you, Sienna."

A moment later they were alone. "It really is good seeing you, Sienna," he said softly.

"You too, Randy."

"Sit down." He indicated the chairs in front of his desk. He went around to his and sat.

"You look good," he said.

"You, too."

He did. He'd been a nice-looking man back then, with broad, pleasant features and a steady, reassuring gaze. He'd grown into those features, becoming truly handsome.

She cleared her throat. "You never contacted me. I thought you might."

"I didn't know how. I asked your dad for your contact information and he declined to give it to me. He felt our friendship was inappropriate, and that it would confuse you."

"He was probably right. I was a mess back then."

"You'd been through a lot. He was protecting you."

"Yes." She looked away, then back. "So, besides being supercop, what have you been doing these past ten years?"

"I got married." She opened her mouth to congratulate him; he cut her off before she could. "And divorced."

"I'm sorry."

"Me, too." He shrugged. "It's a hazard of being a cop. I hear you're a chef."

"I am."

"And thinking of setting permanent roots in Tranquility Bluffs by buying The Wagon Wheel."

"That's out already?"

"Oh, yeah. You know the small-town network. Faster than the Internet."

She laughed. "Yes, it is."

He folded his hands on the desk and leaned toward her. "Tell me about these calls you've gotten."

She told him about the first call, then the one from an hour ago. Sometime during her rendition, he took out a notebook and began jotting down notes.

"So, I came here," she finished. "It seemed like my best, heck, my only move. Chief Thompson seems to think it was somebody's idea of a joke."

"But you think differently."

"I'm not saying it's not a joke, just that . . . what if it's not? There's a chance." She twisted her fingers together. "First off, what I thought at the time was not common knowledge. The only folks I told were you, Chief Thompson, and my family."

He shrugged. "True. But people talk. Somebody told the wrong person, suddenly everyone knows."

She forcibly relaxed her hands. "What if I was right all those years ago and the person who's called me, twice now, murdered Madison?"

"Then I suggest you be very careful."

"What do you mean?"

"Sienna"—he leaned toward her, his steady gaze no longer reassuring—"if the call's for real, ten years ago you were a killer's intended target. And from what I know about crime and criminals, if this person had a reason for wanting you dead back then, he probably still wants you dead."

A chill washed over her. She hadn't thought about that, not really. Her focus was always on proving, mostly to herself, that she wasn't delusional.

"Remember when we talked about the murder being

a crime of passion?" She nodded and he went on. "That means it was personal."

"Yes."

"Then who do we look at, Sienna?"

She realized what he was saying and felt the blood drain from her face. "Not my family."

"Afraid so. Mother. Father. Brother."

"That's crazy. None of them would hurt me."

"If that's true, which I'll take your word for at the moment, where do we look? You didn't have a boyfriend. No angry BFF you'd cut out of your life. Nobody you beat out for a prize or scholarship award, anything like that?"

She shook her head.

"Your dad was a surgeon. Correct?"

"Yes."

"Any botched surgeries? Malpractice suits brought against him?"

"Not that I know of. He was highly regarded in his field."

He made himself a note, then looked back up at her. "What about extramarital affairs?"

She opened her mouth to say her dad wouldn't do that, then shut it as she realized that he had. He'd cheated on his first wife, and ended up divorcing her to marry her mother.

"How about sexual harassment allegations made against him? Or a particularly contentious firing of an employee? Anything like that?"

"No. God, no."

"You say that with such certainty. How do you know?"

"Because I knew my dad." She stiffened her spine. "He wasn't that kind of man."

"You loved your dad a lot, didn't you?"

"Yes, of course. He was an awesome father."

"Exactly. The dad *you* knew and loved wasn't that kind of man. In your eyes, he could do no wrong. Am I right?"

She didn't respond. She didn't have to. He knew he was.

"And, am I also safe to assume that anything as upsetting as a lawsuit against him would be the last thing he would have discussed with you, his fragile daughter?"

"I wasn't fragile."

"But he thought you were, didn't he? That's why he whisked you off to London."

She couldn't deny it or argue, though she wished she could. The implications of any of these scenarios lay heavily on her heart.

Randy leaned forward. "And if all that adds up to nothing, we circle back to your family."

His reasoning made so much sense. But her mother, father, or brother committing such a violent act? Not even possible. Never.

"There's one other avenue you could explore," she said tentatively. "My mother's always insisted that Dad's ex wanted to hurt her through me. Dad cheated on her with my mother."

She couldn't believe she was saying this, repeating the delusions that had tormented her mother for years.

What if they were true?

They weren't. Of course they weren't.

"We're aware of your mother's theories. They're well documented from her many visits to the TBPD."

"Has anyone ever followed up on them?"

"I don't know." He narrowed his eyes and nodded. "It might be worth a shot."

"I'll get you contact information."

"Good. And look, this person has called you twice— my bet is, he'll call you again. When he does, hang up and immediately dial star fifty-seven. Then call me. I'll contact AT&T to retrieve the trace information."

"They won't release it to me?"

"Nope, just a law enforcement agency. And look, don't tell anyone about the calls or our arrangement. This could be anyone around you—even if only a crank caller—and we don't want to tip them off."

CHAPTER TWENTY-FOUR

Sienna checked her phone as she left the police station. Her brother had called, so she dialed him back. "What's up, bro?" she asked when he answered. "I saw you called."

"Just wondering if you were going to need bail money."

"Bail money . . . Oh, you saw Mom's car at the police department."

"Yup. We haven't talked all week, you want to grab a cup of coffee?"

"Definitely. The Java Joint?"

"Perfect. See you there."

Since the coffeehouse was located around the corner on the square, Sienna decided to walk, enjoying the sun on her face and the sound of the crispy snow crunching beneath her boots. When she arrived, Brad was already seated at a table by the window. He sat in profile to her, gazing out at the street. The way the afternoon light fell over him, he looked older than his thirty-eight years.

He'd ordered her a latte and as she sat down the barista walked it over, along with his Americano. "This is nice," she said. "Thanks for suggesting it."

He sipped his coffee, then set the mug down. "When I saw the car at the police department, I worried something was up with Viv."

"Not that, thank God. She's actually been great this week. She even went grocery shopping with me this morning." He looked so dumbfounded, she laughed. "That medication is a miracle drug."

"So if Viv's okay, why visit the police?"

"I've gotten a few crank calls, that's all."

"What kind of crank calls?"

"Nothing to worry about. Just some idiot's idea of funny."

He tilted his head, frowning at her. "They were nothing, but you went to the cops about them? Come on, Half-pint, what's the big secret?"

"There is no big secret." She thought of Randy's warning not to tell anyone about the calls and decided that order excluded her brother. She trusted him more than anyone except Mimi.

She brought the latte to her lips. "Some creep called and said I was right back then."

"Right about wha—" He bit the last back, realizing what she meant. "Holy shit, Sienna. That's not nothing."

"Which is why I reported it. Just in case. But," she hurried to add, "Chief Thompson thinks it was definitely a joke."

"That old geezer should have retired years ago. What if Viv had answered the phone?"

She shuddered at the thought. "Thank God she didn't."

"What's he going to do about it?"

"Nothing. If it happens again, I report it."

"Great."

She leaned toward him. "While I was there, I asked why he reopened the case."

"And?"

"There's no new evidence. He just wanted to take another crack at solving it before he retires at the end of the year. He put Randy Clark in charge."

"You're kidding?" He shook his head. "That guy's the reason you got shipped off to London."

"That's not fair. I was the reason I got shipped off, not Randy."

"He was screwing with your head, sis. You were a kid and he was a grown man."

"I was eighteen, Brad. And I was the one who floated the whole 'maybe it was supposed to be me' idea."

"But he encouraged you. Dad should have had him fired."

Sienna couldn't have disagreed more, but she let it go. She looked at him over the rim of her cup. "Randy's taking it really seriously. He's checking every angle."

"What does that mean?" He frowned. "Every angle? They didn't before?"

"You know they didn't. It makes sense."

"Your crazy-ass theory, that's what you're talking about, isn't it? It never made sense. And *that's* how you ended up in London for ten years."

"Lower your voice." She leaned toward him, hurt and angry. "In terms of police work, it makes sense."

"It's happening again, isn't it?" He reached across the table and caught her hands, holding them tightly. "Being around your mother. It's like she infects you or something."

She thought of her panic attack. Her first in years. Which she most definitely wasn't telling him about. She pushed the thought away. "That's not true, Brad. She's doing really well."

"It's not going to last, you know that, right?"

"Not to be a party pooper or anything," she shot back sarcastically. "Gee, thanks, Brad."

"I just want you to be ready. Liz went through the same thing. A couple times." He paused. "I don't want you to be hurt."

Like Liz had been hurt. And like he, consequently, had been hurt. She squeezed his hands. "Thanks, big brother. I'll do my best."

They finished their coffees in an awkward silence. As they parted at the sidewalk, Sienna remembered to ask him about his real estate attorney.

"I called him about you. He's out of town, but promised to get in touch as soon as he got back."

"Great, thanks."

"Heard anything from Donna and Ted?"

"Not a word. Thought I'd swing by the restaurant now and see where they are in the process. I'll keep you posted."

CHAPTER TWENTY-FIVE

4:15 P.M.

When Sienna arrived home, she saw that all the front curtains were closed. She didn't have to see her mom to know she had taken a turn for the worse.

She paused outside the door, took a deep breath, and dug her keys out of her purse. Her hand shook so badly it took a couple tries to insert the key into the lock. She thought of her brother's warning from just a few hours ago. It had proved true already.

Heartsick, she stepped into the foyer. The silence was deafening. Why did she take all that time to wander in and out of those shops? Why hadn't she just hurried home?

"Mom," she called, reaching for the light switch, "I'm home."

"No lights." Her mother appeared in the dining room entryway. "Lock the door. Fasten the chain."

Sienna wanted to cry. What had happened between when she left her and now?

"This way." She motioned Sienna toward the dining room. She had something in her hand.

A gun, Sienna realized. "Mom," she said, keeping her voice as calm as possible. "Why do you have a gun?"

"They've left me no choice. I have to protect us."

"We've been through this," Sienna said, struggling to stay calm. "I protect us now. That's why I've come home."

"But you weren't here. Where were you?"

Sienna held out her hand, wishing she could stop its trembling. "Give me the gun, Mom. Please."

"I can't do that. They're here."

"Who?"

"Margaret. Her people. We're surrounded." She jerked the gun; Sienna's breath caught. "Move away from the windows, Sienna. It's not safe."

"Let me call the police. They'll protect us."

"They won't. Margaret's bought them off."

"That's not true. A friend of mine's in charge now. He's a good guy. I trust him."

"I said no!" Her mother's voice rose, taking on a hysterical edge.

Sienna recognized how dangerous that edge was and backed off.

Her mouth went dry. "Okay. Where?"

"The back of the house. Too much access to the street up here. The kitchen is safest. And I've taken extra precautions."

Sienna started that way, keeping her movements slow and deliberate. Her mother was in the grip of a full-blown episode. She wouldn't be able to bring her out of it, not without professional assistance. "I'll call Brad. He'll come help us. We'll need his help."

"He's one of them."

Sienna reached the dining room and stopped. Only three of the six chairs sat around the table. She had a good idea where one of them was. "What happened, Mom? You were fine when I left."

"It's been going on for days. They've been calling."

"No, Mom. My friends have been calling. They're happy I'm home. They want to see me."

"Not them. The ones who hang up. Margaret's people."

"A wrong number, that's all. Or kids playing a prank."

She sounded like Chief Thompson, blowing off concerns with a glib comeback.

"No. Three today. And they hang on the line. Just breathing." Her voice rose. "Then there's the van."

"The van?"

"It's white. Passing the house at all hours. I've been keeping a record."

They reached the kitchen. A camping lantern sat on the counter, casting a reassuring circle of light. Sienna's gaze dropped to a dark smear on the floor. Blood, she realized.

"Mom, what— Oh, my God, what have you done to your feet?"

"It's nothing."

"It's not nothing." She grabbed the lantern and bent down to get a good look. Her mother's bare feet were dirty, cut, and bleeding. She looked up at her mother. "How did you do this?"

"I'd do anything to keep them from getting you. *Anything,* Sienna."

Sienna's gaze shifted, following the trail of blood. It led to the door out to the patio—and one of the dining chairs propped there, a makeshift barricade. Shards of broken china were scattered across the floor in front of the door and under each window.

A sound of dismay slipped past her lips; tears burned her eyes. She'd never seen her mom this bad. Ever. Was it a flare-up like this that had finally caused Liz to call it quits?

"If that doesn't stop them, the gun will."

Sienna blinked. "What did you say?"

"I'll kill anyone who comes through that door. Or any other door."

"You can't mean that. Do you even know how to shoot that thing?"

"Your dad taught me. It's his gun. Bradley tried to find it but I hid it too well."

She made a mental note to ask her brother about it. She straightened, returned the lantern to the counter. "I think you might need stitches; I need to call a doctor."

"No doctors."

"At least let me clean and bandage the cuts."

She didn't wait for an answer, instead going to the pantry for the first-aid kit, then to the bathroom medicine cabinet for disinfectant and two clean towels. She retrieved the washtub from under the sink and filled it a third of the way with warm, soapy water, then set it in front of the commode.

Sienna lowered the seat and called her mother to come sit. She did, and Sienna knelt in front of her, easing the foot that looked the worst into the tub.

Her mother winced and squirmed while Sienna gently washed, first the right foot, then the left.

"I have proof," she said. "That what I'm saying is true. The book I've been reading, I've hidden it in there."

Sienna didn't respond, so she went on. "All the times. Day and night."

"For how long?"

"The past week."

The entire time she was celebrating her mother's miraculous progress, her mom had been busy feeding her delusions.

Sienna gently dabbed antibiotic cream on the wounds. "Were you just pretending, Mom? To be better?"

"I haven't been sick."

Sienna looked up at her. "Oh, Mom."

"You got one of the calls, too, didn't you?"

Sienna shook her head as she bandaged the various cuts. "No."

"I know you did. That's why you ran out of here so fast."

"I didn't. That's not why."

"I listened on the other extension. The one in my bedroom. I know what they said."

Sienna's heart sank. She was listening in? No wonder she'd gone completely off the rails. It would've been the proverbial straw that broke the camel's back.

"You don't have to lie to me anymore." Her mom stroked her hair, expression tender. "I know you were trying to protect me. But we're in this together. You and me."

"You're right, Mom, I was trying to protect you. I still am. Just like Dad always did."

"He did," she whispered, the mania seeming to drain out of her. "He always did."

"He wouldn't want you to have that gun, Mom. So, I'm going to take it." She eased it from her mother's grasp. "I'll put it somewhere safe, where no one will get hurt—"

"No!" Her mother launched to her feet, not even cringing at what must have been excruciating. "You can't put it somewhere! We need it!"

"Mom, stop. We don't—"

She grabbed for the gun. "Give it to me!"

Sienna managed to keep ahold of it, but her mother grabbed again, fighting her for it. Wildly, like someone in a life-or-death struggle.

Sienna wondered if it had a safety and whether it was on. And as she wondered, the gun went off.

The crack of the bullet exploding from the barrel was deafening in the small bathroom. Sienna stumbled backward. So did her mother. The gun slipped from both their grasps, hitting the floor.

At first, Sienna thought they'd both escaped injury. Then her mother's face went blank, turning deathly pale. As if in slow motion, she seemed to collapse, crimson red staining her white sweater.

Dark red creeping across brilliant white.

Sienna caught her mother and carefully lowered her to the floor. The bullet had penetrated her mid-section, and Sienna grabbed a hand towel and pressed it to the spot, the way she'd seen done dozens of times in movies.

"Hold this, Mom," she said, and brought her mother's hand to the towel. "Like this. With pressure. I'm going to call an ambulance."

"Am I dying?"

"No—" Sienna's voice caught on a sob. "God, no. Keep pressure on it. I'll be right back."

Sienna located her phone, dialed 911. "My mother's been shot!" she cried when the dispatcher answered. "I need an ambulance."

CHAPTER TWENTY-SIX

6:05 P.M.

The ambulance arrived in under five minutes. A police cruiser moments after. "Where's the victim?"

"In the bathroom." She led the EMTs to the powder room. Seeing her mother sprawled on the floor and as white as death stopped her short. Suddenly light-headed, she grabbed the doorjamb for support.

"Miss? I'll need you to step away from the door."

She blinked. Looked at them. "Of course. Just . . . is she going to be all right?"

"As soon as we know, you'll know. We need to work."

The cop came over, touched her arm, and gently guided her away from the scene. "Ms. Scott, I need to ask you a few questions."

She nodded and followed him, although all she could think about was her mother and what the paramedics were doing.

"Ms. Scott?"

Sienna blinked again, and focused on him. He was young, she realized. Maybe even younger than she was.

"Can you tell me what happened?"

"She had a gun. I tried to get it away from her, but she wouldn't let it go. She suffers from a delusion disorder and—"

"Is she on any medications?"

"Yes, I have a list." Sienna ran to the kitchen secretary, retrieved it, and ran back. She handed it to him. "Everything's there, including her regular physician and her mental healthcare provider."

"Sienna?"

Randy. She let out a cry of relief and ran to him. He gave her a quick, hard hug, then held her at arm's length. "When I heard the name, I came right over. Are you okay?"

"I'm fine. But my mom . . . I think I shot her." She started to cry. "I didn't mean to. I was trying to get the gun away."

"What precipitated the struggle for the weapon?"

"I came home from seeing you and she was experiencing a full-blown paranoiac episode. She had the gun . . . look what she did to the house—" She pointed out the door and windows.

One of the EMTs rushed by, then returned with a gurney. Sienna grabbed his arm. "How is she?"

"The wound looks clean. Can't tell much more at this point. We're transporting her to Saint Anthony's Medical Center."

"Saint Anthony's? No. She needs Evergreen Behavioral Health Hospital."

Randy stepped in. "We have to deal with the gunshot wound first, Sienna. Once she's stable, she'll be transferred to Evergreen. Okay?"

She nodded, her gaze following the EMTs. "I've got to go with her, Randy. I've got to."

"That's no problem, Sienna. Just a couple more questions, then I'll catch up with you at the hospital. Did she threaten you?"

"No!"

"Did she threaten anyone else?"

Sienna hugged herself. "No. Not really."

"What does that mean?"

"It's her illness. The delusions that I'm in danger . . . she was just trying to protect me."

"You're saying she told you . . . what? That she would shoot anyone who tried to hurt you?"

"Yes. Anyone who came through the door. I knew I had to take the gun . . . She was handing it over, then suddenly changed her mind and grabbed for it."

The paramedics appeared with the gurney, her mother strapped to it. She looked deathly pale and terrified. Anyone would be, but her mother—this played into every one of her delusional scenarios.

"I have to go with her."

"Go," he said. "I need to photograph the scene. You have any problem with that?"

She shook her head. "Do whatever you have to do."

"I'll see you at the hospital later."

"Okay." She hurried after the paramedics, grabbing her purse and keys from the entryway table, making it outside just as they were loading her mother into the ambulance. Sienna grabbed her hand. "It's going to be okay, Mom. Don't be scared. I'll meet you at the hospital."

"Miss, we have to go."

She released her hand and stepped back; a moment later, the doors slammed shut.

"Sienna!"

She swung around. Jonathan was jogging across the street.

"Are you all right?" he asked, reaching her.

"I'm fine. I can't talk now."

"How can I help?"

Tears stung her eyes. She shook her head. "I've got to go."

"Let me drive you. You're in no state to—"

"No, please. I've got to go."

She turned and hurried to her car. As she backed out of the driveway, she saw that Jonathan hadn't moved. He stood watching her, brow furrowed and hands stuffed in his pockets.

Sienna couldn't help wondering what he was thinking.

And why he always seemed to be watching her.

CHAPTER TWENTY-SEVEN

7:00 P.M.

Saint Anthony's Medical Center served as the region's trauma center. By the time Sienna got there, her mother had already been admitted and was being seen by the doctor. "Can I see her?" Sienna asked the admissions nurse.

"I'm sorry, she's being examined. Have a seat, I'll let you know when you can go in."

Sienna couldn't sit and used the opportunity to call her brother. She got his voice mail. "Brad, call me. I'm at Saint Anthony's trauma center with Mom." Her voice broke. "She went completely off the rails . . . she had Dad's gun. Call me as soon as you get this."

Not knowing what else to do, she sat and fretted, going over the accident, every step leading up to it. Questioning her every decision. Each minute that passed was agony.

Finally, after what seemed like forever, her name was called. Sienna hurried across to a middle-aged woman in scrubs. "I'm Sienna Scott," she said.

The woman smiled. "I'm Dr. Aronson. I'm taking care of your mother."

"How is she?"

"She's stable. We're prepping her for surgery."

Sienna's head went light. "Surgery?"

"Don't panic. This could have been so much worse. The bullet missed all her major organs and arteries, but we need to go in and make certain there's no gunshot residue and repair any damage caused by the bullet."

Sienna brought a hand to her chest, struggling to control her pounding heart. "So she'll have a full recovery?"

"Surgery always comes with risks, but barring unexpected complications, she'll be fine. We'll know more when we're done."

Sienna let out a pent-up breath. "How long will the surgery take?"

"I don't know for certain because I'm not in there yet. I'll have the nurse direct you to the surgical waiting room. After surgery she'll be admitted to the hospital; the attendant there will keep you informed." The doctor lightly touched her shoulder. "It's going to be fine. If you want to see her, now's the time."

The doctor led her to her mom's curtained room. Her eyes were closed and she looked as pale as the sheets. But still beautiful; oddly so.

Sienna crossed to the bed. "Hey, Mom," she said softly.

Her mother's eyes fluttered open, then focused.

"How're you feeling?"

"Okay," she whispered. "Thirsty."

"You're going into surgery, but the doctor promises you're going to be just fine."

The orderly arrived with a gurney. Sienna bent and kissed her forehead. "I've got to go, but I'll be in the waiting room, and as soon as they let me, I'll be in to see you."

"Sienna . . ." She plucked at her sleeve. "The . . . caller . . ."

Sienna bent closer. "The caller? What, Mom?"

"He was . . . right."

Sienna searched her mother's gaze. "I don't understand."

"Right . . . you were the one . . ."

The attendants cleared their throats, obviously impatient to make the transfer. Sienna understood, but they would just have to wait. "The one who what, Mom?"

"Who was—"

"Ma'am, we need to move your mother."

She looked over her shoulder. "Just one more moment, please."

"—supposed to . . ."

She was drifting off. Sienna leaned even closer. She felt her mother's breath against her cheek. "Tell me, Mom. Supposed to what?"

". . . die . . ."

Stunned, Sienna straightened and backed away. The orderly and nurse took over, expertly transferring her mother from the bed to the gurney, attending to the various bags, drips, hookups, and plug-ins.

A moment later, she was gone and the nurse looked sympathetically at her. "She'll be fine."

"What?"

"Your mother. She'll be fine. You'll see."

But she never has been. Not ever.

"Do you know where the surgical waiting room is?" the nurse asked.

Sienna said she did not, and in a daze, she listened, then followed the woman's directions. There, she helped herself to a cup of coffee, then sank into one of the chairs. Maybe she'd misheard, Sienna thought. Or, her mother was just repeating what she heard when she'd listened in on the call.

But why say that now, that moment?

You were supposed to die.

Sienna closed her eyes. The smell of the burnt coffee wafted up to her nose, turning her stomach. She realized she'd eaten neither lunch nor dinner. But, although she was hungry, the thought of eating was repugnant.

Sienna set the coffee aside and curved her arms over her middle. *It's nothing, Sienna. More ravings from a disturbed psyche.*

But it wasn't the first time her mother had told her that. No, the first time was the night before her father sent her away.

CHAPTER TWENTY-EIGHT

Fifty-five days since the murder

From the window seat in her second-floor bedroom, Sienna saw her brother pull into the driveway. He climbed out of his BMW, looking totally *GQ* in his wool topcoat and aviator sunglasses. The sun glinted off them as he glanced up at her window. He saw her and lifted a hand in greeting. She waved, then hurried down to say hello. He'd been checking in with her every couple of days to see how she was doing, and she felt closer to him than she had at any other time in her life.

She'd always adored him. A sort of hero worship. She remembered shadowing him from the time she was old enough to do so. He'd alternated between being affectionately amused and irritated by the attention. But the nine and a half years between them, and their complicated family life, had kept them from truly connecting. Until now.

Sienna trotted down the stairs, stopping in the foyer to listen for him. She heard the murmur of male voices coming from her dad's study, and headed that way. Her mother, she saw, was curled up on the couch, reading. She didn't even look up, even though Sienna paused a moment to admire how elegant she looked, her fiery hair shielding her face like a shiny curtain.

Sienna reached the study's closed door. She lifted her hand to tap on it, then stopped when her dad said her name.

Her brother responded, but she couldn't make out what he was saying, and pressed closer to the door.

"Dammit, Bradley! I was counting on you."

Her father never cursed, so even a word as benign as that startled her.

"I talk to her almost every day," Brad said. "What more do you want from me?"

"She's hiding something. What is it?"

A lump formed in her throat. *Don't tell him, Brad. You promised—*

"I don't know, Dad. I think you're being paranoid. Maybe you've been spending too much time with Viv?"

"Don't be a disrespectful punk."

"Sorry, Dad."

He didn't sound sorry at all, and Sienna gave a silent cheer.

"Her phone records show she's talking to that man every day."

That man? Who was he—

Randy, she realized. Then, in the next moment, another realization struck. Her father was monitoring her calls? And using her brother to spy on her?

Sometimes her dad could be such a jerk. Overbearing and plain unreasonable. But spying? And forcing Brad to help him do it?

She'd never done anything to cause him not to trust her. Hadn't stepped out of line even once, never wanting to be an additional burden to him.

"—I didn't know that. She doesn't tell me everything."

"But she tells you some things, doesn't she? Like about this campus cop."

"I know she talked to him once, about the murder investigation."

"But you didn't tell me?"

Her face went hot. The way he was interrogating Brad wasn't fair—and it pissed her off.

"What's the big deal, Dad?"

"The big deal?" Her father's voice rose. "She's a vulnerable young—"

Sienna had heard enough and marched into the study. "Stop, Dad! If you want to know something about my life, just ask *me*."

He looked momentarily surprised. "I don't know what you think you heard—"

"I heard everything. Using Brad to spy on me? Checking my phone log. That's disgusting."

"You're my daughter. You live under my roof. I have the right to—"

"But no *reason* to, Dad. None."

"It's my responsibility to know what you're doing and who you're seeing."

"Then ask *me*." She pressed her fist to her chest. "I'll tell you. I've always been honest with you."

"You've been calling that campus cop—"

"Randy Clark."

"—every day. Why?"

"He's nice. Why shouldn't I talk to him?"

"He's too old for you."

"We're not dating. We're talking."

"About what?"

"About the investigation. He's keeping me updated. That's all."

His expression softened. "Why didn't you ask me? I talk to Fred almost every day."

"I didn't want you to worry. With Mom, you have too much to worry about already."

"You're my daughter." He held out a hand. "I care about everything that has anything to do with you."

She made a sound of frustration. "Can't I just keep some of my thoughts to myself?"

"Not from me, no."

She looked from her father to her brother, and back. "That's not fair. I'm eighteen, and I should have your trust."

"I do trust you, but it's complicated."

"Because of Mom? And maybe because you're afraid I'm just like her?"

He looked shocked, then angry. "This is nonnegotiable. I pay for that cell phone, and I can take it away. Why are you talking to Officer Clark?"

"I told you, it's nothing!"

"Then why won't you tell me?"

She curled her hands into fists, tears burning her eyes. "Because it's just stupid. That's why!"

Brad jumped in. "It's true, Dad. That's exactly what I told her. She thinks the killer was after her, not Madison Robie."

Several emotions raced across her father's features—surprise and concern, then a dawning realization. It broke her heart.

"I'm not like her, Dad," she said quickly, wanting to reassure him. "The idea's not as out there as you might think."

"Is this about you two having the same coat?"

Her cheeks heated. "Partly."

"I thought I told you that was nothing."

She twisted her fingers together. "There's the timing, too. I walked that way every Wednesday night at midnight. Madison didn't. So, why was he there waiting for her?"

"Wait." Her father looked from her to Brad, and

back. "Who said the killer was 'there waiting' for her?"

"Nobody. It's the presumption."

"The chief's never said that."

"She's right."

They all turned toward the doorway. Her mother stood there, pale as a ghost, eyes wide, blinking at them as if she'd just awakened from a deep sleep.

"Viv," her dad said calmly, "I don't think you understand what we're talking about."

"Yes, I do. I knew it from the moment I heard about that murder."

"For God's sake, Viv." He dragged a hand through his graying hair. "Sienna, stay here. I'm going to help your mother upstairs."

But when he moved to take her arm, she shook him off violently. "No! I'm not going to shut up, and I'm not going upstairs. Sienna needs to know!"

She whirled to face Sienna, and Sienna took an involuntary step backward. "Mom, please stop."

"You need to know!" She grabbed Sienna's hands, clutching them so tightly she thought her bones would break. "It *was* supposed to be you. I told your dad, but he wouldn't listen."

"Let me go." Sienna tugged against her grasp. "Mom, you're hurting me!"

Brad jumped in, yanking her free of her mother's grasp. Simultaneously, her dad sprang forward, and dragged his wife against his chest, arms circling her in a bear hug.

Like an enraged animal, she fought his grip, howling with fury. "No matter what they say, Sienna, you're supposed to be dead! Do you hear me? It was supposed to be you!"

Sienna stood frozen, watching in horror as her

elegant mother devolved into a woman she hardly recognized, kicking out, clawing at her father's arms. Wailing, as if Sienna actually had been killed.

"Bradley," her father barked, "take your sister upstairs. Stay with her until I get your mom calmed down."

"She's not *my* mom," he muttered, and curved his arm around her. "Don't worry, Half-pint," he whispered against her ear, "I've got you."

Sienna climbed the stairs with Brad, the sound of her mother's ravings in her ears—and the words thundering in her head like a drum.

It was supposed to be you.

It was supposed to be you.

It was supposed to be you.

Madison Robie wasn't the one who was meant to die, Sienna acknowledged.

She was.

CHAPTER TWENTY-NINE

Present day
8:35 P.M.

When Sienna returned to the waiting room, she saw that Brad had arrived. He rushed to her side and pulled her into a tight hug.

"Are you okay?"

"I'm fine."

He held her at arm's length. "When I got your message . . . All I could think was that it could have been you."

"I'd be lying if I said I wasn't scared. She was out of her mind. Completely irrational."

"You look exhausted. C'mon, let's sit down."

They did. He took her hand. "Tell me what happened."

So she did, starting with noticing the curtains were drawn and ending with their struggle for the gun. "It went off." Her voice shook. "I don't know if I pulled the trigger or she did. I didn't even know that she'd been hit until—"

She bit the last back, her head filling with the image of the circle of red growing on the white sweater, and her mother falling backward. That image morphed into another, of dark blood creeping across the bright snow.

The murder. It always came back to the murder.

Sienna shook her head in an attempt to clear it. "She's in surgery now."

"What are they . . . what's the prognosis?"

"Good." She twisted her fingers together. "She was lucky, considering the bullet struck her torso. The doctor wasn't sure what she would find so she didn't know how long it would take."

He searched her face. "Are you okay?"

"Define 'okay.'" She tried to laugh; it came off as a soft sob.

"I bet you haven't had anything to eat, have you?"

"Not since breakfast."

"I'll see if the cafeteria's open. Since she's in surgery—"

"I'm not leaving."

"Sienna—"

"I'm not. She's here because of me; I'm not leaving."

"She's here," he said softly, "because of her mental state. Not because of anything you did, or didn't do." He must have seen by her expression that she wasn't going to budge, because he sighed, then capitulated. "Okay. I saw a Subway in the lobby. How about I go get us both something and bring it back here?"

She nodded. "That'd be good."

"You're going to be okay while I'm gone? I shouldn't be too long."

She said she would and sat back down. The minutes ticked past. Ten became twenty. Twenty became thirty. She stared at the clock, wondering what was taking him so long. She wondered how the surgery was going. And she wondered how she was going to face tomorrow.

"Sienna?"

She turned her head. Randy, heading her way. She stood to meet him.

He gave her a quick hug, then searched her expression. "I understand your mother's in surgery. And that the doctor's expectation is a full recovery."

She nodded, feeling numb from head to toe. "That's right."

"Do you have a few minutes to talk with me?"

"Right now, I have nothing but time. Do you mind if I sit?"

"Not at all."

She did. "Brad's here. He went to get us both a sandwich. Should we wait for him?"

He looked at her oddly. "Was he there at the house when the accident occurred?"

"No."

"Then no, my questions are for you alone." She nodded and he went on. "Were you aware that your mother was in possession of a firearm?"

"No. I had no idea."

"Have you ever seen your mother with a gun?"

"Never."

"So, she's never threatened you or anyone else with a gun? That you know of?"

"Not that I know of."

"Any idea what precipitated this episode?"

"Yes." She looked down at her hands, then back up at him. "The phone call I told you about, I didn't realize it but she was listening on the other extension. And, apparently, there have been a number of hang-ups recently. Which also fed into her paranoiac delusions. She said she kept a log of the dates and times of the calls, but I haven't seen it."

"I'd like to take a look at it."

"I'll make certain to get it to you." She rubbed the back of her neck, at the tension that had settled there.

"You're exhausted," he said softly, forehead creased

with concern. "Maybe you should head home, get some rest."

"You know I can't do that, Randy."

Just then, Brad returned. He saw them and strode over, expression thunderous. "What the hell are you doing here?"

Randy seemed unaffected by the confrontation, but Sienna made a sound of distress. "He had a few more questions for me, that's all."

"I'll bet."

Randy ignored the barb and looked at Sienna. "We've cleared the scene. You can go back and do whatever you need to do."

She nodded, picturing what awaited her at home. The blood. The broken china. She shuddered and Brad put an arm around her shoulders.

"I'll call you tomorrow, see how your mom's doing. And check on you, too."

"The hell you will, you son of a bitch."

"Brad! What's wrong with you?"

Randy took a step back. "Apparently, he doesn't realize you've grown up."

"Stay away from my sister, you hear me? Or I'll have your badge. You ruined our lives once, I'm not going to allow you to do it again."

Randy smiled and gave her a small salute. "Talk to you tomorrow, Sienna."

For a moment, she thought her brother would go after him. His body tensed, and he moved his arm from her shoulder to his side.

"Don't," she said softly. "Please. It's okay."

"No," he said, voice so tight it hurt to hear, "it's not."

"He didn't ruin my life, Brad."

"Then maybe he ruined mine."

She tipped her face up to his. "I don't understand. Why?"

He met her eyes. "You being sent away was the worst thing that ever happened to me."

CHAPTER THIRTY

1:15 A.M.

Sienna stayed with her mother until she was out of surgery, settled in her room, and fast asleep. She didn't want to leave then, but Brad convinced her a few hours of sleep would help her care for her mother the following day. The night nurse promised to call if there was any change.

Sienna didn't bother putting the car in the garage, just parked in the drive, right in front of the house. She climbed out, all but vibrating with shock and fatigue. She simultaneously felt numb and as if she'd been used as somebody's punching bag.

She let herself into the house and just stood there, surveying. The drawn drapes. The pieces of shattered china. The dining room table, half its chairs missing.

Practically nothing compared to what awaited her in the kitchen.

She flipped on the entryway chandelier. Light spilled over every inch of the grand foyer. Boot tracks from the EMTs. The faint outline of a bloody footprint. Hers, she saw. From when she ran to let the paramedics in.

She looked down at herself and made a sound of dismay. Blood on her shirt cuffs, smeared across the front of her shirt. On the knees of her jeans.

Overwhelmed, she brought her hands to her face. She didn't know what to do, let alone what she should do first.

At the tap on the front door, she jumped, then whirled around. It came again.

"Sienna, it's Jonathan."

She went to the door and opened it.

"Hey," he said, holding up a bottle of wine, "I thought you might need this. And maybe some company, too."

For a moment, she just stared at him. Then she burst into tears.

In the next instant, his arms were around her and she was sobbing onto his shoulder.

He was awkwardly sweet, murmuring sounds of comfort and trying to pat her back despite the bottle of wine in his hand.

She finally eased out of his arms, missing them the moment she did.

He met her eyes, expression sheepish. "I don't usually have this effect on women."

She sniffled. "I'm sorry."

"So, I guess my timing's good?"

"It's perfect. But I cried all over your jacket."

"I have other jackets."

"I don't know what to do. The blood . . . it's everywhere. The house . . . what she did."

Her chin quivered and he cupped her face in his palms, looked her in the eyes. "How about you change clothes? Maybe wash your face? That might make you feel better."

It would, she thought, relieved. "I'll be right back. You'll wait?"

A smile touched his mouth. "I'll wait."

Ten minutes later she returned, hands and face scrubbed clean, and wearing ancient blue jeans and a chenille sweater the color of butter. He stood exactly where she'd left him, looking more handsome than a man should.

He held out his hand. She took it and he led her to the couch. They sat. She rested her head on his shoulder. For the first time since arriving home and seeing the drapes drawn, she felt safe.

They sat that way for several minutes. He broke the silence first, motioning toward the bottle of wine. "You want a glass? And look, a convenient, and very classy, screw top."

She smiled. "You're funny."

"I sing and dance, too."

She laughed, amazed that she could. "I'll get a couple glasses."

"You sit. I'll get them. Just tell me where."

"I don't want you to see that."

"What's that?"

"What she did. It's sort of horrifying."

"I was in the military for four years, I know horrifying."

He'd mentioned the military before, but not how long he'd served. "What branch?"

"Army."

"Where?"

"Iraq."

He did seem like the strong, silent type. Steady in a crisis. The kind of man a woman could lean on when things got tough. The kind of man her father had been.

"I thought I'd make it a career, but things didn't work out."

"What happened?"

"Problems back home. They needed me."

Family issues. She made a sound of sympathy. "I certainly understand those."

"You want to talk about what went down tonight?"

Did she? It would change the mood. Steal this moment of sweetness and peace.

It already had, she realized. Just his mention of it brought the horror of the night back.

She must have stiffened, because she felt him tip his head to look at her. Then he let out a breath that sounded like regret. "I'd take that back if I could."

"It's okay." She stood, held out her hand. "I'll show you instead."

He took it and she led him back to the chaos that was the kitchen. He walked silently through, examining the scene with the thoroughness of a crime scene investigator.

She watched, and something about the still but intent way he moved, taking it all in, fascinated her. Like a predator in the wild, cautious but confident. Missing nothing.

He had been in a place like this before.

She followed him to the bathroom, but didn't step inside. She didn't want to look at it. She couldn't, not just yet.

He exited. "The police collected the weapon?"

She hadn't even thought about it, but of course they must have. She wondered how he knew a gun had been involved. "I suppose so."

"How's your mom?"

"Stable. She had surgery to repair damage caused by the bullet."

"It's not your fault."

"I know."

"It's not your fault," he said again. "None of it."

A lump settled in her throat. She swallowed past it. "Her mental illness didn't . . . it didn't present until after I was born. The doctors say the pregnancy triggered it."

"But it was there all along. It wasn't *you,* Sienna."

"Then I appeared looking just like her. Her little mirror image."

"And that means what?" He turned her to face him. "Nothing. It means nothing."

"Does it? Or does it mean—"

He stopped her words with a kiss. The tenderness of it shattered her—and his strength put her back together again. Awareness of him rolled over her: his clean, male scent; the sound of his breathing; the beat of his heart against her hand pressed to his chest.

How could something so magical happen at such a nightmarish moment? She couldn't wrap her mind around it, but she was glad it had. So very glad.

He broke the kiss, but didn't let her go. She rested her cheek against his chest and listened to the runaway beat of his heart. Finally, regretfully, she moved out of his arms.

"Thank you," she said softly. He drew his eyebrows together slightly, in that way he did, and she smiled. "For helping me forget for a moment."

He cupped her face in his hands and kissed her again, this time with more urgency. When he stepped away, he looked troubled. "You're asleep on your feet. I should go."

She caught his hand. "Please don't. Not yet, anyway. I don't think I can be alone here."

He could have taken advantage of her request. Kissed her again. Drawn her deeper. And she wouldn't have simply acquiesced, she would have reveled in their lovemaking.

But he didn't take advantage. Instead, he led her to

the couch and told her to sit. She did, and he grabbed a couple of throw pillows and plumped them. He propped one behind her head and handed her the other. She hugged it to her.

"Would you like a glass of wine? It might help you sleep."

She said she would and watched him leave the room. She didn't know what was happening between them, whether it was the trauma of the night, her bleary-eyed exhaustion, or the fact that he was calm and strong when she needed both more than anything, but at this moment, she felt as if they belonged together. As if she'd met the person she was meant to spend forever with.

Because tonight, she couldn't imagine her life without him.

He returned with a glass for her but not himself. She didn't question it. Minutes passed as she sipped her wine, her eyelids growing heavy.

The quiet should have felt weird, she thought, shifting to curl into his side. But it didn't. It felt comfortable. And good. Really good.

He gently took the glass from her hand and set it on the coffee table. She nestled into his side, and he trailed his fingers through her hair, rhythmically stroking.

"You awake?" he asked softly.

"Mmm-hmm."

"There's something I need to tell you."

She heard the words, but as if he were calling to her from far off; they were muted. She moved her head slightly, in response.

"I should . . . told you . . ."

Even as she struggled to listen, his voice faded away as she sank into a deep sleep.

CHAPTER THIRTY-ONE

6:00 A.M.

The smell of coffee penetrated Sienna's dream. In it, she was running from window to window. Looking for something, although she wasn't certain what. Something important. Something she had missed.

Her feet were bare. Cut and bleeding.

The smell of the coffee grew stronger. Someone called her name. She opened her eyes.

Jonathan. He stood in the doorway to the living room, holding two mugs of steaming coffee.

He smiled. "Good morning."

"Morning," she managed, voice thick with sleep. She sat up and pushed the hair away from her face. "What time is it?"

"Early." He crossed to the couch and held out a mug. "I hated to wake you, but you said you wanted to be at the hospital first thing."

She nodded. Sipped the coffee. "Mmm. This is perfect."

"I'm going to take off. Give you a chance to wake up, get cleaned up."

She didn't want him to go, she realized. She wanted him to stay. But she couldn't ask, not again. Not now, with daylight on the horizon.

"I could make us breakfast?"

"I already ate."

"Oh. Okay, good." She stood up, shocked at how wobbly she felt. "I can't . . . thank you enough for last night."

"I'm sorry you had to go through all that."

"Yeah," she said, "me too." Except for his parts of the night, she acknowledged. If not for her mother's episode, those parts might not have happened.

"Good luck today."

"Thanks. I'm sure I'll need it."

He cleared his throat. "Mind if I take my coffee with me?"

"Go for it."

"I'll bring the mug back."

"I look forward to that."

He grinned. "You're flirting with me right now, aren't you?"

"Maybe." She cocked an eyebrow. "If I am, what are you going to do about it?"

"How about I let you know tonight?"

"That'd be good." She shifted her weight from one foot to the other.

"Should I just let myself out?"

"I'll walk you. Got to lock the door."

"Smart girl."

But she wasn't smart, she acknowledged as she walked him to the door. She was as smitten as a starry-eyed teenager. And worse, she had the feeling he knew it.

She mustered her good sense and didn't linger at the door, didn't watch him go, hoping he would take one last glance back at her.

Instead, thoughts turning to breakfast, she started for the kitchen. Knowing the chaos that awaited her,

her heart thumped a little faster with every step closer she came. She dreaded seeing it this morning. Not just because it would be a harsh reminder of the events of the night before, but because the chaos gave a clear picture of her mother's mental state.

But instead of chaos, she found calm. Someone had swept up all the broken glass and china. Her bloody footprints had been wiped away. The dining room chairs sat back around the table, where they belonged. The drapes had been opened to reveal the dawn.

Not someone. Jonathan.

Tears flooded her eyes at the sweetness of it. Hoping to catch him before he reached his house, she ran back to the front door and yanked it open. But his name died on her lips.

She didn't catch him before he got home, but she was just in time to see a white van with tinted windows rolling slowly by her house.

CHAPTER THIRTY-TWO

6:20 A.M.

Sienna watched the white van cruise past. Could it be the one her mother had told her about? She said she'd recorded its comings and goings.

Sienna understood her mother's illness. This was what she did: took ordinary occurrences—like an unmarked van passing the house—as proof that her wild imaginings were truth, not fiction.

So, why did this feel different?

Get a grip, Sienna. It's just the timing. Or exhaustion.

She pushed away from the door and hurried to the kitchen. Her coffee was cold, so she dumped it and poured a fresh cup, then popped a couple slices of whole-grain bread into the toaster.

Once they had toasted, she slathered them with almond butter, sprinkled them with cinnamon, and added some sliced banana. Her stomach growled and she realized just how hungry she was. As she shifted her gaze, it landed on her mother's book.

Randy wanted to see it, but she supposed she should take a look first. She collected it, noting the book's title: *Eye of the Storm: Coping With the Mentally Ill Family*

Member. She shook her head. And all this time she'd thought her mother was reading a novel.

She carried it and her breakfast to the table. There, she took a big bite of the toast, then turned the book over and read the back cover. Written by a therapist who worked specifically with families dealing with mental illness, it promised coping mechanisms and de-escalation strategies, as well as tips on maintaining calm in the midst of chaos.

Sienna tilted her head, chewing thoughtfully. Interesting choice. As if her mother wasn't the one with mental illness.

Taking another bite of toast, she opened the book. The food lodged in her throat. Tiny notations, made in pencil, covered the inside cover, the title page, and the margins of the first fifty pages.

They were extremely organized and completely legible. Dates. Times. Observations. A continuing column with the heading PHONE, and another headed with VAN. According to the notations, both had begun the day after Sienna arrived home.

Could this be accurate? Sienna wondered. She counted the occurrences of the van passing. Four times a day. Day after day. Like clockwork.

She sipped the coffee, then started on her second piece of toast. That was a lot; the consistency was weird. She flipped through the pages. The times varied only slightly. Early morning. Midday. Evening. The nighttime occurrences varied wildly: ten P.M., midnight; one at four A.M., for heaven's sake.

Those crazy night hours excluded the option of the van being a service vehicle, like a painter's. It didn't exclude the option of the van belonging to someone who lived on the street.

Sienna polished off the second piece of toast, and turned her attention to the hang-up calls. These lacked consistency. Two one day, four the next. The times spanned the gamut of the day, some in the early morning, others late at night. And everything in between. But too many to chalk them up to coincidence.

Sienna shut the book and stood. She might be able to deal with the van question right now, before she went to the hospital. All it would take was a bit of investigation.

Twenty minutes later, she was cleaned up and dressed for the day, bundled into her coat, gloves, and boots, and on the sidewalk.

The day was cold and crisp, the sky a cloudless blue. She would have been less conspicuous in the car, but most of the homes on this street had detached garages behind the house, like her mom's did. If the van had pulled all the way up, it would be easier to spot on foot.

She walked the entire street, up one side and back on the other. No white van in any drive. She could've missed it driving off while she ate breakfast, then dressed, or it could be parked in a garage.

As she neared Jonathan's, she started to cross back to her side of the street, hoping he didn't see her.

He did, and stepped out onto his porch.

"You lose something, Sienna?"

Only her mind, she thought. She stopped at the end of his walk. How did she explain this without sounding alarmingly like her mother? She could lie, making up something about a cat she didn't own being missing, but lying felt even crazier than the truth.

"Did you see a white van drive by about a half hour ago?"

"Can't say I did. You having some work done today?"

She shook her head. "No. It's just—"

She stopped. Her looking for her delusional mother's white van wouldn't make sense to him. It didn't even make sense to her.

Rip off the Band-Aid, Sienna. Just tell him.

She cleared her throat. "Last night Mom told me about a white van constantly passing the house . . . she's been noting its comings and goings—"

He cocked an eyebrow. "A white van?"

"That's what she does, sees something ordinary and turns it into something—"

"Alarming?"

"Yes. Something conspiratorial." She took a deep breath, then let it out. "But anyway, this morning, after you left, I saw a white van passing and—"

And what, she wondered. She was babbling, for God's sake.

"—I wanted to be able to tell her it was nothing. A neighbor's van. Or workmen in the neighborhood. To reassure her."

He drew his eyebrows together. "Nothing, huh?"

"No sign of it."

He stomped his feet and rubbed his arms. She realized he wasn't wearing a coat.

"I'll watch for it, if you like?"

"Would you? Thank you, Jonathan. It might help."

"You're welcome."

"I better go. I've got to get to the hospital." She lifted her hand in goodbye, then stopped and turned back. "If you can, get their license plate number, too."

As the words passed her lips, she wished she could grab them back. She saw something cross his features, something she recognized from years of seeing it on people's faces when they looked at her mother.

The truth of that crashed over her, stealing her

equilibrium. Stammering something about her mother and the hospital, she hurried to her car.

As she backed out of her drive, she noticed that for once, he wasn't watching her drive off.

CHAPTER THIRTY-THREE

8:00 A.M.

When Sienna arrived at her mother's hospital room, a tall, trim woman was exiting. The woman saw her and smiled warmly. "You *have* to be Sienna," she said. "The resemblance is startling."

"People used to call me her little mirror image," Sienna said. "And you are?"

"Dr. Pamela Margery, your mother's psychiatrist." She held out her hand. "It's good to finally meet you."

Sienna shook her hand. "Likewise. How is she?"

"Groggy and confused. But both are to be expected. She asked for you. She's worried for your safety."

Of course she was. "Does she remember what happened?"

"Yes. And no. I'd love to hear your version and to chat a bit about how things have been going."

"Until last night, they were going pretty well." Sienna sighed. "Let me know when and where, and I'll be there."

Dr. Margery glanced at her watch. "How about now? It won't take long."

"I should say hello first, so she knows I'm here. And safe."

"Of course. I have some calls to return anyway. I'll be in the floor waiting room."

Sienna nodded and entered her mother's room. The television was on, but her mother wasn't watching. She was sitting up in bed, seeming to stare at nothing.

"Hey, Mom," Sienna said softly. "How are you doing this morning?"

Her expression brightened. "Sienna! Thank God, you're okay."

"That's what I should be saying to you." She bent and kissed her cheek. "I'm fine."

"I dreamed you were shot."

"You were the one who was shot, Mom. Do you remember what happened?"

She frowned slightly. "I was having an episode, a really bad one."

"Yes."

"I'm sorry about that. But you're safe, that's all that matters."

"Mom . . . you stopped taking your medication, didn't you?"

Her gaze shifted guiltily. "Yes."

"You lied to me."

"I wanted to make you happy."

"But you see the way that turned out. I can't live this way, Mom. You have to take your meds."

"Can we talk about this later? I'm really tired."

"Of course." Sienna tucked an errant wave behind her mother's ear. "I ran into Dr. Margery on my way in. She wants to talk to me for a few minutes. How about you take a rest, and I'll be back after?"

She agreed, and by the time Sienna left, her mother was already dozing. After a brief conversation with the nurse, Sienna headed to the waiting room. Empty save for Dr. Margery, it was equipped with a coffee maker, as well as drink and snack machines. A television on the wall was tuned to the local news.

The psychiatrist ended her call and pocketed her phone. "Thank you for agreeing to speak with me," she said, motioning to a couple chairs at the far end of the room.

They sat, angling in the chairs to face each other.

"First off, how are you, Sienna?"

The question took her by surprise. "Me?"

"Yes." The doctor smiled. "Last night must have been traumatic."

"It was definitely that. I'm a bit shaky, but on my feet."

The psychiatrist didn't respond, and silence stretched between them. Sienna cleared her throat. "I do worry," she said, shifting her gaze for a moment before returning it to the doctor's, "that my being here isn't good for her. I've thought about going back to London."

She nodded. "I understand that."

"But, a part of me, a big part, feels like that's running away." She cleared her throat. "I think she needs me."

"I know she's worried about you."

Sienna let out a short, brittle laugh. "That's an understatement, Dr. Margery. Don't you think?"

The psychiatrist responded with another question. "How was your mother when you first arrived home?"

"Excited to see me. Happy, but . . . anxious, too. She was certain Margaret and her 'people' would discover I was home and come for me."

Sienna paused, then went on. "I guess I should have expected that, and maybe I did. The romanticized version, anyway."

Dr. Margery nodded slightly, as if understanding.

"I didn't realize until I was home how much her

disorder had come to control her life. She rarely leaves the house and keeps all the drapes and blinds closed so no one can spy on her, and is obviously not taking care of herself physically."

Sienna clasped her hands together. "Did you know about her fall down the stairs?"

"She tripped on some loose carpet, correct?"

"That's what she initially said, then confided in me that she was pushed. She didn't tell Brad because she believes he's one of 'them.' She doesn't sleep at night, but when she does, she barricades herself in her room."

Sienna let out a long breath. "She and I had a heart-to-heart and I convinced her to take her medicine. The turnaround was like a miracle. She was calm. She voluntarily opened the drapes. I even convinced her to run errands with me. Then last night happened. Of course, I now know she was only pretending to take her medicine."

The doctor reached across and patted Sienna's clasped hands. "It's difficult, I know. Especially after being away from it for so long."

Tears flooded her eyes. She blinked furiously against them. "What should I do, Dr. Margery? I don't know what to do."

"Your mother and I talked about what happened last night, but I think I should hear your version."

Sienna nodded and began with arriving home to a dark house, and finishing with the gun going off and calling 911. "I shouldn't have fought her for the gun, but I was so afraid she was going to hurt someone. If someone had come to the door . . . Brad, a neighbor, the police . . . she was in such a state . . . she could have killed them."

"Sienna, look at me." She did. "You did nothing wrong. Vivienne was in the grip of an acute paranoiac episode. You were right, she very well could have used that weapon on someone. Let go of any feelings of responsibility or guilt you're carrying about it. Okay?"

"I'll try."

"Let me ask you this: Do you have any idea what triggered this episode?"

"I think I do." Sienna explained about the call her mother had listened in on, then bent and took her mother's book out of her tote. "But that call was the final straw. Apparently, a white van has been passing the house several times a day, and there's been an inordinate number of hang-up calls, all starting since I've been home."

"Or so she says."

"Yes." Sienna held the book out. "She kept a record of each time."

Dr. Margery took the book, flipped it open. Several moments later, she met Sienna's eyes. "Would you like some good news?"

"Are you kidding? I'd *love* some good news."

"Your mother is aware of how extreme her behavior became last night, and she expressed regret for what happened. Frankly, she scared herself bad enough she's agreed to a fourteen-day inpatient program at Evergreen Behavioral Health Hospital."

Sienna could hardly believe what the woman was saying. "She agreed to that? Voluntarily?"

"Yes. She's afraid you'll return to London if she doesn't. Frankly, she's ready to do whatever's necessary to keep you in Tranquility Bluffs. But," she cautioned, "when the shock wears off and her memory of her frightening behavior dims, she could very well change her mind. It's up to us to continue to encourage her."

Her mother's visits to Evergreen, or other places like it, had always involved mandatory stays of twenty-four to seventy-two hours, enough time to defuse whatever episode had spurred her dad into calling for help, and to stabilize her medication.

"Of course," Sienna said. "Anything I can do."

"She doesn't want to lose you again," Dr. Margery said. "She wants to make whatever changes are necessary to keep you in her life."

"I'm not going anywhere, Dr. Margery. Not this time."

"Good. Later today, we'll move her to this hospital's psych unit, and by the end of the week she should be cleared for the move to Evergreen."

CHAPTER THIRTY-FOUR

4:10 P.M.

Sienna spent the rest of the day with her mother, leaving only after she had been moved to the psych unit. Then, once her mother was settled in, she had been asked to leave. From this point, visiting hours were fewer, and strictly adhered to.

Sienna exited the hospital, shivering as the cold surrounded her. She hurried to her car and climbed in, then cranked the engine.

While the engine warmed, she checked her phone for messages. Word had gotten out about what had happened—of course it had—and a few old friends had called to see if there was anything they could do. Her brother had texted to check on her mom's condition— and hers as well.

And that was it. She frowned slightly, surprised she hadn't heard from Randy. He'd wanted to see the notations in her mother's book; she'd thought he might stop by the hospital for it.

When warm air finally began streaming out the car's vents, Sienna backed out of the parking spot, then headed out of the lot. As long as she had to pass by the police station on her way home, she might as well take the book to Randy.

Fifteen minutes later, Sienna entered the Tranquility Bluffs Police Department. It was busier than she expected: a patrol officer booking a drunk; two other officers executing their version of conflict resolution with a married couple at war with each other; and half a dozen dejected-looking folks seated in the waiting area, two of them, Sienna saw, in handcuffs.

So much for the tranquility in Tranquility Bluffs.

She made her way to the desk officer. "Is Detective Clark in?"

"He's with someone right now. You want to take a seat?"

"You'll tell him I'm here? Sienna Scott."

"When he's done." He shifted his gaze behind her. "You! Sit your ass down."

She glanced over her shoulder. The guy the officer was reprimanding was big, bald, and had a scar that ran the length of the right side of his face. She returned her focus to the desk officer. "Do you know how long Detective Clark might be?"

"No idea. Stay or go, your choice. We're a little busy here."

"I'll wait," she said, seeing that the officer had already moved on anyway.

She took a seat by the door. After only a couple minutes, a commotion drew her attention. A man burst out of one of the back offices, voice raised in anger.

"Are you sons of bitches ever going to leave me alone? Ten years, nothing's changed!"

Sienna recognized him and caught her breath. Reed Shepard.

And Randy. He was the picture of calm juxtaposed to Shepard's fury. "We're reviewing every lead—"

"Bullshit! You never followed the one I gave you. Why is that, Detective?"

Two uniformed officers joined Randy, obviously ready to step in if necessary.

Randy held out a hand. "If you'll just calm down—"

"Fuck that. I'm done here."

"Thank you for coming in today, Mr. Shepard." Randy nodded to his colleagues. "The officers will escort you—"

"Get your hands off of me! Don't worry, I want to get far away from here as fast as possible."

He turned and strode out. Without questioning the wisdom of her actions, Sienna hurried after him. "Reed! Wait."

He stopped and looked back, glowering at her.

Her steps faltered. He looked not only like he could hurt her, but like he wanted to, as well.

"What?" he demanded.

"I don't know if you remember—"

"Yeah, I remember."

"What you said in there, about them not following a lead, what did you mean?"

"What does it matter?" He turned to his car and unlocked it. "Leave me alone."

"Talk to me, please."

He yanked open the car door. "Fuck off."

"Wait! They didn't follow my lead, either."

He stopped. Frowned at her. "What lead?"

"Madison and I were wearing the same coat. If she was in the wrong place at the wrong time, it's because that was my place and time."

He stared at her a moment, then nodded. "Not here," he said. "Follow me."

"Where?"

"Not so anxious to talk to me now, huh? Suspected killer that I am."

"Just being smart. Where?" she asked again.

"There's a place I go. Hanson's Hideaway. It's right before the Illinois state line."

Even as she questioned the sanity of what she was about to do, Sienna nodded. "I'll follow you."

Hanson's was a hole-in-the-wall place tucked away between an all-night package store and a un-marked warehouse, the most welcoming thing about it, the bright neon sign, flashing: BEER. HERE. BEER. HERE.

Shepard didn't wait for her, just hopped out of his truck and headed inside. He either hoped she would give up, or he needed a drink that badly.

Sienna followed him in, heart pounding wildly. Judging by the few cars parked outside, the place was nearly empty. She was on her own, facing down the man widely believed to have stabbed his girlfriend to death.

She stepped inside. The lighting was dim; the place reeked of cigarettes and booze. A large U-shaped bar, surrounded by old-school stools made of dark wood and upholstered in red leatherette, dominated the space. A half-dozen tables and a row of booths took up the rest of the main room. A lit doorway at the back appeared to lead to a pool room.

Shepard was standing at the bar; he'd bought her a beer. When he saw her, he jerked his head toward the row of booths.

He picked one and she slid onto the bench across from his. He pushed the beer her way, then took a long swallow of his.

"Thanks for the beer," she said.

He didn't respond, and she went on, "It must have been hard, all these years, having people believe you killed her."

"You think? Maybe?"

The short response dripped sarcasm born of bitterness.

"I know what it's like to be judged because of someone else's actions."

He finished his draft and pointed at hers. "You going to drink that?"

"Probably not." She nudged it in his direction. "You can have it."

"Thanks."

She watched him throw back half in one swallow, then said, "In my case it's my mother."

"Heard she's crazy," he said.

"And that I'm just like her? You hear that, too?"

He said he had, and she understood his bitterness—she had her own to contend with. "Because I look just like her." She glanced away, then met his eyes once more. "I'd hear the whispers behind my back, see the averted gazes."

"How about folks crossing to the other side of the street to avoid you? You get that, too?"

"Not me. My mom a lot."

A glimmer of what she thought was respect came into his eyes. "You moved far away. You were smart, doing that. Not so smart coming back, in my opinion."

"Why did you stay?"

"Don't know. Maybe I wanted to be here when they found the bastard who really did it?"

She nodded. She understood that. It made a twisted, soul-stealing kind of sense.

"I broke up with her, not the other way around. Nobody likes to talk about *that*."

He finished that beer and, like magic, the bartender appeared with two more and a shot of whiskey.

"Everyone said you and Madison were fighting that day."

"Yeah. I found out she was stepping out on me."

She thought she must have misheard him. "Did you say—"

"Yeah, I did. She had somebody on the side. He sent her flowers. She lied about it and I broke up with her."

"I never heard that before."

"'Cause the cops swept it under the rug. Said I was making it up."

Her hands shook and she dropped them to her lap. "That can't be right. The other guy could've been the one who killed her." The last part caught in her throat, came out thick.

"They never followed up on it."

"That doesn't make sense. They must have had a reason—"

"They had a reason, all right. I was their guy."

"What did you know about him?"

"What does it matter?" He threw back the shot and chased it with beer. "He's long gone by now."

"You don't know that."

"Who'd hang around? You go berserk and stab your girlfriend eighteen times, you gonna hang around?"

Another reason he had stayed, she thought. To prove to everyone he was innocent.

His words slurred slightly. If he kept hitting the alcohol that way, soon he wouldn't be able to walk, let alone talk.

"What was his name?"

"Don't know. Got the feeling he wasn't a student . . . that he was older. Must've had money."

"Why would you think that?"

"The fancy flowers. What college student can afford roses like that?" He stopped, stared into his beer for so long she wondered if he'd decided he was done talking. Then, suddenly, he looked up. "Called her a whore," he muttered, mouth twisting into bitter grimace. "Every-body heard *that*."

"What'd she say about the guy?" Sienna leaned toward him. "During that fight?"

"It doesn't matter, don't you get it? Leave me alone." He dropped his head into his hands. When he lifted it, there were tears in his eyes. "They've started up again. Questioning everyone. Digging it all up. It's never gonna go away."

"It'll go away if they catch the real killer. Let me help you, Reed. I'll help you, I promise."

"Just go away. You can't help. Nobody can."

"Please. Together—"

"Don't you get it? I'm fucked. From the day I met her . . . God, I wish I'd never met her."

He dropped his head into his hands again, and Sienna knew she wasn't going to get anything else out of him.

She slid out of the booth, looked down at him. She'd always felt sort of sorry for herself. For being the one who found Madison—and the chain reaction of events that followed. But now she understood she was just one of the many victims of this crime—and that her resid-ual trauma was small, indeed.

"I'm sorry this happened to you, Reed. If you change your mind about my help, call me."

He didn't look up, and she jotted her cell number on a napkin, folded it, and laid it on the table.

Without another word, she turned and walked away.

CHAPTER THIRTY-FIVE

By the time Sienna arrived home, it was completely dark. Once again, she parked in the drive instead of the garage, finding the glow of the porch light inordinately reassuring.

She collected the few groceries—including a rotisserie chicken—she'd picked up on the way home, and climbed out of the car. She glanced over her shoulder at Jonathan's place. Lights glowed from every window, and she wondered what he was doing and if, after this morning, he'd decided she was too much crazy to bother with. She hoped not, because she really liked him. More than she should, she supposed, considering everything going on right now.

She let herself in, locking the door behind her. Then she stopped and listened. Utter silence. Not even the hum of the furnace. But still, there was something . . .

Goose bumps prickled at the back of her neck. It felt wrong. Like the atmosphere had changed or someone's energy lingered, someone who didn't belong.

Her mother's frantic claim popped into her head.

"I didn't fall. I was pushed."

Sienna shook her head, annoyed with herself. *Stop it, Sienna. You're being ridiculous.*

She hung her coat in the closet, catching a whiff of cigarette smoke. She brought the sleeve to her nose, then made a sound of distaste. The smell of the bar clung to her. Even her hair, she realized, holding the strands to her nose.

A shower, she decided. Then food. After depositing the groceries in the kitchen, she headed upstairs. The second floor was colder than the first, which she found odd.

She realized why when she went into her bedroom. Her window was cracked open. She stared at it, a chill that had nothing to do with the temperature racing over her. She didn't open that window. Why would she have, it was too damn cold outside.

Her mother. Of course.

Sienna hadn't even been upstairs last night, and this morning she must have been so distracted, she didn't notice it was open.

She marched across the room. As she bent to close it, she glanced outside. And realized she had a clear view of Jonathan's front window. And as she stared, he walked into view.

She froze, unable to tear her gaze away. Like some creepy stalker, or voyeur, she watched as he stretched, imagining his sweatshirt lifting, revealing a glimpse of his flat, muscled belly dusted with dark hair. Imagined the hair trailing under his waistband then . . . lower.

Remembering if she could see him, he could see her, she yanked the window down, locked it tight, and pulled the drape.

Was that what her mom had been doing? Spying on Jonathan? It wouldn't surprise her—of course not much would after last night.

She turned away from the window, gaze landing on her desk. Two notebooks, papers, her psychology textbook. And journal.

That wasn't right. The journal had been in the drawer. She'd looked at it, then put it back.

Or had she? She drew her eyebrows together. Maybe her mom was reading it. But why? Anything in it was ten years old.

Deciding to ask her mother about it, she collected the items she needed and headed to the bathroom to shower.

Twenty minutes later, she towel-dried her hair, the smell of tobacco replaced by the fruit-and-honey scent of her overpriced shampoo. Deciding to forgo the blow-dryer, she slipped into dorm pants and an oversized sweatshirt, then headed downstairs for food.

The doorbell sounded as she landed on the bottom step. She checked the time, then went to the door. "Who's there?" she asked.

"Jonathan."

She looked down at herself. And here she was looking like a college student wannabe.

"I come bearing gifts."

He could be bearing arms, she'd probably still let him in, she thought, and cracked open the door. He smiled at her, and her heart skipped a beat. Dangerous, she thought. It had been a long day; she was tired and hungry. And he was sexy as hell.

He held out a thermal bag. "Sustenance."

She frowned, surprised. "You mean food?"

He laughed. "Yeah, I mean food. Have you eaten?"

"No. And I'm starving." She took the bag. "You want to come in?"

"It *is* a little cold out here."

She stepped aside so he could enter, then in a move

she'd seen her mother make a million times, she peered around him at the street, before shutting and locking the door.

"What is it?" she asked, catching the aroma of something spicy.

"My famous chili."

She cocked an eyebrow. "Famous?"

"Yes, ma'am." He unzipped his jacket. "Not to brag, or anything."

"You know I'm a chef, right?"

He slid his hands into his front pockets and smiled. "Heard that. But I'm not scared."

She laughed and several minutes later she understood his confidence. The chili was delicious. Meaty. Made with three kinds of beans and with a depth of flavor that didn't come from a seasoning package or a can.

They sat side by side at the kitchen island, bowl of chili and glass of the previous night's wine in front of them, eating in a comfortable silence.

"This is good," she said, scraping the side of the bowl with her spoon. "And it's just what I needed."

"There's more."

She laughed. "I would if I wasn't afraid I'd pop."

He smiled, obviously pleased. "How's your mom?"

"Doing good. Surgery went well; her prognosis is excellent." She sipped the wine, feeling her tension slipping away. "I'm hopeful, too. She's voluntarily committing herself to a behavioral health hospital for fourteen days. If you've ever dealt with someone with mental illness, you know how huge that is."

"I'm guessing it's similar to dealing with an addict. Rehab isn't high on their to-do list until they hit rock bottom and have no place else to go."

"Your mom?"

"Yeah." He took another bite of the chili. "Good times."

"That's the thing about her form of psychosis. Her fears, the imminent danger, are absolutely real to her. But nobody else sees it."

"It sounds lonely."

She hadn't thought of it that way before, but he was right, it would be. She hurt for her mother.

"When you opened the door, you looked surprised to see me."

"I was. I thought that maybe, after the thing with my mom and then my hunt for the white van this morning, you'd decided it'd be smart to keep your distance. I half expected to see a For Sale sign in your yard when I got home."

He laughed. "It takes a lot more than that to scare me away."

She opened her mouth to respond when the doorbell sounded.

He glanced at his watch and frowned slightly. "You expecting someone?"

"No." She laid her napkin on the bar and slid off the stool. "Excuse me."

Randy, she saw, and opened the door.

"Hi, Sienna," he said. "Is this a bad time?"

She thought of Jonathan and wished she could say yes, but didn't, and stepped aside so he could enter. "No, this is fine. What's up?"

"I'm sorry I missed you at the station earlier."

The book. Of course. She'd forgotten all about it. "It was a busy place this afternoon."

"You left so quickly—is everything okay?"

She some reason, she didn't want to say anything about talking to Reed Shepard, at least not right now.

"Everything's fine. I was tired from being at the hospital all day, and figured I'd catch up with you later."

"And here I am." His gaze shifted to a point behind her. She looked over her shoulder. Jonathan, lounging in the kitchen doorway, arms folded across his chest, head cocked as he studied Randy.

She had no reason to be embarrassed, but her cheeks heated. It was just the way he looked, so comfortable standing there, exuding something decidedly territorial.

Jonathan smiled and strolled over. He held out his hand. "Jonathan Hart."

"Detective Randall Clark, Tranquility Bluffs PD." He took his hand. "I know most folks around town, don't know you."

"Jonathan's my neighbor. He lives across the street."

"No kidding." Randy's eyes narrowed slightly. "You have a job, Jon?"

"Jonathan," he corrected. "Currently, it's renovating the house."

"One of those flippers, huh? That's what you do?"

"Right now it is," he responded, tone deceptively mild.

It was as if they had both taken an instant dislike to each other, which she didn't understand. "I'll get Mom's book."

She returned with it a few moments later. It appeared as if the two men hadn't moved a muscle. They studied each other silently, as if preparing to go into battle.

"Here it is," she said, grateful to break the tension. "I saw a white van this morning. I searched the neighborhood to see where it landed, but came up empty."

Randy frowned. "I don't think that was a good idea."

"Why not?"

"Somebody's messing with you, and you have no

idea why." He looked at Jonathan. "Maybe even some-one you know. Or *think* you know."

She didn't know what to say, so she cleared her throat. "Keep the book as long as you like. Mom's vol-untarily committed herself for fourteen days. She's not going to need it."

"Thanks. Maybe we'll have the whole thing figured out by then."

"Or maybe there's nothing to figure out," Jonathan said.

Randy ignored him. "Walk me out, Sienna?"

She did, stepping out onto the front porch with him. He closed the door behind them, obviously to keep Jon-athan from hearing what he said next.

"It pays to be careful, Sienna." He leaned toward her, lowering his voice even more. "Really careful."

"Now you sound like my mother," she said, forcing a light tone.

"No," he countered, "I sound like a cop. You don't know this guy, don't forget that. If you do, you may live to regret it."

Hugging herself against the cold, Sienna watched Randy drive off. He was right, she didn't know Jona-than. He could be the nice guy he purported to be, or one with an agenda.

What Reed Shepard had said popped into her head.

"She was stepping out on me with another guy. Someone older."

Someone older. When he said that, she'd thought of a professor. Someone in a position of power. Jonathan, she guessed, was more her brother's age. The age of a graduate assistant. Or a young professional.

It would be more likely that Madison would have been seeing someone like that.

Sienna shook her head, scolding herself for letting

her imagination run away with her. None of it had anything to do with Jonathan. At that time, he most likely would have been stationed in Iraq.

She slipped back inside and found Jonathan waiting for her, expression thoughtful.

"What was that all about?" he asked.

She couldn't quite meet his eyes. "Which part?"

"The 'walk me out,' then close the door behind him part."

"Nothing."

"Really?" He cocked an eyebrow. "My guess is, he was warning you about me."

She couldn't deny it. "He's a cop and a friend. I guess I couldn't expect anything different."

"Friends? I don't think that's what he thinks you are."

She tried to laugh it off; it caught in her throat. Maybe once upon a time something had been growing between them, but that was long dead. "You're reading something from nothing."

"He said someone was messing with you. What's that all about?"

"I've gotten a couple crank calls. That's all."

"It was nothing, but you thought enough of it to take it to your buddy Detective Clark?"

"Why all the questions?"

The words came out sharply. He drew his eyebrows together, studying her a moment, then nodded. "Right you are. It's none of my business."

"I didn't mean it that way."

"I think you did. It's time for me to go." He plucked his coat from the coat stand and shrugged into it.

"Jonathan"—she held out a hand—"don't leave yet."

He crossed to the door. "You wanted to know why all the questions? I thought something was happening here, between us. Something kind of great."

He stopped, looked back. "But you can't have that without trust. You're not ready, I get that. So, I'll see you around."

He let himself out. The door snapped shut behind him, the sound seeming to reverberate through the empty house.

Like Randy said, she didn't know him. Not his family or history; not his successes or failures, not his dreams for the future. But she did know he was thoughtful. And funny. That he made great chili and liked red wine. She knew he was kind, and when he kissed her her mind emptied of everything but his mouth on hers. And she knew she liked being around him. She liked that a lot.

She didn't want him to go.

If that was foolish, she was willing to take the risk.

She grabbed her coat, not bothering with gloves or boots, neither locking the door behind her nor taking the time to gather her keys or phone. She didn't look back, not at her house or the vehicle that turned onto her street and rolled slowly past.

CHAPTER THIRTY-SIX

8:50 P.M.

Jonathan swung the door open before she knocked; Sienna didn't give him the chance to turn her away. "You're wrong," she said, voice breathless to her ears. "I am ready for great."

For a moment, he simply held her gaze. Her heart seemed to stop beating, then, when he held out his hand, it started again, thumping almost painfully against the wall of her chest.

She took it. His fingers, warm and strong, curved around hers, and he drew her inside and into his arms. As the door clicked shut, he kissed her.

Sienna leaned into him, flattening her hands against his chest, feeling his runaway heartbeat under her palm. What did she do with this? She wanted him in a way she hadn't wanted before. Closer. Deeper. But it was as if the deepest part of her wouldn't be deep enough.

It was thrilling.

And terrifying.

Because that didn't come with sex alone. Not even mind-blowing sex.

As if he read her mind, he broke the kiss, rested his forehead against hers. "Your move, Ms. Scott."

He was offering her a choice. Proceed in this direction,

or choose another. She appreciated the choice more than she could express.

She met his eyes. "Thank you." He didn't have to ask for what. He knew. She took a step back, feeling the loss of his body acutely, wanting nothing more than to move back into his arms and take this thing between them to its natural conclusion.

Instead, she shrugged out of her coat, then caught his hand, lacing her fingers with his and leading him to the folding chairs. They both sat. She began without preamble. "You asked me how Randy and I became friends."

She looked down at her feet, then back up at him. "You've been in Tranquility Bluffs long enough to have heard about a murder that happened on the Fredricks campus. A girl named Madison Robie."

He nodded, and she went on. "I was a freshman at Fredricks and I—" She took a deep breath; she couldn't bring herself to look at him. "I found her. On my way home from the library that night."

He didn't comment, and she went on. "Randy, Detective Clark, was the first one to come to my aid. He was a campus cop at the time."

"That seems an odd basis for a friendship."

"I know. My father certainly thought so." She paused, gathered her thoughts. "It didn't happen naturally, not really."

"How could it?" he asked. "There was nothing natural about that situation."

Sienna nodded. "After that night . . . I couldn't stop thinking about Madison. About the murder. I kept telling myself that I'd be able to move on once they caught the guy."

"But they didn't."

"No, they didn't. And as the days and weeks went by, I started worrying that—"

She bit it back, hesitant to share, afraid he'd think she was as crazy as her mother was. But like he said, great only came with trust. And that door swung both ways.

"I started worrying that it was supposed to have been me."

He looked at her, eyebrows drawn together in confusion. "I don't understand what you're saying."

Of course he didn't. Her father hadn't wanted that part of the story to become public. It was part of the reason he sent her away.

Sienna shifted her gaze, not wanting to see his expression while she explained. "I started worrying that I was the one who was supposed to be dead."

She quickly explained about the coat, the location, and the timing. "I tried to talk to my dad, but he . . . it freaked him out too much. Because of Mom and her illness. He told me the coat was a coincidence and that they hadn't found a killer because it was a random crime."

Beside her, Jonathan shifted, as if agitated. Or as if he wanted to say something, but held back.

"I tried to convince myself of it, but I couldn't. I needed to talk to somebody who would know what was going on with the case, so—"

"You went to see Clark."

"Yes. He explained how this type of murder is highly personal. Because of the way Madison was killed, the number of stab wounds. It definitely wasn't a random crime."

"I agree."

She looked at him. "You agree?"

"From what I've heard, and what you told me just now." He drew his eyebrows together. "And come on, a guy with a knife just happens upon a girl walking alone at midnight, in a blizzard no less, and he decides to kill her? That makes no sense. Didn't then, doesn't now."

She drew her eyebrows together. "What do you mean, then?"

"What?"

"You said it didn't make sense 'then.' As if at the time of the murder."

"Sorry. I meant when I first heard about it. So, that's how you became friends with Clark?"

"He promised to ask around, try to find out what was going on with the investigation and keep me posted."

"He didn't know what was going on?"

"He was campus police, the case was turned over to the Tranquility Bluffs police."

"Gotcha."

"My dad found out I was communicating with Randy and why, and basically flipped out. He thought I should go stay with his mother, my grandma, in London."

"And you went?"

She looked down at her clasped hands, then back up at him. "Yes."

"Did you fight it?"

A lump formed in her throat. "No."

"Why not?"

She'd asked herself that a thousand times. And every one of those times, she'd come up with the same answer. One she wasn't proud of.

She hedged. "It was only supposed to be for a little while."

"You were gone ten years." He paused. "You went without a fight. And you stayed without a fight. Why, Sienna?"

A lump settled in her throat; she struggled to speak around it. "I don't know."

"Bullshit."

He said it softly. Not a condemnation. Not a challenge. Just stating a fact.

She clasped her hands in her lap. She'd never said the words out loud, not even to Mimi. "I wanted to go," she said, looking him in the eyes. "How's that for the truth? I wanted to get away from her."

"Your mom?"

She nodded. "Yes. From her delusions and her constant hovering, from the anxiety of waiting for her next flare-up."

"You don't have to feel guilty about that."

"Don't I? I left my dad and brother holding the bag. I'm not proud of that."

"You didn't run away, Sienna. You were sent away."

"But I never came home."

"You're here now."

She was. Here and in the thick of it. Fighting the urge to pack up her stuff and run back to the calm and safety of her life in London. "I was afraid. As much as anything, that's why I left."

He angled toward her, covered her clenched hands with his own. "What were you afraid of?"

"That I was just like her. When I looked into a mirror, I didn't see myself, I saw her. The same as everybody in Tranquility Bluffs did."

She paused. "And that fear's why I'm home, too. Not for my mom. Not for my brother. For me, Jonathan. I'm being completely selfish."

He cupped her face in his hands, looked her in the eyes. His were a deep, endless brown. She realized she could lose herself in them.

"I see *you,* Sienna. Not some distorted mirror image.

I see a beautiful, smart, and caring woman. One I enjoy being with way more than I should."

She probably should ask him what he meant by that, but she didn't want to. She didn't want anything—or anyone—to mar how she was feeling right this moment.

He stood and drew her to her feet, against his chest. "Where do we go from here?" he asked, his gaze searching hers.

"Your bedroom," she said simply.

"You're sure that's what you want?"

Randy's warning rang in her ears, but the pounding of her heart drowned it out. "I don't think I've ever wanted anything more."

Jonathan took her hand. Silently, almost reverently, he led her downstairs to the basement apartment. They sank together to the bed, wrapped in each other.

There, all restraint evaporated. Passion exploded between them. They tugged at each other's clothing, hungry for the feel of skin against skin, warmth to warmth. He plundered her body, and she his.

She hadn't realized the extent to which she wanted him—or how much she needed this. This connection. This release. And this tether. To the world and to her physical self.

Worries about her mother's mental illness and fears of her own; concerns about white vans and anonymous phone calls, they all disappeared. Leaving sensations: his breath against her ear, him inside her, her body arching up. Her cry of release meeting—and matching—his.

As she tumbled back to earth, still clinging to him, Randy's words popped into her head out of nowhere.

"You don't know this guy, don't forget that. If you do, you may live to regret it."

Too late, she admitted, tangling her fingers in his dark hair and smiling up at him. Being careful, or playing it safe, was the last thing she wanted to do with this man.

CHAPTER THIRTY-SEVEN

2:50 A.M.

Sienna awakened to realize she was alone. She reached for Jonathan anyway and found the bed not only empty but cold. Shivering, she pulled the blanket up to her chin, listening intently, thinking any moment she would hear the toilet flush or the sound of his footfalls as he returned to the bedroom.

Nothing.

She reached for her phone to check the time, only to remember she had left it behind in her hurry to get to Jonathan. She'd also left behind her purse, her house keys in it.

She swore softly and climbed out of bed. She found her clothes, and quickly dressed. How could she have been so careless? What if the hospital had needed her? And with everything going on, to leave the house unlocked was just plain stupid.

"You don't know this guy, don't forget that. If you do, you may live to regret it."

Heart in her throat, she looked wildly around her for her coat. She found it, snatched it up, and darted out of the bedroom.

And ran smack into Jonathan. "Sienna?" He looked sleepy and way too sexy. "What's going on?"

"I've got to go."

She started by him; he caught her arm, searched her gaze. "What's wrong?"

"Where were you?"

"I couldn't sleep. I didn't want to wake you." He eased her against his chest. "I'm sorry. Where do you think I'd have gone in the middle of the night?"

She felt like an idiot. "I woke up and realized I left my phone at the house. And if the hospital tries to reach me—"

"I'll go get it. Just give me your keys and tell me where it is."

"That's the thing. I left my purse and keys behind, too."

"The house is unlocked?"

She nodded.

He leaned back so he could look her in the eyes. "No way am I going to let you go alone, in the middle of the night, to a house that's been unlocked for hours."

"I guess I wasn't thinking clearly."

"I guess you weren't."

She smiled up at him. "But it was your fault."

"Mine?"

"Mmm-hmm. Taking off that way. Leaving me pondering 'something great.'"

"And was it? Great?"

"You know it was."

"Sometimes a guy just needs to hear it."

She stood on tiptoes, leaning suggestively against him. "It was better than great, Jonathan."

He grinned broadly, but set her firmly away from him. "Enough of that. First, your phone and keys."

In the end, they went together. Jonathan did a thorough search of the house. She followed behind him as he went from room to room, checking closets and under beds. Even the attic.

Once they were convinced the house was secure, she checked her phone. "Oh."

"Did the hospital call?"

"No. Reed Shepard did."

"Reed Shepard?"

"The boyfriend of the girl who was murdered."

"I remember."

She frowned. Did she tell him that part of the story last night? Or did he hear it from folks around Tranquility?

"Newspaper," he said, as if reading her mind. "I remember from the newspaper article. Said he was the prime suspect."

"He wants to talk to me."

"What the hell for?"

The animus in his voice surprised her. He must have realized how he sounded because he added, "The guy got away with murder."

"I don't think he did it. Not anymore, anyway."

"What does *that* mean?"

Sienna explained about going to the PD to give her mother's book to Randy and hearing Shepard's outburst. "He accused the police of not following up on the lead he gave them. I was curious, and followed him outside."

He frowned. "And he told you, just like that?"

"Not quite. He didn't want to talk there, and told me to meet him at a place called Hanson's Hideaway."

He looked disbelieving. "All you know about this guy is that he's the prime suspect in a murder and you follow him, just like"—he snapped his fingers—"that?"

"I was careful. I had my own vehicle and we were heading to a public place. I wouldn't have gotten out of my car if it looked sketchy." She hoped he didn't know Hanson's, because it was about as sketchy as places got.

"Apparently, at the time of the murder, Madison was seeing another guy. That's what they fought about the day she died and why he broke up with her."

Jonathan looked doubtful. "It sounds awfully convenient."

"Reed said he told the cops, but they never followed up on it."

"And you believe that?"

"I think I do. For a couple reasons. First, I never heard anything about there being another guy in Madison's life, and second, Shepard was miserable. He didn't seem like someone who was hiding something. More like an innocent man whose life had been ruined by a lie."

"No disrespect, but maybe he's miserable because he killed Madison and didn't get away with it?"

"It could be. But again, that's not the impression I got."

"Did he say anything else?"

"Just that he got the idea the other guy was older and might have money. He clammed up then, but I offered to try to help him. I gave him my number and told him to call me if he was willing to talk to me some more."

Jonathan looked at the ceiling, as if asking for answers or patience, then back at her. "You gave him your number?"

She shrugged. "My mom's listed. He could find me easily."

"What did his message say?"

"That he'll tell me everything he told the cops."

"You don't think you could just ask your buddy Detective Clark?"

It was a good question, so Sienna ignored its edge.

She considered it a moment, then shook her head. "Truthfully, I don't know if he'd even be able to tell me. He wasn't with the Tranquility Bluffs police at the time. Even if he could, there's a good chance he wouldn't. Not everything, anyway."

"Because cops only tell you what they think you need to know."

She looked at him in question. "You don't like cops very much, do you?"

"Not true. It's just some cops I don't like."

She started to ask him why, then decided it would be better to wait until they were both rested.

"I'll go with you to see Shepard tomorrow," he said.

"You don't have to do that."

"Yeah, I do." He reached for her and eased her into his arms and against his chest. "Think of me as a bodyguard with benefits."

"Mmm, sexy. How could I refuse that offer?"

"I hoped you'd say that." He kissed her, then set her away from him. "But right now, I need to grab some shut-eye."

"You could stay?"

"I don't think we'd sleep."

She tried to hide her disappointment, obviously unsuccessfully, because he drew her back into his arms. "Let me rephrase that. I really, really want to. But I have to be up in a few hours. Flooring's being delivered first thing. Rain check?"

She stood on tiptoe and kissed him. "I think I can manage that."

Moments later, she stood at the door, shivering against the cold as she watched him cross the street. When he reached his door, he turned, lifted a hand in goodbye, then disappeared into his house. Almost immediately, his lights went out.

And she was left staring at his dark windows. Giving herself a shake, she shut and locked the door. Thoughts filled with him, she flipped off her own lights, starting with those in the kitchen.

When she returned to the foyer and the stairs to the second level, she stopped, a feeling of dread coming over her. She thought of her open window, her journal, and her mother's claim that she'd been pushed down the stairs, and her mouth went dry.

Don't be stupid, Sienna. Jonathan checked up there. Take. One. Step.

She did, one after another. A third of the way up, she stopped. Looked down and across to the living room. Her gaze landed on the couch, and she thought of the overstuffed cushions, how comfortable they were. How soft her mother's chenille afghan was.

Acknowledging that she was being ridiculous, she gave in to her fears and headed for the couch. As she pulled the afghan over her, headlights cut across the front window. Followed by the rumble of an engine.

The white van, she thought, and jumped to her feet. She raced to the window, like her mother making a note of the time.

But it wasn't a white van. It was a truck.

Jonathan's truck.

Her breath seemed to lodge in her throat. She took an involuntary step back from the window, hurt spiraling through her.

Jonathan had lied to her. Why?

CHAPTER THIRTY-EIGHT

7:40 A.M.

The scream of the cell phone awakened her. Sienna bolted upright, and grabbed the phone off the coffee table. "H'lo?"

"What the hell were you thinking?"

It took her a moment to get her bearings. "Brad?"

"Yes, 'Brad.' Who the hell else would it be?"

"Stop swearing at me, and tell me what's wrong."

"I just got off the phone with my mother. Apparently, the police have been by to question her."

Sienna pushed the hair away from her face and stood. She made her way to the kitchen, thoughts as much on coffee as on the call. "What about?"

"In regards to Madison Robie's murder."

Sienna stopped in her tracks. "What?"

"That's right. They're exploring other avenues, and apparently, someone in the *family* suggested my mother might have information about the murder. . . . Considering her reported animosity toward your mother."

Sienna frowned. "I still don't understand what your mother could have to do with Madison's murder."

"Not a damn thing! It has to do with *you,* Sienna."

She switched the coffee machine on. "I still don't

under—" But then she did understand, and bit the words back. After that anonymous caller, she had urged Randy to at least explore "other avenues." And he'd warned her it would mean investigating her family.

Her cheeks heated. And what had she done? Offered up her mother's paranoid delusions as that other avenue.

It *was* her fault.

"I'm sorry, Brad. I got this phone call. The caller said I was the one who was supposed to die. I went to Randy with it and he—"

He cut her off. "I don't care. All these years my family's put up with Viv's crazy claims. Her letters and calls. Her threats. The private investigators she's hired. And so have I. But now you, Sienna? It's too much."

"I'm your family, too, Brad."

"Are you? Right now you're acting a lot more like Viv than like me or Dad."

The blow struck its mark, and she flinched. Nothing he could have said could have hurt her more. She wanted to deny it, but couldn't—for heaven's sake, last night she was afraid to sleep in her own bed.

"You remember Margie White?" he asked.

"Dad's old office manager?"

"Yeah. Police called on her, too. I heard from her a couple days ago, but didn't put two and two together. They're investigating Dad, Sienna. *Dad,*" he said again, emphasizing the irony of it. "He must be rolling over in his grave."

Sienna crossed to a chair and sat down hard. She fought against dissolving into tears. "I'm sorry. I didn't mean for all this to happen."

"Well, it did. Call your pet monkey off, Sienna. Do it now."

He hung up, and Sienna was left with the phone to her ear, the sudden silence mocking her. She laid the phone on the table, and went back to the coffee maker. She went through the steps, pouring the water, measuring out the grounds.

Before the coffee even began to drip, the landline rang. She snatched it up. "Hello?" Met with dead air, she tried again. "Hello?"

A soft click.

Her hands began to shake. She held the phone a moment, then, remembering Randy's instructions, hung up and immediately dialed star fifty-seven.

That done, she poured herself a cup of coffee, and hurried to get dressed. She needed to let Randy know about the call, but she needed to see him in person.

Twenty minutes later, showered, dressed, and hair pulled into a high ponytail, Sienna stepped out onto the front porch. Her gaze landed on Jonathan's truck, sitting in the driveway.

A lump formed in her throat. She'd forgotten about his middle-of-the-night trip, but in the light of day her worry seemed silly. The poor guy could have gotten an emergency call or realized he needed something for first thing in the morning. Like coffee.

Longing to be with him again rolled over her in a wave. To be with him now. To ignore all the questions and conflicts pressing at her and march across the street—and have her way with him.

Shaking her head at her own thoughts, Sienna unlocked her car and slid inside. She let the engine warm a moment, then rolled out of the drive.

Traffic was light, and within minutes she was parked and crossing the police station's threshold. Randy stood talking to a uniformed officer, a mug of steaming coffee in his right hand.

He saw her and smiled. "This is a surprise. It's not even nine yet."

She forced a smile. "What I needed to discuss can't wait."

His expression became concerned. "Is everything all right?"

"Could we chat a moment? Privately?"

"Of course." Randy looked at the other officer. "Excuse us."

He signaled her to follow him. As they passed the desk officer, he said, "We'll be in interview room one."

A moment later he escorted her into a small, windowless room with a wooden table and two chairs. A video camera was mounted from the ceiling and pointed directly at the table.

"It's not on," he said, noticing the direction of her gaze.

She nodded and took a seat. He did as well, and folded his hands in front of him on the table. "How can I help you today, Sienna?"

"I got a hang-up call. This morning." She took a note-card from her pocket and handed it to him. "As you instructed me to do, I immediately dialed star fifty-seven. The exact time of the call is on that card."

"Good." He laid it on the table, his gaze never wavering from hers. "But you could have taken care of this with a phone call. So, why are you really here?"

"To undo a mistake I made." She looked down, then back up at him. "I shouldn't have made a stink about that crank caller."

"The one who said you were the one who was supposed to die?"

Hearing the words, she shifted uncomfortably in her seat. "Yes."

"Why do you think coming here with that was a mistake?"

"You were right. It was somebody's idea of a joke."

"But at the same time, you want me to collect the trace on this number?"

"That's for my mother. Obviously, someone's been messing with her."

"But they're not messing with you?"

"All that . . . about me being the intended victim, it's just, like I said, a joke."

"Remind me," he said softly, "back then, did you make your suspicions known?"

"You know I did. To you. And my family."

"Nobody else?"

She saw where he was going with this. If others didn't know she'd ever considered herself the intended victim, how could the call have been a random prank? "It wasn't common knowledge. But I'm sure word spread. You know how small towns are."

"I do, indeed."

"I'd like you to stop nosing around my family."

His eyebrows shot up. "Excuse me?"

"It's my fault you are; I take responsibility. That whole thing about me being the person the killer was really after—I was young and under the constant influence of my mother's delusions. Is it any wonder my imagination ran away with me?"

"What you just said, you don't believe it."

She twisted her fingers together. "Yes, I do. All of it."

He leaned toward her, expression sympathetic. "It's uncomfortable, I know. People get testy."

"My dad, Randy? You're asking questions about him?"

"We never followed this lead, which I believe was a mistake. One I'm remedying. I intend to pull every thread."

"He was above reproach."

"Was he?"

Her breath seemed to lodge in her lungs. "You didn't find anything?"

"No, I didn't." He paused. "The point is, of course you'd say he was beyond reproach because of your relationship with him."

"There are no threads to pull, Randy. I was a naïve young woman in the middle of something pretty horrifying. I lived under the constant barrage of my mother's paranoid delusions. That influenced me. I couldn't see it at the time. Which is why my dad sent me off to London."

"What if you were right?"

Why wouldn't he believe her? "Let this go, Randy. Please. For me."

"Your brother called you, didn't he?"

She hesitated a moment, then agreed that he had. "How did you know?"

"He called me, too. Mighty pissed off."

"He's put up with a lot." Her voice grew thick. "I don't blame him for being angry."

"Then you'll be happy to learn, Brad's mother won't hear from me again. I cleared her of any suspicion in Robie's death."

"Did you really think you'd find anything?"

"You suggested I look her way."

"I know I did. And I regret it."

Sienna looked down at her clenched hands, forcing herself to relax them. She wondered if her mom ever had these moments of crystal clarity. Moments when she thought: Dear God, what have I done? When she realized just how far outside reality she had wandered.

"Your brother's in financial trouble."

Her thoughts snapped back to Randy. "Excuse me?"

"Your brother, he's in financial trouble."

"That's not true. Brad's very successful."

"I'm sorry, Sienna. I really am. I thought you'd want to know."

She stared at him a moment. "Even if it is true, what business is it of—"

Then she realized how he'd gotten the information. "Now you're investigating *him*?"

"He's part of the puzzle. If you were the intended victim—"

"I wasn't."

"But what if you were?"

It was bizarre, hearing her own thoughts—her own imaginings—parroted back at her. And to now be the one on the opposite side of the theory, frustrated and helpless to get through to him.

She tried a different tack. "Why haven't you followed up on Reed Shepard's lead?"

He cocked his head, expression surprised. "What lead would that be?"

"That Madison was stepping out on him with another guy. That's why he broke up with her. It's what they were fighting about the day she died."

"And where did you get this information?"

"I talked to Reed. Last night."

"You followed him out of the police station."

It wasn't a question, but she answered him anyway. "Yes."

"I wondered where you went."

"How come the police never pulled that thread?"

"Who says we didn't?"

"He did."

"The number-one suspect?"

She lifted her chin a notch. "You mean the number-one suspect who was never charged? Yes, that's who said it."

"As you know, I wasn't a member of the TBPD at the time. But when Thompson put me in charge of re-opening the investigation, I reviewed all the old case notes. We did follow up, Sienna. We interviewed Madison's family, friends, sorority sisters, coworkers at the library, and not one of those many people we talked to corroborated his claim of another guy."

"No one?"

"That's right, not a single person. Don't you think she would have told someone? A trusted girlfriend? Girls don't keep that kind of thing quiet."

They didn't. Madison would have shared it with *someone*.

His expression turned sympathetic. "Madison Robie was not seeing anyone else at the time of her murder, Sienna."

"Then why, yesterday at the station . . . why was he making such a scene about it?"

"When people are under the microscope, especially the law enforcement microscope, they say all sorts of things. Anything to deflect the attention from themselves. Like I said, it's an uncomfortable place to be."

She thought of her brother. "Just leave my brother alone. Please, Randy."

"I'm sorry, Sienna. The lid's off the box, I can't put it back on."

CHAPTER THIRTY-NINE

9:10 A.M.

Sienna sat in her car, engine running, thoughts chaotic. The Tranquility Bluffs police had investigated Reed Shepard's claim of another boyfriend. And found it wasn't true.

So, why would Reed still be singing that song? She thrummed her fingers on the steering wheel. Randy's explanation made sense, but . . .

Ten years had passed. The police had looked into the claim and come up empty. It seemed to her, if the story wasn't true, he would have given up telling it long ago.

Wouldn't he have?

Sienna's thoughts jumped to her brother. Brad, in financial trouble? Could that be true? Why would Randy lie about that?

He wouldn't. It was something he'd uncovered while investigating her brother. For some reason, he thought she should know about it. She frowned. Again, why? It had nothing to do with her.

She leaned her head back and sighed. What could she say to her brother? Nothing. She'd asked Randy to back off, and he told her it was too late.

"The lid's off the box, Sienna. I can't put it back on."

Her phone sounded; she answered without looking at the display.

"Sienna, this is Dr. Margery."

"Good morning. Is Mom okay?"

"She's good. In fact, that's why I'm calling. The surgeon has cleared her to move over to Evergreen."

"That's great. When?"

"This morning. I was hoping you could bring by some things she's going to need. Comfortable clothing, toiletries, and any personal articles you think she might enjoy having near her during her stay."

"Of course. Should I meet you at Saint Anthony's or Evergreen?"

"Saint Anthony's, please. I'm afraid that now that the move is happening, she might refuse to go. I'm hoping your presence will remind her why she agreed to this in the first place."

Sienna told her she hoped so, too, and promised to be there within the hour.

A short time later, Sienna turned onto her street. A delivery truck was parked in Jonathan's driveway; he stood beside it, directing the men as they unloaded boxes.

He saw her and jogged over. "Good morning," he said.

At his smile, all questions about his honesty or his middle-of-the-night trip flew out of her mind. "Good morning."

"Everything okay?"

"Better than okay. Mom's being moved. I'm pulling together some things she needs for her stay." She pointed toward his place. "I see it's a busy day for you."

"Very. See you tonight?"

Her heart skipped a beat. "I'll make you dinner."

"It *is* your turn."

She laughed. "Gonna be tough to beat that chili of yours."

He bent and kissed her. His lips, cold from being outside, warmed against hers. Longing took her breath.

He broke the kiss. "I'll see you then." He took a couple steps, then stopped. "Wait, I realize you don't even have my cell number." He took his phone from his pocket. "In case you need me."

She experienced a rush of warmth. She did need him, she admitted. Like a flower needed sunshine or a hummingbird nectar.

"Ready?" she asked. He nodded and she rattled off her number. A moment later, her phone rang. She dug it out of her purse, checked the display. "Got it."

"Don't lose it, okay?"

No worries of that, she thought, watching him cross back to his own driveway and the deliverymen, cooling their heels while they waited from him. He took one glance back, as if to see if she was gawking like a lovestruck teenager—which of course she was.

When he was back in his own driveway, she hurried into the house. After shedding her coat and boots, she went upstairs and straight to the walk-in attic for a suitcase.

From there, Sienna turned her attention to filling it. She started with undergarments, counting out enough for a full week. Next, she pulled out two robes, slippers, and seven pairs of cozy socks. Since her mother was always cold, Sienna included layering pieces with the softest tops and sweaters—all things Sienna hoped would make her feel more comfortable.

Sienna turned to her mother's walk-in closet. She smiled, remembering it used to be a favorite hiding place of hers when she was little. Anytime Brad babysat, they'd play hide-and-seek. And he would pretend not to be able to find her, even though she always chose the same spot—behind the row of her mother's dresses.

If that had been today, she would have had to find a different spot. Her mother had become a bit of a pack rat, with boxes and storage containers tucked into every available nook, cranny, and corner.

Her secret spot was no different. Peeking out from the dresses was a large plastic storage container marked FOR SIENNA.

Mementos, no doubt. She wondered which things her mother chose to save, and if they would be the same ones she would have chosen.

She'd have to find out later, she saw, checking the time on her phone. She'd promised to meet Dr. Margery at the hospital within the hour; with travel time, she was already late.

CHAPTER FORTY

1:30 P.M.

"Thank you for everything, Dr. Margery," Sienna said as they exited the behavioral hospital together.

"It's I who should be thanking you. I'm so encouraged, Sienna. I believe if we get your mom on a consistent med schedule, and she commits to weekly therapy, we can greatly improve her quality of life. And yours."

"I hope so, but I have to say, leaving her this way is tough. She looked so lost."

The doctor patted her arm. "This is a good thing. You'll see."

Sienna watched her walk away, then climbed into the Buick. She'd purposely left her phone in the car, and when she checked it, she saw she had missed three calls from Reed Shepard. While the car's engine warmed, she listened to his messages.

"The cops are liars. They want me to be guilty, they never looked further. And I can prove it. Call me back."

In the message, his words slurred slightly. He'd been drinking already, she thought, and checked the time of his call—not even lunchtime.

She listened to the second message.

"You said you believe me, why haven't you called me back? Please call me. I'm home."

By the third message he'd gone from a desperate drunk to an angry one. *"You're a liar, too, aren't you? I should have known."*

And he hung up.

She dialed him back. It rang six times, then went to voice mail. "Reed, it's Sienna Scott. I do want to talk to you. I've been tied up with my mother. Call me back."

But he didn't call her back. After deciding on a dinner menu, she made a grocery run. Then, while unpacking the items, she called him again, leaving another message. When, after she'd assembled the marinade for the pork loin, he still hadn't returned her call, she dialed him again, leaving a third message.

Something wasn't right.

She paced from the back of the house to the front, peered out at the street and the flooring company truck in Jonathan's driveway, then strode to the kitchen. Reed Shepard's messages replayed in her head. Not just the words, but the way they'd run together, becoming more garbled with each one. And the emotions behind them, evolving from last night's cockiness, to this morning's despair, followed by anger. Directed toward her.

An anxious knot settled in the pit of her stomach. She had to do *something*. He said he was home, but she didn't have a clue where he lived. The phone book. Old-school but effective—*if* he had a landline, and if he had a listed number, his address would be there.

Her mother kept the phone book where she always had, in the drawer in the kitchen secretary. She found a dozen Shepards listed in the area, but no Reed Shepard.

That only meant he didn't have a landline, which didn't surprise her. She accessed the Internet from her cell, called up the white pages, and found him. He did indeed live locally. But she had to pay to access his address.

Hanson's Hideaway. Of course. That was a neighborhood bar; she would bet money Reed lived close by. And she'd bet the bartender knew where.

All she had to do was convince the man to give her the information.

Sienna grabbed her coat, purse, and keys. Jonathan would definitely not like her doing this alone, but he had his hands full. And this couldn't wait.

Hanson's parking lot was fairly full. She scanned the lot, but didn't see the truck Reed had been driving the night before. She was disappointed; she'd half expected to find him here.

She hurried inside, pausing a moment for her gaze to adjust to the dim interior. When it had, she saw that the bar patrons were split between men and women, although they all appeared considerably older than she. And they all stared at her as she crossed to the bar.

As luck would have it, she recognized the bartender as the same one who'd been on duty the night before. "Hi," she said, slipping onto a bar stool.

"Hey."

"I was here last night. With Reed Shepard. Do you remember me?"

"Sorry, sweetheart. What can I get you?"

"Nothing to drink. I was looking for Reed."

"He's not here. Hasn't been in yet today."

"It's really important that I talk to him."

"So call him."

He started off; she stopped him. "I did. He's not answering."

"There's probably a reason for that."

"No, he asked me to call. And now I can't reach him. It sounded like he was drinking."

"He always is, these days. But give the guy a break." He shook his head. "Talk about being dealt a shitty hand."

"You know where he lives, right?"

"So?"

"I'm worried. I want to check on him."

"You a cop? Or a reporter?"

"Neither. I'm a friend."

"Fuckin' fat chance of that."

"Yo, Ed! Brew down here."

The bartender looked that way, then back at her. "I've got customers. Order something or get outta here."

"I'll have a Coke."

"A Coke," he repeated. "Great."

He plopped it down in front of her, not making eye contact. Sienna sipped it, deciding on her next move. Watching the warm way the man interacted with his patrons convinced her he cared about them on a level deeper than just the money they spent in his bar.

Which gave her an opening. She waved him back over.

"He really does want to talk to me."

He sighed. "Coke's on me. Hit the road."

She called up Reed's contact number and held the phone out. "Look." He did, and she went on. "That's his number, right?"

"Doesn't mean anything."

"Then listen—"

"Girlie—"

"I think he's in trouble. Just listen to the messages he left me. Please."

He made a sound of irritation and held out his hand.

She handed him her phone, cued up to this morning's messages.

She watched his expression change as he listened, then he scowled as he handed the phone back.

"You promise you're not the press or the law?"

"I promise."

He hesitated a moment more, then nodded. Grabbing a cocktail napkin, he jotted down the address. "It's two blocks from here."

"Thanks, Ed. You won't regret this."

She hoped she could say the same for herself.

Reed lived in a small, square house at the end of a disreputable-looking street. His mailbox leaned right, as if Reed had been drunk when he'd installed it. Blades of bright green poked out of the melting snow, the contrast somehow accentuating the forlorn quality of the home.

His truck sat in the drive. Which meant he was home. She didn't see a doorbell, and knocked. "Reed," she called. "It's Sienna Scott."

She knocked again. Still nothing. She decided to try the back, and followed a walkway around the side of the house.

The back door stood slightly ajar. She found that odd, as cold as it still was. She pushed the door farther open and stuck her head inside. The kitchen, she saw. "Reed? You here? It's Sienna Scott."

She stepped inside, heard the hum of a television turned down low. Letting out a breath she hadn't realized she was holding, she moved her gaze over the room. An open cereal box sat on the counter, milk carton beside it. A stack of dishes in the sink. Some sort of spill on the floor—dry now—next to the garbage can, its lid balancing precariously on overflowing garbage.

She turned in the direction of the television, a prickle of unease at the back of her neck. She shouldn't be doing this. If she was concerned about Reed's safety, she should call . . . Who? 911? Randy? And say what? That a known drunk left her messages that sounded like he'd been drinking?

She'd sound like an unbalanced woman reading something into nothing.

That was what she was doing, wasn't it? She was going to find Reed passed out. And when she did, she would tiptoe back out and pretend this had never happened.

She found him sitting in front of the television. On the TV tray table next to him were a bottle and a glass. Jack Daniel's, she saw. The bottle all but empty. She saw the top of his head over the back of the chair.

Of course she did. She brought a hand to her mouth to hold back her nervous laugh. Right now she felt like a complete idiot.

She took a step toward him. "Reed, it's Sienna. I'm sorry to barge in like this, but I was worried." She took another step closer. "I got your messages—"

It was then that she noticed the dark stain on the back of the tan-colored chair. She frowned. What was . . .

Blood. She froze, the image of dark red creeping across brilliant white filling her head. She recalled the sting of the snow against her cheeks. The cold seeping through her layers of garments.

She started to shake. This couldn't be happening. Not again.

As if with a will of their own, her legs propelled her forward. Around the chair. The whole time, she told herself this was all a mistake. He could be alive.

He probably was. That wasn't blood on the back of the chair, it—

But of course it was. His head, what was left of it, lolled against the recliner's back. She dropped her gaze. A gun, in Reed's own hand.

She was too late.

Her stomach lurched to her throat, and she ran for the door, managing to make it outside before she threw up.

CHAPTER FORTY-ONE

4:15 P.M.

Randy was the first to arrive, even before a cruiser. She ran to him and he hugged her tightly.

"Dear God, Sienna, what're you doing here?"

"Reed called me, left a message. He said he had proof. Begged me to come by."

"Proof of what?"

"That Madi was seeing another guy."

"I told you this morning that wasn't true. That the original investigation found absolutely no evidence of that." He searched her gaze, expression wounded. "You didn't believe me?"

"I did. He just sounded so bad. Desperate and . . . sad. I wanted to make sure he was okay."

"I understand that." He squeezed her shoulders. "You're a good person, Sienna."

She didn't feel like a good person. If she'd taken her phone into the hospital with her, he might still be alive. He probably would be.

"Sienna?" She blinked, met his gaze. "What happened when you got here?"

"I rang the bell and knocked." She took a breath. "When he didn't answer, I went around back. The back door was cracked open."

"Why didn't you call me?"

"I thought I was overreacting, that you'd think—" She cleared her throat. "You know, that I was . . ."

"Like your mom."

"Yes. So I poked my head inside and called out. He didn't answer, but I heard the TV. So, I just . . . went to check on him."

"And found him dead."

She nodded. "I think he shot himself."

Randy's gaze seemed to sharpen. "Why do you think that?"

"He had a gun in his hand, and his face—" She couldn't say it; she knew from past experience that voicing a nightmare made it more real.

Two cruisers pulled up; Randy squeezed her shoulders. "I need to direct the guys. Are you going to be okay?"

She nodded, though she wasn't sure if she was. "Can I just go home?"

"Not yet. After I look at the scene, I'll need to ask you a few questions. I won't be long, I promise."

"I won't be long, I promise."

He'd said that to her another time. Made her that exact same promise. She drew her eyebrows together. But when?

"You could wait in one of the cruisers," he offered. "You'll be warmer."

The memory crashed over her, bringing with it a cold sweat.

The click of all four doors locking. Realizing she was trapped inside. Pounding, screaming for help . . .

"Sienna," he said, "are you okay?"

"No." She shook her head. "I'm staying right here."

CHAPTER FORTY-TWO

5:10 P.M.

Sienna huddled deeper in her coat, watching the coming and going of law enforcement personnel. Two more cruisers. The crime scene van. Coroner's wagon. She alternately stomped her feet and clapped her gloved hands together to keep her blood moving.

Her cell phone went off. She saw it was Jonathan.

"Hey," he said. "I was just checking what time for dinner and whether I should bring red or white?"

She'd forgotten. Tears flooded her eyes. "I don't know."

"What?" He sounded amused. "The time or the wine?"

"Either," she managed, and started to cry.

"Sienna? What's wrong?" His lighthearted teasing became concern. "Talk to me."

"Reed Shepard's dead."

For a moment she thought the call had dropped. Then he cleared his throat. "Dead? Oh, my God . . . what happened?"

"I don't . . . I'm not sure. I found him."

"Did you call the police?"

"Yes," she managed. "They're here."

"Where is 'here,' Sienna? I'm coming for you."

"Reed's house."

"I don't know where that is, babe."

"Maple Street." She looked over her shoulder, at the number beside the door. "One-eleven. Hurry."

Jonathan arrived just as the coroner's investigator was leaving. Neither man seemed to notice the other as they passed; Jonathan's gaze never wavered from hers.

Just his presence comforted her, crowding out other, ugly things. She made a sound of relief as he reached the porch and drew her into his arms and against his chest.

Sienna clung to him, shivering from the cold and from shock. Minutes ticked past. Little by little, his warmth seeped into her, chasing out the cold.

"Thank you," she whispered.

"For what?"

"Holding me."

He didn't respond to that, instead asking softly, "What happened?"

"Reed . . . he left me three messages, and in each one he sounded more . . . I don't know, desperate. He wanted to talk to me so . . ."

She knew how reckless that sounded and let the last part trail off.

When he didn't comment, she went on. "I think he . . . killed himself." The words came out thick. "He had a gun in his hand. There was a lot of—"

She bit it back, a decade-old image filling her head. *Red staining white. Bitter-cold hands cupping her cheeks.*

"You should have called me. I would have come with you."

She wiped her nose with the back of her hand. "I know."

"What are you doing here? This is a closed scene."

Sienna looked over her shoulder at Randy. "He came to be with me."

Randy's face turned a deep red. "Sorry you wasted your time, buddy. Turns out I'm not going to need to keep her any longer."

Jonathan narrowed his eyes. "So you left her waiting out here in the cold, for nothing . . . *buddy*?"

"I offered her the cruiser. She declined."

"He did," Sienna said. "For personal reasons, I chose the cold." She turned back to Randy. "So, I can go?"

"Yeah. It's pretty clear what went down here. We will need your phone to get transcripts of his voice messages."

"My phone? You mean take it?"

"I'm afraid so."

Sienna looked at Jonathan, then back at Randy. "For how long?"

"We'll have it back to you tomorrow. I'll make sure of it."

"But what if my mother or Dr. Margery need me?"

"You can pick up a cheap burner phone at any drug store. Or just stay close to the house. Your mom has a landline."

He was right. She nodded. "Give me a minute to let Evergreen and Dr. Margery know they won't be able to reach me at this number."

She made the two calls, then handed over the device, feeling like she was losing an appendage. "If only I'd responded to his calls sooner, maybe this wouldn't have happened."

Randy dropped the phone into his pocket. "Shepard was one messed-up dude, Sienna. A drunk. And judging by his suicide, probably a killer, too."

"How do you figure that, Clark?" Jonathan asked.

"Why else kill himself? Seems to me, the guilt finally got to him. He couldn't live with himself and what he'd done anymore."

"But what about his calls to me?" Sienna asked. "He said he had proof there was another guy. Why would he say that, then go kill himself?"

"Don't know. Could be he figured you were his last chance, and when you didn't buy his bullshit, he realized nobody would."

Jonathan cocked an eyebrow. "So which is it? He killed himself because he couldn't live with the guilt? Or because he was despondent that no one believed him?"

Red started at Randy's collar and spread upward. "We'll release an official statement after the coroner's report. Until then, the investigation is ongoing."

"Doesn't seem that way to me," Jonathan said softly.

The other man stopped and looked back over his shoulder at them. "Maybe I should be investigating you, Mr. Hart? Pretty coincidental, you showing up in Tranquility Bluffs the way you did. Buying the house across the street from the Scotts'. Insinuating yourself into Sienna's life the way you have."

"Feel free. But what I find even more curious, Detective Clark, is how *you* insinuated yourself in Sienna's life. That's an odd friendship, don't you think? An older guy. One who absolutely shouldn't have been fraternizing with a student. No wonder her dad sent her to London."

The animus between the two men was palpable. Jonathan had the upper hand, and clearly, Randy didn't like it.

He opened his mouth to respond, then shut it and

turned his gaze to Sienna's. The cold in his eyes caused her to shudder.

"I told you not to get involved with him, Sienna. There's something not right going on here. You'll see."

CHAPTER FORTY-THREE

7:25 P.M.

By the time she and Jonathan got back to her house, Reed's death was all over the news. And so was her name. The phone hadn't stopped ringing—old friends, neighbors, and even a reporter wanting to get "her" story.

She'd taken calls between bites of the sub sandwiches they'd picked up on their way home. Sienna finally turned the ringer off, too exhausted to speak to one more person.

Then the doorbell rang.

She peeked out, saw it was Brad. She swung open the door and he hugged her hard. "I saw it on the news, sis. I couldn't believe it."

He held her at arm's length, searched her expression. "How're you holding up?"

"By my fingernails. C'mon in."

He did. And saw Jonathan. Although obviously surprised, he recovered quickly. "Hello." He stepped forward, held out his hand. "I'm Brad Scott. Sienna's brother."

"Jonathan Hart. Sienna's friend."

Sienna stepped in. "Jonathan bought the Collinses' old house."

"You're that flipper." Brad smiled. "I keep up with all things real estate in Tranquility Bluffs." He turned back to Sienna. "I tried to call. Your cell and here. I was starting to panic."

"Police have my cell and the phone was ringing off the hook here, so I—"

"Whoa, back up. The police have your phone?"

Jonathan jumped in. "Since I've heard this story, I'm going to take the opportunity to head out."

"You're leaving?" Judging by her brother's expression, he didn't miss the disappointment in her voice.

"The cabinets are being delivered tomorrow, and I'm not quite ready for them." He kissed her, then whispered against her ear, "I'll be back."

He headed toward the door. "Good to meet you, Brad."

"Likewise, Jonathan."

As the door snapped shut behind him, her brother looked at her. "So, when did *that* happen?"

"Since I got home."

"Obviously, sis. And deliberately vague."

"I'm all grown up, Brad."

He cocked an eyebrow. "Also obvious."

"You don't need to worry, I know what I'm doing."

"But what do you know about him?"

She rolled her eyes. "Not you, too?"

He shrugged out of his coat and hung it in the front closet. "What's that supposed to mean?"

"Randy warned me about him, too."

"I never thought I'd like anything that guy had to say. I've proved myself wrong."

She folded her arms across her chest, and sent him a stern glance. "I know everything *I* need to know about him. So, how about we call this subject closed?"

"I guess you have grown up." A grin spread across

his face. "You have anything to drink around this place? We need to talk."

A few minutes later, they sat across from each other in the living room, he with the remnants of her and Jonathan's wine, and she with a hot chocolate.

"How's Viv?" he asked.

"Transferred to Evergreen this afternoon. Dr. Margery is hopeful for good progress."

"I hope for that, too. For all of us." He paused a moment, eyebrows drawing together slightly. "You never told me what happened today or why Clark has your phone."

She filled him in, sharing about Reed's calls, then how she got his address, and then, finding him dead. "The rest," she said, "will be repeated on the ten o'clock news."

"Not sure I like the idea of you driving over to a murder suspect's home like that. Could have had a very different ending."

"But didn't."

He nodded. Looked down at his glass, then back up at her. "Sorry about earlier today. Some of the things I said—"

"Were downright mean?"

"Yeah. When it comes to my mom, I can get . . . protective. It hasn't been easy for her."

"Or you."

He nodded. "Or me." He paused a moment. "It's not true, what I said. You're not like her."

She swallowed past the knot in her throat. "Thank you."

"Can you forgive me?"

"Of course." She reached across and covered his hand with hers. "You're my big brother. I'd forgive you anything."

He blinked and looked quickly away, and she realized he had tears in his eyes. Which caused her own to fill. She, too, looked away, not wanting to cry.

After a minute, he broke the silence. "I heard something today that I thought you'd want to know."

"What's that?"

"There's another party interested in buying The Wagon Wheel."

She set down her mug. "What?"

"I heard through the real estate grapevine. It's somebody with deep pockets."

She felt the words like a blow. "Donna and Ted all but told me I had it. They were contacting a broker, and were going to get back with me with a price."

"Calm down, sis. You still may have it, if you can meet their price."

"They have a valuation?"

"I made some calls. And yes, the valuation is in."

"And?"

"Eight fifty."

She felt as if all the wind had gone out of her sails. "Eight hundred fifty *thousand*?"

"The lion's share is the property, sis. The restaurant itself isn't worth a lot, because their business has fallen to a trickle. If it was still booming, the price would be a lot higher."

"It still seems high to me. Crap."

She stood, started to pace nervously. "There are still all the costs of updating and refurbishing. That can cost upward of a million dollars. Then advertising and marketing. Stocking the place, everything from cookware to the pantry."

"And time to build word of mouth and a clientele."

"Yes." She stopped, looked at him. "Maybe they'll come down?"

"Maybe. But if someone else is interested . . ."

True. Why would they? This was their retirement, for heaven's sake. "I could still do it."

"How?"

"My inheritance and loans."

"Half-pint—"

"Don't call me that. Not now." She pulled a hand through her hair. "Dad left me one point five million. I'm certain the investments have grown, right? You manage the account."

"Right, of course."

"How much has it grown?"

"Don't know off the top my head, sis. But I'll let you know."

She nodded. "Good. With that amount of capital, I should be able to secure a loan to cover the rest."

Brad stood and crossed to her. He put his hands on her shoulders and looked her in the eyes. "Think this through. You're twenty-nine years old. Do you really want to use every penny you have to do this? Do you really want to tie yourself not just to all that debt, but to this town as well?"

"It's home, Brad."

"Is it?"

"I could get investors."

"You could. But take it from me, that's not as easy as it sounds."

Sienna thought of what Randy had told her, about Brad being financially strapped. "Is everything okay with your business?"

"Of course." He dropped his hands. "Why would you ask that?"

No way was she going to bring up Randy now, not when they'd just smoothed things over. She would have to tell him sometime, just not now. "The other day you said something about trying to line up investors, and what you just said about it being hard—"

"It is hard. But this is about you. I'm fine." He paused, searching her gaze. "I know you wanted this and that you're disappointed. Just promise me you'll really think about your next move before you make it. This decision will alter the course of your life, you don't want to rush it."

She let out a resigned-sounding breath. "Okay, I promise. Let me know if you hear anything else about the other buyer."

"Of course." He retrieved his coat from the closet. "And you'll come to me before you make your final decision?"

"I will." She walked him to the door, and as she opened it, her gaze automatically went to Jonathan's.

Her brother noticed and grinned. "He seems like an okay guy."

"What?" She blinked and looked at him.

"Your friend. He seems like a good guy." He kissed her forehead. "I'm glad you found someone who makes you happy."

CHAPTER FORTY-FOUR

9:15 P.M.

Within minutes of Brad walking out her door, Jonathan walked back through it. "I thought he'd never leave," he all but growled, kicking the door shut behind him and pulling her into his arms.

"Me, too," she said against his mouth, pushing his coat off his shoulders. It landed in a heap on the floor.

"Where?" he asked between kisses.

"Upstairs."

Cupping her derriere, he lifted her. She wrapped her legs around his waist and her arms around his neck, clinging to him and nibbling on his ear as he climbed the stairs.

"You're not making this easy," he said, voice thick. "Watch it or we won't make it to the bed."

"That's okay with me."

It was a challenge. One he accepted. There at the top of the stairs, nothing but her mother's cherished Oriental runner to cushion them, they tugged and tore at each other's clothing until they were half dressed but wholly accessible.

She pinned him to the rug and straddled him, then, holding his gaze, slowly sank onto him. He groaned and thrust; she cried out in an instant, shattering orgasm.

It was the first of three. Two consecutively, there in the hallway, the third in her childhood bed, brought on by his slow, exquisite exploration of her body.

Long after she had returned the favor by exploring and savoring his every muscled angle and plane, they lay side by side under her girlish quilt.

She rubbed herself against him, like a cat, all but purring. He smiled at her. "Happy?"

"Very."

"Me, too." He yawned and moved his gaze over the room. "It's a pink explosion."

She smiled sleepily. "You look good in ruffles."

"You think so, do you?"

"Mmm-hmm." Her eyelids drooped, but she forced them back open. She didn't want to miss a moment of being with him. "Stay, tonight?"

He didn't respond and she lifted her head to look at him. "Please."

He nodded and she lowered her head once more. The seconds ticked past, and the silence stretched between them, warm and sleepy.

"Sienna?" he said softly. "We need to talk."

"Mmm . . ."

"There's something—"

He threaded his fingers through her hair. Even though the movement felt relaxed, she sensed tension in him.

"I need to tell you . . . what Clark said about me . . ."

She didn't know what he meant to say, only that she didn't want anything to shatter this wonderful moment between them.

"Not now." She trailed kisses over his chest and up to his mouth. "I know you're a good guy."

"How?"

She rested her head against his chest, her cheek over his heart. "Like the beat of your heart, I feel it."

Her lids drooped; she dozed a moment, then stirred. "Jonathan?"

"Hmm?"

"I'm sorry. For dragging you into all this drama."

"You didn't, babe. Believe me."

She was unsure what he meant by that, but smiled to herself, pleased with the endearment. "I wonder . . . do you think Randy . . . has feelings for me?"

He shifted, tipped his face down to see hers. "That seems an odd question, considering."

She yawned. "It's just the way he . . . acts around you. Angry . . . and like he's . . . jealous."

"Yeah," he murmured. "I think he does."

Which gave her the power to hurt him, something she didn't want. It made her sad to think she might have already. So for now she wouldn't think about it at all. Tonight she would only think about Jonathan and the very real possibility that she was falling in love with him.

CHAPTER FORTY-FIVE

Sienna awakened to the sun streaming through the blinds and Jonathan smiling down at her.

"Morning, sleepyhead."

She yawned and stretched. "What time is it?"

"Almost seven thirty."

"Still early."

He smiled. "Not that early. The cabinets could come as early as nine."

"You're saying you have to go soon."

"Afraid so."

She pouted and he laughed. "How about I make us some coffee?"

"I'll get up. We'll make it together."

She climbed out of bed, but instead of the kitchen, they ended up in the shower. By the time they were dry, dressed, and sipping coffee, there was no hot water left in the tank and the clock was pushing nine.

"How about some toast? I have almond butter."

"Sounds good." He pointed at the answering machine and its blinking light. "Looks like you have messages."

She winced. "I should have turned the ringer back on."

"I'll do it."

She popped four slices of bread into the toaster. "Hit the Play button while you're there."

"Not sure I remember how to do this. Do they even make these anymore?"

In the next instant, the mechanical voice announced: *You have eighteen new messages.*

Sienna groaned. "Eighteen?"

Hi Sienna, this is Donna Meyers. We have the valuation on the restaurant and building. Call me.

Beep—

The toast popped up. As she slathered the bread with the nut butter, the machine played back a hang-up and a solicitation for a lower credit card interest rate.

"Only fifteen to go," Jonathan teased, coming up behind her and kissing her neck, then reaching around her and snagging one of the pieces of toast.

You can lower your mortgage rate—

"Fourteen," she said, taking a bite.

Beep—

You're not answering your cell . . . tried this number . . . I just figured it out. I know who killed her. Call me. Don't tell anyone. If they find out I know—

Beep—

Sienna dropped her toast. Hearing Reed Shepard's voice was like being visited by a spirit from beyond the grave. Goose bumps raced up her arms, and she looked at Jonathan. He appeared as stunned as she.

"That was Shepard, wasn't it?"

"Yes. Oh, my God . . . he said he figured it out."

Jonathan reached around her and hit Rewind, then replayed the message. Once, then again.

"What's that noise in the background?" he asked.

"A bar? Hanson's Hideaway?"

He played it again, turning the volume up. "Yeah, maybe. It could be."

"Check the time stamp."

"Eleven fifteen."

"I went to Hanson's Hideaway after that and the bartender said he hadn't been in."

"He could've been lying."

"Could have. But I don't think he was. After all, he did give me his address." She pursed her lips in thought. "Play it again."

He did and she strained to hear. "Could that be his TV?"

He nodded. "Definitely."

"He was in front of his TV," she said. "That's where he shot himself."

"Which doesn't mean anything."

"It could mean something," she murmured. "He said in the message that he *just* figured it out. *Just*," she repeated. "Maybe something he was watching triggered a memory? Like the news?"

"Maybe. What channel was he watching? Do you remember?"

She thought a moment, then shook her head. "I could get Randy to—"

"No. Shepard said not to tell anyone."

"But he's dead. What difference does it make now?"

"Sienna, if Shepard was being truthful, it means he didn't kill Madison. And that whoever did is out there. The last thing we want to do is clue the killer that we're on to him. Or, at the very least, that we suspect Reed's death wasn't a suicide."

"But we don't." Her toast had grown cold and soggy; she took a bite anyway. "Do we?"

"Here's a question for you: If Shepard figured out who really killed Madison—"

"—why kill himself?" she finished for him. "It makes no sense. He finally had a way to prove his innocence and get out from under the cloud of suspicion that ruined his life, and he shoots himself?"

"Exactly." Jonathan finished his first piece of toast and reached for the second. He took a bite, chewing thoughtfully. "But we can't go to the police."

"Then what do we do?"

"We need to find out what show he was watching when he died. In case it did trigger a memory."

"He could have changed the channel between when he left the message and when he died."

"He could have. The pathologist will call the time of death."

"Which isn't exact," she said. "All this sounds like a crazy long shot."

"Maybe he wrote something down. Or left some other clue?"

She cocked an eyebrow. "One the police wouldn't have collected? I don't know, sounds unlikely."

"Do you trust me?"

"Yes."

"Good. Don't tell anyone about this. I'm going to make a plan."

She frowned, not liking the look in his eyes. "What kind of plan?"

"I'm not sure yet." He glanced at the time and swore. "I've got to go. Don't worry." He kissed her. "It's all going to be okay."

Then why, she wondered, watching him go, did she feel like it most definitely was *not* going to be okay?

CHAPTER FORTY-SIX

Sienna stared disbelievingly at Jonathan. "Are you out of your freaking mind?"

He shrugged out of his jacket. He was dressed head to toe in black. "Just hear me out."

"I think I did. Your plan is, we break into a dead man's house to search it for clues we don't even know will be there?"

"Brilliant, huh?"

"No. It's twisted." She crossed her arms. "And how do you know how to break into a house?"

"Like it's hard? C'mon, Sienna, we're not talking about getting into some wired-to-the-nines mansion. In that neighborhood, nobody's calling the cops. And Shepard's dead, so we know he won't show up and try to kill us."

It did sound exciting. And reckless.

Which was exactly why she should refuse to participate.

His voice turned coaxing. "We turn on the television and see what channel was playing when he died, and, if his remote has a Back button, the one playing before that."

"It's such a long shot."

"True. But while we're there, we also scour the place for anything that might give us an idea what he was thinking."

She frowned. "You're really into this. How come?"

"Don't you want to know the truth? Finally? Maybe you were right, and it was supposed to be you? Maybe if you see or hear the name, you'll know?

"Or," he went on, "you'll realize that it wasn't supposed to be you."

She did want to know. She wanted to be certain, once and for all, of the truth.

"Consider this, Sienna: my instinct tells me the cops are going to use Shepard's death to close the investigation. They're going to call him the guy who killed Madi, and put the case to bed. Is that good enough for you?"

It wasn't, she realized. And it wasn't fair to Madi or her family. Or to Reed.

"Okay," she said. "I'm in."

They waited until late. Eleven on a weekday night seemed good—not so late that they'd call attention to themselves, but not so early there'd be many folks out and about.

Jonathan parked his truck a couple houses down from Shepard's. Even from this distance they could see the bright yellow crime tape. Sienna's stomach knotted.

"I don't know if I can do this."

"You can, Sienna."

"The man's dead. It just seems so . . . disrespectful."

"In my opinion, it's the opposite of disrespectful." Jonathan angled in his seat to face her. "This guy's life was colored . . . no, it was ruined, by allegations he murdered his girlfriend. Unsubstantiated allegations. If he found something that would clear his name, don't you think we owe it to him to find it and bring it to light?"

She'd always wanted this answer. The unsolved murder, her personal questions surrounding it, had hung over her like a cloud. Not as dark or as heavy as the one that had hung over Reed's, but it had shadowed her life, nonetheless.

And what of Madi's family? They deserved the truth. And Madi herself, didn't she deserve justice?

She unfastened her safety belt. "Let's do this."

The street was relatively quiet. The small homes were spaced tightly. Several had lights burning, but not those on either side of Shepard's. From somewhere past Reed's came music and the sound of laughter.

Jonathan indicated they would enter around the back, the same way she had the day before. Unlike the front, no crime scene tape stretched across that door—she wasn't sure why that made her feel better, but it did.

The door wasn't even locked, a pretty clear indication what the police thought of this case and Reed Shepard. Or maybe they were just that sloppy. Either way, Sienna was glad they didn't have to actually break in. If they got caught, maybe that would work in their favor?

Jonathan flicked on his penlight. They stepped inside. She wrinkled her nose at the hint of something foul in the air. She moved her gaze over the room; nothing had changed: the dishes still piled in the sink, the milk carton still on the counter, the same crusty spill on the floor.

Of course it hadn't changed. The one who would have done something about them was dead.

"Put these on."

He held out a pair of medical gloves.

"You're serious?"

"Absolutely. In case we find something. We don't want to contaminate the evidence."

She almost laughed, but didn't. "Are you a cop?"

"Nah. I just watch a lot of *CSI.*"

Sienna took the gloves, fitted them on. He handed her a flashlight. Together, they made their way from the kitchen to the living room. Her stomach lurched when she saw the chair, the stain set now, dark and ugly.

Jonathan circled around to its front; she followed. Reed had bled a lot, and the mess on the upholstery was worse from this side. Sienna blinked and in that instant, she pictured him there.

Slumped. Neck arched, head against the chair back. Blood dripping. Gun in his hand.

She swallowed hard against the bile that rose in her throat.

"Steady," he murmured.

She nodded, fighting for it.

"The TV was on?"

"Yes."

"Did you look at it? What was playing?"

"I did, but I don't remember."

"Close your eyes. Try to picture what you saw."

"I can't." The words lodged in her throat. She tried to clear them. "I just see him there . . . dead."

"What did you hear?"

"I wasn't listening . . . I—"

"Clear your mind. Deep breaths."

She did, putting herself back in those moments. Entering the room. Noticing the television. Glancing at it.

"Bruce Willis," she said. "Something exploding."

He picked up the remote, switched the set on. "FXM," he said. "Fox Movie Network. We can check the schedule online." He pointed the remote, hit the

Back button. The channel changed; the AMC logo appeared at the bottom of the screen.

"More movies," Jonathan murmured.

"He spent his last day here," she said softly. "Watching movies, drinking. And making phone calls. It's so sad."

"Yeah, it is. Not the way I'd want to go, that's for sure.

"They no doubt have his phone." He looked at her. "Which means Randy will know how many calls he made to you, be they to your cell, which he has, or your mom's landline."

The thought of it made her uncomfortable. Like she was being spied on.

"Tomorrow morning, you go down to the police station and tell Randy or the chief about Shepard's call to the house and the message he left on the recorder. Offer to bring in the machine."

She frowned at him. "That just seems so . . . over the top."

"Somebody's dead. Until the death is classified, they'll want everything. Just like they wanted your phone. That way he won't suspect you're keeping things from him."

"I'm not." She realized how ridiculous that sounded, as she stood there in a dead man's living room wearing crime scene investigator gloves. "Not really, anyway."

"Promise you'll do it first thing."

"Of course I promise, but I'm confused. You're acting like you think Randy—or the cops—are guilty of something."

"I don't trust anyone, Sienna. You shouldn't either."

She wondered if that meant she shouldn't trust him, then rejected the thought. "What do we do now?"

"I'll search the chair and living room. You try the bedroom and kitchen."

"I don't know what I'm looking for."

"Just trust that you'll know it if you see it."

It wasn't much to go on, but she figured as long as she was here, breaking and entering, she might as well throw herself into it. She thought back to the mysteries she'd read and the police shows she'd watched, and imitated what she'd learned from them.

She started in the bedroom, checked drawers, the pockets of jackets and trousers, even turned over his work boots. Nothing.

She moved on to the kitchen. She leafed through the couple old issues of *Field & Stream* magazine, and the stack of mail—a bunch of unopened bills and expired sale circulars.

A Bible sat on the top of the refrigerator. A King James version, she saw, well worn. She opened it. His name was scrawled on the inside cover, the handwriting childish. Beside the name, a date—*May 15, 1998*.

Sienna wondered if the book had been a birthday gift. Or maybe a gift celebrating a faith milestone, like confirmation?

As she went to set it back on the top of the refrigerator, she saw a paper tucked between the pages, almost at dead center.

An old newspaper clipping, she discovered. From the one-year anniversary of Madison's murder. It was a rehashing of the crime; all their names were in it: hers and his, Fredricks College cop Randall Clark; TBPD Chief Fred Thompson. Even her own dad and mom were mentioned.

Sienna didn't have to read the article to find all the names—Reed had circled them with a red pen.

"You found something?"

She looked over her shoulder at Jonathan, standing in the doorway. "A newspaper article about the murder. Everyone's mentioned by name. Even me."

He crossed to take a look. He scanned it. "Interesting that he circled everyone's name."

"Why do you think he did that?"

"I don't know. Maybe familiarizing himself with all the players. Keep it."

She folded it and put it in her pocket. "How about you, you find anything?"

"Nada."

She turned back to the Bible, and saw that it was open to the twenty-third Psalm.

The Lord is my Shepherd—

Shepard. The Good Shepard. Not a murderer.

Someone else. Someone whose name was circled in that article?

Sudden light shone through the side window. A light from the house next door. A face peering out a window.

"I think we should get out of here," Jonathan said, snapping off his flashlight and starting for the kitchen. "Now."

Sienna agreed and followed without comment. They made it to Jonathan's truck, and drove off without incident. As they did, she looked back, a later verse from that same psalm popping into her head, one about walking through the valley of the shadow of death.

Chill bumps raced up her arms as she realized that was exactly where she had just been.

CHAPTER FORTY-SEVEN

The next morning Sienna awakened late. Jonathan had gone, leaving a note by the coffeepot. He'd headed home to take care of a few things in advance of his subcontractors arriving. He'd drawn a heart at the bottom of the note, and she stared at that sweet, silly little heart, feeling as if her own had sprouted wings.

She was in love with him. Crazy as that was, considering the short time they had known each other, but she'd never felt this way about anyone else.

Judging by the bowl in the sink, it looked like he'd fixed himself some cereal before he left. Deciding he deserved better than that, she set about cooking them both a real breakfast.

Forty-five minutes later, her mother's old picnic basket and a blanket in tow, she rang his bell. It took several minutes, and when he swung the door open, he looked preoccupied.

"Hey," she said. "Is everything okay?"

"Yes." He stepped aside so she could enter. "Dealing with some billing hiccups, that's all."

"I hope you're hungry?"

"Is that a trick question?"

"Maybe." She held up the basket. "I bring real sustenance."

He laid out the blanket, then she unpacked the basket. She'd brought everything they'd need, from silverware and cloth napkins to a bud vase with a daisy.

He touched the bloom and grinned. "Silk?"

"From one of Mom's old centerpieces. Sometimes you have to improvise."

His eyes met hers and something in them caused her heart to skip a beat. He broke the connection. "It smells amazing."

She uncovered his plate and set it in front of him. "Veggie and Swiss omelets and crispy bacon." She did the same to hers, then lifted out a small towel-covered basket. "Drop biscuits with whipped honey butter. And finally—" She held up a dainty glass pitcher. "Fresh-squeezed orange juice."

"You're an angel," he said, leaning across and kissing her. "Thank you."

It seemed like no time at all before they'd consumed every crumb, and Jonathan was checking his watch. "I'm sorry," he said, "I still have a lot to do before the cabinets go in."

"I totally understand." She started repacking the basket. "I should get going, too. First on my list, Randy and the answering machine."

"Perfect." He stood and folded the blanket. "Do you want to take a look at the kitchen before you go?"

She did, of course. Kitchens were her favorite room in a house; for her, truly the heart of a home. His was off to a beautiful start—light and bright, with big windows and soft white walls. He showed her the samples for the muted gray cabinetry and white quartz countertops.

"I could cook in here all day, every day," she said. "It's lovely."

"Not as lovely as you." He cupped her face in his hands and kissed her. She didn't know how—or why—it felt different, but it did. "God, I'm going to miss you."

"I'm only going across the street."

He smiled against her mouth. "Promise."

"Well, I might run into town, too."

He laughed and dropped his hands. "Keep me posted on . . . you know."

She did know, and nodded. He walked her to the door; as she was stepping through a thought occurred to her. She looked back at him. "What was it you wanted to tell me last night when I was falling asleep?"

His expression froze. "I don't remember."

He was lying. The realization felt like a slap. She struggled not to let it show. "Oh. You made it sound sort of important at the time. Something about Randy, something he said."

"I'm sure it was important." He grinned. "At the time. What made you think of it?"

"I don't know, it literally just popped into my head."

"I'm sure I'll remember, probably a minute after you leave."

He smiled and all thoughts of him being untruthful evaporated. He'd been surprised, that's all.

His next words seemed to confirm that. "Then you can tell me later."

"I look forward to it."

After one last kiss in the doorway, she started across the street, only to see Randy waiting for her in the driveway.

Her heart sank. He would have seen her and Jonathan kiss at the door, and if he felt about her the way she suspected, his feelings would be hurt.

"Good morning," he said stiffly when she reached him.

She forced an easy smile. "Good morning to you."

His gaze dropped to the picnic basket and blanket, then returned to hers, the expression in them hard. "A little cold for a picnic, isn't it?"

Was that hurt in his tone? Or disappointment?

"I brought Jonathan breakfast."

A muscle jumped in his jaw. "He's a lucky guy."

She didn't know how to respond to that, so she didn't. "Come on in. I was going to run by the police station this morning, you saved me a trip."

He followed her inside. She carried the basket into the kitchen and set it on the counter.

"Can I get you a cup of coffee or an orange juice? It's fresh squeezed."

"They teach you how to do that in chef school?"

"Squeeze orange juice?"

"Pack perfect picnics for lucky guys across the street?"

She didn't deserve the barb, but she let it pass. "What brings you here this morning?"

"Reed Shepard."

Her mouth went dry. "What about him?"

"We collected his phone from the scene."

"Makes sense."

"There were a lot of calls to you."

"I told you that."

"There was one I don't think you mentioned, made to the house. I wanted to ask you about it."

"Exactly why I was coming to see you."

His eyebrows shot up in mock surprise. "Really?"

"Mmm-hmm. That and to see if you'd finished with *my* phone."

"I have." He took it out of his inside coat pocket and

handed it to her. "Sorry it took a little longer than I thought it would."

The device was warm from being inside his coat and close to his body. She didn't know why, but it felt like a violation.

She set it on the counter. "No problem. So, the other reason I was coming to see you this morning is the day Reed died—"

"Killed himself," he corrected.

She stopped, confused. "You're sure of that now?"

"Pathologist called it. Classified it a suicide, and unless new information emerges, which I find highly unlikely, the case is closed."

His nonchalance didn't sit right with her. A man was dead, a man who had suffered greatly for a murder she didn't believe he had committed.

"The day he died," Sienna went on, "he called my cell phone, but he also called here. He left a message."

"And you're just telling me about it now? Too busy playing house to make the time?"

"Excuse me?"

He nodded in the direction of the basket. "Picnics and all."

She flushed. But she wasn't going to apologize, or stammer out some lie or evasion. She and Randy were friends, nothing more.

She folded her arms across her chest. "I think you're going to be interested in hearing the message. Feel free to take the machine with you."

"How about I just listen to it now, see if it changes anything."

"Sure." She'd already cleared all the other messages, and hit the Play button.

You have one saved message.

You're not answering your cell . . . tried this number . . . I just figured it out. I know who killed her. Call me. Don't tell anyone. If they find out I know—

Beep—

Randy sighed. "You don't believe that garbage, do you?"

"What if it's true?"

"It's not true." He crossed to her. Laying his hands on her shoulders, he looked her in the eyes. "Sienna, Reed Shepard was a drunk, a liar, and I believe—as does Chief Thompson—a murderer."

"But you don't have any proof."

"Not for a court of law, but now we don't need one."

"Because he killed himself."

"Yes. Driven by guilt. It makes sense."

"Even after listening to that voice message?"

"Especially after. The dude was desperate." He snatched his gloves off the counter. "Get back to your . . . *diversions,* Sienna, and leave the police work to us professionals."

First playing house. Now diversions? He had crossed the line, big time. She needed him to know he was her friend, not her lover, and he had no right to judge her personal choices.

"Randy, wait."

She went after him, caught him at the door. He looked at her, eyebrows raised in question.

"We're friends, right?"

"I hope so."

"I think of us that way. You're . . . special to me. You were there for me when no one else was."

His expression softened. "I thought you'd forgotten."

"Never, Randy. That was one of the most difficult and confusing times of my life."

"Mine, too."

"Those kinds of bonds aren't erased by time or distance. By marriages—"

"Or boyfriends."

She smiled. "Exactly."

"I'm sorry I was sharp with you—"

"It's okay. I should have told you before. When Dad sent me to London, things between us—"

"Were so different."

"Yes." She brought a hand to her chest. "I feel like an idiot."

"Me, too," he said softly, and kissed her cheek. "I'll see you later."

"I'd like that."

As he walked away, she smiled to herself. That, she decided, was way easier than she thought it'd be.

CHAPTER FORTY-EIGHT

2:00 P.M.

Sienna sat across the worn booth from Donna and Ted Meyers. The restaurant was empty except for a couple servers filling salt-and-pepper shakers.

"It's worth more than we thought it would be," Donna Meyers said, beaming at her husband.

"More than we dreamed possible," he added. "There was a time we feared we'd never be able to retire."

Donna nodded. "Ten years ago, the property was worth a pittance, less even than what we're asking for the restaurant now."

"Congratulations," Sienna said. "That's such good news for you."

Donna's face fell. "But not for you, I'm so sorry. Is it out of range now?"

"No." She didn't sound confident, even to herself, so she said it again. "No, I'm most definitely still on board."

"Oh, good!" Donna smiled at her husband. "We're so glad."

Sienna folded her hands on the table in front of her, hoping she looked calm and professional. "Originally, you indicated you weren't in a hurry—"

"That's changed," Donna said. "We have another interested party—"

Ted elbowed her. She stopped and frowned at him. "I'm not going to keep it from her."

"Well, you don't have to flaunt it in her face."

"I already knew," Sienna said. "My brother heard it through some of his real estate contacts. Is this buyer ready to act?"

"According to our broker, yes."

Donna jumped back in. "But we promised you first refusal and we keep our promises."

"And we would truly love for a local to take it over."

"Let me ask you this, is there any wiggle room in the price?"

Their faces fell. "Not at this point, no."

Meaning if the other buyer was willing to pay asking price, they would go with him, local loyalty be damned.

"What about a partial lease purchase?"

"I don't think so." Donna cleared her throat. "Sienna . . . I wish we could help you out, I really do. But this is our retirement. It's all we have. If something should happen and you went under . . ."

"Too risky," Ted said. "We're not young anymore. If this was our only offer, the situation would be different."

"I get it, I do." Sienna looked from one to the other. "I'm just exploring the various options."

She scooted out of the booth. "Can you give me a couple days? I need to talk to my financial adviser about my next steps and to the bank about a loan. Then I'll know how to proceed."

"Of course." The couple stood, all smiles once more. They walked her out, happily chattering.

After promising to be back in touch soon, Sienna

headed to her car. She slid behind the wheel, then let out a breath she hadn't even realized she was holding. She wanted this so bad. The location was perfect. The price was good. Yes, higher than she hoped it would be, but she would *own* the property. A restaurant—even one as worn-out as The Wagon Wheel—would be upward of two million in a more upscale region.

This was perfect. She could make this work.

She started the car, then dug her phone out of her handbag. She dialed her brother. She had tried him before meeting Mr. and Mrs. Meyers, even fantasizing that he would offer to come with her, but he hadn't answered so she'd left a message.

Once again, he didn't answer. "Hey big bro, met with Donna and Ted. They're not budging on the price and won't consider a lease purchase offer. I wanted to discuss how to proceed. Call me back."

Frustrated, she set her phone on the console, and backed out of the parking lot. This waiting was hell. She just wanted to know what she had to work with, and what her options were.

She didn't want to cook for anyone else. She wanted her own place. A place she could put her stamp on and grow.

The light ahead turned red. She rolled to a stop and sat, tapping her fingers on the steering wheel. That's when the realization struck.

She didn't have to wait for her brother to call back. Her dad's longtime financial planner was also a close family friend. He and her dad had gone to school together. Henry Barnes. His office was on the corner of Sycamore and Spruce, just a half-dozen blocks from here.

Hoping he hadn't retired, she made a U-turn and headed back the way she had come. The building hadn't changed, she saw. Redbrick. Green door. Same wooden shingle hanging above it.

BARNES INVESTMENTS.

Sienna parked in front and climbed out. His was an old-school outfit. A three-person staff, all family. They knew each of their clients personally, sent birthday cards, and delivered home-baked cookies at Christmas-time.

At least that's the way it used to be. She hoped it hadn't changed.

Sienna stepped inside; a welcoming bell announced her arrival. The gray-haired woman at the desk looked up—and broke into a big smile.

"Oh, my Lord, as I live and breathe. Henry!" she called, standing up and coming around the desk. "Little Sienna Scott is here."

She came around the desk and hugged her. "Look at you, just as beautiful as I knew you were going to be."

Sienna hugged her back. "Hi, Mrs. Barnes. It's good to see you."

"Mrs. Barnes? Call me Millie. You're all grown up now."

Her husband appeared at his office door. "What's all the commotion—Sienna! Oh, my goodness."

He gave her a bear hug. She hugged him back, swamped with memories of her dad. And of these two men at the kitchen table, laughing and swapping stories about the "good old days."

He had more waist and less hair since she saw him last, but otherwise he hadn't changed a bit.

"It broke my heart that I missed the service for your dad. Millie and I were on a Mediterranean cruise, cel-ebrating our fortieth anniversary."

"He knew you loved him," she said, voice thick. "He would have been happy for you two."

"It broke both our hearts," Millie said. "Losing him so suddenly."

"He was the last person I'd expect to have a bad heart. Now me"—he patted his substantial belly—"I'm a different story."

"How's your mother?" Millie asked, changing the subject.

"The same. That's the main reason I'm home, so I can help Brad take care of her."

Henry nodded. "Heard about your brother's marriage breaking up. It's a shame. But it's good you're here now."

"Do you plan to stay?" Millie asked.

"I do. And that's the reason for my visit today. Could we talk, Henry? It's business."

"Of course. Millie, hold my calls."

She smiled and shook her head. "He loves saying that, the old goat."

Henry ushered her into his office. Sienna sat in the upholstered chair in front of his desk, while he took the one behind. "What can I do for you today, Sienna?"

"I'm looking at opening my own restaurant where The Wagon Wheel now is. I wanted to know how much money I have in my investment account."

He frowned slightly. "You mean your mother's account?"

"No, mine. The money Dad left me."

"Your brother moved that account over a year ago."

"That can't . . . Dad always invested with you. He didn't trust anyone else, he always said so."

"Apparently, your brother wasn't happy with my service."

She could see that the move had hurt his feelings. Yes, it was business. But Henry had been more than a business partner to their family. A lot more.

"I'm . . . shocked. He didn't discuss it with me."

"As executor, he had the right to make the move. But, considering, I would have expected him to get your okay."

Sienna struggled to wrap her head around this news. Yes, she had given Brad written permission to act on her behalf. At the time, she'd been devastated by her father's death, living in London and in school; truthfully she'd been relieved not to have to worry about it. But to make this kind of decision without consulting her?

"What about Mom's account?"

"That I still manage. As I understand it, Viv refused to let him move it."

"Do you know who he invested with?"

"I have the paperwork on file. I'm sure Millie can put her hands right on it."

Sure enough, moments later the woman handed the papers to him. "Okay," he said, "we transferred the funds to Pershing and Miller Investments. I'm not familiar with that group, but they're CFP certified, I double-checked."

"Can you tell me how much was in my account at the time?"

"The original insurance benefit invested was one point five million. The market was booming and we made some very smart investments for you." He slid the paper across the desk. "As you see, we transferred two million and change."

Over two million? She could hardly believe it. "I'm . . . thrilled. This is wonderful."

"Yes, it is." He opened his mouth, then shut it, as if uncertain whether he should say what he wanted to.

"Go ahead," she said. "What is it?"

"If I remember correctly, your father appointed Brad

to be the executor of the estate, managing your portion until you were twenty-eight."

"That's right."

"And you're how old now?"

"Twenty-nine. Almost thirty."

"It's time for you to take charge of your own finances."

He said it gently. And with a smile. But she understood what he was really saying: it was time for her to grow up.

She could have taken offense or made excuses. She did neither. He was right. It was most definitely time for her to grow up.

She started now.

CHAPTER FORTY-NINE

4:30 P.M.

Sienna left Barnes Investments and just drove. She visited all her old stomping grounds. New neighborhoods and parks, an elementary school, more fast-food joints. The drive-in where she used to order blueberry slushes and chili-cheese fries.

She cruised the Fredricks campus, went by her high school, and then to the place she'd gotten her first kiss. She stopped at the Baskin-Robbins ice-cream shop for a double scoop of her two favorites: mint-chocolate chip and Jamoca almond fudge.

And while she devoured the treat, she checked in with Dr. Margery about her mom's progress. If the woman heard her smacking, she made no comment.

It was time to grow up. Adults didn't eat chili-cheese fries—at least not regularly—they didn't slurp slushes or devour ice-cream cones while on business calls.

And they certainly didn't let their brother manage their money.

Ice cream gone save for sticky fingers and mouth, she drove by her brother's office. The lights were out; his car was nowhere in sight. She checked the dashboard clock—after five now; he could be home. If not home, perhaps she would try that pretty Max's restaurant.

Brad was not going to take this well. She instinctively knew that. She had to make him understand that taking charge of her finances wasn't about him, but her.

As luck would have it, he was home. The townhouse community he lived in was one of his developments, and it was stunning, well treed and beautifully landscaped—a feat for this time of year—and designed to blend with the natural surroundings.

She found his unit, glad he had shared his address with her previously, and went to the door. She rang the bell, and he answered, still dressed for the workday.

"Half-pint," he said.

She smelled liquor on his breath. "Can I come in?"

"Of course."

She stepped inside. The interior was just as fabulous as the exterior. She met his eyes. "You didn't call me back."

"Rough day. Sorry."

The old Sienna would have asked why it was rough and tried to make him feel better. There was nothing wrong with that, but tonight, she had to stay focused.

Time to grow up.

"Can we talk?"

"Sure." He motioned her toward the living room. "Want a drink?"

"No, thanks."

He refilled his glass and turned to find her watching him. "So, you spoke with Donna and Ted."

"Yes."

"I think they're asking too much. In this environment—"

She held up a hand. "Stop it, Brad. I want to do this. I think a restaurant, my restaurant, in Old Town is a good bet."

His mouth dropped. Her all-business approach had obviously caught him by surprise.

"Industry," she went on, "is booming here. Specifically tech, the right kind of industry. Property values are up, because demand is up. These are high-paying jobs for people with urban, sophisticated palates."

"The Wagon Wheel—"

"Does not meet the needs of that clientele. And you know it. That's why I'm buying the location, not the concept."

"I think you're being hasty."

"Why?"

"You're twenty-nine years old. What do you know about running a restaurant?"

"A lot. I've been working in the industry for almost ten years now."

"But that's not the same as—"

"Why did you move my money from Henry Barnes to another investment firm?" His expression said it all. "Yeah, I know. I went to see him today."

He opened his mouth, then shut it. "You gave me the authority to make these kinds of decisions on your behalf."

"You're right, I did. I'm rescinding that now."

He looked dumbfounded. "Why are you doing this to me?"

"It's not about you, Brad. I love you and I appreciate all you've done for me. And my mom. But I'm an adult. I need to take charge of my life."

"I don't understand."

"I'm buying The Wagon Wheel and opening my own restaurant."

"Dad wouldn't want you to do this. He'd want me to keep you from doing this."

"That's bullshit, Brad. And it's low to pull the 'Daddy would be disappointed' card. I need to know how much money I have."

He downed his drink and went for a refill. "He made me executor to save you from making mistakes that would cost you your nest egg."

"Until I was twenty-eight. I'm twenty-nine, thirty in May. How much money do I have? Right now?"

"I don't know."

"I want to see a statement, Brad."

"Did Barnes put you up to this?"

"This has nothing to do with Henry. I want a statement. The most recent one, please."

"I don't have one. Not here."

"Then get online. I want that number. It's my money."

"I'm not set up to do that."

"Bullshit. Someone in your—"

She bit the last back. Someone in his position would be acutely aware of finances. He would know exactly what he had and what he owed at any given moment. He would have to.

A nauseated feeling settled in the pit of her gut. One that brought a sour taste to her mouth. She swallowed hard. What she was thinking couldn't be true. It *couldn't* be.

"How much money do I have, Brad?"

He didn't answer. The sour taste burned.

"Henry transferred over two million a year ago; I presume it's grown since then?"

He didn't look at her.

She repeated the question. "How much money do I have, Brad?"

"Right now?"

"Yeah, right now."

"You've got nothing. Less than fifty thousand."

Her knees went weak. "Very funny."

But he wasn't laughing. She rested a hand on the back of a chair to steady herself.

"You're serious?"

"Unfortunately."

She fought to catch her breath. It was as if her world was crashing out from under her feet. Her plans of buying The Wagon Wheel—or any restaurant—were shattered. Reduced to what he'd called them the other day—pipe dreams.

Different emotions battered her. Anger. Disbelief. That her brother could have been so careless. That he could care so little for her. Despair. What was she going to do now? She would have to find a job, and soon. She couldn't live with her mother forever. She didn't even own her own car.

Sienna wanted to cry. She wanted to shout at him. She did neither, holding tightly to her emotions. "How could you lose it like that? It was two *million* dollars. How?"

"I didn't lose it. I'm not stupid, Sienna."

Even now, arrogance. "Then what, Brad? What did you do? Did you steal it from me?"

"I'm not a thief. I just borrowed it."

The words sank in. It took her a moment to wrap her head around those four words. "You borrowed it?"

"It was a loan, that's all."

"I want it back, Brad. Give it back."

"I can't."

Breathe, Sienna. Just breathe. "You can't?"

"Not yet. But I will."

"When?"

"The market shifted. The investors . . . Everyone's pulled back."

"Your Door County Resort development?"

"Yes." He tossed back the rest of his drink. "We don't need to panic. Just stay calm."

He was reassuring himself as much as her. And if his shaking hands were any indication, he wasn't taking his own advice. If anything, desperation was all but seeping from his pores.

"I don't understand, Brad. How does what you do work?"

"I put everything, all my available cash, into the perfect spot for this resort community. I got loans to clear the land, put in roads and infrastructure."

She felt sick to her stomach. "That sounds . . . expensive."

"It's a fortune. But I had investors on board. With their cash, I could keep up with the debt service and complete the infrastructure. As soon as that's done, I can start selling plots."

"But the investors backed out?"

"Yes, the sons of bitches."

"So you used my money to finish the infrastructure?"

"No. For debt service on the loans."

"I don't know what that means." Even as she said the words, she feared she *did* know what it meant.

"The loan is a balloon note, but every month there's interest I have to pay."

Sienna looked at him in disbelief. And disappointment. "You used my inheritance to pay *interest*?"

"You were supposed to be in London. You wouldn't even have known. I would have secured the funds I needed and put it back."

The phone call she'd overheard the day she popped into his office to say hello. His agitation. Desperation.

"Is this why Liz left you?"

"Of course not."

But his expression said otherwise. The subtle shift of his gaze. "Even after you showed up, I was sure it would be okay. Then you got this harebrained idea to buy The Wagon Wheel—"

"She left you because you were stealing from your family."

"No."

"You're my brother. I trusted—"

"No!" he shouted, and threw his glass. It whizzed past her head, hit the wall, and exploded. "My family stole from *me*!"

Shocked, she took an involuntary step backward.

"Your mother's delusions! My mother's anger. Dad's obsession with 'protecting' Viv. And then you. His little princess. So beautiful. So sweet. But so *fragile*."

The bitterness in his voice cut her to the quick. "Randy told me you were in financial trouble. I didn't believe it but—"

"How the hell did Randy Clark—"

"—even if it was true, I never for a moment considered you would resort to stealing my inheritance."

"You have him investigating me? The way you encouraged him to investigate my mother?"

She shook her head. "I didn't encourage him to investigate anyone. That wasn't what I wanted him to do. I went to him because of the anonymous caller, I thought he should know, considering—"

"Shut up! Don't you hear yourself!" He pressed

the heels of his hands to his eyes, then dropped them. "This is why Dad did what he did. This is why he made me executor—of all the money he left *you*. And your mother. A one-and-a-half-million-dollar policy for you, and two million for Viv. You know what I got? A measly two hundred fifty grand, that's it. Because I could take care of myself. Because I didn't *need* it."

This was a surprise. She'd never asked. She'd been told how much her father left for her, and the conditions he put on her receipt of the money. She'd just assumed he'd left the same for Brad.

She couldn't see her father doing this. It didn't sound like the fair-minded man she'd known.

And she imagined how much that must have hurt Brad's feelings.

Brad looked at her then, the animus in his eyes startling her. "It was always about protecting you, Sienna. 'Bradley,'" he mimicked bitterly, "'watch out for your little sister. That's your job, son.'"

He dragged his hands through his hair. "I even had to protect you from your own mother. How many times did he tell me to take you upstairs, to shield you from her meltdowns? 'Take care of your sister, take care of your sister'—my God, I can still hear his voice in my head. What about *me*, Sienna?"

His words, like fists, pummeled her. She curved her arms protectively around her middle. "All these years, you resented me? My big brother whom I *adored*?"

He seemed to flinch, then stiffened. "He thought you were like her. He told you he didn't, but he did."

At that, the most violent blow of all, Sienna brought a hand to her mouth to hold back a cry. Her father thought she was like her mother. Her brother thought it. Like everyone around town always had. Like deep down, she'd always feared.

"That's why he shielded you, coddled you. That's why he sent you away to live with Mimi. He saw it happening here. He wanted to buy you time, he told me, give you a chance to develop away from Viv. And it's why he left you all that money. He didn't think you'd ever be able to take care of yourself. The way your mother can't take care of herself—"

"Stop it! It's not true!"

"It is true. Ever wonder why Dad picked twenty-eight as the age you could access your money? Because Viv's mental illness fully presented at twenty-five."

Sienna struggled to process what he was saying. A safety net. If she was fully functioning by twenty-eight, her dad figured she would be in the clear.

That he'd thought so little of her was devastating.

"Viv had you, then totally lost her shit. But don't blame yourself. It really had nothing to do with you. The psychosis was always there. Visible in little things. How suspicious she was of people. Of their motives. How she would sometimes believe she was being spied on. Or followed."

"That's not me."

"No? Some poor girl gets killed and you think it was supposed to be you. That's pretty out there, don't you think?"

He was being as cruel as he could be. Hoping to wound her as deeply as possible.

He had succeeded.

"Do you hate me so much, Brad? It's not enough that you stole my inheritance, but you had to break my heart, too?"

He didn't respond. She shook her head, holding back tears. "I didn't do anything to you but love you."

"I'll get the money back. I just need time."

She collected her coat and purse. He still didn't have a clue. For him, it was still just about the money. For her, she'd lost so much more than that. An essential part of her had been ripped out, leaving behind a bloody, gaping wound that would never heal.

CHAPTER FIFTY

6:40 P.M.

As Sienna drove, it began to rain. One of those cold, early-spring rains that chilled to the bone. As the rain came, so did her tears. She pulled to the side of the road and allowed herself to simply sob.

The tears finally stopped, leaving her drained. Brokenhearted. And in need of Jonathan's arms around her. His warmth and his strength.

She found her phone, sent him a text:

Are you home
Yes. What's up
Can I come by
I'm in the apartment. Come to the down-
stairs entrance

Ten minutes later, she stood at his door, shivering and soaked to the skin from her run from the car to his door.

He saw her and his welcoming expression became one of concern. "My God, Sienna, what—" He drew her inside. "Your hands are like ice."

"I didn't have an umbrella."

He rubbed her hands between his for a moment, then

helped her out of her wet coat. "I'll get some towels and a blanket."

She just nodded, teeth chattering.

In moments he was back. He also had a big, soft sweatshirt emblazoned with U.S. ARMY and a pair of woolly socks. "If you need them," he said, and handed them to her. "Go ahead and change, I'll get you something warm to drink."

Sienna's clothes ranged from wet to uncomfortably damp. She removed everything but her undergarments, grateful for the over-sized sweatshirt and socks.

She folded her things, then went in search of Jonathan. He was putting the finishing touch—a squirt of canned whipped cream—on two hot chocolates. They carried them to the small living room and curled up together on the love seat, afghan draped over them.

Sienna clutched the mug and stared down at the melting cream. She sensed him watching. Waiting for an explanation for this latest round of drama. "My family's a train wreck."

He chuckled. "Mine's no Caribbean cruise. Unless the ship crashes into port and sinks."

She laughed. "I'm sure that's not true, but thank you anyway."

"You want to talk about it?"

She let out a deep breath, not certain she did, but feeling like she needed an explanation for her bizarre behavior. She opened her mouth, then closed it, the words just not wanting to come off her tongue.

"Is it your mom?"

"For once, no. It's Brad."

"Your brother?" He sounded surprised. And why wouldn't he? She'd never portrayed him as anything but a steady Eddie, and their one meeting no doubt reinforced that image.

She nodded. "You know I was hoping to start my own restaurant, here in Tranquility Bluffs."

"You were thinking of buying that old place on Main—"

"The Wagon Wheel, yes." She took a sip of the chocolate. It was sweet, warm, and comforting. "I met with Donna and Ted Meyers this afternoon; they're ready to sell."

She took another sip of the beverage, then set the cup aside. "My dad left me some money when he died. Quite a lot of money, actually. I knew mine had been the payout from an insurance policy of which I was the beneficiary. And Brad was the executor. I wasn't to get control of the funds until I turned twenty-eight."

"Okay."

From the way he drew out the word, she suspected he knew what was coming next.

"It would have been nearly enough to buy and refurbish the restaurant and property. And with that much capital, getting loans for the rest wouldn't have been a problem. The restaurant I've dreamed of was . . . that close."

"Was, Sienna?"

"The money's gone. All but fifty thousand."

"That son of a bitch. What did he do?"

"Got overextended. Lost investors on a project, and used my money to keep things afloat."

"So your plans are—"

"History."

"Do you have legal recourse?"

"I don't know. And honestly, right now losing the money isn't even the worst part."

He didn't comment, just let her gather her thoughts. "He told me how he really"—her voice wobbled— "feels about me. That he resents me. That he's angry

Dad always made him watch out for me. He called me a coddled princess."

"I'm sorry," he said softly. "That hurts."

"Apparently, Dad took out life-insurance policies for all of us. Mine was for a million and a half bucks, but Brad's was less than a quarter of that. More reason to resent me."

"It is a pretty messed-up thing to do. Why would your dad do that?"

"According to Brad, he was afraid for me." She had to force the words out. "Afraid the psychosis that imprisoned my mother in her midtwenties would do the same to me. He didn't think I'd be able to take care of myself. The way my mom can't."

He didn't comment, and Sienna wondered what his silence meant. Was he second-guessing their relationship, the wisdom of getting involved with her? If so, who could blame him?

"Brad thinks the same thing. He always said he didn't, but today—"

Jonathan gently turned her face to his, looked her directly in the eyes. "What do you believe, Sienna?"

What *did* she believe? She didn't know anymore.

She swallowed past the lump in her throat. "I always worried . . . I mean, I look just like her. And that whole thing with Madison Robie's murder . . . and me thinking it was supposed to be me . . . How sane is that?"

"You didn't answer my question. I didn't ask what everyone else thinks. Or what you fear. You, Sienna. I asked what *you* believe."

She gazed at him, into those deep brown eyes. "I'm not like her, Jonathan. I know I'm not."

The words were freeing. She felt as if a thousand-pound weight was lifted from her. She'd told herself the words before. But half-heartedly. With false bravado. As if rebelling from reality. But there'd always remained a grain of . . . uncertainty.

Not now. Not anymore. This was her truth, spoken emphatically. To him. Jonathan. That it was he didn't surprise her. She trusted him with everything. Her heart and life, her fears and dreams.

And now, her truth.

She cupped his face in her hands and kissed him. "Thank you."

He smiled. "For what?"

"Being here. Being you."

He rested his forehead against hers, gaze serious. "You need to talk to the lawyer who executed the will."

"Why?"

"Because it might not be true."

"What part?"

"Whatever part."

She started to deny her brother would do that, then stopped. That was her old relationship with Brad, the one she'd imagined she had.

"I'm sorry," he murmured, caressing her cheek.

"He wasn't sorry," she said softly. "He jammed a stake in my heart and never flinched."

"You may be surprised. He was caught red-handed. Lashing out at you was his way of justifying his own behavior."

"He was all I had."

"You have me."

At that moment, she realized how little she knew about him. His family. The things he hoped for the future and the shadows of his past. And, she acknowledged, none of that mattered.

Because she was head-over-heels, caution-be-damned in love with him.

CHAPTER FIFTY-ONE

Sienna awakened alone. She'd slept fitfully, awaking intermittently, aching with loss. Her brother had betrayed her. Stolen from her. Broken her heart. The only thing that lessened the ache was Jonathan. His arms, his murmured words of comfort. The warmth of his body curved against hers.

She reached for her phone, checked the time, and sat up. She saw that he had dried her clothes; they were neatly folded and sitting on the dresser. Climbing out of bed, she dressed, and went in search of him.

She smelled coffee and headed for the small efficiency kitchen, thinking she might find him there. She didn't, but he'd left a sticky note by the coffeepot; this time, instead of a heart, he'd drawn a smiley-face sun and scrawled *Good Morning*.

Smiling, she tucked the Post-it into her pocket and poured a mug of the coffee, doctored it, then sipped. She headed to the stairs that led to the main house.

"Jonathan, you up there?"

He didn't respond, although if he was in the middle of anything, he might not have heard her. She went back for her shoes, then headed upstairs to look for him.

"Jonathan?" she called again when she reached the top. The silence told her he wasn't working up here, so she wandered from room to room, sipping her coffee and admiring his progress.

Coffee nearly gone, Sienna headed back downstairs. Jonathan was right—she needed to contact her father's attorney and confirm the details of his will, just to make certain Brad had told her the truth.

She'd leave him a note, she decided, and headed to the small desk set up in a corner of the living room to look for paper and pen. Besides a laptop computer, the desktop was littered with folders, mail, a stack of invoices, and a set of blueprints.

A legal tablet peeked out from the stack of folders. Sienna attempted to ease it out from beneath them, and in the process she sent several manila folders tumbling to the floor. The contents of one of them spilled out, and squatting down, she started gathering up the pages.

One of them caught her eye—a printout of a news story.

Not any news story. One about Madison Robie's murder, from the day after it happened. Sienna's gaze went to the only type highlighted in yellow.

Her name.

She felt light-headed, and breathed deeply to right herself. *This is nothing, Sienna. He did a little research after meeting you.*

She rifled through the papers, and saw that hope dashed. This was no sudden interest sparked by their acquaintance. It looked as if the entire folder was devoted to the murder. And to everyone involved. Her. Reed Shepard. Randy. The chief. Even her mother, brother, and father. And others whose names she wasn't familiar with. An investigative reporter from

Rockford. Phone numbers. Names beside them. Research on delusional disorder.

Her face heated. What was he, some kind of investigative journalist? A cop? Private detective?

One thing she knew for sure: he wasn't who he said he was.

Betrayal tasted bitter on her tongue. She started to stand, then saw one last page under the desk. She retrieved it; saw it was a list of names.

One name was scratched out.

Reed Shepard.

Reed was dead. By his own hand, according to the coroner's office.

What if he didn't kill himself? Maybe someone made it look like a suicide? Someone who was afraid he'd been found out?

Not Jonathan. No, that thought was completely crazy. She and Jonathan went to Reed's home, looking for evidence. He talked her into it. Why would he do that if he was the one who . . .

Goose bumps raced up her arms. To look for evidence. Not just any evidence, something that incriminated him.

No. She stood, carefully laid the reassembled folder on the desk. Her hands shook so badly, she was surprised she didn't send it sailing to the floor again. None of this was right . . . it couldn't be.

Put it together, Sienna. A timeline. The way a cop would.

That night she talked to Reed, that was the first night she and Jonathan made love. The next morning, she'd told him what Reed said. About Madison stepping out on him with another guy. Someone older.

He'd looked strange after. And been distant . . . distracted.

The next afternoon she found Reed dead. And after, who had called her, then come to comfort her?

Jonathan.

The next morning, who had listened to Reed's message? The one in which Reed claimed he had figured out who killed Madison?

Jonathan.

No. She brought a hand to her mouth. At the time of Madi's murder, he'd been deployed. Out of the country. Iraq.

Or so he'd said. He'd lied to her about other things—made clear by a folder stuffed with information about her, her family, and all aspects of the murder—why not that?

She heard the rumble of his truck; the slam of the vehicle's door.

He was back. A squeak of terror passed her lips, and she ran for her coat and purse. Her phone, she remembered, and darted back to the bedroom for it. She grabbed it off the bedside table, stuffed it in her coat pocket, and turned to find him standing in the doorway, holding a coffee caddy from the Java Joint, a newspaper tucked under his arm.

He took one look at her face and frowned. "What's wrong?"

Don't confront him, Sienna. The newspapers were littered with stories of women who made that fatal mistake.

"It's Mom," she managed. "She . . . Evergreen . . . called." She started for the door. "I've got to go now."

"Is she okay?"

"A flare-up . . . she needs . . . They want my input."

He was frowning. "I'll drive you."

"No, it's better if I go alone."

"You're obviously upset, Sienna—"

She started past him; he caught her arm. "It's safer if I drive you."

She struggled to keep her act together. "Please, Jonathan, just let me go."

He held her arm for a moment more, then released it. "Sure, if that's what you want."

He sounded hurt. And for a second, she forgot the folder and her suspicions. "Thank you," she whispered. "I . . . I have to do this myself."

"If you need me, you know where I am."

Without looking at him, she nodded. She made it across the street and into her car. Out of her drive and his range of vision. Out of his life.

Because even if she was wrong, which she prayed she was, he would never forgive her for what she was about to do.

CHAPTER FIFTY-TWO

10:10 A.M.

The desk officer stared at her like she was totally off her rocker. Sienna didn't doubt she not only sounded the part, but that she looked it as well. Her hands were shaking, and she hadn't even combed her hair since getting out of bed. Her eyes were red from crying, the mascara she hadn't taken off the night before smeared under them.

"Detective Randy Clark," she said again, as calmly as she could manage. "I must speak to him. It's urgent."

"And as I already told you"—he said the words extra slowly, as if she couldn't understand English—"he's off today. But I'm sure one of the other officers will be happy to speak with you."

This was how people spoke to her mother, she realized. It'd always made her feel bad for her mom but also embarrassed for herself. Now she understood how it made her mother feel.

"No!" Her voice rose. "It has to be Randy. Call him. Tell him it's Sienna Scott."

"Ma'am—"

"Or just tell me where he lives, and I'll go there. We're old friends."

One of the patrol officers overheard their exchange

and came over. He was older and had kind eyes. "Can I help you, miss?"

"Yes, please. I have to speak with Detective Clark. No one else. He'll understand."

"Okay," he said quietly, "just tell me what this is about."

"Randy and I are friends. His number should be in my phone, but a recording keeps telling me it's no longer in service."

"She asked me to give her his address." That came from the desk officer, who all but rolled his eyes.

"I'm sure you understand we can't give out our officers' addresses."

"I understand. But if you call and tell him Sienna Scott—"

"Scott? You any relation to Vivienne Scott?"

"She's my mother, yes. But this has nothing to do with her. I have new information about Madison Robie's murder. And the Shepard case, too."

The older officer told the younger one to call. Both were clearly surprised when Randy informed them to set her up in an interview room and offer her a cup of coffee; he was on his way in.

When he strode through the door, she jumped up. "Thank God you're here."

He gave her a quick hug, and motioned for her to sit. He took the chair across from her. "What's going on?"

"I don't think Reed Shepard killed himself." He opened his mouth as if to stop her then, so she raced on before he could. "I think he was murdered because he figured out who killed Madison."

"Sienna," he began, "we went through this the other day."

"Hear me out. Please."

He nodded and sat back in his chair.

"I say that because I think—" Her voice thickened and she cleared it. "I know who really killed Madison."

"Not Shepard?"

"No. My . . . neighbor. The one you met."

"The lucky guy across the street. Jonathan something?"

"Hart. Yes." Sienna took a deep breath. "He has a folder filled with information about the murder. I discovered it by accident this morning."

He frowned. "What do you mean?"

"I went to his desk, to write him a note . . . and this folder, I knocked it off and the papers went everywhere. When I started gathering them up, I saw what they were."

"Back up a minute. You say this happened this morning?"

"Yes."

"You were at his house?"

"Yes."

"And where was he?"

"I didn't know. I woke up and . . ."

The way he was looking at her made her feel dirty, and she flushed. A split second later, the look was gone, replaced by that of the objective cop.

"And," she went on, "he was gone. I meant to write him a note. I went in search of paper and pen, and that's when it happened."

He looked down at his notepad. Picked up his pen. "It, being the folder going over the side of the desk?"

"Yes."

He didn't look up. "And what were these papers?"

"They were all about Madison's murder. Copies of what looked like every article published about her murder, the investigation. Even about us."

He stopped writing, met her eyes. "Us? What does that mean?"

"You. Me. My family. Everyone who worked on or touched the investigation. There was even research on delusional disorder."

"This is interesting, Sienna, but it doesn't mean he's a killer. Maybe he's writing a true crime book?"

She clasped her hands together. "Maybe. But I told him what Reed said about there being another guy Madison was seeing, one who was older. And then Reed was dead."

"Shepard's death was ruled a suicide."

"But what if it wasn't?"

"Sienna—"

"Maybe he made it look like a suicide. That's possible, isn't it?"

"Yes. But it takes a lot of skill to pull something like that off." He leaned forward slightly. "There was gunpowder residue on his hand. Shepard fired the weapon, there's no doubt about that."

"Maybe he forced him to hold it?"

He smiled slightly. "And pulled the trigger? There were no signs of a struggle."

"He could have incapacitated him somehow." She was sounding more and more like her mother, insisting something was real when all the facts pointed toward the opposite.

"Like with drugs?"

"Yes."

"Which would have shown up in the toxicology report."

She twisted her fingers together. "There are other ways to disable people, right? What about a Taser or stun gun?"

"You really want this guy to be guilty, don't you? What did he do, break up with you?"

"No!" She slammed her hands on the table. "It's the last thing I want, I just know there's more to this than . . ."

She let the words trail off at the pitying look in his eyes. She shook her head. "And there was this list."

"A list? From the folder?"

"Yes. It had everyone's name on it."

"What do you mean, 'everyone's'?"

"Mine and yours. My mother, brother, and dad's. Reed's. Even the chief's. A few people I didn't recognize. And one was crossed out."

"Reed's?"

She nodded.

"It was the only one?" When she nodded again, he frowned. "You wait here a minute, I'm going to check a few things out." He stopped at the door and looked back. "You comfortable?"

"I'm fine."

"Need anything?"

"Is there a vending machine? I didn't eat."

"I'll get you something."

She thanked him, and a few minutes later, the officer with the kind eyes came in with another cup of coffee and a plate with two donuts. It wasn't exactly the breakfast of champions, but at least it was something in her stomach.

She ate the first donut quickly, the second slowly, watching the clock. The time ticked by, five minutes becoming ten, becoming twenty. At forty-five, when she got up to go find the restroom, he walked in.

"Sorry, that took longer than I thought it would."

"Did you find something?"

"John Hart is a popular name. Jonathan Hart, not as much."

"So, you didn't find him?"

"I did not. And I have a theory why."

"What is it?"

"That Jonathan Hart isn't his real name. I've sent a cruiser to bring him in for questioning. I'll keep you posted."

CHAPTER FIFTY-THREE

Sienna couldn't sit still. She'd left the police station, pulling out of the parking lot as the patrol car carrying Jonathan pulled in. Their eyes met as the two vehicles passed, and the look on his face made her cringe.

In the hours that had passed since, the more she thought about what she had done, the more certain she was that she'd made a mistake.

About the time she thought she would go crazy waiting, Randy called.

"He may be a liar, Sienna. But he didn't kill Madison Robie. Or Reed Shepard."

Twin emotions went to war inside her. Relief. Joyous relief. Then regret. So bitter it burned. "You're sure?"

"Positive. He really was in Iraq the night Madison was killed. And the day Shepard died, he was overseeing a work crew at his place. He never left his house."

"But the folder? All that information—"

"That's the rest of the story. He's Madison Robie's brother, Sienna. Half brother, actually. Same mom, different dads."

She grabbed the back of the chair for support. "Her brother?"

"Legal name's Andrew Jonathan Hart. He figured if

folks didn't know who he was, they'd be more likely to answer his questions."

When she didn't respond, he went on. "I know you feel pretty foolish right now."

Devastated. She felt devastated. But she wasn't about to share that with him. He seemed to be enjoying this too much.

"But better safe than sorry. If one of Ted Bundy's neighbors had come forward, think how many girls' lives would have been spared."

She had accused the man she loved of being a murderer.

"I'm going to go now, Randy. Thank you." She managed the last, though the words tasted sour on her tongue.

"No problem at all." He sounded almost happy. "By the way, fair warning, I'd expect a chill in the air next time you see him. He was pretty pissed off."

She ended the call, feeling as if she had been stripped of everything but despair and self-loathing. What was wrong with her? How could she have even entertained the idea that he had killed two people?

When her doorbell sounded, she knew it was Jonathan. She longed to take the coward's way. Hide. Avoid. Lick her wounds, some of them self-inflicted. But not all.

He had things to answer for, as well.

Sienna smoothed her hands over her hips, a move she had seen her mother make hundreds of times before, when she had been readying herself for whatever, be it visitors, a doctor's consult, or a confrontation.

It didn't mean she was like her mother. It didn't mean anything.

Sienna crossed to the door, pausing to take a deep, steadying breath, then swung it open.

He looked as if he had been battered. Not physically, but emotionally. They just stared at each other a moment, his gaze on hers cool and distant. As if she was an unpleasant stranger he was being forced to deal with.

She felt as if her heart were breaking.

"I'm sorry," she said.

"Not good enough."

"You want to come in?"

"Not really. But I don't think either of us want to have this discussion outside. What if a white van drives by?"

She flinched at the barb, and swung the door wider. He stepped through, angling his body so it wouldn't brush against hers. A lump of tears formed in her throat; she swallowed it and closed the door.

He faced her. "After everything we shared, did you really think I could be a murderer?"

"I didn't know what to think." She twisted her fingers together. "You lied to me, Jonathan."

"Is that your defense for thinking I could *kill* someone?"

"If you'd been upfront with me, I wouldn't have had the opportunity to misinterpret—"

"Don't." He lifted a hand. "That's so convenient, you accusing me of your very own actions. If you'd simply asked me what that folder meant, I would have told you."

"But I—" She bit what she was about to say back; in light of the facts, it was too awful.

But he read her mind. "But you thought maybe I would have killed you?"

Tears flooded her eyes. She hugged herself. "Why didn't you tell me?"

"I started to. Twice."

"Now look who's being convenient." She lifted her chin. "That doesn't count."

"So, here we are."

"I was falling in love with you."

"Right." He looked away, then back, expression fierce. "Falling in love with me? You told the police I killed two people."

"I didn't know . . . what to think. I just . . . the coincidences . . ."

"Coincidences? What are you talking about?"

"That I told you about talking to Reed Shepard, how he told me about Madison dating another guy who was older, then he was dead. And that phone message, and your insistence that we go to Reed's and look for evidence. That was the clincher. I couldn't fathom why, looking at everything, you would urge me to do that."

The anger, which moments before had glinted in his eyes, disappeared. Replaced by sadness. A cavernous regret that made her want to weep.

"And now you see why? The whole reason I'm in Tranquility Bluffs is to try to figure out who killed Madi. If Shepard truly had information, I couldn't let it slip away."

"Why didn't you tell me?" She held back tears. "When I was spilling my guts about my mom and the murder, you already knew everything!"

"She was my *sister,* Sienna. And I lost her."

In his shoes would she have handled things differently? She wasn't so sure. "Where do we go from here?"

He seemed to freeze, and Sienna held her breath. She wanted more than anything to start over. Give them another chance.

"We both made mistakes," she said, holding out

her hand, praying he would take it. "Can't we start over? Forget the past and go on?"

He caught her hand, but instead of grasping it, he brought it to his lips for a last kiss, then let it go. "I really did think we had something great going. But you can't have great without trust."

"That's not fair!" she cried. "You didn't trust me either. All this time, you were spying on me and my family. Manipulating me. When I shared my heart with you, were you taking notes?"

"I'm not abdicating my responsibility in all this. I made mistakes. But I don't think I can get over this. Goodbye, Sienna."

And then he was gone.

CHAPTER FIFTY-FOUR

1:40 p.m.

The next several days passed at an agonizingly slow pace. Sienna rumbled around her mother's house without direction, doing a little of this and a little of that. She would catch herself at the window, looking across the street, hoping to catch a glimpse of Jonathan.

And sometimes she did, and the longing inside her cut so deep she winced. And no matter how hard she willed him to look her way, he never did.

His place had been a bevy of activity. All manner of work and delivery trucks—subcontractors, appliances, bathroom fixtures. She suspected he had stepped up the pace of the renovation so he could leave Tranquility Bluffs—and her—as soon as possible.

Her brother hadn't called, and she hadn't called him. Frankly, she didn't know what she would say to him. Good morning, you detest me and stole my inheritance, but have a good day?

She had been in daily contact with Dr. Margery—who each time said her mother wasn't ready to see her yet. And she hadn't heard a peep from Randy, though she wasn't surprised. He'd stuck his neck out for her, and ended up looking like a fool.

No, she thought. She had ended up looking the fool.

But today, she was forcing herself to get out of the house. As Jonathan suggested she do, she'd made an appointment with her dad's lawyer. She wanted to know the terms of her father's will, and to discuss what legal recourse she had against her brother, if any. Although, even if she did, she wasn't certain she was going to pursue it. What would it solve? If the money was gone, it was gone. Like her relationship with her brother, she'd never really had it at all.

Sienna stood outside the Becker, Becker, & Gregory law offices, wearing her spring trench coat, rain splattering on her umbrella. The law office was located downtown, in one of the shiny new office buildings that had sprung up in her absence.

She lowered her umbrella and stepped inside. The rush of warm air welcomed her, as did the door attendant, who offered her an umbrella bag. He directed her to the elevators that would take her to the fourth-floor law office.

Swanky, she saw, as she reached them. All glass and sleek, dark wood.

"I'm here to see Samuel Becker."

"Junior or Senior?"

"I'm thinking Senior."

"Then you must be Ms. Scott." She smiled and stood. "Right this way."

Several moments later she was shaking the hand of a portly, gray-haired man.

"Mr. Becker, thank you for seeing me."

"Happy to, Ms. Scott." He indicated she should take the chair in front of his desk. "How have you been?"

"Good. And you? Your family?"

"Good. I'm a grandpa now." He pointed out the photos of two cherubic youngsters that graced his desk.

"They're adorable," she said.

"Best thing that ever happened to me," he said, folding his hands on the desk in front of him. "Now, to business. You said on the phone that you wanted to talk to me about the terms of your father's will."

"Yes, that's right. I know I'm ridiculously past due, but better late than never."

"Exactly. I've made you a copy." He slid it across the desk. "Why don't you review it, then I can answer any questions you have."

She nodded and did as he suggested. It read very much as Brad had explained it to her. There were little things: the house and its contents were her mother's until death, then she and her brother would sell them and split the proceeds. Unless she was unmarried, in which case the house was hers to use until her death.

Unless she was *unmarried*? She reread the condition, thinking she must have misunderstood. But no, she hadn't. Had her father thought so little of her capabilities? Or was he just that big a sexist?

She felt a pang of sympathy for her brother. She'd already been left more than four times the money as he—but then this, too? The expectation that because she was *unmarried,* he should take care of her as well as Viv. No wonder he resented her.

But it didn't excuse his behavior. She was not going to give him a hall pass on this. No way.

Sienna read on, to the details of the various insurance monies, the reasoning behind them, and that upon Viv's passing Brad would inherit whatever was left. At least he had that, she thought, and laid the document aside.

"You have a very expressive face, Ms. Scott. Was there something unexpected?"

"I guess I didn't realize just how old-fashioned my dad was. I'm a little shocked by the sexism."

Becker chuckled. "Can't teach old dogs new tricks. Especially when it comes to their daughters."

"I'm going to be honest with you. I knew what my father left me, and that my mom was also taken care of, but I didn't ask about Brad. I just assumed . . . It doesn't seem fair."

"Maybe not, but these were your father's wishes." He leaned slightly forward. "I advised him to go in another direction, but in the end, that's all I can do, advise."

"Of course."

"You'd be surprised how often I see situations like this. And worse, much worse."

"Worse than this?"

"A will can be used as a weapon, Ms. Scott. A final blow delivered upon death. This was not that, and we can be thankful for it."

But it had been received that way. Like a blow.

"Sometimes," the attorney went on, "the beneficiaries make their own arrangements."

"What do you mean?"

"They make things more equitable after the fact."

They talked a short while more, then minutes after that, Sienna was in her car. Donna and Ted Meyers were also on the day's to-do list. She owed them an answer, and she felt it only right to do it in person. She supposed they would be disappointed—but not nearly as disappointed as she.

They greeted her with smiles. The smiles faded as she delivered the bad news. "I'm sorry, I really wanted to buy your restaurant. In fact, I wanted to quite badly. But it's not possible right now."

"Would a little more time help?" Donna ignored her husband's elbow. "I know we said we were in a hurry, but if you need—"

"It's not going to help, Donna. And I don't want you to lose the other buyer." She stood and held out her hand. "Thank you for the time and your consideration."

Ted shook her hand, but Donna gave her a big hug. "I wish things had turned out differently," she said.

"Me, too, Donna."

As she exited the restaurant, she took a last glance at the building. She had to let go. But just because this dream wouldn't come true, it didn't mean another wouldn't.

She thought of Jonathan. Could almost hear him saying exactly that to her as he drew her into his arms.

Holding on to the thought, she slid into the car. She'd left her cell phone on the console; it was buzzing. She snatched it up. "Jonathan?"

"Sienna, is that you?"

The connection wasn't the best, but the voice was a woman's, not a man's. "Yes?"

"Hello, my darling girl!"

"Mimi!" she cried, delighted.

"Who else would call at this time of night?"

"Mimi, it's afternoon here."

"All the better. How are you?"

"I've missed you and London terribly."

"I and it miss you as well. I have news."

Sienna frowned slightly. Her grandmother sounded giddy. "What kind of news?"

"Anthony proposed!"

Mimi was seventy-five—though she always claimed five years less—and Tony was sixty-eight. Not too old for love, but marriage? "Proposed? I didn't know you two were that serious."

"I didn't know either. Until I did, that is." She laughed, the sound more youthful than Sienna felt. "It turns out your timing for returning to the States was perfect. I'm selling the London flat and moving in with Tony."

Until this moment, Sienna hadn't realized she had been holding on to the belief that she could go back, return to London and her old life there. And holding tightly, at that.

With each passing second, that grasp was being pried painfully loose.

"Moving where?"

"Portugal. He has a home and family there. And at our age, being near family is important."

"Yes," she managed. "It is. Congratulations." She sounded anything but congratulatory; luckily her grandmother didn't seem to notice.

"How are you, Sienna? Are things good? And your mother, she's doing well?"

Sienna wanted to cry. She wanted to tell her everything, weep on her shoulder and hear Mimi tell her everything would be all right. She wanted to hear *"Come home. There's a place here for you."*

But there wasn't, not anymore. That ship had sailed. Like her love affair with Jonathan. Like her dream of buying The Wagon Wheel, and her relationship with her brother. And it had left her stranded here, alone and without a plan B.

"Sienna? Sweetheart, are you still there? Is something wrong?"

She wouldn't take the glow off her grandmother's happiness. "Yes, Mimi, I'm here. Everything is fine. Mom still struggles, but is heading in a good direction. I miss you and London, but I'm acclimating."

"Are you working?"

"Not yet. I'm going to start looking next week."

"I know you'll land somewhere amazing, my darling

girl. Keep me posted on everything, and I'll do the same."

After promising she would and congratulating her grandmother again—this time enthusiastically—Sienna ended the call.

The rain had turned into snow: lovely, fat flurries that hit the windshield and disappeared, each flake becoming just another rivulet cascading to the ground.

If letting go of a dream was a necessary part of growing up, she was well on her way to adulthood.

But if this was adulthood, it sucked.

CHAPTER FIFTY-FIVE

Sienna couldn't sleep. She tried reading and watching TV. She drank a cup of chamomile tea, but still lay staring at the ceiling, thoughts racing, a headache growing behind her eyes and at the base of her skull.

She finally gave up. She wasn't going to sleep; she might as well do something productive. Her mother had completed her first full week at Evergreen, and this afternoon, the two of them were to be reunited.

It sounded weird, their being "reunited" after just a week apart, but Dr. Margery explained that her mother had been doing intensive inner work without triggers from beyond the center's walls, and that her re-introduction to family and the outside world had to be handled delicately.

The psychiatrist had instructed her to bring a couple of mementos to the session. Ones evoking memories of good times between just the two of them. Times before her disorder became a wall separating them. A photo. A favorite bedtime storybook. A saved ticket stub from someplace special.

Pouring herself a glass of wine, Sienna started with the photos. Framed ones on the fireplace mantel, her father's desk, her mother's dressing table. There were none of just the two of them. Sienna alone or with Brad, brother and sister, her hand clasping his much bigger one.

She sipped her wine, moving to the upstairs hallway. There, graduation pictures, family portraits, portraits of her parents' wedding—and their parents' weddings. All a lovely trip down Memory Lane, but not what she needed.

The game room storage closet, she thought. She seemed to remember a box of snapshots stored in there. Sure enough, she saw, and eased the photo box out from under Brad's old science kit. She sat cross-legged on the floor, going through the snapshots.

Here there were many. Casual shots of her and her mother: when Sienna was learning to walk, when she was starting school, dressed for her first junior high mixer. And her mother was there in those. Smiling brilliantly. As if no dark cloud of uncontrollable fear hung over her head.

One glass of wine led to a second. Sienna gathered together a small stack of possible choices, then returned the box to the closet.

Next item, she decided, a storybook. When she was little, her mother read to her every night. And every night, as she would read "The end," she kissed the top of Sienna's head.

Smiling at the sweet memory, she recalled one book in particular that she'd asked for again and again. About a little field mouse who loved to daydream. And how those dreams fed his fellow mice through the cold, spare winter.

She couldn't remember the title, but knew she would remember the book on sight.

It wasn't in the bin of books in the playroom, not on the family bookshelves, not with the books stored in her bedroom closet. Surely her mother wouldn't have tossed that one?

Then she remembered the plastic bin in her mother's closet, the one marked *For Sienna*. She collected her wine and headed back upstairs to her mother's walk-in closet.

Sienna eased the container out and lifted the lid. And there, right on top, was the book. *Frederick* by Leo Lionni. And beside it, *Alice's Adventures in Wonderland,* a favorite from when she was older. How she'd loved the story of Alice and the bizarre, magical world the White Rabbit drew her into.

She set both aside, then saw her favorite lovey, a soft pink elephant with big, silky ears. Worn, but still soft; she caressed those silky ears. Below those, a layer of brown paper, then her christening gown and cap. The ridiculously tiny shoes, with their satin soles.

Another layer of paper. Wrapped in cloth, a sterling silver rattle engraved with her name and birthdate, and her little comb and brush set, also engraved. Sienna ran her fingers over the brush's baby-fine bristles before setting it aside.

Next, a petite ceramic box, shaped like a tooth. She didn't have to guess what was inside, but lifted the lid anyway. Her baby teeth. She'd never really understood why mothers saved them, but weirdly, she did now.

She counted them. Twenty. Was that all of them? she wondered, deciding to Google that sometime and find out. But, if she used her baby book as evidence of her mother's thoroughness, she had a feeling it would be. Every page had been filled in with her mother's scrolling but precise hand.

No sign of mental illness here. No warnings. No jotted observations about white vans or hang-up calls.

Only love. A mother's love.

Sienna wiped tears from her cheeks. She supposed she always knew her mother loved her, but having a relationship with someone who suffered from mental illness was challenging. Like a roller-coaster ride that never ended. The moment the car steadied and slowed into the straightaway, along came another curve or climb that stole your breath—and your equilibrium. Until finally, you just wished the ride would end. You longed to get off and find a quiet, calm place to catch your breath.

London. Mimi. Her quiet place.

Ten years' worth.

Sienna peeled away yet another layer of the brown paper, smiling at the now-familiar crinkling sound.

Her smile faded.

Dark red creeping across brilliant white.

A sound passed her lips. Horrified, she stared at the item in the box.

Her coat. The one she had been wearing that night. Neatly folded.

Stained red.

With shaking hands she lifted it from the bin and held it up. Dried blood smeared across the front. Her gaze shifted. The hood, the faux fur rimming it, matted and rusty red.

She closed her eyes, recalled it all. Tripping, landing on her knees, her hands sinking into the dark, wet snow. Pushing back her hood to see.

Her shock when she realized what she was looking at. Frantically wiping her hands against her jacket. No, not her hands. Gloves.

Sienna dropped her gaze. There they were.

The gloves. They'd been soaked, and they were stiff, crusted with Madison's blood.

The contents of her stomach lurched to her throat. Sienna jumped to her feet and ran to the commode. There, she retched until she couldn't anymore, then sank to the floor and sobbed.

CHAPTER FIFTY-SIX

3:10 A.M.

Much later, cried out and chilled to the bone, Sienna stood and crossed to the sink. She hardly recognized the reflection staring back at her. Eyes red and swollen from crying, face blotchy. As she gazed at herself, her reflection shifted and she was staring at her mother.

Eyes on fire with something feral. Like a cornered animal who would fight to the death if necessary.

"I'd do anything to protect you, Sienna. Anything."

Sienna shook her head, and the image of her mom disappeared. Alice down the rabbit hole, she thought. What bizarre turn came next?

She rinsed her mouth and splashed water on her face. In the morning, she would call Dr. Margery. Ask her what she should do. How she could wrap her mind around this. But for now . . . sleep. Or try to, anyway.

As she reached the closet door, she stopped, gaze drawn back to the parka, lying right where she'd left it. The gloves on the floor beside it. Why did her mother save them? Yes, they were mementos of a big moment in her life—but not one she wanted to relive.

Suddenly angry, she strode across to the box. Everything else packed in this container was precious. Not the coat. Not the gloves. They were profane. They belonged in the trash, where they should have gone before.

She went to snatch them up, and noticed something she hadn't before. An object wrapped in brown paper, at the bottom of the bin.

She frowned. A part of her was curious, while another part of her wanted nothing to do with anything else she might find in that box.

Morbid curiosity won out, and she bent and picked it up.

And wished she hadn't. She recognized the feel of the object, the weight of it in her hand. She was a chef, she knew what it was—but refused to accept it. It wasn't possible; her mind was playing tricks on her. Exhaustion, the shock of seeing the bloody coat and gloves, the loss of the past days, it all conspired to twist her thinking.

Lay it down, Sienna. You do not want to do this.

But she had to. The last object in the box. A clean sweep, she told herself. If nothing else, afterward she could scold herself for her crazy thoughts.

Hands trembling, she carefully unwrapped the object. The breath hissed past her lips. Her mind hadn't been playing tricks on her.

A small chef knife. Someone had obviously attempted to wipe the six-inch blade, but hadn't done a good job. The stainless steel was smeared, and where the blade met the handle she saw residue.

"You're right, Sienna. It was supposed to be you!"

She pictured her mother lunging at her, eyes alight with fanaticism. Her father grabbing her, keeping her away from Sienna, ordering her brother to take her upstairs.

The sound of her mother screaming those same damning words after them.

It was supposed to be you . . . It was supposed to be you . . . It was supposed to be you . . .

Sienna pulled in a deep, steadying breath. This wasn't what it looked like.

Then what was it? A sick joke? Did her mother think she, her daughter, wouldn't find this until she died? Then what? *"Surprise! Look what I have for you?"*

No, not what I "have" for you. What I "did" for you.

There had to be another explanation. But she couldn't think of one.

The coat. The gloves. The knife. All placed in a bin marked "For Sienna." Her mother, tormented by delusions. Tormented by the notion that she, only she, could protect Sienna from those who sought to hurt her.

"I'd do anything to keep them from getting you."

Would "anything" include *killing* the very one she wanted to protect?

A memory came crashing back. From a short time after the murder. It had been late, long after her parents usually turned in. She'd gone down for a snack, when on her way past their door, she'd stopped at the sound of their raised voices.

"Where were you that night, Viv?"

He'd sounded shaken. In a way that was uncharacteristic of him.

"You already know where I was."

Defiance in her mother's.

"For the love of God, Viv. Tell me you didn't do this."

Fear now. Almost a plea.

"I did what I had to. I had to protect—"

"Shut up! I don't want to hear another word."

Sienna remembered backing away from the door, not wanting to hear more. She had heard a variation of that same argument dozens of times before.

Or so she had thought at the time. Now, it took

on a new significance. Could her father have known something? Found bloodied clothing or . . .

He would have gone to the police. He was a good and honorable man. Law abiding. If he thought his wife was a murderer he would . . .

Do nothing. Sienna lowered her gaze to the knife. How many times during the course of her childhood did she wonder at how irrationally devoted he was to her mother? How many times a day had she heard him say he loved her?

He would have protected his beloved, no matter what.

Sienna rewrapped the paper around the knife, careful not to touch any part of it, folding the paper exactly the way it had been, then placing it back in the bin.

Her mother would have had to be waiting for her. At midnight. In a blizzard. That made no sense. How would she have even known where Sienna would be and when?

Because she'd told her, Sienna remembered. Not directly, not that night. In anger. Weeks before.

"Mom, do I really have to do this?"

"Yes. This is a condition of you being allowed to live on campus."

"Dad!"

He sat at the kitchen table, reading the paper. He looked up. "You agreed to the condition."

"But it's stupid! I'm eighteen years old!"

She thought she saw sympathy in his eyes. But as usual, it didn't matter. He took his wife's side.

"You made the deal. Live with it."

"Grab your things, Sienna. I'll be in the car."

Sienna watched her mother exit the kitchen, then turned back to her father. "It's embarrassing, Dad. She's made a map of the campus."

"She wants you to know your way around. So you won't get lost."

"You know that's a lie. She wants to show me all the places I shouldn't set foot because they're dangerous."

"It's only a morning."

"It's humiliating, that's what it is."

And it was humiliating. And embarrassing. Her mom had paraded her around campus, pointing out all the places to avoid. Because she could be ambushed. Or snatched. Or overpowered.

The cut-through from the library to the dorm had been one of them. Unlit. Shielded from view. Close to a parking lot so an attacker or kidnapper could make a quick getaway.

Sienna didn't argue, not then. She didn't challenge her. But she promised herself she would do every one of the things her mother ordered her not to. She would take this cut-through—and every other one her mother pointed out that day—every chance she got.

She kept that promise to herself, and at the first opportunity that came along, she threw it in her mother's face. Including that she took that "very dangerous" cut-through every Wednesday night after study group let out at midnight.

CHAPTER FIFTY-SEVEN

4:05 A.M.

Sienna waited for Randy in the driveway. She'd called 911. Asked for Randy by name. No one was hurt, she assured them. But yes, it was an emergency. A cruiser arrived first, lights flashing. The patrol officer stepped out, identified himself, and informed her he had been ordered by Detective Clark to wait with her until he arrived.

In an attempt to ward off the cold, she stomped her feet and hugged herself. She wondered if she would ever be warm again—and if spring would ever come. She glanced toward Jonathan's and saw him standing at his door. Drawn, she had no doubt, by the blue lights. He was probably congratulating himself on being rid of her and all the drama associated with her.

Longing took her breath. To run to him, have his arms encircle her, to feel the beat of his heart against hers.

And what would she tell him then? That her mother had killed his sister?

Even if they could manage to overcome their past mistakes, they couldn't overcome this. Every time he looked at her, he would remember. His sister was dead instead of her. Because of her.

And she would have to be the one to tell him.

Sienna looked away, teeth beginning to chatter. Maybe it wasn't true. Another of her wild imaginings. Or the perverse joke she originally thought it was.

Ironically, at this moment she wished she *was* delusional like her mother. The police would exchange pitying glances and humor her, until Brad—or a representative of Evergreen—came to collect her.

Poor, crazy Ms. Scott, they would say. *Just another one of her spells, nothing more.*

Brad, she thought. Another gaping hole in her heart. She would have to tell him, too. Swallow her hurt and anger, reach out to him.

Randy arrived. He parked behind the cruiser and climbed out. She didn't run to him. It had been so awkward between them the last time they spoke. He'd been angry with her. Disillusioned. Now, he just looked tired.

"It's the middle of the night, Sienna," he said when he reached her. "You want to tell me what's going on?"

"I found something. It couldn't wait until morning."

"Where's your boyfriend?"

"If you mean Jonathan, we're not together anymore."

"Sorry to hear that."

He wasn't, of course. And this line of questioning was completely inappropriate. But then, their relationship had been inappropriate from the beginning. "I thought we were friends, Randy. We talked about it."

"Right." The one word communicated layers of meaning. Disappointment. Disgust. Hurt.

He took a notebook and pen from his pocket, now all business. "What did you find?"

"A knife. I think . . . it's the murder weapon."

He looked up from the notebook. "Excuse me?"

"The murder weapon. The knife used to kill Madison Robie."

His expression turned disbelieving. Suspicious. Not of her. Of her sanity.

"Where?"

"Upstairs. My mother's closet."

Randy called for the patrol officer, asked him to follow. She led them into the house and up to her mom's walk-in closet. The bin was where she had left it, the items spread out.

She wrung her hands. "I was supposed to meet with Mom and her psychiatrist later today. Dr. Margery asked me to bring a couple things with me that represented"—the words caught in her throat—"good times."

She fought falling apart. Fought dissolving into tears. Neither would solve a thing. "The last thing in the bin, it was a knife."

He fitted on scene gloves, and squatted beside the box. "This."

He pointed, she nodded.

"You opened it?"

"Yes. When I saw—" She cleared her throat. "I rewrapped it and put it exactly as I found it. I thought . . . that's what you would want me to do."

He didn't comment. Sienna watched as he took it from the container and carefully lifted away the paper, one corner at a time. Until there it was, completely revealed.

The breath hissed past his lips. "Damn."

Tears flooded her eyes. "It could be nothing, right?"

He met her eyes. "Yeah. Of course."

He turned to the patrol officer. "I've got evidence bags and a camera in my console. Grab them for me."

He turned back to Sienna. "Did you know your mother had saved the coat and gloves?"

"No. God, no."

"Anything else in the box that—"

"No. All sweet. What you'd expect a mother to save for her child."

He stood. "Chief Thompson's going to want to see this."

She nodded. "This doesn't seem real. I don't understand how my mom—"

"Who else had access to this closet?"

"Besides me?"

"Yes."

"Brad, I suppose. His wife, Liz. They're divorced now."

"That's recently."

"Yes."

"You have no idea when this bin was created. All you know for sure is that these could have been stored her since Madison's murder, ten years ago."

"That would mean my dad—"

"Would have had access as well, yes."

She frowned. "What are you suggesting? That my father or brother could have placed those objects in the bin?"

"Remember what we discussed, way back? That this murder was highly personal?"

"Yes, of course I remember."

"So, if DNA comes back and proves this was the knife that killed Madison, in my opinion, we have three suspects."

Her mother, brother, and dad. "This can't be happening," she said. "It just can't be."

He patted her shoulder. "We'll figure this out, Sienna. Why don't you wait downstairs. Make yourself some breakfast or coffee. When I'm done up here, we'll need to talk some more."

She nodded numbly and started for the door. He stopped her when she reached it.

"Sienna?"

She looked back at him.

"Looks like you could be right: you really might have been the one who was supposed to die."

CHAPTER FIFTY-EIGHT

6:20 A.M.

Chief Thompson arrived. Sienna heard him, but didn't leave the kitchen to go out and greet him—she didn't have the energy or the heart. She had made a pot of coffee and scrambled some eggs. The eggs turned her stomach, so she settled on a couple handfuls of granola, straight from the bag.

More people arrived; she peered out a side window and saw a crime scene van. Not long after that, Randy and the chief appeared in the kitchen.

The chief crossed to her and put his hands on her shoulders and looked her in the eyes. "You doin' okay?"

"Define okay."

He smiled grimly. "I don't know what's going on here, but I knew your dad. He was a good man."

"Yes," she agreed, "he was."

Randy stepped in. "We need to ask you a few more questions, Sienna. To try to make sense of what we've got here. Is that okay?"

"Of course."

Chief Thompson took over. "How about we sit down? An old man like me needs to conserve his energy."

She directed them to the kitchen table. "How about right here?"

"Excellent."

When they were all seated, the chief began. "Randy explained that you found the items in a bin in your mother's closet, and that you were looking for some childhood mementos."

She glanced at Randy—he was taking notes—then looked back at Chief Thompson. "That's right."

"So you were aware of the bin's existence?"

"I saw it a couple weeks ago. I had to pull together some clothes to take Mom, for her stay at Evergreen."

"Here's what baffles me. The perpetrator of Madison Robie's murder had to have been either lying in wait for his—or her—victim, or it was a crime of opportunity. Meaning, their paths crossed, and our killer saw the opportunity and took it."

She nodded and he went on. "Early on we eliminated the notion of this crime being random. Because of the weather that night and the passion with which Ms. Robie was killed.

"So, tell me this," he continued, "on the night of the murder, how would your mother—or any member of your family—have known exactly where you would be at that time?"

"My mother and I had an argument. As you probably know, she was . . . super-protective of me." He nodded and she went on. "She had forbidden me to take that cut-through, because it wasn't safe."

"Was that the only one she warned you about?"

"Lord, no. But it's the one I threw in her face."

"What do you mean by that?"

"Like I said, we were arguing about her 'safety rules.' I told her I took that shortcut every Wednesday after study group. And that nothing had happened to me."

As she relayed the story, Sienna could hear her

youthful self, her belligerence. If only she could take it back, do it differently.

The two men exchanged glances. The chief cleared his throat. "Did anyone overhear that argument?"

"I don't know. Maybe Dad. Maybe Brad. I can't recall if either of them were home. Dad usually ran interference between me and Mom. Or had Brad do it for him."

"I hear you and your brother had a falling-out."

"How did you—" She bit the last back because it didn't matter. Small towns made it their business to be in yours. "Yes."

"May I ask about what?"

"It was personal."

"Heard, too, you're not buying The Wagon Wheel after all."

"That's right. And again, for personal reasons."

"Something to do with money?" Randy asked.

She stiffened. "What does my decision to purchase, or not purchase, a restaurant have to do with what was in that bin?"

The chief sent Randy an irritated look. "Nothing, just establishing time and place."

She opened her mouth to ask what he meant, but before she could, the chief fired off another question. "Back then, were you aware of anyone following you?"

"Following me? You mean around campus? No, never."

"You're certain?"

"Yes. Absolutely."

"And everything was all right with the family?"

"You were a family friend, Chief. Everything was as all right as it ever was. You know, with Mom and her illness."

Chief Thompson sat back, meeting her eyes over

steepled fingers. "You're right, I did know your family well. Your father loved his family, and would do anything for you. And your mother, despite her troubles, was the same way."

She frowned. "What are you saying?"

"I have a hard time picturing Viv out there in the snowstorm, waiting for you with that big knife. Why would she do that? Her life's goal was to protect you."

"I know. I struggled with that, too. But she always said she'd do *anything* to keep me from Margaret . . . In her twisted mind, could she have taken it that far?"

"You mean, kill you to protect you from Margaret?"

"Yes. It's twisted thinking, but Mom . . ."

She let the thought trail off; the chief didn't pick it up, but went in another direction.

"The writing on the bin, *'For Sienna,'* was that in your mother's hand?"

Sienna tried to picture the bin, the label affixed to the front. "I don't know. I didn't look at it that way—"

"Randy. You took pictures. You have a shot of the label?"

Randy called it up on the camera and handed it to her. She looked at it and frowned. "No. I don't think so. Her handwriting has a lyrical quality to it."

"Is it your dad's?"

"No. Definitely not. His was almost machine-like, it was so precise. This is clumsy and a little messy."

"Maybe rushed?"

"Could be," she agreed.

"Heard Viv fell down the stairs a couple months ago. Hurt her arm."

Goose bumps prickled at the back of her neck. "I learned about it when I got home. She tripped on some loose carpeting at the top landing. Brad had it repaired."

"She tells a different story, doesn't she?"

Sienna glanced at Randy. Obviously, he had shared what she'd told him with the chief. "Not at first, but later . . . she told me she was pushed."

"What do you believe? Was she pushed?" Chief Thompson asked.

She moved her gaze between the two men. Where was this heading? She'd been interviewed by the police the night of the murder, but it hadn't been like this. Tonight, it was as if they were taking a random, twisting path. But she suspected they knew exactly where they were going, and there was nothing random about it.

But if their goal was to keep her slightly unbalanced, it was succeeding.

"No, I believe Brad. As you know, my mother sees villains around every corner."

Randy spoke up. "Those hang-up calls; I got the star fifty-seven back."

She looked at him in surprise. "Whose number was it?"

"Bradley Scott's."

She stared at him, shocked silent. "That can't be right."

"I'm sorry, Sienna."

"But his number's programmed in the phone. He called me right before . . ."

"He blocked the number and called you back. It's as easy as two numbers first."

Brad? Calling and hanging up?

"I think we have enough to get a warrant for his phone records. My bet is he was behind all the calls."

"Why would he do that?"

Randy arched his eyebrows. "I think it's obvious. He wanted your mother to respond exactly as she did. She could have ended up dead. You could have as well."

Sienna shuddered at the memory. The sound of the gun discharging. The circle of red on her mother's white sweater. Catching her as she went down.

Her hands trembled and she clasped them tightly in her lap. "Are you saying he predicted her response?"

"There's the van, too," Randy said. "I chased them down. Your brother hired them to cruise past the house several times a day."

Brad knew Viv's triggers. But why do it? So she would forget about buying The Wheel and run back to London before she found out he'd taken her money? The thought made her feel sick. But it rang true. He had discouraged her from staying in Tranquility Bluffs, and from buying the restaurant.

And not for her own good, as he'd wanted her to believe. For his.

Chief Thompson sent her a sympathetic look. "I see by your expression, what we're saying is starting to make sense to you."

She now understood where this twisting, turning road was taking them. They didn't think her mother killed Madison.

They thought her brother did.

"No. It will never make sense to me." She glared at them, suddenly angry. "This is my brother you're talking about."

"Better your mother?"

The question came from Randy; it cut her to the quick. "No. But at least I'd have a reason for it, one out of Mom's control. But with Brad . . . the reason—"

Sienna bit those words back, and chose others. "I remember overhearing a conversation between Dad and Mom. It was shortly after the murder. He was upset. He asked her where she was that night. And asked what she had done." She curved her hands into fists, and repeated the last: "What she *had* done."

"You think she murdered Robie and he found out?"

"It's possible."

"And he didn't come to me, his friend?"

She looked at the chief. "He would never give her up like that. He spent his life shielding her from herself."

The two men fell silent. They just looked at her, as if waiting. For something from her. Something more.

"I love my mother. But all these things, they add up!" She covered her face with her hands, using the moment to collect herself. "What should I think?" she demanded, looking at them once more. "I really don't know!"

"Here are some other things to consider," the chief said softly. "It's never been a secret that your brother was jealous of you."

She dropped her hands. Looked at him. "What? No, I never knew that. Never. Not until—"

"Recently," Randy offered. "Your falling-out with him."

It wasn't a question, so she didn't respond. The chief took over once more. "Your father and I were quite close, Sienna. He shared things with me. Private things." He paused. "Like how he intended to write his will. And why.

"And I happen to know that your dad shared his plans with Bradley, and that your brother was quite upset. They had a terrible fight."

Sienna couldn't look at him. She didn't want to know any of this, didn't want to hear any more.

But she didn't have a choice.

"Do you know when your dad had the new will drawn up?"

"No," she said, tone resentful. "But I have a feeling you're going to tell me."

"Not long before Madison Robie's murder."

"My brother would never hurt me."

"But he has already, hasn't he?" Randy said. "What was your falling-out over?"

She didn't answer, didn't look at him, instead shifting her gaze to a point over his shoulder.

"Why did you pull out of buying The Wagon Wheel?" Randy's voice turned coaxing. "You were really excited about the prospect of opening your own place, right here in Tranquility Bluffs."

When she didn't respond, he went on. "It's because you couldn't afford it, isn't that right, Sienna?"

They already knew that Brad had used her money, that it was gone. "It doesn't mean he . . ." She choked on the words. "That he could . . ."

"Kill someone? No, I guess it doesn't. But enough circumstantial evidence makes a damn strong case."

Chief Thompson concurred. "We're sending the knife to the state lab. If DNA tests prove this was the knife used to stab Madison Robie, it might be enough to charge him. Who knows, maybe they'll even get a fingerprint?"

"How long?" she asked. "When will you hear back?"

"Forty-eight to seventy-two hours." They both stood. "You'll be the first to know."

She followed them to their feet. "What do I do until then?"

"I suggest you just go about your life as if nothing's happened."

CHAPTER FIFTY-NINE

"Go about your life as if nothing's happened."

Sienna paced from one end of the house to the other. As she did, Chief Thompson's words kept coming back to her. And each time, they rankled a bit more. How, exactly, was she supposed to do that? The police believed her brother was a murderer. That he'd been so jealous, so resentful, of the terms of their father's will, that he'd lain in wait for her that snowy night, attacked "her" from behind, and in a frenzy stabbed her eighteen times.

She couldn't wrap her mind around it. This was the big brother she'd adored, the brother who she'd looked up to and relied on.

He always seemed to love her back.

Sienna's thoughts turned to the knife. The debris on the knife would turn out to be the remnants of a Sunday roast beef dinner, she decided. The whole thing was a sick joke. Perpetrated by Liz, bitter and angry over the end of her marriage with Brad. A hateful parting shot to end all parting shots.

Sienna brought the heels of her hands to her eyes. She was grasping at straws. In the pit of her gut, she knew she'd found the murder weapon.

But even if it came back negative—no DNA, no

fingerprints, nothing—then what? Back to square one? Or would they hound Brad the way they had hounded Reed? Certain they had their man?

And would she ever be able to look at her brother the same way again? She honestly didn't know.

Sienna checked her phone for the third time in as many hours. She needed to call Dr. Margery, beg off the two o'clock meeting with her and her mother. Claim she had the flu, which wasn't far from the truth. She felt like she did—she ached everywhere, her head hurt, and her stomach roiled, as if even her body rejected the idea that her brother hated her so much.

Sienna thought back, recalling that night. Back at the house. Brad showing up drunk. He'd been out with his buddies, drinking, she remembered. She'd smelled the liquor on him. No way he should have been driving, let alone in such bad weather, and her dad had been furious.

Wouldn't his friends provide an alibi? She searched her memory for the amount of time that had passed between Madison being killed and Brad showing up at the house. Three hours maybe?

Enough time to commit the murder, get himself cleaned up, meet friends, and get stinking, fall-down drunk?

It seemed unlikely. Unless he'd faked inebriation? But again, wouldn't his friends remember that night? Although it occurred ten years ago, it had been made more memorable by tragedy.

Sienna stopped pacing, certainty crashing down on her. Brad didn't do it. She knew he hadn't. And she didn't care how much circumstantial evidence the police thought they had.

That left her mom. Or her dad. *If* the DNA came back positive.

Sienna became aware of her surroundings. She stood in the center of the kitchen, facing the long counter between the stove and the refrigerator. She blinked, her vision focusing on an item on the counter.

The wooden butcher block that held her mother's knife set. She'd used the set, with its wooden handles, for as long as Sienna could remember.

Wooden handles. Not composite.

Sienna's heart began to thump violently against the wall of her chest. She crossed to the counter; drew one of the knives from the block. Chicago Cutlery.

Not Henckel.

It was a full set. The biggest and best money could buy. That's the way her dad had been. Especially when it came to his wife. She checked the set; it included both a large chef's knife and a small one.

Realization hit her with the force of a wrecking ball. No way her mother could have committed the murder. Her mother's episodes weren't calculated. She didn't plan them. They just . . . happened.

The crime she suspected her of was one of passion, but also highly organized. Buying a knife. Knowing when to wait and where. Planning her escape strategy—leaving the scene, cleaning up, getting back in bed. And finally, acting shocked when she "learned about the crime," then *feigning* an episode afterward.

Sienna shook her head. No possible way.

So, by her reasoning, if DNA proved the knife in the bin with her coat and gloves was, indeed, the murder weapon, there were two possible suspects. Brad, who, like her mother, she'd already eliminated. Or her dad, which was beyond inconceivable to her.

"Go about your life as if nothing's happened."

Screw that, Sienna decided, and checked the time once more. She wasn't going to cancel the session with her mom and Dr. Margery. The meeting would be the perfect opportunity to ask her mom about the plastic bin—and the things she'd found in it.

If DNA proved that knife was the murder weapon, she wanted to be ready to prove that every one of her family members was innocent.

Forty minutes later, storybook and photo tucked into her handbag, Sienna stepped into Evergreen's cozy meeting room. He mother stood up and, beaming, held out her hand. "Sienna, sweetheart."

"Mom. You look wonderful!"

And she did. Rested. Her eyes and skin bright. Her smile genuine. And she even appeared to have put on a little weight.

"I *feel* wonderful," she said.

"And your wound?"

"Sore. But the pain medication makes it bearable."

Dr. Margery motioned her toward the chairs. "I'm glad you could make it."

Sienna found the comment odd, as if the woman had somehow been privy to her earlier thoughts. "Of course I'm here."

She squeezed her mother's hand, then released it. They all sat, she and her mom next to each other.

"Viv's worked really hard," Dr. Margery began. "And she's excited to reconnect today and share her insights with you."

Her mother angled in her chair to face her, expression eager. "The first thing I want to do is apologize—"

"You don't need to—"

"Yes, I do. I want to. Not for my disorder. I can't help that. But for lying to you about taking my medicine.

That wasn't fair to you. And it wasn't the best for me, obviously."

She rubbed her hands on her thighs. "I have to listen to the people I love and trust. And I love and trust you." Her voice turned thick and her eyes glistened with tears. "I've been working on trust during my stay here. And Dr. Margery and I have come up with some self-monitoring strategies."

She looked at the therapist as if for confirmation, then back at Sienna. "And we talked about the part you'll need to play in me implementing them." She paused, then went on. "If you see me veering off track, you tell me. And I promise to trust you."

Sienna glanced at the doctor, then back at her mom. "I can do that. We'll work on this together."

"I don't want you to go back to London, Sienna. I'm so sorry about what happened!"

"It's behind us now." Sienna curved her hand around her mother's. "But you have to take your meds, Mom. That's a deal-breaker for me. Do you understand and accept that?"

She let out a long breath. "I do."

"You're right about having to trust me. I promise that I'll make certain you're taking the right medicine in the right dose, just like Dr. Margery ordered. Do you think you can do that?"

Her lips trembled and she pressed them together and nodded.

"You trusted Dad. Remember?"

"I did. Completely."

"Do you think you can learn to trust me the same way?"

"I'll try." A tear rolled down her cheek. "Will you forgive me when I fail? Because I will, I know it."

Sienna did, too. Her disorder couldn't be cured, just controlled. There would always be triggers. Always be episodes. But they would face them together.

"I will, Mom." She released her hand. "I brought something fun for us to look at today." Sienna reached in her purse for the book, then held it out.

Her mom's face lit up. "*Frederick*! Where did you find it?"

"A bin in your closet. You don't remember putting it there?"

She thought a moment. "That's right, I remember now."

"You marked the box 'For Sienna.'"

"I did?" She shrugged, as if accepting Sienna's words but having no actual memory of the act. "How many times did we read this?"

"Too many to count," she said softly. "And do you remember that every time after you read 'The end,' you'd kiss the top of my head?"

Her mother's eyes grew teary. She ran her fingers over the pages. "I do. It was my favorite time of day."

Sienna watched as she flipped the pages, her mouth moving as she silently read. When she closed the book, she sighed. "I'm so glad I saved it."

"Me, too."

"What else was in the bin, I can't remember."

Sienna's chest tightened, her head filling with the image of the bloodied coat and gloves. The knife.

Nothing but expectation registered on her mother's face: no apprehension, trepidation, or even sly recognition.

"Let's see," she began. "My christening gown and a little tooth box with my baby teeth in it."

"I kept every one," she said. "And your baby book," she said.

"You filled out every page."

"Oh, I wish you'd brought it."

"Next time."

"Promise?"

"I do." Sienna ticked off the other items in the box, until *the* three remained. She opened her mouth to ask, then shut it. How could she? Things were going so well, the last thing she wanted to do was trigger an episode.

But the police planned to question her, and they wouldn't be nearly as gentle as she.

"I was wondering, when did you start that bin, Mom?"

"Years ago. After your dad passed."

"After Dad died?" Her mother nodded, and it felt as if a crushing weight was lifted from her shoulders. It proved her father couldn't have had anything to do with the murder.

Viv went on. "I needed something to occupy me, and I wanted to make certain the important things were together. I don't know why I stopped."

The important things? Like a bloodstained coat?

"I wondered about something, Mom."

"What's that?"

"How come you saved that coat?"

"What coat?"

"From, you know, *that* night."

"What night?"

Her mom seemed genuinely confused. But Sienna had to ask; there was no getting around it. "The night the girl was murdered."

A sound of surprise came from Dr. Margery. "Sienna," she said sharply, "could I speak with you out in the hall—"

"Your white parka?" Her mother's expression changed

from confusion to disbelief. "Why would I . . . how could you think I would do . . . that?"

"You didn't put it in the plastic bin? To save it for me?"

"No!" She looked from Sienna to Dr. Margery. "That would be . . . sick. Besides, I never saw that coat again. And if I had, I would have disposed of . . . Wait—" Her eyes widened. "Are you saying the coat was in the bin?"

"Sienna," the therapist interrupted, voice brusque, "we really need to discuss this before you go any farther."

"Nonsense," Viv said sharply. "I'm not a child." She turned back to Sienna. "Was it in the bin?"

"It was."

She shuddered, rubbed her arms. "Who would do something so perverse? So . . . vile?"

"That's what I'm trying to find out, Mom. When's the last time you looked in that bin?"

She thought a moment. "A couple years, at least. Since just after your dad's death— No, wait . . . About a year ago, I ran across a little bag with all your baby teeth in it. So Liz went out and bought the cutest little porcelain box for them."

"Did she put it in the bin for you, Mom?"

"No. We did it together."

CHAPTER SIXTY

6:45 P.M.

Hours later, Sienna stood at her front window. Dr. Margery had been furious that Sienna would compromise her mother's progress by bringing up that disturbing memory. She had been less so after Sienna explained herself. Still, the therapist had scolded her, warning her never to do something like that again without consulting with her first.

Sienna sorted through the things she'd learned from her mother, adding them to the pieces she already had, working to fit them all together. Liz was the latest piece of the puzzle. But the more she worked to create a clear picture, the more confused she became.

Liz had known about the bin and where it was stored. Liz had access to the house. But as far as Sienna knew, Liz hadn't even lived in Tranquility Bluffs ten years ago. How would she have come into possession of the coat and gloves?

Brad. He was the obvious answer, but she'd already eliminated him as a suspect.

For the murder, but not of planting the coat and gloves in the bin. But why would he? Perhaps the same reason he had made the calls and hired some guys to drive a van past the house? To unhinge her mother and send Sienna scurrying back to London?

That worked only if the knife proved to be a prop.

On the coffee table behind her, her cell phone vibrated. She didn't recognize the number but answered anyway.

"Sienna, it's Mom."

"Mom?" She frowned. All communications from the facility by her mom were scheduled. "This is a surprise. I didn't expect a call."

"They let me use the phone. I promised to make it quick."

Her voice had the secretive, hushed tone it sometimes took on when her delusions came out to play. A knot settled in the pit of Sienna's stomach. "Are you all right?"

"I'm fine. I had a thought, about what we were talking about this afternoon. About who could have planted your coat in the bin."

"Okay. Who?"

"The same person who pushed me down the stairs."

Sienna felt as if she'd been sucker-punched. Although it didn't bring her any closer to knowing the person's identity, it made complete sense.

"My time's up. I've got to go. Goodnight, Sienna."

Sienna pocketed her phone, thoughts spinning. She couldn't make sense of this, not on her own. There were too many pieces—and they were all tightly intertwined with her feelings.

She thought about calling Randy, but his allegiance was to the TBPD and its investigation, not her or her family. She crossed back to the front window. Light shone from Jonathan's front window, like a welcoming beacon.

Jonathan. It was his sister who was dead. Her murder was why he'd come to Tranquility Bluffs. He had studied all the players in this drama, studied the crime, evidence, the facts and rumors. Like she did, he wanted the truth—not just an arrest.

Besides, he deserved to know what was happening, even if telling him was going to be one of the hardest things she'd ever done.

She grabbed her coat and slipped it on, then stepped outside. The weather was warming, the snow melting. Earlier, she'd noticed tips of green emerging from what was left of the snow. Spring was coming. But one thing she knew from many years of living in Wisconsin: the change of seasons was anything but predictable. And its unpredictability could be brutal.

He answered the door, and longing for him, for what they'd shared, swamped her. "Hey," she said, mouth going dry.

"Hey."

"Can I come in?"

He hesitated, then stepped aside. As she passed him, she fought the urge to touch him. It was agony.

From what she could see from the foyer, the progress he'd made on the remodel in the last two weeks was amazing. "It's really come together," she said. "It's stunning."

"Thanks." He shut the door behind him. "It'll be ready to put on the market May first."

She longed to ask him what he planned to do then, where he planned to go, but knew she had lost that right when she accused him of being a murderer.

"Congratulations," she said.

"Funny, I don't feel like I won anything."

Neither did she. Instead she felt like she had lost everything. "Jonathan—"

He cut her off. "I have plans, so if there's a specific reason for this visit . . ."

Get to it. Right. It hurt, but what did she expect? Flowers? She'd come to do the right thing and, hopefully, get advice; she wasn't about to let hurt feelings get in the way.

"We better sit down. I'm not sure I can do this while standing."

His eyebrows shot up, but he nodded and jerked his head in the direction of the folding lawn chairs.

Sienna headed for them, slipping out of her coat. He didn't offer to take it; obviously he didn't intend for her to be here long. She laid it over the chair's arm and sat. She looked at him, and the memory of that first night they had sat next to each other on these very chairs filled her head and took her breath away.

She had begun falling in love with him that night.

She looked away quickly, afraid he would read the longing in her eyes. And the despair.

He cleared his throat. "It's your party, Sienna."

He had said those very words that first night, and she wondered if he, like she, was remembering it.

The thought gave her confidence, and she turned back to him, meeting his eyes. "There's been a break in Madison's case. They have a suspect. But I don't think he did it."

"Your brother or your father?"

She made a sound of surprise. "How did you—"

"The commotion over at your place last night. And not just a cruiser. You had a detective and the big cheese himself, Chief Thompson. Knew your mom's still at Evergreen, you weren't taken out in cuffs, and no EMTs came to the scene. And now you're here, saying there's a suspect. One who's a 'he.'

"So," he finished, "which one is it? Your dad or your brother?"

"My brother." The two words came out thick with emotion. "But he didn't do it."

"You're certain of that?"

She lifted her chin. "Yes."

"You found something in your mom's house that caused you to call the police. What was it?"

"My bloodstained parka and gloves from that night. In a plastic bin marked 'For Sienna' in Mom's closet."

"That's it?"

"Why do you think there's something else?"

"You called the cops, that's why. In the middle of the night. The coat and gloves were your property, no need for the cavalry."

"A knife."

He seemed to freeze. An expression of anguish came over his features. "*The* knife?"

"Maybe. The police sent it out for DNA testing. Results are due back in two to three days."

He stood, strode to the window and, fists on hips, stared out. She couldn't take her eyes off him. She breathed in and out, deep and slow. The way he'd told her to when she was having the panic attack.

"Go on," he said, not looking at her.

"It was a small chef's knife. Six-inch blade. Obviously . . . used. Not one of my mother's."

She clasped her hands together. "At first I thought it was . . . her. Her delusions, the things she said about doing anything to keep 'them' from getting me. How she'd agreed it was supposed to be me when she overheard me telling Dad."

"But?"

"Her episodes are triggered, not orchestrated. The planning involved in the crime, including buying a knife that wouldn't be traced to her, doesn't fit her diagnosis."

"Agreed. Why not your father? Maybe he was the older guy Shepard claimed Madison was seeing."

"Mom didn't even start the memento box until after Dad died."

"Which leaves your brother. He was jealous of you and angry over the terms of your father's will."

"Yes."

He looked at her then, the expression in his eyes hard. "Then why do you think he's innocent?"

"Besides the fact I just know it?"

"Afraid so."

She clasped her hands together. "I was remembering that night. He showed up at home drunk. Totally smashed. Dad was furious. I did the math—no way he could have committed the murder, gotten cleaned up, and headed out with his buddies to get wasted."

"Can I show you something?"

She frowned, confused, but nodded.

"I'll be right back." He went toward the back of the house, then she heard him going downstairs. Several moments later he came back with a battered padded envelope.

Photographs, she saw, as he carefully extracted a bundle of them. "This is one of my favorites," he said, gazing lovingly at it a moment before handing it to her. "Me and Madi at my graduation from West Point."

He looked so handsome in his uniform, so happy. And Madi was beaming up at him. With pride. And love.

Madi had adored Jonathan.

The way Sienna adored Brad.

Her chest was so tight, she had to struggle to breathe.

He shared more photos. The two of them holding hands, Madi barely walking, he the devoted brother. Holiday photos: carving pumpkins, with Easter baskets, and standing awkwardly in front of a decorated Christmas tree.

Him at her side, protective and patient.

He handed her another. He and Madison stood on either side of a woman she guessed was their mother. Jonathan looked to be fifteen—and uncomfortable in his suit and tie; Madison was a vision in a pink-and-white dress.

She studied the photo. The woman was lovely. Jonathan got his dark hair and eyes from her.

"Mother's Day?" she asked, noting the woman's corsage. "Or birthday?"

"Mother's Day."

"You look like her."

"She adored us both. Especially Madi. They were very close."

"What's her name?"

"It was Pamela."

"Was? Did she change it?"

"She passed away."

"Oh . . . I'm so . . . sorry."

"You didn't know." He cleared his throat. "I told you she battled alcohol addiction. She turned to booze after Madi's . . . death, to numb the pain. Then, she decided the alcohol wasn't fast enough."

"Fast enough?"

"It was killing her too slowly. So, she took a bottle of pills."

Sienna tried to speak, but was too overcome with emotion to do more than mumble a platitude.

"I should have shared all that with you way before . . . this. But it didn't seem important at first. The last thing I expected to do was get involved with you." He looked directly at her. "And truthfully, I hoped to get information from you."

"Information like what I just shared?"

"Yes. A private investigator I hired talked to one of your brother's old girlfriends. She shared a story I hadn't heard. That you thought the killer might have been targeting you, not Madison. She told him your dad sent you to London because of it.

"I was intrigued. Since every other lead had been a dead end, I decided to follow this one. I asked myself what if you were right?"

"That's why you bought this house."

"Conveniently located across the street from your mom, yes. I tried to get to know her, but she would have none of it. Slammed the door in my face. It didn't deter me. I started asking questions around town, not direct questions, neighborly ones."

"Small-town folk like to talk."

He looked at her, then away once more. "That they do. Heard a rumor your brother was jealous of you, 'cause your dad always favored you."

"Apparently, I was the only one who *didn't* know that."

"Lots of speculation that the jealousy had something to do with money."

"You think he did it?" It hurt to force the words out. "That he meant to kill me and killed Madi instead?"

"Didn't say that."

"Then what do you think?"

"I think I agree with your assessment."

"You do?"

He smiled slightly at her incredulity. "I do. I looked his drinking buddies up. All but one of them remembered that night. They swore he was with them the entire time. Your brother all but got in a fistfight with one of them when they tried to take his car keys."

"So you think he's innocent?"

"Didn't say that either. Maybe there was a reason he didn't want to give the keys over. Maybe he was afraid of something they—or somebody else—might see in the car?"

"Like what?"

"Maybe the clothes he changed out of."

She felt as if the wind had been let out of her sails. "I don't want to think that."

"I know."

What could she say? If it was proved that her brother had brutally taken Jonathan's sister from him, how could he even look at her? Her brother would have wielded the knife, but she—her entire family—was also culpable.

"I'm so sorry. Do you hate me now?"

"No, Sienna. I don't hate you." He stood up, signaling it was time for her to go.

She put on her coat; he walked her to the door. "Thank you for telling me this, Jonathan."

"You deserved to know."

She stepped outside, then stopped, looked over her shoulder at him. "One last thing. Brad's ex-wife—"

"Liz."

"You know her?"

"We met one day, when she was leaving your mom's."

"Oh." Sienna digested that, uncertain why it made her feel uneasy. "I just . . . I found out today that she knew about the bin. She and Mom put something in it together."

His eyebrows shot up. "Something?"

"My baby teeth."

"Weird."

She smiled; she couldn't help herself. A moment later, the smile faded. "Mom thinks if I want to know who put the coat and gloves in the bin, I should find the person who pushed her down the stairs."

He was quiet for a moment. "She has a point, Sienna. *If* she got pushed down the stairs at all."

CHAPTER SIXTY-ONE

10:10 A.M.

Every morning when Sienna opened her eyes, the question crashed down on her: Would today be the day she learned whether the knife was a murder weapon or a perverse hoax?

And every day, she would watch the hours tick past. Waiting. Anxious. Unable to truly focus on anything else. Hoping, praying, that her gut was lying to her. That it wasn't true. Then, exhausted, she would sleep. Only to awaken and repeat the process.

Not today. Not a repeat. She pressed the cell phone tighter to her ear. "What did you say?"

"The results are positive, Sienna. The DNA sample from the knife matched Madison Robie's."

"Oh my God." She found a chair and sank onto it, the nightmare becoming fully real. "This can't be happening."

"I'm sorry, Sienna."

She struggled to speak. "What . . . happens next?"

"We bring your brother in for questioning."

Tears stung her eyes. "Are you . . . going to arrest him?"

"We have the right to hold him for twenty-four hours without an arrest. That's all I can say right now."

"What about my mom?"

"We'll need to question her as well."

Sienna squeezed her eyes shut, picturing it. Her mother being questioned by Randy and Chief Thompson, breaking down, having a full-on psychotic episode. This was her every delusion come to life. Reality, the ultimate trigger.

"She'll fall apart. You know how she is."

"I can't help that, Sienna. We have to find out what she knows."

"Let me question her then. Or Dr. Margery."

"We can't do that, I'm sorry."

"I've talked to her about the coat and bin already." Sienna heard the desperation in her own voice. "She didn't even start the bin until after Dad died. And she didn't know anything about the coat."

She heard him expel a long breath. "Did you say anything about the knife?"

"No."

"Good. I'm sorry, Sienna. We have to question her."

"Then, not at the police station." To hell with pride, she decided. She would beg if she had to. "Please, Randy. Promise me. You know how she is."

"I do." His voice softened. "And so does the chief. We will take that into consideration."

"I'll have to be there—"

"That won't be possible."

"Or her psychiatrist. This will trigger an episode, I'm sure of it."

"She's still at Evergreen?"

"I'm picking her up today. She's coming home."

"Good to know. I'll talk to the chief."

"Promise me, Randy."

"I'll try, but I can't promise, Sienna. And I'll let you know what we decide—"

"Wait! Don't hang up."

For a long moment, silence stretched between them. She fought falling apart. She had to say this. "He didn't do it, Randy. If you ever cared about me, trust me. I know he didn't."

"I appreciate that he's your brother, Sienna. And that you're loyal to him, but—"

"This isn't that. Not just that, anyway. Find his ex-wife. Elizabeth Talbot. I think she might be—" Sienna heard a click as he hung up, but finished her thought anyway. "—involved." She held the phone to her ear a moment, heart thundering, panic taking her ability to think.

No, Sienna. Deep, even breaths.

She followed her own order. Deep breath in through the nose, out through the mouth.

What to do?

Again. In. And out.

In. And out.

Call Brad. Do it now.

She punched in his number. He answered immediately. "Sienna, thank God. I'm so sorry—"

"The police are coming for you, Brad. Call a lawyer. Now."

"I'm working on getting the money back. One investor—"

"This isn't about the money, Brad. They think you killed Madison Robie."

"What? That's crazy—"

"Call your lawyer," she repeated. "And don't talk to them until he gets there."

"You're scaring me, Half-pint."

"You should be scared. They found the knife used to kill Madison in Mom's closet."

"That can't be . . ." She heard the sound of strident

voices in the background, then her brother's "Oh my God . . ."

"They're there, aren't they?"

"Yes. I've got to go. I'll call you back later."

CHAPTER SIXTY-TWO

10:50 A.M.

Sienna had promised Jonathan she would share the DNA results with him as soon as she knew them. She could have called or sent a text, but the truth was, she needed to see him. Just to look into his eyes, maybe for the very last time.

She fully expected him never to want to see her again.

When he didn't answer his doorbell, she knocked loudly, waited, then tried again. Finally, she had to admit he wasn't home. She turned to go, just in time to see a white van coming down the street.

Acting on instinct, she ran toward it, waving her arms and calling for it to stop. Even with tinted windows, there was no way the driver didn't see her. Yet, instead of stopping, the driver gunned the engine and roared past her.

Sienna chased after it a moment, then stopped, out of breath and frustrated. The driver had obviously seen her. Then why not stop?

Obviously because he, or she, either didn't want to answer her questions or didn't want to reveal their identity. Or both.

Randy had told her that her brother paid some guys to drive by her mother's house several times a day for the same reason he'd been calling and hanging up—to trigger a delusional episode. But why would he still be doing it? Her mom had been institutionalized for the past two weeks.

She looked over her shoulder at the rumble of an engine. Jonathan's truck, she saw. He turned into his driveway, and Sienna headed his way. She reached the truck just as he swung out of the cab.

"What's going on?" he asked.

"What do you mean?"

He frowned slightly. "You were standing in the middle of the street, Sienna."

"Oh, that." Her cheeks heated. "The white van just passed. I tried to get the driver to stop, obviously without luck."

His frown deepened. "You ran into the street?"

"Waving my arms and shouting. It was sort of impulsive."

"I'll say." He reached into the cab and came out with a couple grocery bags. "You hear from the cops about the knife?"

"This morning. I was on my way over to tell you when I saw the van."

"And?"

"Results were positive. They're questioning my brother now."

"Damn." He looked away, then back. "Thanks for letting me know."

"Jonathan . . . He didn't do it."

For a long moment he said nothing, then he nodded. "I hope not. See you around, Sienna."

She watched as he headed inside, praying he would glance back, the way he used to. Her prayers went unanswered. Feeling as if her heart had shattered into a billion tiny pieces, she headed back across the street.

Sienna used the twenty-minute drive to the behavioral hospital to calm herself and collect her thoughts. Her mom had worked hard to get healthy the past couple of weeks; Sienna owed it to her to give her as drama-free a homecoming as possible.

Dr. Margery was waiting for her. Sienna greeted the woman. "How's Mom today?"

"Doing well. Excited to be going home." The doctor eyed her, a concerned frown creasing her brow. "How are you?"

"Truthfully? A bit anxious."

"That's understandable. Let's talk a moment."

She indicated Sienna should follow, and led her to a consult room. The room's interior was a soothing mix of beach colors, like sand, sea foam, and blue, its fabrics all cozy and reassuring.

They sat and Sienna resisted the urge to hug one of the soft, squishy throw pillows to her chest, although she didn't doubt many an anxious family member before her had done exactly that.

"How can I help you, Sienna?"

Sienna resisted releasing the nervous laugh that wanted to spring from her lips. "How about you tell me everything's going to be okay?"

She nodded, expression understanding. "I can't promise you that, but I think it will be. And I know things will be better. The medication is already helping."

She set two vials on the coffee table between them. She held up the first. "This is Zyprexa, the same antipsychotic drug she was taking before, although we've adjusted the dose. It's helping restore the balance of chemicals in her brain, so she's experiencing less anxiety and agitation. It's also helping her think more clearly, and has decreased her paranoiac tendencies."

"Here in the bubble," Sienna said.

Dr. Margery smiled. "That's true. But I expect you to see the same results at home. She must take this every day, as close to the same time as possible. She's adjusted very well to this dose, exhibiting limited side effects."

"Which are?"

"Weight gain and insomnia. Which brings me to the second medication I'm prescribing, Sonata. This is a sleep aid, but it's only to be used when she's too agitated to sleep. We discovered that's she particularly fearful at night, which keeps her from resting. Lack of sleep then increases her paranoia. Obviously, creating a vicious cycle."

"Thank you." Sienna collected the vials and put them in her handbag.

The therapist crossed her legs. "Do you have any other questions or concerns?"

"Besides making certain she takes her medication, what can I do to help her?"

"You know her triggers. Be cognizant of them without enabling her."

"Can you give me an example?"

"Of course. Her fears revolve around your safety. Just let her know where you're going and when you'll be back. If you're running late, let her know."

"Like I did when I was a teenager."

She smiled slightly and nodded. "Yes. As you know, your mother has an Axis I psychotic disorder. The medication helps her manage the illness, it doesn't cure it. Encourage her to share her fears with you, then gently focus her on reality. She can call me anytime, as can you."

"Thank you. I'm sure you'll be hearing from us."

The therapist cocked her head. "Is something else worrying you? You seem distracted."

"I am." Sienna clasped her hands together in her lap. "Remember the situation we discussed the last time I was here? The bin and the bloodstained coat?"

She inclined her head and Sienna went on. "What I didn't tell you is, there was a knife in the box as well."

"A knife?" Her unnaturally smooth brow furrowed. "I don't understand."

"One that looked like it could be a murder weapon. *The* murder weapon."

She seemed to recoil slightly as Sienna's words sank in.

"I didn't mention it because I'd hoped it wasn't what I thought it was." Sienna cleared her throat. "But lab results confirmed that it was, indeed, the knife used to kill Madison Robie ten years ago."

"Dear God."

It was the most ruffled Sienna had ever seen the woman.

"They don't think your mother—"

"No. My brother."

"Your brother?"

Sienna leaned forward. "I believe he's innocent, and I wouldn't be telling you all this now, except the police insist they'll have to question Mom."

For a long moment the therapist was quiet. "When?"

"Soon, I suspect."

"That makes me nervous. I don't know how she'll react."

Sienna twisted her fingers together. "I couldn't dissuade them—believe me, I tried. What can we do?"

"Not much, I'm afraid. Let me call a judge who's a friend of mine, ask her advice. For now, the important thing is for you to be calm. Focus on your mom and her homecoming."

"You mean, pretend none of this is happening?"

"Essentially. If you act normal, she'll follow your lead."

Act normal, Sienna thought ten minutes later as she collected her mother. A neat trick considering her brother was a murder suspect, the murder weapon had been discovered in her home, an unmarked van kept cruising by her house, and she'd fallen in love with a man who happened to be the brother of the woman her brother was suspected of murdering.

Normal, things were not.

CHAPTER SIXTY-THREE

9:10 A.M.

"You at that window again?"

Sienna looked over her shoulder at her mother. "Just looking out at the day."

"Really?" Her mother joined her at the front window, handing her a mug of freshly brewed coffee. "And last night, you were just staring out at the dark street?"

"Yes, what else?" She took a sip of the coffee.

"You really want me to answer that?"

"How did you sleep?" Sienna asked, turning and crossing to the couch.

Her mother didn't fall for the diversion. "He's very handsome."

"Who?" she asked, feigning ignorance.

"Really, Sienna? We're going to play that game? Jonathan. Across the street."

"You know his name?"

"Of course. He introduced himself." When Sienna didn't reply, she went on. "Are you seeing him?"

"I was."

"What happened?"

"I made a mistake. A big one."

Her mother brought her mug to her lips. "Tell him you're sorry."

"I did. Sorry didn't cover it."

Her mother came and sat beside her. "What could be that bad?"

"Suspecting someone of being a murderer."

Sienna would have laughed at her mother's expression, if it didn't hurt so bad. "It's a long story," she said.

"It seems like we have lots of time."

Sienna set her coffee on the side table. "I saw something when I was over at his place, and it gave me the wrong idea."

"Well, that's clear as glass."

Sienna couldn't help smiling. "Funny, Mom." When her mother didn't respond, she sighed. "Jonathan is Madison Robie's brother. I saw some pictures of her and thought . . ."

"Oh." Viv set down her coffee as well. "Were you . . . are you in love with him?"

"It doesn't matter." She blinked against sudden tears. "It's over now."

"Are you sure? I made a lot of mistakes and your dad—"

"You and Dad were special. Let's talk about something else. Okay?"

Her mother didn't even have to agree, because the doorbell sounded. She sent her mother an amused glance and stood. "Saved by the bell."

It was Chief Thompson, she discovered. "Hello, Chief." The words came out tight, and she told herself to breathe.

"Sienna." He looked past her. "Viv. Can I come in?"

Her mother stepped forward. "Of course, Fred. Let me take your coat."

He shrugged out of it, then tugged off his gloves and stuck them into a pocket. He handed them over.

She smiled. "I just brewed some coffee. Would you like a cup?"

"I would. Thank you, Viv."

As soon as her mother cleared earshot, Sienna turned to him. "What's happening?"

He didn't have to ask about what. "We released your brother. We didn't have enough to charge him."

Which meant he still thought he was guilty. "He didn't do it."

"I wouldn't expect you to say anything different."

Of course he wouldn't. "You need to find his ex-wife."

"We did."

Her heart seemed to miss a beat. "And what did she say?"

"She readily admitted she knew about the bin, and told us the same story your mother told you about the tooth box."

"But—"

He held up a hand. "She said the bin was maybe a quarter filled. She told Viv she would help her add to it if she liked. Your mother declined."

In other words, no coat and no gloves.

"We asked her why her marriage to your brother ended."

She folded her arms. "And?"

"She couldn't deal with his anger and bitterness over your father's will anymore. Apparently, when business was booming, it wasn't a huge issue. But the minute he ran into financial difficulty, he changed. She told us it broke her heart."

"What are you two talking so seriously about?" Viv asked, appearing in the doorway with a tray carrying coffee service and a plate of muffins.

"Nothing much," he said, his voice big and warm. "And what do you have there, Vivienne Scott?"

"Sienna made these," she said, smiling proudly. "They're pistachio-chai. But don't let the name scare you off, they're delicious."

She waved him toward the living room seating area. "Come, let's sit down."

They did. He prepared his coffee—with a frightening amount of sugar and a splash of cream—then took a sip. "Viv, you always did make a mean cup of coffee."

Sienna sat back a moment, watching as they laughed and reminisced, listening as they discussed the old days and the things they'd done as couples. He was, quite simply and deliberately, charming her. And her mother was . . . delightful. The woman, Sienna imagined, her father had fallen in love with.

As her mother chatted with her old friend, Sienna acknowledged she'd never seen her this way before, so lighthearted and free. Or if she had, she'd forgotten, those memories crowded out by darker ones.

When did her mother's psychosis take over? Was it a gradual overtaking, or did a switch inside her just flip one day? Maybe the day she gave birth to her daughter?

Sienna hoped not. She would hate being the one who'd extinguished this beautiful light.

"Viv," Chief Thompson said, tone turning serious, "I needed to ask you a few questions. You think you're up to that?"

Sienna held her breath, realizing what he meant and where this conversation was going.

"From you, my old friend, of course."

"I appreciate that, Viv. Thank you." He paused a moment. "Sienna tells me she shared with you about finding her old coat in a bin in your closet."

The twinkle faded from her mother's eyes, and Sienna wanted to jump up and shout *"No!"* She didn't want to lose the bright, happy woman she'd just discovered.

"The coat she was wearing *that* night," he continued.

Viv set her coffee on the table and folded her hands in her lap. "The night Madison Robie was murdered."

"Yes," he agreed. "When was the last time you saw that jacket?"

"The last time I saw Sienna wearing it, I suppose. Probably the weekend before the murder."

"I stopped by home at least once every weekend," Sienna offered.

"After Robie's murder, did Dan ever mention it?"

"The coat?"

"Yes. That he had retrieved it from the police, anything like that?"

She thought a moment, then shook her head. "No. Never. Other than saying that it had been entered into evidence. But I do remember buying her a new one." She looked at Sienna. "What color was it? Pink?"

"Neon pink."

"You and I always look our best in pink." She smiled at the chief. "It's our hair."

"And beautiful it is." He smiled. "Do you have any thoughts on how the coat and gloves may have ended up in a plastic bin in your closet?"

"I do."

Sienna couldn't hide her surprise. "You do, Mom?"

"Yes, I already told you. Find the person who pushed me down the stairs, and you'll find the one who had the coat."

"Viv," Fred said gently, "Brad maintains you tripped and fell down the stairs."

"That's what I told him, but I lied."

"Why?"

"I didn't want him to think I was crazy."

In another situation, Sienna might have laughed at the irony. The whole town thought her mother was crazy for things much less serious.

Fred leaned toward her. He lowered his voice. "Maybe it was Brad himself who pushed you down the stairs?"

"Bradley?" She arched her eyebrows. "Oh, no. It wasn't him."

"How do you know?"

"He loved his father too much. Besides, why would he?"

"If you die, he inherits the money Dan left you."

She thought a moment. "No, it wasn't him."

"What about his ex-wife? Maybe she was angry over her and Brad's marriage breaking up, and decided to make you and him pay for hurting her?"

"She wasn't even part of the family back then. How would she have come into possession of the coat?"

Sienna couldn't hide her surprise at her mother's calm, rational responses to the chief's questions. She realized that when someone suffered with mental illness you started to see them as less able, or less intelligent, but that wasn't the case at all.

"I know it was neither of them," she said. "Neither of them smell like that."

"Like what?" Chief Thompson asked.

She looked at Sienna. "You know how sensitive my nose is. Right before I was pushed, there was this smell. Like fresh-cut pine. But sweeter."

For a long moment, the chief seemed to digest that. "And neither Bradley nor his ex ever smelled like that?"

"Never."

"Interesting." His cell phone sounded; he checked

the display, then declined the call. "Seems folks are looking for me. I better move along."

"But you haven't even touched your muffin," Viv said.

"That is a shame," he said. "How about I wrap it in a napkin and take it along for later?"

Her mother insisted on wrapping up enough to share when he got back to the station. When she went to the kitchen to get them, Sienna turned to the chief. "Thank you for being so careful with her. And thank you for doing it here and allowing me to be present. Randy didn't think that was going to be possible."

"Detective Clark doesn't speak for me. I do things my way."

"I'm sure glad you do." Sienna lowered her voice. "You didn't mention the knife. That was what I worried most about her reaction to."

"Didn't think I had to. Might sometime in the future, but not today."

"Here we go." Her mother returned with a small basket of the pastries covered with a pretty towel.

"You're an angel, Viv," he said, taking the basket from her. "This is going to be a real treat for my officers. They'll need one, with this nasty weather moving in."

"Weather's moving in?" Sienna opened the door. Sure enough, just in the time since Chief Thompson had arrived, the temperature had dropped and the sky had turned a heavy gray.

"Big system out of Canada, supposed to dump a whole lot of snow on us, starting this afternoon. It's been all over the news the last couple days. Meteorologist says to expect blizzard-like conditions."

"Guess I've been a little distracted." Sienna looked at her mother. "I better make certain we have all the necessaries, in case the power goes out and we're snowed in."

The chief stepped outside. "I think that's a good idea. Things are going to get real bad."

They watched him climb into his car and drive off. When he had disappeared from view, her mother sighed. "Well, you know what they say, when March comes in like a lion, it goes out like a lamb."

CHAPTER SIXTY-FOUR

10:30 A.M.

Sienna made a list of items to pick up, everything from bottled water to batteries, canned soup and stew, to snacks for when the stir-crazy-blizzard-munchies set in.

"I'm going to pick all this up, Mom, then stop and see Brad."

Her mother nodded in agreement, but looked anxious. "How long will you be gone?"

"I'm not sure—the store's likely to be a madhouse and who knows how long it'll take to locate batteries. But I'll keep you posted." She looked her in the eyes. "Trust me, Mom. Okay?"

Viv took a deep breath. "I can do that."

"Good. You could come along, but there's no sense in both of us being out in the weather." She searched her mother's expression. "Are you sure you're okay with this?"

"Yes. Absolutely. Just keep me posted."

Sienna promised she would and headed out. And, as she expected, everyone else in Tranquility Bluffs was doing the same thing she was. And as she feared, the shelves holding batteries, bread, and bottled water had been picked clean.

It took three stops, keeping her mom posted on each, to purchase everything on her list. By that time the wind had picked up and long dark clouds crowded the sky.

Sienna dialed her mother. "I've got everything and am on my way to see Brad."

"I'm thinking you should come home. It's looking pretty bad out there."

Sienna heard the distress in her mother's voice and worked to calm her. "Mom, it hasn't even started snowing. I've got the radio on and am getting constant updates, and promise I won't put myself in harm's way."

"Is he at his office or home?"

"The office, I hope. I'll let you know for sure. I thought I'd ask him to ride out the storm with us. What do you think?"

"I like that idea. I'll wait to hear from you."

Unfortunately, Brad's office was dark and obviously locked down tight. Which meant she'd have to make the trip to his place, along winding, much less traveled roads.

She checked the dash clock. It was twelve forty-five and the storm wasn't supposed to hit until two; plenty of time, she decided.

She called, left him a message, and headed that way. Twenty minutes later, she saw that his place looked as unoccupied as his office. She went to the door anyway, rang the bell, then pounded.

"Brad," she called, "it's me! If you're home, answer the door."

Just as she gave up, he came to the door. He looked like hell. "Visiting the enemy camp? And on a day like today, no less."

"You're not the enemy, Brad. Can I come in?"

He stepped aside, then closed the door behind her.

Without inviting her to sit, he crossed to the couch and slumped onto it. "I screwed everything up. Our relationship. My marriage. Your future. Mine." He lifted his head, looked at her. "I'm so sorry."

He started to cry. She'd never seen him cry, not even as a child. He'd been one of those guys who pulled himself together and soldiered on, too proud to let her— or anyone else—see his pain.

A lump formed in her throat. She swallowed hard and crossed to the couch, taking a seat beside him. Putting her arm around him, she rested her head on his shoulder.

Minutes ticked past, silence stretching between them. He broke it first. "I love you, Half-pint. From the first moment I saw you, I never wanted to be anything but your hero."

He tipped his face to hers. "So how could I be so jealous of you? So resentful?"

He didn't expect an answer and went on. "I hated myself for it. I hated Dad for favoring you, but didn't blame him. I favored you, too." He let out a long, sad-sounding breath. "How screwed-up is that?"

"It sounds completely human to me," she said softly. "I'm sorry I didn't know. That I didn't see. I'm sorry I was so involved with myself, and my fear of being like Mom, that I took you for granted."

She paused. "You *were* my hero, Brad. You were the one who was always there for me. Always a cushion between me and Mom. And now I see that wasn't fair. Not at all."

"I would never try to hurt you, Half-pint. Let alone . . . kill you?" The word came out choked, as if he had to force himself even to say it. "Oh my God, the questions they asked . . . they kept hammering and hammering at me . . . They don't believe me. They let me go, but they still think I did that."

"I don't." She turned to him, caught both his hands. "I know you, despite the money stuff . . . you're kind. You're a good man, just like Dad was."

He started to cry again, and this time she did, too. When they both stopped, he hugged her. "Can you forgive me?"

"I already have."

"I'm going to get your money back. I already have one investor who's back on board—"

"Let's not worry about that now. We've got bigger fish to fry."

His expression turned pensive. "How'd that stuff end up in the bin?"

"Mom's convinced whoever pushed her down the stairs did it."

"They accused me of that, too," he said bitterly. "So I could get her money."

"And we both know you didn't. Mom, too."

"That surprises me. Last time you and I talked, she'd lumped me in with the 'the bad guys.'"

"She's better now. Her stay at Evergreen worked wonders." Sienna glanced at her watch. "She said something interesting. That whoever pushed her smelled like pine."

"Pine," he repeated. "Like a cleaning solution?"

"I hadn't thought of that, but it could be. I'd focused on an aftershave. She described it as pine, but sweeter."

He drew his eyebrows together. "That'll give me something to think on during the storm."

"Come stay with me and Viv. We'll ride it out together."

"I'm not fit company."

"You're family. You don't have to be good company."

He laughed. "I'll think about it."

She stood. "Don't think too long." She indicated the wall of windows across from them. "Look, it's started snowing already."

CHAPTER SIXTY-FIVE

2:40 P.M.

Sienna gripped the steering wheel tightly. The snow fell so heavily she could barely see the road, and with every gust of wind, she had to fight to keep her vehicle from drifting out of her lane.

She couldn't believe how quickly the snowfall had changed from Christmas morning dream to winter nightmare. She crept along, acknowledging that she was out of practice when it came to driving in these conditions, and being thankful for how little traffic was on the road.

It took her almost three times as long to get back to the Tranquility Bluffs city limits from Brad's as it had taken her to get there in the first place. She breathed a sigh of relief, knowing that at least if she went off the road now, help would be close.

The light ahead turned yellow, then red, and the car ahead of her, unable to stop in time, skidded through the intersection. In horror, Sienna watched as it spun off the road and slammed into a tree. With a sickening crunch, the car's front end folded like an accordion.

"Oh my God!" Sienna resisted the impulse to slam on the brakes, and eased to the side of the road, nearly sliding off and into the ditch anyway. She climbed out of her car and, battling against the snow and wind, made her way to the other car. A young woman sat behind the wheel and deflating airbag, bleeding from her nose and mouth.

Sienna rapped on the window. "Hey! Are you okay?"

The girl turned her head and stared blankly at Sienna, obviously in shock.

"Hold tight! I'm calling nine-one-one."

Sienna hurried back to her car and made the call. The dispatcher asked her to stay with the victim but cautioned her not to try to move her. Before she left the car again, Sienna sent a quick text to her mother, then trudged back, the wet and cold seeping through her boots. Her lightweight knit gloves were no match for the weather, and her fingers began to go numb. She clapped them together, scolding herself for leaving the house so unprepared.

When she reached the other vehicle, she saw the driver was crying.

"The police are coming!" Sienna said, shouting to be heard above the wind and through the glass. "Hold tight. Try not to move."

Her words didn't reassure, and the teen's tears turned to sobs. She tugged on the door handle. "Let me out! I have to get . . . please help me!"

Sienna didn't know what to do. The 911 dispatcher had instructed her not to move the victim, but she was so agitated, Sienna feared she would hurt herself if she didn't help her get out of the car.

"Try to calm down. My name's Sienna. What yours?"

Her level of hysteria seemed to drop. "Mandy."

"Okay, Mandy. The police are on their way. I promise you, help will be here any moment."

"I want to get out. The door's stuck." She tugged on the handle again.

"Check the lock, Mandy. Where is the lever for—"

As she said the words, she heard the faint cry of a siren. A moment later she saw the flash of blue and red.

"They're here!" Sienna cried. "Look!"

In the next instant, both a cruiser and an ambulance arrived. Teeth chattering, Sienna stepped aside so they could do what they needed to do.

She could have gone back to her car, could have left, for that matter, but something kept her riveted to the spot. The police officer was businesslike but gentle, his gloved hands quick but steady as he freed the teen from the safety belt and all but lifted her out.

The teenager crumpled against the officer, clinging to him and sobbing. Was that how she had been that night? Sienna wondered. Both hysterical and in shock, if such a thing was possible. She remembered Randy, then unknown to her, just another campus cop, how he had calmed her.

An image from that night filled her head. Of Randy, stooping beside the body, then reaching out, pressing his fingers to her neck, checking her pulse.

"Miss?"

She blinked and the image evaporated. The cop's face came into view. She saw the paramedics were with the teenager.

"We've got this. She's going to be fine. Thank you for your assistance."

She nodded, but didn't move.

He frowned. "Are you okay? Feel steady enough to drive?"

"What?"

"You able to drive? The roads aren't getting any better."

She pulled herself together and forced a confident nod. "Yes. Thank you."

Sienna made her way back to her car. After stomping her feet and brushing off as much snow as possible, she climbed in. She'd left it running so it was nice and warm. She pulled off her wet gloves and held her hands up to the vent.

As she did, her thoughts tumbled back to that night. Of being so cold she thought she'd never be warm again. Of Randy tugging off her wet, bloodstained gloves, then guiding her hands to the vent, to warm them just this way. She remembered how cold his hands had been, how chapped from the elements.

Sienna jumped at the short, shrill scream of a siren. The police officer, signaling her to go. She lifted a hand in acknowledgment, then eased back onto the road.

CHAPTER SIXTY-SIX

Sienna almost cried in relief when she caught sight of home. The drive from where she'd witnessed the accident to here had been harrowing, the number of cars and trucks in the ditch sobering. Light spilled from the front windows, and as she turned into the drive, she saw her mother peering out. A little too anxious to be home, Sienna gave the vehicle too much gas, and the big old sedan fishtailed. She overcorrected in response, spun off the drive and into the lawn.

With an exhausted squeak, she rested her forehead on the steering wheel. It could have been worse. So much worse.

Deciding it made more sense to leave the car where it was, she collected the groceries and climbed out. And sank into calf-high snow. Her mother met her at the door with a towel and slippers.

"I was so worried," she said, taking the bags.

Sienna shrugged out of her coat and yanked off her boots. "Me, too. I can't tell you how happy I am to be home." She searched her mother's expression, looking for the telltale signs of an impending meltdown. "Are you okay? No dark thoughts?"

"A few," her mother admitted. "But ones involving

traffic accidents and hypothermia, not vicious ex-wives plotting to harm my only daughter."

Sienna smiled slightly. "I can live with that."

"Me, too. Bradley's not coming?"

"He was going to think about it, then decided to stay put."

Viv nodded. "Why don't you go change? I'll put the groceries away and heat us up some soup."

Sienna nodded. "That sounds good, I'm starving." She started up the stairs, then stopped and looked back. "I'm going to take a hot shower, too. I won't be too long."

Twenty minutes later, warmed to her core from the shower, and dressed in her softest flannel pants and favorite old sweatshirt, she dug a pair of woolly socks from the bottom of her sock drawer. As she bent to put them on, her gaze landed on something sticking out from under her desk.

Her journal, she saw a moment later. How did it end up on the floor? Frowning, she retrieved it. As she did, a receipt fluttered to the floor. She scooped it up, noting it was from Jimmy's Hardware downtown, then tucked it back into the book.

"Sienna," her mother called from the bottom of the stairs, "soup's ready!"

"Coming," she called back, then tugged on her socks and headed down.

They ate their grilled-cheese sandwiches and soup at the breakfast counter. Halfway through, the power went out, and they finished their meal by candlelight. Afterward, Sienna made a fire and they sat in front of it, her mother flipping through old magazines while she amused herself browsing online and playing Candy Crush Saga. They took turns jumping up to look nervously out at the mounting snow.

The hours dragged by. Sienna's thoughts kept turning to the accident she'd witnessed that afternoon. She kept picturing that cop freeing the teenager from her car, something about it plucking at her.

But what? The cop had been efficient and professional. So why did it feel wrong?

From there, her thoughts skipped to this morning, to Chief Thompson's visit. His showing up that way had been pleasant, but seemed sort of weird now. Him stopping by with a big storm moving in, the leisurely way he'd questioned her mother. Taking all that time and care to charm her.

And for what? A couple quick questions about the coat and gloves. Ones that could have been easily answered by phone. Sienna turned the things he said over in her mind. Nothing jumped out as unusual, and yet she had this feeling she'd overlooked something important.

"What's wrong?"

Her mother was looking at her, her eyebrows drawn together in a small frown.

"Nothing, really. Just thinking about the chief's visit this morning."

Viv's frown faded. "It made me think of the old days. And your dad. I miss him so much."

"What's the chief's wife like?"

"Carol? She's very nice. We used to be friends."

"Maybe you could be again?"

Her mother looked at her in surprise. "Do you think so?"

"Why not? The Vivienne Scott I saw this morning would be fun to hang out with."

"I don't know. Maybe."

"If you got out more, maybe you'd meet someone."

"To date?"

She sounded horrified, and Sienna smiled. "Why not?"

"It's not that I wouldn't be interested, but the truth is, your father was the only man who could put up with me. I come with a heck of a lot of baggage."

Sienna laughed and touched her hand. "Don't we all?"

"Not like mine."

Sienna rested her head against the couch back, face tipped toward her mother's. "I love you, Mom."

Her eyes grew misty. "I love you, too."

"Why don't you go to bed? I'll keep watch."

"I won't be able to sleep. I'm too anxious."

"Take a sleeping pill. I think Dr. Margery would approve."

"I don't know." She wrung her hands. "What if I sleep through something important?"

Sienna grinned. "And what would that be? Me snoring on the couch? Or the power coming on in the middle of the night? Besides, Dr. Margery said this medication provides a light sleep. I'll wake you up if there's an emergency."

Her mother agreed. Sienna walked her up to bed, setting a small flashlight on the night table.

"Night, Mom," she said. "See you in the morning."

"Leave the door open, would you, sweetheart?"

"How's this?" she asked, leaving it cracked halfway open.

Her mother approved, and Sienna headed back downstairs, amazed at the dramatic change in her mother. Just a few short weeks ago, her mother not only insisted on closing and locking the door, she'd barricaded herself in, as well.

Sienna crossed to the front window and peered out. Still snowing heavily, she saw. Deeper than ever.

And still no signs of life at Jonathan's place.

Was he there? She wondered. Hunkered down, the way she was, waiting for the storm to pass and the new day to dawn.

She missed him. Missed the way they laughed together. Missed his arms, his smile, his gentle touch. Missed making love. The passion he'd awakened in her that no one else had.

Her eyes burned and she blinked against the tears. Stupid tears. Crying didn't help. She'd blown it. And there wasn't a damn thing she could do about it now.

She marched to the couch, angry at herself. She sat and flipped through one of her mother's magazines, then tossed it aside, frustrated. She laid her head back and stared at the ceiling.

The wind howled. The house creaked and groaned. The branch of the big old maple tree tap . . . tap . . . tapped on the window. Her thoughts turned once again to the accident. The officer. The girl's bloodied face. Her white coat blemished with dots of red.

Dark red creeping across brilliant white.

Dammit. Sienna jumped up, strode to the front window, once again gazing across at Jonathan's place. As if doing so would provide answers. Something about the events of today was still niggling at her, like the buzz of an insect she couldn't seem to shoo away.

She thought of her dad. They used to work on jigsaw puzzles together. He loved them—and she'd loved spending time with him. Truthfully, she always wondered if he'd found them reassuring because he was able to create order out of chaos, one piece at a time—a control he couldn't exert over his life because of her mother's mental illness.

"Sienna," he would say when she got frustrated, "clear the clutter in your head and visualize the picture you're creating. Calmly focus on the picture and how each piece fits in."

That was it, she realized. What she needed to do. After all, what was this but a puzzle? She took a deep, calming breath, closed her eyes, and pushed away worries about the storm and thoughts of Jonathan; cleared her mind of frustration and grief.

And focused on the events of the day.

She and her mother talking. Chief Thompson at the door. Her mother, the charming, gracious hostess. The chief, asking about the coat and gloves. Her mother's answers, then the bombshell about the smell of pine.

Pine cleaner. Who smelled like that? A janitor? A nurse?

She reined in her thoughts, backed up. She was going too fast, going for the big picture before examining the small pieces.

The chief at the door. Her mother, taking his coat. Him, stuffing his gloves into his coat pocket. The muffins, her mother's pride; the way the lawman had cajoled her mother.

His questions. Every one of them about the bloodstained parka and gloves.

He'd zeroed in on them.

Why? What was he thinking?

Sienna left those questions, and moved forward. The pending storm. Running errands, gathering supplies. Visiting her brother.

A lump formed in her throat. He was devastated. Ashamed of what he'd done. But not a murderer.

Snow falling, god-awful conditions. The accident she witnessed. Sienna pictured it in her head: the vehicle skidding off the road; fighting her way through the snowstorm to the disabled car; the white coat of the teenager behind the wheel; the drops of blood on it.

Obvious why that would have not only triggered thoughts of the night of Madison's murder, but elicited a similar emotional response as well.

But none of that was what bothered her.

Sienna moved forward. The sound of sirens. The police officer helping the victim. Her standing there, as if transfixed. She'd been staring at his gloves while he worked to free the girl from the car.

The chief removing his gloves.

The officer today, gloved hands nimbly working to free the accident victim.

Sienna's mind spun back in time, to the night of the murder. Randy's hands, chapped from the elements, icy on hers as he tugged off her gloves and brought her hands to the warm air streaming out of the cruiser's vent.

That's what had been plucking at the back of her brain, the piece of the puzzle she'd been searching for.

Randy wasn't wearing gloves the night of the murder.

CHAPTER SIXTY-SEVEN

Sienna spun away from the window. It didn't mean anything. Randy was her friend. He'd been kind to her, had helped her through the most difficult time in her life.

But why would a cop on patrol in a blizzard not wear gloves?

Lack of mobility? The cop today seemed to have no problem with that. All manner of specialty items were manufactured for law enforcement, no doubt gloves were as well.

What if he had removed them? But why would he have?

The same reason she'd removed hers. Blood. His gloves would have been soaked with it.

Bile rose in her throat. Sienna forced it back. She was doing it again, wasn't she? Building a case against someone she cared about. Just like she had with Jonathan, her mother, then her brother.

She had to stop this. Now.

Think of something else, Sienna. The restaurant you'll own one day. Plan the menu.

Yes. The menu. Sienna started to pace again. Recipes. Which favorites would she want to include?

What dishes would she want to be known for? She forced herself to focus. Coq au vin, she decided. Mentally, she pulled out the recipe, began checking off each ingredient.

She made it through the first ten, then she found herself asking something she hadn't before: How did Randy get to the scene so quickly? She'd screamed and he'd appeared.

She drew her eyebrows together in thought. Could he have heard her, parked his cruiser, climbed out, and made it to her side in the short amount of time? Would he even have been able to hear her scream? Windows up, motor running, wind howling?

She stopped, brought a hand to her mouth. Why would Randy kill Madison Robie?

"She was seeing another guy. Someone older."

If Randy was that guy, jealousy. Fury that Madison refused to stop seeing Reed, or even that she called it quits with him instead of Reed?

She twisted her fingers together as she paced. *Think it through, Sienna.* How could Randy have planted the knife, coat, and gloves in the bin? When would he have done it? And where would he have gotten her coat?

The TBPD had taken her coat and gloves the night of the murder.

Sienna shook her head. But that night, the detective told her dad that they would release the items in the next day or two.

Release them to the family.

But what if "the family" never came for them? Nothing, she'd bet. All these years they'd probably been safely tucked away in some evidence locker.

The TBPD. The knot in her chest tightened. Back then, Randy wouldn't have had access to the case evidence. But he did now.

She stopped, took a deep breath, thoughts whirling. So, assuming Randy took the coat and gloves from TBPD evidence, and that he *was* the one who put them in the bin, when would he have had the opportunity?

The night of her mother's meltdown. Sienna left with the ambulance. She'd told Randy to do whatever he needed to.

He'd had complete access to the house for hours. No one would have questioned him being there. He was a cop, investigating a crime scene.

Was she grasping at straws? Manipulating the facts to create her own "truth," the way her mother did?

No. Not this time.

Slow down, Sienna. Take your mind back to that night. Maybe there's something else, something you're overlooking.

She brought the heels of her hands to her forehead. She recalled the cold. Shivering with it. Her teeth chattering, nose running.

She'd asked for a tissue, and he'd handed her a square of plaid fabric.

She dropped her hands. That was it. It'd smelled faintly of pine. Pine . . . the scent her mother caught right before she was pushed.

Sienna brought a hand to her mouth. Which meant Randy had been in the house that night. And that he was the one who had pushed her mother down the stairs.

The realization rocked her. Gooseflesh raced up her arms.

"Keep it. This time of year, I buy them by the dozen."

She had, she remembered. Kept it. She'd still been clutching it when they took her coat. Sometime between the police station and home, she'd stuffed it into a front pocket of her blue jeans.

She had found it later. After laundering the jeans. There, in the washing machine.

She had meant to give it back and tucked it away—and forgotten about it.

Until now.

Sienna grabbed her flashlight, her dad's big old Maglite, and switched it on. It was a long shot, but there was a chance she still had it. She raced up the stairs, stopping in surprise when she saw her mother's door was shut.

Figuring she had changed her mind and closed it, Sienna moved on to her bedroom. Once inside, she stopped. If, after all these years, the hankie was still here, where would it be?

Sienna went to her desk first, quickly checking the drawers, but coming up empty. She then turned to her dresser, carefully going through the few articles of clothing she'd left behind when she moved to London—most everything in the drawers now had been brought back with her.

Her gaze landed on her window seat, and Sienna hurried to it. She set aside the cushion, lifted the lid. The flashlight beam illuminated the contents as she sorted through them. Favorite old sweatshirts. The teddy bear she'd gotten for her fifth birthday. The sketchbook from the year she had been determined to be a clothing designer. The Disney princess blanket she'd outgrown but couldn't bear to part with. And her black Nike Gym-sack.

She opened the bag. Earbuds. Athletic socks. A pony for her hair and an ancient bottle of moisturizer.

And the square of plaid fabric.

Of course. She used to pass campus police head-quarters on her way to math. She'd planned to pop in and leave the handkerchief for Randy. Obviously, she'd forgotten.

Now, she was grateful she had.

Hand trembling, she brought the square of fabric to her nose.

The very faint scent of pine.

With a soft cry, she backed up, sank onto the corner of the bed. The truth ricocheted through her. That's why he'd gotten to her side so quickly. And why he hadn't been wearing gloves. But no one ever questioned any of it. Of course they hadn't. He was a cop.

She looked at the square of fabric. His explanation of why Madi's murder was personal and not random had been so convincing. No wonder.

And she'd believed everything he told her. Without question.

In a way, she'd helped him get away with murder.

No more. She jumped to her feet. She had to call Chief Thompson. Now. Urgency propelling her, Sienna scrambled for the desk and her phone. As she snatched it up, the receipt from earlier caught her gaze.

She pointed the flashlight at it.

It was dated today.

That couldn't be. That would mean . . .

He had been here. In the house. In her bedroom. *Today.*

Heart thundering in her chest, she lowered her gaze to the list of items purchased.

Road salt. Rope. Duct tape. Sand.

With a cry, she laid the flashlight on the bed, snatched up the phone, and hit the Home button. A missed call and voice mail. From four hours ago. She hit Play and brought the device to her ear. "Sienna, it's Chief Thompson. I'm sending a cruiser to collect you and Viv. I'll explain when you get here, but you're not safe there. I believe I've identified Madison Robie's—"

The message cut off abruptly. Goose bumps prickled at the back of her neck, and a chill slid down her spine. Four hours. Wouldn't the cruiser have arrived by now? Even with the bad weather?

Something had gone wrong.

Sienna pressed *Call Back*. It went straight to voice mail. "Chief, it's Sienna Scott. Is the cruiser still coming? I think I know, too. I'm scared. Please call me back."

"Hello, Sienna."

At the sound of his voice, her mouth went dry. She turned slowly, the heavy thump of her heart painful in her chest.

Randy stood in the doorway, dressed in tactical gear. On his utility belt she saw a knife, a gun, and a rope. He smiled, the stretching of his lips over his teeth almost feral. "No hello for me?"

She tried to respond, but the words stuck in her throat.

"Why are you scared?" he asked softly, taking a step into the room. "It's just me, your old friend, Randy."

Her knees went weak. She didn't know what to do, so she played dumb. "What're you doing here?"

"That's a silly question, Sienna. I've come to collect you."

CHAPTER SIXTY-EIGHT

10:40 P.M.

Randy took another step into the room, shutting the door behind him.

Fear stole her breath. One way out, that's all there was. And it was through him.

Stay calm, Sienna. Think.

"Did the chief send you?" she asked.

"No, the chief did not send me. You should know that."

It didn't make sense, but he sounded hurt. "It's just . . . he left a message. Said he was sending a cruiser, so I thought maybe you were . . ."

"That cruiser's not coming."

Her heart sank. She told herself to breathe. "Are you sure? Because he said—"

"What he wanted doesn't matter anymore. This is about us. You and me." He moved toward her; she instinctively backed up. "It's ironic that tonight is so like that other night; truly, it's a chance for us to rewrite history."

"How did you get in the house, Randy?" she asked, voice surprisingly steady.

"Same way I always do."

The words sank in. They chilled her to her marrow. "The way you always do, Randy?"

"Back-door key. I took the one your parents stashed in the fake rock beside the door and got a copy made."

How long ago was that? she wondered. Before her father died? His next words seemed to confirm that suspicion.

"Your dad was such an asshole, he left me no choice. I had to be with you, Sienna. It was the only way."

Randy shook his head. "He wouldn't tell me where he'd sent you. Yes, London, but not how to reach you. He even refused to forward my letters to you. I've kept every one. So you could read them. So you could see how much I love you."

"I don't . . . how did a key to the house help with that?"

"I would come up here." He made a sweeping gesture with his right hand. "I would lie on your bed and just breathe you in."

"You're sick," she blurted out. "You need help."

His face turned red, then pinched with fury. "That was mean, Sienna. We don't talk to each other that way. If this is going to work, you're going to have to mind your manners."

Mind her manners? If *what* was going to work? "You killed Madi, didn't you?"

"She forced my hand. I didn't want to."

"Oh, my God."

"I'm surprised you didn't realize it that night, the way I slipped up." He saw she didn't understand and smiled. "The Tranquility Bluffs cop, that prick, he asked the victim's name. And I told him."

For a moment she didn't get what he was referring to, then realization rolled over her. She pressed her lips together to hold back a sound of distress. When she'd asked that same question, just minutes before, he'd said he didn't know.

She'd missed that. Just like she'd missed the suspicious timing of his arrival.

"You look so shocked, Sienna. So disappointed in me. What about how *I* feel? Or how disappointed *I* am? How shocked by *your* behavior?"

She shook her head, fighting panic. She couldn't fall apart. Not if she wanted to live. "What did I do to disappoint you?"

He laughed, the sound hard. "Seriously? You can say that to me? You and I, we were meant to be together."

"No." She shook her head. "I don't know what you're talking about."

"It's there in your journal. You wrote all about me. About us."

"You read my—" She bit the words back. Of course he'd read her journal. How else would that receipt have ended up in it?

"And you slept with him?" His voice rose slightly. He pointed toward the window behind her. "That nobody across the street? I'm your soul mate." He thumped his chest. "Me."

Sienna took the moment to try to dart past him. He caught her easily, and anchored her against his chest.

"Now *that*," he hissed in her ear, "pisses me off."

He shoved her facedown on the bed, then planted a knee in her back to hold her down. She fought to breathe, growing light-headed from fear and lack of oxygen.

He grabbed her arms, wrenched them behind her back. "Why did you"—he tied them so tightly her fingers began to tingle—"betray me?"

He flipped her over, and she gulped in air. Tears

leaked from the corners of her eyes. "Why . . . are you doing . . . this?"

"That night we met, you said it yourself. That it could have been you instead of Madi."

Dead. Snow red with her blood.

"At first it didn't sink in. That you were right, that it was *supposed* to be you," he went on. "Not until after that day you came to see me. We talked about it."

"What? I don't know—"

"We were destined to meet. People's paths cross for a reason. That's when I knew it for sure."

Sienna shook her head, hysteria rising up in her. "Knew what for sure? I don't understand what you mean!"

"I knew it was you who was my soul mate. Not Madi. *You.* My one true love." He bent closer, caressed her cheek. "You and me, it's always been about us, Sienna."

When he started speaking again, his voice had hardened. "But you betrayed me anyway. How could you do that to me? After the way I loved you? The way I waited for you."

Suddenly, she understood. Some sort of psychosis. Not that dissimilar from her mother's. A delusional disorder. Not built around fear, but around love.

It would do as much good to try to talk him out of his belief that they were soul mates as it did to try to talk her mother out of her conviction that Margaret was determined to hurt her. His version of reality was his truth.

Her only chance was to play along.

"But you married someone else," she said, almost choking on the words. "When you told me that, I thought you . . . didn't love me anymore."

"She was a mistake. I thought I'd never see you

again . . . that maybe I could be happy with another. But I couldn't."

"If I'd only known." She looked pleadingly at him. "I thought maybe being with Jonathan could make me forget you . . . and heal my broken heart . . . but it didn't work."

He didn't look convinced, so she used his own words against him. "I thought we were soul mates, but you didn't wait for me. After the way I loved you all these years. After I waited for *you*."

His eyes filled with tears, and he helped her to a seated position. "Why didn't you say something?"

"Why didn't you?"

"How stupid we both were."

She wanted to ask him to free her hands, but was afraid it was too soon and he'd realize her deceit.

He tugged off his gloves. "Look, you've made a mess of your face." He tenderly wiped at her tears, then smoothed her hair. "Your hair's so much prettier than hers."

He brushed his mouth against hers, taking her shudder for excitement. "We've waited so long, my love. But truthfully, I'm glad we did. Before we consummate our devotion, I want you to know everything about that night. And about me and Madi. I don't want anything to come between us, ever again."

He ran his hands over her body, pausing to cup her breasts, and she had to bite her lips to keep from crying out. Finally, he dropped his hands to his lap and sat almost primly beside her. "That night, it was our anniversary. Madi's and mine. We'd been so patient. Keeping our love secret, contenting ourselves with stolen glances. I meant to surprise her."

His voice changed as he sank into his memory, becoming faraway. "The weather predicted snow that night. A storm, not that different than tonight's. Snow, then temperatures plunging into the teens by dawn. Remember?"

She swallowed hard and nodded, sucked into the past and his story.

"The entire force was either working or on call. But seeing her couldn't wait. I'd gotten her a ring. I planned to propose."

"Propose marriage?" she repeated, voice high. "To Madison?"

He took her surprise in a way that fit into his fantasy. "Sounds crazy now, doesn't it? Considering you and me." He paused a moment. "So I went looking for her. That's when I"—his voice thickened—"caught them together. I didn't know his name then, but I do now."

Reed Shepard.

He talked on, and Sienna found herself being pulled into the sound of his voice, the emotion in his words, and she was: the story wrapped around her, drawing her in as if she were there.

CHAPTER SIXTY-NINE

The night of the murder

Randy waited in the shadows, trembling, though not from the cold. No, with disillusionment and despair. With betrayal.

Madi's betrayal. The woman he loved. His one true love.

The image of her in the arms of another man burned onto the back of his eyelids, and he blinked against tears. He was such a fool. A hopeless romantic. He'd written poems for her, sent her flowers. Delivered love notes.

He had made her the very center of his universe, and she repaid him this way?

He brought a gloved hand to his chest, to the breast pocket and the small box nestled there. He recalled the first time her eyes met his. He'd experienced this sensation, this sort of physical trill . . . a high-frequency call that had penetrated to his soul. And then she'd smiled at him, that shy, sweet smile that melted his heart.

And he had *known*. They were meant to be together.

Oh, the plans he'd had for them. A small house in the country. One with a porch and a big oak tree in the yard. Two children, a boy and a girl. The children would want a puppy, of course. He and his beloved would argue about the breed and at what age the kids would be old enough to care for one.

Their future would be perfect.

Until today, he thought she believed the same things.

He lifted his face to the sky. Sometime during the minutes he had been standing here, the drizzle had become snow. The flakes were fat and wet; they fell on his cheeks like the tears he refused to shed.

They'd kept their love affair secret. They'd had to. He understood that. If they'd gone public, he would have lost his job and her parents would have cut her off.

So he'd settled for watching her from a distance. Sending her notes and gifts. And when they passed each other on campus, exchanging longing, loving glances with her.

Soul mates. She was his. And he was hers.

At least he'd thought so. Until today.

He sensed her approach before he caught sight of her. That's how attuned to each other they were. There, rounding the corner by the library, the same as she did every Wednesday night. She wore the white jacket he loved on her, the one that set off her dark hair and warm, brown eyes. Tonight, the hood was up and her head bowed against both the wind and wet.

His resolve melted along with his heart. Maybe it wasn't too late. Maybe what he'd spied had been a mistake. An act. Or acting. Yes! The boy had been rehearsing a part, and he had solicited Madi's help.

Hope burst to life inside him. That was it! The boy had convinced his beloved to help him—but the entire time she'd been wishing to be in *his* arms.

Could he have misjudged her?

He could test her. If she still loved him, she would sense his presence, the way he sensed hers. If she didn't—

The knife burned against the palm of his hand.

She neared where he stood. He called silently to her. *Look at me, my love. Now, sweetheart. One glance and I'll know your love is true.*

But she didn't glance his way. Didn't even pause. His heart splintered into a million sharp pieces.

Blinded by rage, he burst from the shadows and flew up behind her, sinking the blade deeply into her back. The white coat bloomed red. A sound passed her lips. It sounded to him like a cry for forgiveness.

But it was too late. He knew what she was.

He plunged the knife in again and again, both cursing her faithless heart and blubbering like a baby. He slowly became aware of time. And place.

Of who he was.

And what he'd done.

Sobbing, he released her and she crumpled, rag doll–like, to the pavement. He gazed, transfixed by the way the snow landed on her, then disappeared into the gore.

His breath caught and his nose ran. He wiped it with the back of his gloved hand. It came away bloody. He stared at it, earlier rage gone. Replaced by horror. And sorrow. It wasn't his fault. He shook his head and backed away. She was the one who had cheated. She was the liar.

Her fault.

That's not what everyone else would think. They wouldn't understand what the two of them had been to each other. The promises she had made him.

He swiveled his gaze from left to right, heart hammering violently in his chest. He'd had a plan. What was it? He couldn't think. He felt sick, like he was going to puke. No, he couldn't. Not here.

Walk away. His cruiser in the parking lot. Change of clothes there. Baby wipes. A plastic bag.

He put one foot in front of the other. Made it to the vehicle. Changed, cleaned up, stuffed the offending garments in a black trash bag. Shoved the bag under the seat. Noticed there was still blood on his hands, figured he'd clean them in the snow.

And then he heard a scream.

CHAPTER SEVENTY

"*Your* scream, Sienna. And there you were. My real soul mate." He brushed his mouth against hers again. "It's funny how fate works."

She felt him tremble, felt his growing urgency as he kissed her again, more forcefully. It was all she could do not to gag.

"But that's in the past," he went on. "We're together now."

"Yes," she said, forcing what she hoped was a smitten smile. "Soul mates."

"Remember when we first met? You were crossing College Drive, in front of the admin building. It was slick and you fell."

She did. He was nearby and helped her up, then gave her a ride to the infirmary. "I do. I was so grateful for you."

"I met Madi the same day. Somehow, I got confused. It was you all along, Sienna. I'm so sorry. I hope you can forgive me?"

"Of course, my love. But now, you need to go, Randy. Untie me and go quickly. I won't say anything to anyone."

He leaned back to look into her eyes. "Go? Why

would I go? This is where I'm supposed to be. You're who I'm supposed to be with."

"Chief Thompson," she said. "Like I told you, he called. He's sending a cruiser. He knows what you did. Go, I won't tell him you were here. When it's safe, I'll come to you."

"My darling." He cupped her face in his hands. "We don't have to worry about him anymore. Just like we don't have to worry about Shepard."

"What are you saying?"

"The chief was a good man. But he stuck his nose in our business and I couldn't have that."

Was a good man? Sienna struggled to hold herself together. He'd killed him. Because he'd figured it out.

Help wasn't coming, she acknowledged. It was up to her. She had to buy some time. "And Reed? How did you arrange him killing himself?"

"You called that one," he said, beaming at her. "In my office that day. I immobilized him with my Taser, then put the gun in his hand and we held it to his head. Relatively easy."

"Did he figure you out? Is that why you did it?"

"I don't know how he could have. He'd become a thorn in my side, and when he started messing with you, he had to go. That simple."

She drew in a deep, steadying breath. She would deal with the guilt of that later; for now she put it aside. "You pushed my mother down the stairs. Why?"

"As a way to get you home. You came home for your father's funeral, I knew you'd come home for hers. And if she didn't die, I was certain you'd be worried enough about her to come see her. Of course, your thieving brother didn't want *that* to happen."

"And the coat and gloves, did you have them all along?"

"No. They were still logged into TBPD evidence."

She'd been right about that, too. "So you took them?"

"I shouldn't have. It's how Chief figured me out."

That's why the chief had so many questions about them this morning. He'd wanted to be one hundred percent certain before he moved on Randy. Sienna held on to calm, if only by her fingernails. "Why, Randy? Why plant the coat and knife?"

"I was certain your brother or your crazy mother would be charged. The case would be closed and I would be there to help you pick up the pieces. Just the way it was supposed to be."

He grimaced. "I researched. The evidence was circumstantial, but compelling. A jealous brother. A mother who, again and again, claimed she would do *anything* to keep 'the others' from getting her daughter. Another plan Chief Thompson mucked up."

"But what if I didn't find the bin?"

"I knew either you or your mother would. I made sure the bin was clearly visible to anyone who walked into the closet. I even added the label with your name on it. How could you *not* look in the bin?"

Her cell phone display illuminated. A text from Jonathan.

Are you and your mom okay?

Tears burned her eyes. She fought them. She couldn't cry. Not now. If she did, Randy would know the truth.

But it felt as if her heart was breaking. She wondered if she would ever see him again.

A moment later another text arrived.

I have news about the white van. Ran them down. They said a cop hired them to watch your house.

Randy read it and swore. "Son of a bitch. Now I have to take care of him, too?"

She pictured Randy heading across the street, shooting Jonathan when he opened the door. Somehow she had to warn him.

"I should answer him," she said quickly. "If I don't, he'll keep texting."

As the words finished coming out of her mouth, another text arrived.

I can't stop thinking about you. About us.

Randy stared at the phone, a muscle in his jaw twitching.

"He's nothing to me," she said quickly, the words sounding forced. "Just ignore him."

"What's your password?"

She told him and he punched it in, then typed a response. He held it out so she could read it.

There is no us. Don't ever contact me again. Goodbye, Jonathan.

"I call him Jon," she lied. "Not Jonathan. If you call him that he'll think something's wrong and come over. And we don't want him bothering us. This is *our* night, Randy."

He frowned a moment, made the change, then hit Send. "You're right, tonight's our special night. Just like all those years ago, I thought it was me and Madi's special night. And just like then, I have a surprise for you—and I refuse to let a storm or anything else ruin it for us."

He set her phone aside, then got down on one knee. He took a small velvet box out of his pocket. There were tears in his eyes as he flipped it open. The diamond ring sparkled against the black velvet. "We've both waited so long to be together. Sienna, will you marry me?"

As a young girl, she'd dreamed of a moment like this. A ring. The man she loved, down on one knee.

Those most significant, most romantic of all words being asked of her.

But this perversion of love broke her heart.

Sienna forced the words past her lips. "Of course I will. Yes, Randy, I'll marry you."

He let out a whoop of joy and kissed her. Pretending a passionate response was the hardest thing she'd ever done. "Untie me quick," she managed around his kisses. "I want your ring on my finger, it won't be real until then."

He complied, blubbering like a baby. Her hands free, she held out her left, and with her right felt behind her for the flashlight.

He slid the sparkling circle on her finger as she located the Maglite. With a silent prayer, she swung as hard as she could.

Her blow landed badly, but caught him by surprise, knocking him sideways. She was on her feet in a flash, swinging again, catching him in the side of his head, sending him to his knees.

Sienna ran for the door, yanked it open. She darted into the hall and saw her mother's door was fully open, her bed empty.

"Mom!" she shouted. "Get help—"

Randy grabbed her from behind, yanking her backward, off her feet. "If I can't have you, nobody will!"

Over the howl of the wind, she heard a pounding on the front door. A man's voice, shouting for her.

"Jonathan!" she screamed. "He's got a gun!"

The pounding ceased. A moment later the glass sidelight shattered.

"We go together, then," Randy growled against her ear. "You first."

He meant for them both to die. She fought his grasp,

twisting and kicking. Still, he managed to turn the gun on her; she felt it pressed into her side.

A high, blood-chilling cry rang out. Startled, he loosened his grip and Sienna broke free, stumbling forward, grabbing the newel post to keep from tumbling down the stairs. Her mother, face twisted in rage, flew at Randy, a knife in her raised hand.

As her mother sank the knife into Randy's chest, Jonathan burst through the front door, Sienna's name on his lips. Randy's eyes widened in shock. The gun slipped from his hand, clattering onto the stairs. He teetered a moment, then fell backward. Sienna watched in horror as he toppled down the stairs, landing unmoving at the bottom, a circle of red growing around him.

EPILOGUE

Three months later

Sienna stood on the sidewalk in front of The Wagon Wheel restaurant, gazing up at the building's 1920s facade. She smiled. The storm had passed and spring had officially arrived in Tranquility Bluffs. All traces of the fury of that night had melted away, and everywhere Sienna saw signs of vibrant new life.

Especially in her own life.

Randy was dead. Ironically, the pathologist determined it wasn't the knife wound that had killed him, but a blow to the head during his tumble down the stairs.

A part of her wished he'd lived to be punished for his crimes, but a larger part knew that nothing would have been gained by their living through the trial. Life was too short, happiness too fragile.

The police, to her surprise led by Chief Thompson, had arrived shortly after Jonathan. The seasoned cop had planned ahead, and it was a good thing—the Kevlar vest he'd donned before meeting with Randy saved his life.

She'd learned that the chief had grown suspicious of Randy, and had done a bit of digging—and discovered Sienna's bloodied parka and gloves had gone missing from Evidence. He'd visited her mom the morning of the storm seeking to confirm his suspicion before he brought his officer in for questioning. Unfortunately, Randy found him first.

She and her mother had relayed their stories, and Sienna still couldn't get over her mother's bravery. She'd awakened, heard Randy with Sienna, and crept down to the kitchen in search of a weapon. Even though Randy had a gun, she fulfilled her lifelong promise to do anything she had to in order to keep her daughter safe.

Sienna had experienced many sleepless nights since. She'd sought help from Dr. Margery, who had helped her make sense of the events—and understand why Randy had come to believe himself in love with her, and she with him. She had given his disorder a name: erotomania.

Sienna, the psychiatrist reassured her, had done nothing to encourage him but cross his path. To Randy, she'd been a fantasy, not a real person. The same as Madison Robie had been before her. The erotomaniac was driven by the fantastical notion of a perfect, spiritual love. Soul mates, as he'd called them.

Dr. Margery also suggested that recognizing his mental illness and playing along most probably saved her life.

Donna Meyer caught sight of her through the restaurant's front window and waved. She and Ted were busy tying up the loose threads of their lives here, and preparing for their new one down in perpetually sunny Florida.

Sienna's smile widened. She loved this building, everything about it. And to think, it would be hers in just a matter of days. At the same time Donna and Ted's other buyer had failed to secure financing, her brother's investors had come through, and he had managed to repay her half of what he'd taken.

For Sienna, half seemed fair—because in her opinion, the way her dad structured his will wasn't fair. That had been his decision to make, but this one was hers.

And half was enough to get started—although it wasn't going to be easy. She'd had to scale back her plans and put off renovating the living quarters upstairs, but her dream of owning her own restaurant was coming true.

But it wasn't the only dream coming true.

At the rumble of a pickup truck pulling into a parking spot behind her, she turned. Jonathan, smiling like the cat who swallowed the canary.

"Hey, babe," he called out the open window, "sorry I'm late. The closing took longer than expected."

Smiling, she crossed to meet him. He took her in his arms and kissed her. "It's official. I'm a house flipper."

She smiled up at him. "Congratulations."

He kissed her again. "I missed you."

"I missed you, too."

"You ready to do this?"

"Wait." She looked up at him, searching his gaze. "Are you sure?"

He drew his eyebrows together. "About the job?"

He'd agreed to be the contractor for the restaurant renovation, but that wasn't what she was talking about. "No. Are you certain about staying here, in Tranquility Bluffs?"

"Babe, we already talked about this."

"I know, but . . . if it's too difficult . . . if there are too many bad memories—"

He laid a finger gently on her lips. "Your mother's here, your brother—"

"We can go to Chicago or Milwaukee, even Rockford. Someplace close enough to be available but away from the town where . . . it happened."

"This is also the town where I fell in love with you."

"And it's where I fell in love with you, but—"

"I'm certain I want to be with you, Sienna. Are you certain you want to be with me?"

"Of course."

"And this restaurant, are you certain you want to buy it?"

"Yes. But I don't *have* to."

His lips lifted and those sexy brown eyes crinkled at the corners. "And *that's* why I want you to."

He kissed her, then caught her hand. Together they crossed the sidewalk, the past behind them and the future, theirs together, ahead.